A KiLLING
IN THE
VALLEY

By J. F. Freedman

A KiLLING IN THE VALLEY

A NOVEL BY

J. F. Freedman

MADISON
PARK
PRESS™
NEW YORK

Published by Madison Park Press, 15 East 26th Street, New York, NY 10010.

Book design by Christos Peterson

ISBN: 1-58288-224-X
    978-1-58288-224-6

Printed in the United States of America

For Susannah Laurel Freedman

PART I

1

....

THEY DROVE UP Santa Barbara County Highway 154, the road winding serpentine-like over the pass and down into the Santa Ynez Valley, past Lake Cachuma and the ranchlands with their rolling oak meadows, until they came to an even more narrow potholed two-lane blacktop and took it east toward Figueroa Mountain. After a few miles they arrived at a private road that had *No Trespassing/Violators Will Be Prosecuted* signs hanging from poles that flanked both sides of a heavy iron gate. The signs were punctured with rusted-out bullet holes. The wind had come up strong, normal for late summer and early autumn afternoons in the valley.

The gate swung open sluggishly on its sturdy hinges. It made a creaking metallic sound, like iron fingernails on a tin chalkboard.

This road was the only way into this section of the ranch. It was hard-packed dirt overlaid with gravel, oiled and rolled twice a year. Most of the time it was serviceable, but in winter, when it rained for days straight, it would become impassable, sometimes for up to a week. Then nothing came or went on it, unless on foot or on a horse.

The road meandered for almost a mile through stands of live and blue oak, juniper, pine, scrub brush. The driver slowed to a crawl when the ruts got deep, fighting the wheel like he was riding a surly horse. Then they rounded the last turn, and the old house came into view.

There was nobody there. There almost never was. The late-afternoon sun in the western sky was a shimmering, liquid-gold mirage. The driver got out of the car and stretched his back.

"This is it," he said. "End of the road."

The front passenger door opened and the girl got out slowly, looking around, trying to figure out where he'd brought her. She looked past the house and the old orchards and rows of abandoned wine vines in the fields behind it to the low mountains that rose up in the north, about ten miles away.

"This is fucking incredible," she exclaimed breathlessly, as she leaned up against the door of the car, staring.

The fiery colors—the full rainbow spectrum, but deeper and darker—were bleeding across the face of the mountains. This was even more stunning than the sunsets she sometimes saw at Summerland Beach, when it wasn't overcast and the clouds would hang low over the ocean as the sun dripped into the water. She and her friends would sit around an illegal bonfire as evening fell, drinking beer and wine, smoking marijuana and dropping uppers, downers, E, whatever was around. Some of the kids even snorted heroin, although she hadn't gotten to that yet. Those sunsets could be outrageous, but nothing like this. This was like God painting.

She was stoned, and that heightened her perception; in the vague recesses at the back of her mind she was aware of that. But she would have been blown away even if she was completely straight.

"Yeah, it is," the boy agreed, barely glancing at the shimmering hills. His attention was on her. She wasn't perfect—a little chubby, baby-fat, but on her it was sexy. Good legs, tight calves. Maybe she was a dancer, he knew girls with calves like these who were dancers. She was showing cleavage through her thin summer dress and pink Victoria's Secret bra, he could see almost down to her brown nipples. Her honey-colored, heart-shaped face was pretty in the fashion of Penelope Cruz or Salma Hayek. A Mexican Madonna.

"Come on," he said. "I'll show you inside. It's like out of an

old movie." He took her hand and started to pull her toward the
house.

She resisted for a moment longer, her eyes stuck on the mountains, the wine-red burgundies merging into van Gogh sunflower
yellows, into deep eggplant purples, vermilions, aqua. Then she
smiled at him, and let him lead her on.

The house was definitely like a movie, she thought, as she
stood in the center of the dark, high-ceilinged living room. Like
one of those old black and white horror movies they show on
Turner Movie Classics. All the furniture was old and heavy. It
smelled like mold. The carpets were thin in spots, almost so bare
you could see the wood floors under them. The windows were
covered with heavy beaded curtains, like she'd seen in pictures of
European castles. There were clusters of old paintings hanging
from the walls—portraits of Spanish soldiers and ladies in fancy
dresses, like the costumes the rich Anglos wore during Fiesta.
And where there weren't paintings, there were bookshelves,
floor to ceiling. It was dark, the heavy curtains were drawn and
there weren't any lights on, so she couldn't see anything very
well, but the books all looked like they were a hundred years old
or more.

Who lived here, she thought, some crazo who was going to
leap out of a closet with an ax and attack them? The thought sent
a shiver up her back. "Turn on some lights," she whined. "I can't
see for shit in here."

"Aren't any," he said. He was smiling, she could see that well.
He was standing close, practically on top of her.

"What kind of house doesn't have lights?" she asked in a
loopy voice.

"One that was built before electricity was invented," he
answered matter-of-factly.

She was high, so she wasn't thinking clearly anyway, but that
brought her up short. "So what?" she managed to come back.
"There's places in Santa Barbara that were built before electricity
that have it now."

He shrugged. "The owners didn't want to put it in here. They wanted to preserve it as it had been."

"That's stupid," she said. "What about bathrooms?" she asked, suddenly feeling the urge to pee. "Do they have them, or do you have to go in the woods?"

He smiled again. "They have bathrooms."

"That's better than nothing, I guess," she said. "Where is one?"

"Follow me."

He led her through a series of rooms with high ceilings, the walls mostly covered with bookcases that were stuffed with books. Despite her need to relieve herself, she stopped for a moment and plucked one from a shelf. Dust drifted in the air as the book was released from its mooring.

"Does anybody ever read any of this shit?" she asked, crinkling her nose against the dust. She flipped the book open. The paper felt like an old woman's hand under her fingers, like her great-grandmother's hand. So fragile you could almost see the bones and blood vessels through the skin.

"Yeah, the people who lived here did," he answered. "That's what they did before television or computers or video games. Read books. Played cards." He pointed to a small table against a wall. A chessboard was set out, the pieces ready for action. "You had to entertain yourself in those days, Jerry Seinfeld and Jennifer Aniston didn't do it for you."

She put the book back on the shelf. "It sounds, like, incredibly boring. Anyway, how could they, without any electricity?" she asked. "Read books and shit." She thought that was a smart question to ask.

"They used gas lamps," he answered knowingly. "Or candles. You know—like honest Abe."

The name sounded familiar, but she couldn't remember from where. Did he mean Abel? She knew a man named Abel—he was a friend of her uncle's. They had done time in Soledad together.

But no, she thought, he didn't mean Abel Sanchez. How could this guy she had just met know Abel Sanchez? She started to giggle, and put her hand to her mouth to stop herself. She was more stoned than she'd thought, she realized. It felt good. She wanted to do more of his drugs.

The urge to pee came back, stronger. She had a weak bladder; when she had to go, she had to go, immediately. "Where's this bathroom?" she asked.

He took her hand and led her into a bedroom. It had a four-poster canopied bed, the frame high up off the floor. There was more light in here than in the rest if the house; the curtains were lace, not like the heavy material that covered the windows in the other rooms. The late afternoon sunlight filtered in through the thin material. The room smelled like camphor, the way old trunks smelled when her mother or grandmother opened them up to store important clothes, like baptism and confirmation dresses.

"That's a really cool bed," she said, impressed by the bulk of it.

"The mattress is goose down," he told her, plumping it.

"How do you know so much about this place?" she asked, suddenly curious. He was practically a tour guide, the way he was showing her around. "Like, is it a friend's or something?"

He looked past her to the beveled windows at the far end of the room, through which the light from the declining sun was refracted into a soft focus rainbow kaleidoscope, the primary colors melting on the old chenille bedspread. "I've been here before," he answered obliquely. He walked her to a door at the far end of the room and pushed it open. "Here."

The bathroom was big, almost square. All the fixtures—sink, tub, toilet—were old, like everything else in the house. The floor was tiny black and white tiles in a checkerboard pattern, like the one in Arnoldi's, an old Italian restaurant in town where her father and uncles played bocce ball out back. This room, too, was dark, but the window opposite the toilet was bare, so there was enough light for what she needed. For a second, she panicked that there wouldn't be any toilet paper and she'd have to wipe with her hand, or her panties, but there was an almost-full roll on the holder. She wondered how long it had been there. If it was as old as the rest of the shit in this house, it might be really scratchy.

She touched it. It was soft, like the Charmin her mother used. Thank God for small favors.

He stood in the doorway. "You okay?" he asked.

"Well, yeah, as soon as you close the door," she answered, feeling embarrassed. "Like I'm not going to let you watch me pee."

"Privacy's important," he agreed, shutting the door behind him. He was going to have the pleasure of her in a minute anyway, he didn't need to see her squatting on the john, no matter how sexy an ass she had.

While he waited for her he went back outside to the car and got the rest of the bottle of Patron, the baggie of grass, and a pipe. When she came out of the bathroom, the sound of the old pipes groaning loudly after she flushed, he had packed the pipe and poured two shots of tequila into crystal snifters he had taken from a cabinet in the kitchen.

She put the pipe to her lips and he lit it for her. She sucked in the thick smoke, holding it in as long as she could, which wasn't long, it was harsh, then coughing it out. "Shit," she said, her eyes watering. She could feel her high coming back, even stronger. "That is really good grass," she enthused.

He helped her up onto the bed, then got on with her. They each took another hit off the pipe, chasing it with more tequila. The bottle was almost empty. He had bought it after he'd picked her up. She had drunk a lot more of it than he had, which was his plan.

They started making out. Her soft body moved easily under his. He could taste the tequila and marijuana in her mouth. Her lips were pillows, her tongue moving inside his mouth a soft, sensuous snake.

One of his hands went under her dress, caressing the soft, warm skin of her belly. She twisted her body up off the mattress so he could slip her dress over her head. Then the bra, unhooking it with one hand, sliding it off.

He began sucking one of her brown, puckered nipples. She moaned softly. He pulled his shirt off, chucked it onto the floor. Then his OP shorts, his Big Dog boxers. His free hand slipped under the elastic of her panties, his fingers caressing the slick curly hair of her vagina, slipping a finger into her moistness, then another.

After a minute of stimulating her with his hand, he put himself into her mouth. Her head bobbed up and down on his shaft like she was riding a carousel horse. He could feel the wave building rapidly. Pulling his tumescent penis out of her mouth, he turned her around on her hands and knees. He rolled the condom on, preparing to enter her from behind.

"Fuck!" she called out suddenly, rising abruptly into the air.

"What . . ." he started to say, but she was off the bed and running for the bathroom.

She barely made it to the porcelain toilet bowl. He staggered into the bathroom after her. "Are you all right?" he called out to her heaving back.

On her knees, bent over the toilet bowl, her body was shaking as she retched into the toilet. She nodded distractedly, her hands holding her long hair back to keep it from getting splattered with the vomit. He turned and went back into the bedroom.

After she finished discharging whatever had been in her stomach, she flushed the toilet, wiped the edges of the bowl clean, gargled with water from the sink, splashed more cold water on her face, and staggered back into the bedroom. He was lying on his back on the bed, playing with his erection. He wouldn't kiss her while he was fucking her now, but that didn't matter. They had done plenty of kissing already.

"You all right now?" he asked blandly, as she stood at the foot of the bed. Her skin was blotchy. A cold film of sweat had formed on her stomach and chest.

She nodded weakly. "Too much tequila on an empty stomach," she told him.

"Hey, it happens," he said magnanimously. It wasn't like she had gotten sick deliberately. He patted the sheets next to him.

She stared at him. "Are you shitting me?" she asked. Her voice had taken on a hard, angry tone.

"It's okay," he said. "I've had my elephant-breath days. Everyone has." He patted the bed again. "Come to papa."

Wordlessly, she grabbed her panties off the floor and slipped them on. Then she got down on her hands and knees, looking for her bra, which had landed under a chair when he had chucked it across the room.

He sat up. "What're you doing?" he said to her ass, the closest part of her to him.

Still on her hands and knees, she looked up at him over her back. "What does it look like I'm doing? I'm getting dressed." She found her bra and put it on, reaching behind her to fasten the snap. "You might as well, too. Party's over for today. Sorry," she said, without any remorse.

Now he was off the bed, on his feet. "What the fuck are you talking about?"

Hands on hips, she stared at him like he was the village idiot. "You think I feel like having sex after I just barfed my guts out? No way, José."

His jaw dropped. All the foreplay, the whiskey, drugs, that pair of earrings he had bought her at the mall, and now she was turning off the tap? "You little bitch," he snapped at her. "You're not getting away with that shit."

She stared at him gimlet-eyed. "Getting away with what? I didn't make you any promises, man." Seeing the anger rising in his face, she backed off on her attitude. "It's not like I don't like you or nothing. I want to do it with you. Just not now, is all. I can't, I'm feeling too shitty." She tried a placating smile. "Tomorrow, when I'm feeling better, we can get together again."

Yeah, he thought, the rage coming stronger, like you and me are really going to see each other tomorrow, or any other time. Today had been one of those frozen moments in time, when everything came together in a perfect fit. After today they'd never see each other again, he knew that with certainty.

He took a deep breath. "Just calm down, okay? We'll take it easy for a few minutes, you'll feel better, then we'll . . ." He didn't say the rest. He knew that she knew what he meant.

"No," she told him firmly. "I'm done for today with you." She reached down to the floor for her dress. "You need to take me home now. My mother will be worried if I get home too late, it's like an hour's drive almost." She hadn't been paying attention on the drive here, she'd been too spacey, but she knew it was way the fuck out in the boonies.

He put his hands on her shoulders. "We aren't leaving. Not yet." He started to push her down onto the bed. She backed away, then reached back and slapped him across the face, as hard as she could.

"Don't touch me!" she yelled. She was still high as hell, she could feel it, but not high enough that she couldn't take care of herself.

He stared at her for a moment, feeling the color rising in his face. The slap had stung, but the doing of it was the real hurt.

He started toward her again. She backed away, her hands holding her dress in front of her, an instinctive and pitiful act of protection. He grabbed her around the waist, lifting her off her feet. She tried to bite his hand, but he wrapped his fingers around her neck, hard, almost cutting off her windpipe.

"Don't," she tried to choke out.

He threw her onto the bed. One hand tore off her panties, the other covered her mouth to muffle the screaming.

She was back in the living room. She had managed to get her clothes on. She didn't know where he was—somewhere back in the house, that bedroom or the bathroom next to it, where she'd been sick.

She had to get out of here. She didn't know the location; she hadn't been paying any attention during the drive. She did remember they had turned off Highway 154 past the town of Santa Ynez. If she could get to the county road they had turned off to get here, somebody could drive out from Santa Barbara and get her. The way she looked, nobody would pick her up hitch-hiking. She knew that because she had checked herself out in the mirror, after he had finished with her. One eye was almost completely closed, her bottom lip was split and oozing blood.

She reached into her purse, took out her cell phone, and started to dial.

"Who the hell are you calling?"

She jumped, turning toward the voice. She hadn't heard him come up behind her. "Nobody," she said instinctively. That was an obvious lie, the phone was in her hand and she had been punching in numbers. "My mother," she improvised. "To tell her I'm gonna be late."

His head shook slowly, back and forth. "You were dialing 911, weren't you? You were going to call the cops on me." He reached out for the phone. "Give it here."

She started backing away. "No."

He came toward her, stepping slowly. Except for his boxer shorts, he was naked. "Give," he ordered her, holding his hand out.

She stopped and stared hard at him. What more can he do to me, she thought with suddenly clarity. She felt powerful all of a sudden. "What are you going to do if I don't?" she asked in an aggressive tone of voice. "Kill me?" she taunted him. "That's all that's left for you to do to me. You've done everything else already."

He stared back at her. He had gone too far, way too far, and he knew it. "Look," he said, trying to placate her, "I'll drive you back to town and drop you off and you'll never see me again." He forced a smile. "I'm sorry."

Her smile back at him was like the grim smile of a death's-head. "You don't know how sorry you're gonna be, you shit-bird." She started to dial again on her cell phone.

"Don't call the police!" he yelled at her. "That won't do either of us any good."

She momentarily stopped dialing. "The police?" She laughed in his face, that was such a lame idea. "You think the police would do anything for me against someone like you? My word against yours, whose are they gonna believe?"

What she was saying was true, he knew that without her having to spell it out. She had come here with him willingly. They had done drugs and drunk almost an entire bottle of tequila together. He'd bought her a pair of cheap earrings at the mall, which could be construed as payment for sexual favors. Most importantly, she was working-class Latina and he was an Anglo college boy. No way the cops would believe what had happened wasn't consensual.

"I don't need the police to help me." She resumed dialing again.

"Then who are you calling?" he asked suspiciously. "And don't give me that bullshit about your mother."

She paused in mid-dial. "You really want to know? *You really want to fucking know?*" she screamed at him. "I'll tell you, asshole. I'm calling my uncle. He runs with the gangs in Ventura and Oxnard, from way back. He's going to come get me, then he's gonna fuck you up so bad you'll wish I *had* called the police."

Involuntarily, he began to shake, his body trembling as if he was standing on an electric grid. His mind's eye flooded with television and magazine images of tattooed prison inmates from gangs like Bloods, Crips, Mexican Mafia, Aryan Brotherhood. If she really had an uncle who was connected to any one of those gangs, he was in serious trouble.

He lunged for her, grasping for the phone. Surprisingly nimble for someone who had been drunk, stoned, thrown up, raped, and assaulted, she pivoted away from him, running across the room, continuing to punch in numbers.

The gun, an old revolver, was lying on a small table near the fireplace. In the darkness, neither had seen it. She grabbed it off the table and pointed it at him.

He froze. Very deliberately, as if trying to calm a wounded, frightened animal, he asked, "Are you going to shoot me?" Even more deliberately: "You're not actually going to pull the trigger on that thing."

She backed away, her head shaking back and forth. Her gun-hand was shaking so violently she could barely keep it pointing at him. "Not unless you force me to," she told him. "I want to get out of here, that's all. You let me walk out of here, and I won't do nothing to you."

Except call the cops, or your uncle, or someone else equally disastrous, he thought fearfully.

He took a step toward her. Pointing to the gun in her quivering hand, he said, "That piece of shit won't shoot anybody. It's as old as this house. It probably hasn't been fired in a hundred years. The only thing that will happen if you pull that trigger is that it'll blow up in your hand and take your arm off." He reached his hand out. "Come on. Give it to me. I'll make this up to you, I promise."

As she backed away from him she stole a quick glance at the weapon. She didn't know anything about guns, but it was obviously ancient, as he had said. And he was also probably right about how it would perform.

"It'll shoot fine," she said with false bravado. "You don't want to test whether it will or not."

"Neither do you." He took another step toward her. "Put the phone and the gun down, and we'll talk this out." He paused. "I can pay you good money. Neither of us wants the world to know about this."

He was closer to her now. Deliberately and cautiously, he held his hand out. For a moment they were frozen in place, trying to stare the other down. Then with a sudden, violent move, he grabbed for the gun.

The explosion was deafening.

2

FOURTEEN HOURS EARLIER

JUANITA McCOY WAS a daughter and a wife of ranchers, and a rancher herself. She was a direct, tenth-generation descendant of one of the original land-grant families in central California, their holdings conferred upon them by the king of Spain, at the beginning of the eighteenth century. Two hundred years of marriage outside the original Spanish community had bred out most of the Mediterranean-looking characteristics in her lineage. She was fair-skinned and blue-eyed, and before her hair turned its present silver it had been blonde. But the old Spanish connection was still the essential part of her heritage, rather than that of the English-Scottish-German sea captains, prospectors, cattle ranchers, and get-rich-schemers who migrated to California generations later and intermarried with the original Spanish families, including hers.

She lived by herself in a small house on Rancho San Gennaro, the old family ranch in the Santa Ynez Valley, which was on the other side of the low mountains from the city of Santa Barbara, forty miles to the south. The property, 18,000 acres, was the second-largest ranch in the county. She had grown up on the ranch with her parents, brothers, and sisters, other family members. Back then, their operation ran over a thousand head a year.

After her father passed away in the early '60s, she and her husband, Henry McCoy, a prominent lawyer and social activist in the community (dead now going on five years), took over the ranch. Over the subsequent decades, as corporate ranching gobbled up many independents, the operation shrunk considerably. Her current herd was two hundred and fifty cows, and fourteen bulls to service them.

Although Juanita had lived in Santa Barbara for most of her life, she was worldly and well-educated. She went to Stanford, where she met her husband. They traveled extensively. She was a patron of the local arts. Considered a great beauty when she was younger, she was still highly attractive, despite the inroads of age. Although she had lived on a ranch for most of her life, her skin had few lines or wrinkles. She wore her silver hair long, usually wrapped up in a braid or bun, except at night.

Over the past few years, since her husband's death, she had dropped most of her social activities. She had become accustomed to her solitude. When she needed companionship there were still friends to be with, but she was comfortable keeping her own company. She was at peace with everything in her life; with one important exception.

The issue that upset her, that she dwelled on but had no solution for, was knowing that when she died, this way of life, passed down ten generations, would be over, because neither of her children were interested in maintaining stewardship over the land. Her son managed a Nissan dealership in Tucson, Arizona, and her daughter and son-in-law owned a chain of natural-food grocery stores in northern California. Her heirs would subdivide the property. The mini-estates would sell for millions of dollars, and her descendants would be rich. But the land would be gone from them.

The sky was a black canopy of stars and a three-quarters moon when Juanita woke up. She put on a pot of black coffee and clicked the television to the weather channel. The forecast was for hot, dry conditions, with the possibility of evening Santa Ana winds—no change for several weeks now.

Juanita was particularly vigilant about keeping trespassers off her property during this time of year. One careless match, one overturned lantern, and thousands of acres could light up the sky in a hellish fireball. That had happened many times in the past, and would again; nature was more powerful than man. But the heedful landowner didn't help nature destroy itself. You protected your property, and by doing so, you protected everyone else's.

The fear of fire wasn't the reason Juanita was up earlier than usual this morning, however. Over the past week, on two separate occasions, her vegetable garden had been plundered by a vicious, cruel marauder. Both times, her dog had chased the intruder away, but not until considerable damage had been done. This time she was going to be awake and ready when it returned to continue its violation.

She drank a cup of black coffee, waiting impatiently. If she didn't stop it, the culprit would come back until there was nothing left to devastate. She itched to go outside to lie in wait, but if the wind was blowing the wrong way her scent would carry and spook her prey. The instant her dog started yelping she'd rush out and confront the bastard.

She glanced at the clock over her stove. Almost five-thirty. First light would soon be on the horizon, and then the chance for success would be gone, because this was a night prowler who did its damage under the cover of darkness.

Her dog's frenzied barking was loud and intense. She raced to the door, grabbing her father's old lever-action Winchester 30-30, which she had loaded with 150-grain bullets the night before. Flinging the door open, her eyes scanned the edges of the garden for her prey.

A boar or a sow, she couldn't tell from this distance, the moonlight wasn't strong enough. But there it was, its purplish snot rooting deep in her turnips. Her dog, no coward but no fool either, was dancing about at the edge of the garden, keeping his distance from the intruder, barking nonstop.

Juanita whistled up her dog. She chained her to her doghouse, so she wouldn't frighten the intruder away again. Then, bearing the rifle high in her hand like an Indian brave on the warpath, she ran full-tilt across the back grass to the garden, her hair a mane of glimmering silver streaming behind her. She wore only a light summer nightgown and was barefoot, but she could care less about how she looked. She could be stark naked, there was no one around to see her for miles.

The feral pig was dark brown, with scattered, mottled pink and gray patches on its rump. A set of lethal-looking tusks protruded from the corners of its mouth. It shook its massive, hairy head, as if tossing off fleas.

She circled around so that she was downwind of it—pigs can't see well, but their senses of smell and hearing are keen. She got to within seventy-five yards of the predator, then stopped. It was a boar, she could see that now, it was too big to be a sow, and there were no tits hanging from its underbelly. It was a fine if ugly specimen; it would weigh over two hundred pounds, maybe close to two-fifty.

Snorting through massive nostrils, the boar rooted through her hard-won garden. As Juanita had done countless times before, from long ago, when her father had taught her to hunt as a young girl, she dropped to one knee and brought the rifle up to her shoulder in one graceful movement, the worn wooden stock pressed tight to her cheek. Her left eye squinted shut while the right, her shooting eye, narrowed to its target. Her finger squeezed the trigger without a moment's hesitation.

The bullet ripped through the boar's shoulder. The beast ran a few steps on instinct; then it stood still, wavered for a moment, and dropped in its tracks.

She got up and walked to it, prepared to spend a second bullet if the first hadn't killed it—she didn't want it to suffer. But it was dead. She had done the job right.

She prodded its massive belly with the end of her rifle barrel. Later, she would notify her ranch foreman to come fetch it. Right now, she needed another cup of strong coffee.

Juanita ate her breakfast of oatmeal, toast, and the rest of the coffee on the back porch. The now-rising sun was casting pale yellow tendrils on the low hills, shadowy patterns moving across the face of the limestone outcroppings. Next month, she and her ranch foreman would trek into the back-country section of the ranch and hunt for deer and wild turkey. One good-sized buck and a few big tom turkeys, along with this pig, would provide a sizable portion of her winter's meat, which she would dress with the help of a nearby rancher who was good at butchering. The meat would go into her freezer. She only killed what she ate.

Back inside, she caught up with the stock market on CNN, went through the e-mail on her computer, planned a shopping trip into Santa Ynez for her weekly stocking-up, and called her foreman to come get this winter's pork.

Before she knew it, it was midmorning. She walked outside and crossed the yard to the stable. Her dog, an Aussie Shepherd bitch, followed at her heels.

The stable was dark, quiet, cool. It smelled of hay and manure. Shafts of sunlight shone through gaps in the roof, which needed to be sealed before winter. Her mare, hearing her come in, snickered in greeting. The dog jumped and played in the sunbeams.

She fed and watered her horse. Then she led her out of the stall and slid on the bridle. She threw the blanket on her back, the saddle on top of it.

Her saddle was almost sixty years old. It had been a high school graduation present from her parents. She had other saddles, but this one remained her favorite.

"Time to get you two some exercise," she called out to the animals as she mounted the mare. They started off at an easy walk, the dog running ahead of them, then circling back, then running on again.

The trail meandered through low stands of oak, pine, and juniper. Even after living here for three-quarters of a century, Juanita still savored the sights, the smells, the essential feeling of her land. Partway to her destination, she stopped to pick an armful of wild sage. The fragrance was pungently redolent in her nose; on impulse, she decided she would invite a few neighboring ranchers for dinner over the weekend and barbeque some sage-rubbed chickens. She hadn't had a dinner party all summer—the thought of preparing for it energized her.

The original *casa* had been erected in the 1830s, when California was still part of Mexico. It was adobe, the clay coming from their property. Over decades, new sections, also adobe, had been added to the core. The last addition, in the 1880s, had enlarged it to its present twelve rooms. At the time it was constructed there was no running water in the house and, of course, no electricity. Around the turn of the twentieth century, the house was plumbed, but there was still no electricity.

No one had lived there for decades, since Juanita's grandparents died. Despite its age and benign neglect, however, it was still a grand old place—a living link to the past, not only for Juanita's immediate family, but for the history of Santa Barbara County.

She approached the house from the back, riding through the abandoned orchard. Dismounting, she tied her horse to the hitching-post, stretched for a moment to loosen the kinks, and went inside.

As usual, the house upon first being entered had a musty, slightly damp smell and feel to it, as if the lid on the jar that was preserving it hadn't been screwed on tightly enough. She threw open some windows to air the place out, then made her way to the small library at the rear, a room that had been her grandfather's study.

The task she'd set for herself today was to go through some of the old photo albums that chronicled the ranch's genealogy, going back to the 1860s. Alexander Gardner, one of Matthew Brady's principal associates, had spent a month on the property shortly after the Civil War. Edward Curtis, the famous Indian portraitist, a ranch guest around the turn of the century, also took hundreds of pictures, many of which still existed in the albums and scrapbooks that her mother, grandmother, and the women before them had lovingly maintained and preserved.

Sitting at her grandfather's old pigeonhole desk, Juanita leafed through the volumes of old images, jotting down notes in the small pocket notebook she had brought with her. Later, when she got home, she'd transcribe the information into her computer.

She heard the sound of a vehicle approaching on the gravel road. She marked her place, closed the book, and stood up. The single road into this section of the ranch was guarded by a locked gate. Only a few people had access to the combination to the lock, and none of them were supposed to be here today.

Her encounter with the boar should have been enough excitement for one day—she was a strong woman, but she was also seventy-six years old. But she would have to deal with this, she couldn't hide from the intruder—her horse tied up in front and her dog scampering around the yard revealed her presence.

She hadn't brought the rifle with her from her house, but there was enough firepower in this old house to deal with a battalion of intruders. She crossed to a gun cabinet that was built next to the walk-in fireplace, unlocked the door, and opened it. An impressive array of shotguns, rifles, and handguns were lined up inside. None of them were contemporary; many had not been fired in decades. They were part of the ranch's heritage, like the books in the library and the paintings on the walls. A couple times a year, on special occasions, the cabinet would be opened and the old arms would be put on display.

She certainly didn't want to shoot anyone, but a gun was a useful tool. The mere show of arms was usually enough to scare off an unwanted visitor. Reaching into the cabinet, she took hold of an old Colt revolver. The weapon felt heavy in her small hand. She carefully parted the curtains and peered out the window.

A mud-splattered Nissan Pathfinder rounded the corner. As she watched it approach, her hand involuntarily tightened on the pistol's grip. The Pathfinder stopped at the edge of the driveway. There was a moment while the dust cleared; then the driver's door opened, and a young man stepped out, shading his eyes against the sun. The dog ran around him in circles, yapping at his heels.

Juanita put the gun down and flew out the door. "Steven!" she cried out in delighted surprise. "What are you doing here?" She leaned up and gave him a dry kiss on the cheek.

The man, tall and lean, in his early twenties, scooped her up in his arms. "Hey, Grandma," he said. "Hi."

Another man, the same age as Juanita's grandson, got out of the passenger's side and walked over to them, grinning at the old lady's unrestrained show of affection. Steven made introductions: "Tyler, this is my grandmother, Juanita McCoy," he said. "This is my buddy, Tyler Woodruff," he told Juanita.

The other boy came around and shook Juanita's hand. The old woman was shaking, she was so excited. "Come sit with me, boys," she said in a voice that hadn't sounded so high and girlish in decades. She led them to a small gazebo outside the kitchen that was canopied by trellises overgrown with red, orange, and purple bougainvillea. "Tell me what you've been up to."

Steven McCoy was the youngest child of Juanita's son and daughter-in-law. Her youngest grandchild, and her favorite. He had been visiting the ranch with his parents since he was barely old enough to be lifted up on a horse. A fluid, natural athlete, by the time he was seven he could ride as well as most of the cowboys Juanita and Henry hired to help out during roundup. He enjoyed life on the ranch, more than his father had.

"We've been tooling around the past couple of weeks," Steven told his grandmother. "Nevada, Idaho, Oregon. After we leave here we're heading straight home. School starts the beginning of next week."

Steven was a biology major, an honors student about to start his senior year at the University of Arizona. Next year he planned on going to medical school. His future was wide open, boundless.

"Well, I'm pleasured you stopped by," Juanita said. "Although I wish you had given me notice, so I could have planned something."

"We've been road-tramping it, Grandma," Steven explained, "so I didn't know when we'd get here. I knew we'd stop by, though. You know that this is one of my favorite places on earth."

"How did you get in here?" Juanita asked. "The gate wasn't unlocked, was it?"

"It was locked," he reassured her. "I memorized the combination when I was out here last Christmas."

"Okay, then," she said, mollified. "What are your plans?"

"We want to spend the night here."

"Here? In this old house?"

"Is that a problem?" A cloud of worry crossed his face. "It might be my last chance. Sleeping with all the ghosts."

"No, no," she declared. "Not at all. What about dinner?" She remembered the sage she had picked earlier. "I could barbeque, and make biscuits. Fresh corn and tomatoes from my garden."

"Can we do breakfast instead?" he asked. "I want to show Tyler around Santa Barbara. Go to Brophy's for dinner. I'm hankering for seafood."

"Breakfast it is," she agreed, masking her disappointment. "How early?" she asked. "I'm up before the chickens," she said with a laugh.

"Early's good," he said. "We're going to need an early start." He stood up. His friend Tyler followed suit. "Going to go now," he told her. "See you mañana." He gave her a kiss on the cheek.

"Don't forget to lock the gate behind you," Juanita called, as the boys walked back to their truck.

Steven raised a nonchalant thumb in acknowledgment. They got into their Pathfinder and drove off down the road.

3

HIGH SCHOOL HAD been back in session for less than a week, and already Maria Estrada was bored. What more could she learn that would do her any good? She wasn't going to UCSB or city college, which some of her friends were planning to do, so it didn't matter if her grades were any good.

The social side would be excellent. She was looking forward to the benefits of being a senior: the parties, dances, shopping with her friends, coffee in the mall, sleeping over with her friends on the weekends, more shopping. Shopping was one of the things she did best, she set the styles for her girlfriends.

And boys. Maria had been a boy magnet since the seventh grade, and she had never been stingy about sharing her favors. By now, though, none of the boys her age had any luster, they were too young and immature. For the past year she had turned her attention to older guys, like the Marine she had met over the summer, Dennis Montoya, who had been home on leave from Iraq. He'd had money, a plentiful supply of drugs, and he was crazy-wild. The way he explained why he acted like he did was, once you've looked death in the face, nothing scares you.

He was gone now, back to Iraq, or somewhere else. She had tried to stay in touch with him, but he hadn't answered any of her letters or e-mails.

Classes were over for the day. Maria sat at one of the outside picnic-style tables at Chico's, a taco stand near her school. For once, she was by herself. Her two best friends, Sonia Garcia and Jeannette Lopez, who she usually had lunch with, were trying out for the volleyball team. Maria didn't want to be on the team—too much commitment, you had to go to practice regularly, you had to go to all the games, a million stupid rules. She had played volleyball in junior high, but she wasn't good at it—her serve was weak, and she couldn't jump very high. If she couldn't do something well, she didn't want to do it at all. Which was why she wasn't doing any extracurricular activities this year, not even drama, which she actually did like and was good at. There were too many girls who would be trying out for the same parts she'd be trying out for. And the drama coach had a prejudice against Latina girls, the Anglo girls always got the best parts. You couldn't prove it, but everybody knew it was the truth.

Two guys came from the pickup window carrying baskets of food and bottles of beer. After glancing around to see if there were any vacant tables, they walked over to hers. "Mind if we sit here?" one of them asked.

She looked up at him, shielding her eyes against the sun at their backs. He was tall, thin, ropy-muscular. Dirty-blond hair, green eyes. He was hot, she thought immediately. Handsome and casually arrogant, the way she liked her men. His friend was not as tall, but good-looking enough. They carried themselves with an easy self-assurance.

"Okay," she said after a pause, like she owned the table and was doing them a favor by allowing them to share it with her.

They sat down across from her. The one who had spoken to her took a bite out of his taco and washed it down with a mouthful of beer. "Are you from around here?" he asked her, trying to strike up a conversation. He smiled—his teeth were perfectly straight.

She nodded. What would she be doing around here otherwise?

"I'm Tom," the boy said. "This is Bill. And you're . . ."

"Maria," she answered.

Immediately, she wished she hadn't given him her real name. Not that it mattered—they were just sitting here, sharing a table.

"Go to the high school, Maria?" Tom asked, still smiling at her.

She nodded again. "I'm a senior."

"You look old for a senior," he told her. "I don't mean you're old-looking, you look kind of sophisticated for high school. I would have guessed college."

He was bullshitting her, but in a nice, flirty way, so that was okay. "I'm on the cusp," she said, "I turned eighteen last week. I'm one of the older ones in the class." She sipped some coffee— it had gone cold. "I'm going to college next year. City college."

"That's smart," he said. "Good way to get started."

"So, like, you're in college?" she asked. That was pretty obvious, but she had to keep up her end of the conversation.

"Yep. We're in college." He nodded at his friend, who nodded back.

UCSB, she thought. Unless they went to one of the schools down south, like UCLA or USC. They had that L.A. look about them. "What year?" she asked.

"Seniors," he answered. "Our last year until going out into the real world."

Hers, too. The thought suddenly depressed her. Only nine more months of mindless fun.

The boy who was doing the talking leaned forward on his elbows. "What're you doing the rest of the afternoon?"

Okay, there it was, he had officially hit on her. "I don't have nothing planned," she said, trying to sound like she wasn't that interested in him, but wasn't totally disinterested, either. That she could be persuaded, if he knew how to be charming.

He glanced around. No one else was close to their table. "Do you . . ." He put his thumb and forefinger to his lips and sucked in slowly.

She smiled. "Well, yeah. If it's good."

"It's good," he told her, his smile broadening. "Better than good. It's outstanding." Leaning in closer, he said in a soft voice, "Got some E, too."

This day was going to be okay after all, she thought with a fluttering of excitement in her chest.

"So you want to take a drive?" he asked.

"Sure," she answered, not pretending to be blasé now. "I'll meet you around the corner, okay?" She couldn't chance anyone she knew seeing her leaving here with two strange older guys she had only met ten minutes ago. Particularly Anglos; her mother would not like that, any of it. The two of them had been at war for years.

"Okay," he agreed. He hesitated a moment, then asked, "Do you have a friend who could join us?"

Maria sat back. That was a problem.

Looking around, she spied a girl sitting alone on the other side of the patio. This girl was also Chicana, but she didn't know her, although the girl looked vaguely familiar. "Wait here," she told the guys.

She got up and walked over to the other girl's table. The girl looked up as Maria hovered over her. "Hello?" she said tentatively.

Maria picked up on the girl's accent. She wasn't from California, or anywhere in the United States. Mexico, or somewhere else deeper in Central America.

"Hi," Maria said easily. Without waiting for an invitation, she sat down at the girl's table. "I'm Maria Estrada," she said, favoring this new girl with an assured smile. "I've seen you around. What's your name?"

The girl seemed flustered. "Tina," she said. "Tina Ayala." She hesitated. "We're in English together."

Maria nodded knowingly. "I knew I knew you from somewhere. You're new around here, right?"

The girl named Tina nodded. "We moved to Santa Barbara this summer. From L.A.," she added.

"Cool," Maria exclaimed, as that explained everything. "So, like, who do you hang out with?"

"Nobody in particular," Tina answered self-consciously. "I haven't met many people yet. School's only started a week."

"Yeah, it's tough coming to a new school, especially your senior year," Maria said sympathetically. "Maybe we could do stuff together," she casually offered.

The new girl almost blushed, either from embarrassment at not having any friends or chagrin at being an outsider, Maria didn't know. Or care. She was available, that was what counted.

"That would be . . . nice," Tina said in a soft voice.

Maria moved in for the kill. "So what're you doing now? Do you have any plans for this afternoon?"

Tina shook her head. "No."

Maria smiled at her, as if an idea had just come to her. "Hey, listen. Me and a couple friends are going to hang out for a while." She turned and looked at the two guys who were sitting at her table. "We can get them to score some beer or tequila. They have marijuana, too," she added in a conspiratorial whisper.

Tina didn't do drugs, and she rarely drank beer, or any alcohol. But she didn't want to blow the opportunity to become friends with Maria Estrada before she even had a chance. Maria was one of the most popular girls in the school. She always had a posse hovering around her. Being a friend of Maria Estrada's would certainly help her social position, which was basically non-existent.

She didn't have to smoke any dope, and one beer wouldn't be the worst thing to do in the world. She looked over at the boys. They were older, and Anglo. She had never been out with an Anglo boy; she hardly dated at all, her parents watched her like a hawk.

She was a senior in high school, almost eighteen. This was the way American kids lived. The way she wanted to be. "Okay," she said to Maria. "I'll go with you."

The girls met the boys around the corner, so they wouldn't be spotted by anyone they knew. They picked up a twelve-pack of Dos Equis at an AM/PM minimart and drove up Mission Ridge to Franceschi Park, at the top of the Riviera. "It's an awesome place," Maria promised, as she instructed them how to go. "And hardly anybody knows about it."

Tom drove; she sat next to him. By the time they were halfway there her hand had found a resting place halfway up his thigh. Tina was in back with the other boy. They sat further apart from each other, neither one comfortable in making the first move.

The park was empty except for the four of them. Maria and Tom led the way down a narrow trail, the other two lagging behind.

"You were right. This is a fantastic view," Tom remarked, as he looked down at the entire city laid out below them. He opened a can of beer and handed it to her, then cracked one for himself.

"It's really pretty at night," Maria told him. "All the city lights shining, and the harbor."

"I'll bet," he answered. It *was* pretty, but he hadn't come up here for the scenery. "You wanna smoke?"

"Well, yeah," she answered, like he even had to ask. Wasn't that why she was here with him, among other reasons?

He took a pipe that was already packed from his shirt pocket. He lit it, took a hit, passed it to her. She inhaled deeply, sucking a lungful of smoke down her throat. She held it in for a few seconds, exhaled in a raspy cough, swallowed a mouthful of beer. "That's good," she croaked. She took the pipe from him and hit it again. She could feel the high coming on, like she was floating.

He pulled her to him in a hard kiss. She pressed her body up against his. Through his pants, she could feel his erection. She broke the kiss off and led him around the corner of the trail. As soon as they were out of sight of the other two, she turned to him and they started grinding against each other.

Behind them, Tina and the other boy stood together awkwardly. "Do you want a beer?" he asked her.

His name was Billy. The way he'd said it when he first introduced himself made her think it probably wasn't his real name, just like she didn't think the other boy's name was Tom. It didn't matter—she was here to become Maria's new friend, not to cozy up with a boy she almost certainly would never see again after today.

Although he was nice, surprisingly. He hadn't tried to grope her in the car, and he wasn't pushing her now. It was hot, and she was thirsty. She could drink a beer. "Okay," she said to his offer. "I would."

They sat down on a flat rock. He pulled a thin joint from his pocket, held it up. She shook her head. "Maybe later," she told him apologetically. She felt kind of stupid about that, because everyone did it. But she wasn't going to get high with a boy she didn't know. "You go ahead."

He toked up. They drank from their cans of beer in silence for a few moments. Then he put his arm around her shoulder, drew her to him, and kissed her. For a moment she panicked, but she fought back the urge to fight him off. He was a good kisser; gentle, not rough, not pushy. She leaned into his body and kissed him back.

Maria and Tom smoked another pipeful and drank a couple more beers apiece. She was high, and she was horny. This boy—more a man than a boy—knew how to touch her the right way, in the right places. Normally she wasn't into having sex out in the open, but no one else was around, except Tina and the other guy, who were into their own thing, out of sight around the corner, so she let him pull up her top and push the bra off her breasts, then put his hand between her legs under her skirt and snake a couple of fingers inside her panties, into her vagina.

She unzipped his fly and grabbed his erection. "Put on a rubber. I don't fuck without protection. I already had to get rid of one baby, I don't want to go through that shit again."

"Fuck." He sat up. "They're in the car." Clumsily, he zipped his pants up. "I'll go get one. Don't go anywhere."

She giggled. Like she was going to move an inch. "Okay, but hurry."

"Be right back." He started running up the trail to the parking lot.

Tina was having a panic attack. The kissing had been nice, slow and gentle. Even his hand on her breast, on top of her blouse, was all right. But then his hand had slipped under her blouse onto her bra, and then it was under her bra, on her bare skin. Swallowing her nervousness, she let him caress her there; it felt good, she couldn't deny that. But when his hand slipped up her legs before she could stop him, his knee between her thighs so she couldn't close them, that was too much.

"Please," she whispered into his ear. "Don't." She squeezed her legs together as hard as she could, trying to stop his hand from getting inside the elastic around her waist. Nearby, she could hear Maria and Tom getting ready to have sex. The sound was carrying clearly in the narrow canyon. Hearing them increased her terror.

"It's okay," he whispered back. He pushed his hand up harder, trying to get a finger inside the panties.

"No," she said more firmly. "I don't want to."

The hand stopped moving.

"I'm sorry." She was afraid she was going to start crying. "I can't."

"Why not?" he asked.

"Because . . ." *Because I don't know you. Because you're white and I'm Latina. Because I'm a virgin, and I'm not going to give myself to a boy I don't know, the first time. To any boy I don't love.* "I can't. Not out here, in a place like this. Not with other people around."

He sat back. "Okay," he sighed in resignation. "I guess I understand," he told her, although his body language said otherwise.

"Thank you." She sat up and rearranged herself, pulling her brassiere back into place, smoothing her blouse out. "You need to take me back now."

They drove down the winding road into the city. The silence was oppressive. Maria had blown up at Tina when the other boy told them they had to take Tina back. She and Tom hadn't been able to do anything—the condom was still in the package, in his pants pocket.

Tina, sitting as far in the corner of the car as she could, was miserable. She could feel the anger rising from Maria like heat off a griddle. But she couldn't help that, she had to be true to herself. If having sex with a boy she didn't even know was what it took to be a friend of Maria Estrada's, then she wouldn't be her friend. She had never been Maria's friend anyway, so it wasn't like she was losing something important.

Still, she knew it was going to be a long year.

Maria wanted to go to Paseo Nuevo, the large shopping mall on State Street. They drove into town and parked half a block from the entrance. Tina got out of the car and walked away, back to where the boys had picked her up. Tom and Maria talked on the sidewalk for a minute, while Billy waited in the car. Then Maria crossed the street and disappeared into the mall.

4

....

A GIRL'S VOICE called out from across the plaza: "Tyler?"

Steven and Tyler turned and looked as a cute, athletic-looking girl with short, red, wildly curly hair and a face full of freckles, came running toward them. She wearing running shorts, a *Property of UCSB Women's Swimming* T-shirt, and Dr. Scholl's clogs.

"Serena!" Tyler called back with the happy yelp of a puppy whose master just walked in the front door. "What are you doing here? I haven't seen you in . . ." He stared at her.

"Three years," she finished for him. "I go to UCSB now. I transferred last year. They have a really good environmental studies program, which is what I'm majoring in."

"I didn't know that." He stared at her with a dumbstruck expression on his face.

She grinned at him. "You can't know where your old friends have gotten to *if you don't keep in touch*!" She gave him a bop on the bicep. "But now you do, so no more excuses." She looked at Steven. "Who's this cute guy?"

Tyler laughed at her friendly brashness. "This is Steven McCoy, my roommate at Arizona. Steven, Serena Hopkins. We went to high school together in L.A."

"Hello, Tyler's roommate," Serena said nicely to Steven. Turning back to Tyler, she asked, "How long are you in town for?"

"Just till tomorrow. We've got to be back in Tucson by the weekend, for registration."

"Too bad," she said coyly.

This girl definitely liked Tyler, Steven could clearly see that. And Tyler liked her, that was obvious as well. What the hell. He hadn't done his good deed for today. "Why don't you two hang together for awhile?" he suggested.

Tyler, taken by surprise, turned to Steven. "What'll you do?"

"I have a girlfriend who I'm sure would like to join us," Serena piped up, smiling at Steven.

"Thanks, but I'm sure I can find something to occupy my time—or someone to do it with," Steven drawled. He winked at Tyler. "You guys don't need me horning in."

Tyler's hand rested lightly on Serena's back. "Sounds like a plan," he said, almost too eagerly. "How are we gonna hook up later?"

"We'll meet back here." Steven smiled at Serena. "Be nice to him. He needs some TLC."

"I know how to do that," she replied brightly.

"Okay, then," Steven said. He gave Tyler a thumbs-up, and walked into the crowd.

Tyler sat on one of the heavy pine benches near the multiplex movie theater. The mall was packed with people out for an evening on the town. He looked up as Steven approached, walking rapidly. "Where have you been?" he asked peevishly. "It's after eight."

Their plan had been to meet up at seven. Steven was over an hour late.

"Around." Steven slumped onto the bench.

"Wasn't your phone on?"

Tyler had tried calling Steven on his cell. He had been sitting here for almost an hour by now, waiting for Steven to show up. A wasted hour he could have spent with Serena.

"I turned it off when I went to the movies. Sorry," Steven apologized. "How did it go with your cute little friend?"

"Nice." Tyler couldn't hold back a shit-eating smile.

"Dude!" Steven grinned back. "You got laid!"

Tyler put up his hands like he was under arrest, but he didn't stop smiling. "A gentleman doesn't divulge such intimate happenstances."

"You fuckin' got laid, you dog!" Steven clapped Tyler on the back. "So what, you're getting married tomorrow? I didn't pack my tux."

Tyler laughed self-consciously. "We had fun, that's all. What'd you do?"

Steven shrugged. "Nothing as good as you." He turned away to look at the streaming pedestrian traffic. "Went down to the beach for awhile, had a few brews, went to a movie. Very unbig deal."

Tyler looked at him sympathetically. "Too bad. I thought you'd try to . . ."

"Meet the girl of my dreams and fall in love, like you? No such luck." Steven stood up. "Let's go. I could eat a bear and two of her cubs."

They sat at an outside table at Brophy's, scarfing down oysters on the half shell, clam chowder, fried clams, fish and chips. Several bottles of Sierra Nevada slackened their thirst. By the time they drove into the valley and got back to the ranch, it was almost eleven. Steven pulled off the county blacktop onto the gravel road. He drove through the open gate, stopped the Pathfinder, got out, swung the gate closed, and slammed the lock home.

"Did we forget to lock the gate behind us when we left earlier?" Tyler asked as Steven got into the car again. "I thought we did."

Steven shook his head. "Guess we didn't, obviously." He grimaced. "Don't tell my grandmother on me, okay? She gets uptight over ranch security. Like anyone's going to come in and steal anything out of this old place," he said cavalierly. "If you didn't know it was here, you'd never find it."

They drove up the narrow, dark road, parked outside the house, and went in. Steven gave Tyler the nickel tour. They navigated by the light of their flashlights, but it was too dark to see very well.

"Are we sleeping in here?" Tyler asked, when they reached the back bedroom. He stared at the old, massive furniture. "This is like out of *Gone With the Wind*."

Steven hoisted himself up onto the edge of the high bed. This had been his great-grandparents' room, way back when. He had slept here a few times when he was a little boy. The mattress felt like sleeping on a cloud, he remembered, as he laid back on it for a moment.

"Nah," he said, pushing himself back up. "Too stuffy. And we can't smoke in here."

He took a long, slow piss into the high porcelain toilet in the bathroom. Too much beer, he thought, as he pulled the flush chain. The old pipes banged as the water circled down the bowl.

Back outside, they unrolled their sleeping bags on the grass under the gazebo and fished fresh beers from their cooler. Steven lit up a blunt. He toked deeply and passed it to Tyler.

"This shit could paralyze an elephant," Tyler wheezed as he coughed out a lungful of smoke. "Somebody didn't have a tolerance for it, it could knock them flat on their ass." He took a pull from his beer. "Hell, I've been smoking it since we've been on the road, and it's *still* wasting me."

Steven didn't answer. He was in the moment, enjoying the sensation of being high. It was a clear night; the black sky was a blanket of millions of tiny, shimmering lights. They passed the joint back and forth, lying on their backs, staring up through the vines covering the gazebo to the stars over their heads.

By the time the boys woke up the following morning, Juanita was already cooking pancakes and frying bacon on the wood-burning stove in the old kitchen. The oilcloth-covered table was set with heavy ranch plates, flatware, thick coffee mugs.

The boys staggered inside, barefoot in jeans and T-shirts, hair unkempt, mouths dry. She placed two glasses of freshly squeezed orange juice in front of them, and two cups of steaming, tar-black coffee.

"You two look like you had quite a night on the town," she commented, not disapprovingly.

"Have the belly dancers left yet?" Steven said, yawning and scratching his stomach. "And the mariachis?"

Juanita hovered at his shoulder. "Did you have a good time?" she asked, eager to share any part of his life. It had been a long time since she had been around young people. She enjoyed their company, their carefree enthusiasm.

"He did," Steven said in a mock-grouchy voice, cocking his head toward Tyler.

"I met an old friend from high school," Tyler explained to Juanita.

"An old *girl*friend," Steven clarified. "I had to practically throw him into chains to dragoon him back here with me."

Tyler laughed and shook his head. "Who was waiting on who?" he countered.

"As long as you both had fun," Juanita said, enjoying their repartee. She lifted the pancakes off the griddle onto two plates, added several slices of thick bacon, and put the food down in front of them. From her apron pocket she produced a bottle of maple syrup, which she put on the center of the table.

"What about you?" Steven asked her, as he doused his flap-jacks with syrup.

"I ate hours ago," she said airily. "Come on, dig in. I've got a bowl of batter that'll go to waste if you two don't finish it up."

Too soon, as far as Juanita was concerned, the boys had finished their breakfast, packed their car, and were ready to go.

Steven hugged his grandmother. "Thanks for everything, Grandma."

Her goodbye hug was firmer. "Don't be a stranger, Steven," she admonished him.

"I'll be back before you know it," he promised her.

"I'm going to hold you to that," she said. She took Tyler's hand. "It was a pleasure meeting you, Tyler. I hope you'll come back, too."

"That would be great, Mrs. McCoy. It's a beautiful place you've got."

She reached up on her toes and kissed Steven on the cheek. The boys got into their Pathfinder and started down the road, throwing a cloud of dust in their wake. She stood in place and watched until the dust had settled and the sound of their engine could no longer be heard.

5
....

KATE BLANCHARD LUGGED the last bulky carton of books up the stairs to her daughter Wanda's second-floor apartment and dumped it in a corner of the living room. I'm too old for this pack-mule routine, she thought to herself. She was sweaty, dirty, and hungry. She wanted a shower, a mixed drink, something to eat that wasn't takeout. A foot-rub would be divine.

None of those pleasures were going to be afforded her tonight. This forty-eight-hour block of time was for settling Wanda in, making sure the basics were covered: the gas, water, and electricity functioning properly, Wanda's clothing, furniture, personal belongings secure in her new digs. The first night in a new place was a special event. It would set the tone for Wanda's new life. She wanted her daughter to feel good here, because Wanda was going to have enough stress in her daily existence without being anxious about her living space.

The apartment was in the Haight, a few blocks removed from the heavy street action. It had been a lucky find, a last-minute vacancy. Kate, Wanda, and Sophia, her younger daughter, had spent all day yesterday cleaning up the previous tenant's accumulated dirt and grime. This morning they'd hung curtains and lined the kitchen shelves.

The day after tomorrow, Wanda was starting classes at UC San Francisco Medical School. Kate still had a hard time believing the daughter of a working woman and an abusive, absent father, had pulled it off. A girl who during most of her teenage years had been raised (to Kate's burning shame) more by her aunt and uncle than by her own mother. A girl who had won a scholarship to Stanford and graduated with honors, who had worked nights and weekends at a pizza joint to pay for her other expenses, so she wouldn't be a burden to her mother.

When Kate would wake up from the recurring nightmare of her daughters living with her sister and brother-in-law, because she was unable to be there for them during the years when she was going through a brutal divorce while at the same time being fired from the Oakland police department, she would be awash with the sweat of contrition. And yet, despite having been absent on a day-to-day basis during some of the most important years of their lives, her daughters had never questioned her desire to do the best she could for them, an act of charity, forgiveness, and unconditional love that still amazed, humbled, and brought tears to her eyes.

All that was in the past (knock wood). After that series of debacles she turned her life around. She became a private detective in Santa Barbara, which earned her a decent living, restored her confidence, and allowed her to take charge of her family again. Sophia had moved to Santa Barbara last spring, in the middle of her junior year of high school. By then, regrettably, Wanda was in college, so she and Kate had never lived together during her high school years. Kate had never seen Wanda dressed up for a prom, hadn't helped her with her homework, hadn't talked to her about boys, drugs, teen angst, her future.

Yet through all the separation, mother and daughters had stayed emotionally close. And now, they were together again. It had been a long time since Kate had been this happy and content with her life.

"I'm ordering in pizza, Mom," Wanda called from the bedroom, where she and Sophia were putting her clothes away. "What do you want on it?"

"Anything," Kate called back. "Except anchovies." She sagged into a fold-open director's chair. "Can they deliver beer?"

"I guess. If they don't there's a deli on the corner. What kind?"

"Whatever. Something decent. If we're forced to eat pizza we should at least drink good beer."

Sophia walked back into the living room. She looked around at everything strewn about or in yet-unpacked boxes. "This is such a cool apartment," she enthused. "This is how I want to live, when I have my own place. Next year, if I go to Berkeley, maybe I could move in here with Wanda."

Kate looked at her. They were so close, those two, she thought, with a pang of envy. Wanda had chosen Stanford over Brown because she hadn't wanted to be far from her sister. Until Sophia had moved to Santa Barbara the girls had spent at least two weekends a month together, Sophia going down to Palo Alto and camping out on the floor of wherever Wanda was living, Wanda coming up to the city to stay with Sophia at her aunt Julie's place.

Kate thought, still too much, of how things might have been—should have been, could have been—different among the three of them. She had been especially hard on herself about her deficiencies as a mother, as a parent. But that was the past, which she couldn't change. She was going to do the best she could from now on, and try not to beat herself up over her failures.

They sat on the floor, eating pizza out of the box. Kate looked around the apartment. "This was such a lucky find. It's a great location."

"Which I'll appreciate when I'm here, which will be almost never," Wanda said. She stretched out on the floor. "First year of med school. Only the strong survive. The rest get MBAs."

"Well, you'll certainly be one of the survivors," Kate said loyally.

"I know, Mom. I'm not worried." Wanda looked out the bay window to the street below. "So are you guys going to stay over tonight?"

Kate shook her head. "Sophia's already missed two days of school, and it's only the first week. She has all APs, she can't get behind."

Sophia was sitting on the floor, next to Wanda. Kate reached a hand down to help her up. "Time for us to hit the road, kiddo. You'll sleep on the way back."

Reluctantly, Sophia got to her feet. She looked at Wanda, at her mother, then back at her sister. "Mom? Can I ask you a really, *really* big favor?"

The anxiousness in Sophia's voice flew by Kate. "Sure, honey. What?"

"Can I stay here?"

Kate sighed. "We can't, Sophia. You've got to be in class tomorrow, you know that. And I have a court appearance at ten." She smiled wanly. "I wish we could. But we can't, not this time. We'll come back, soon. I promise."

Sophia closed her eyes and inhaled deeply. When she opened them, she looked away from her mother. "I meant . . . permanently," she said in a voice barely above a whisper. "Live here. With Wanda."

Kate's mouth flew open in shock. She turned and stared at Wanda. Wanda shook her head—*I didn't know she was going to say that.*

Somehow, Kate managed to stay on her feet, although the room was reeling. "No, Sophia," she said, trying to appear calm. Inside, she was screaming. "You can't live here." She had to sound rational, she couldn't lose control: "Wanda's going to be gone almost all the time, you aren't enrolled in a school here, it's . . ." She put her knuckles to her eyes. "You live in Santa Barbara now, Sophia. With me."

"You're never home, either."

Kate moaned. "That's not fair."

"You work until seven or eight every night," Sophia blurted out, spinning around to confront her mother. "And you're in law school two nights a week, and Saturday mornings." She was verging on tears now. "I hardly ever see you, Mom."

Where did that two-ton safe come from that had suddenly crashed down on her heart? "That's not . . . true." It wasn't, exactly; but there was too much truth to it not to cut to the bone.

"It is," Sophia came back at her.

Kate inhaled slowly, then exhaled. "Do you want me to quit law school? Is that it?" she asked.

As soon as the words were out of her mouth she started to shake inside again. She had been going to the law school, nights and Saturday mornings, for two and a half years. In another year and a half she would have her degree, six months later she'd take the bar, and she would be an attorney, instead of a private detective who worked for attorneys.

"No, Mom," Sophia protested. "No. It's just that . . ."

"I can take a year off," Kate said. Her heart was beating like a hummingbird's. "Next year you'll be in college. I've waited this long already, one more year isn't going to make that much difference."

Maybe it would, maybe it wouldn't. Emotionally, of course it would. It would be wrenching. But she needed to be with her daughter more. They had so little time left.

"No, Mom." Sophia's eyes were tearing up. "Really, I don't want you to quit, not even for a year. It's not that. It's . . ." An *arrrgh* of pain came from her gut. *"I hate it there, okay?"* she wailed. "I *hate* Santa Barbara! It's totally plastic. I hate the high school, it's all shitty little cliques." She was crying now, bawling. "I don't have any friends there, Mom. It's like I'm a fucking ghost. They already have all their friends, there's no room for me. All my friends are here, in San Francisco. I haven't had one date since I've been there. And I don't even have a car, so I can't go anywhere, I'm stuck. I *hate* it. I hate my life!"

"Ah, Sophia . . ." Kate was reeling, she was going to black out. She grabbed the sofa to support herself.

"I know you want me to be with you, Mom!" Sophia cried. "And I want to be with you, I do. But my life there is horrible.

Why don't you get it? I got there too late. I can't help that. I wish I could, Mom. But I can't." She slumped to the floor in a heap.

Kate stared down at her. "I . . . you just can't live here with Wanda," she said in a shattered voice. "Not like this, with no preparation. And you couldn't anyway, it's not the way things are. I'm sorry, I don't know . . ." She trailed off.

Wanda knelt down and put her arms around Sophia. "Hey," she said softly. She looked up at Kate. "Can we talk for a minute, Mom? She and I?"

"Sure," Kate answered numbly. Her spirit and brain were fried. "I'll take a walk."

"Not for long," Wanda said. "Just a few minutes."

Kate hiked down to Haight Street and went into the first joint she came across. She sat alone at the end of the dark wooden bar, drinking a vodka martini, straight up. She hadn't smoked a cigarette in fifteen years, but if smoking was still permitted in California bars she would have lit one up without hesitation.

She milked her drink, because she knew two would be over the top. Finally draining it to the last drop, she gathered her change off the bar and trudged back up the street to Wanda's apartment.

The girls were waiting for her. Sophia had washed her face and redone her lip gloss. She smiled wanly at Kate, who was shaking inside.

"It's okay, Mom," Sophia said in an even, steady voice. "I know I can't stay here." She turned to her sister for a moment, then looked at Kate again. "I need to be with you." She paused. "We need to be with each other."

6

WHEN MARIA ESTRADA didn't come home by ten o'clock at night, her mother tried her on her cell phone, but got the recorded message. After she dialed two more times with the same result she started calling Maria's friends, trying to find her delinquent daughter. But none of the usual suspects knew where Maria was, and after an hour of fruitless trying, Mrs. Estrada gave up and went to bed.

This wasn't the first time Maria hadn't come home at night over the past few months; during summertime, kids slept over at each other's houses as much as they slept at their own. But now, although school had started again, Maria was still gypsying around. She'd show up at home when she felt like it, blithely announcing that she'd been at this or that friend's house and had forgotten to call, or had tried and the line was busy, or that she'd lost track of the time and it was too late to call—the usual litany of lame excuses that she knew her mother didn't believe but didn't have the energy to get into a fight over. Mrs. Estrada was pretty sure that Maria had a boyfriend she was keeping secret, probably an older man the family wouldn't approve of. She knew that Maria had been sexually active for at least two years, because she had found a discarded condom mixed up in her daughter's underwear (she was always cleaning up after Maria, a worse-than-usual teenage slob) in the spring of Maria's tenth-grade year, and had angrily confronted Maria about it. Maria had flown into a rage at the invasion of her privacy, declaring that if she wanted to have sex that was her business, she was almost six-teen and every other girl in the universe was doing it, and that her mother ought to be glad she was using protection.

They hadn't spoken to each other for almost a week after that blowup, and from then on Maria's sexual activities weren't mentioned. Her mother put her head in the sand about the subject, and they managed to coexist under the same roof. As long as Maria didn't get pregnant, come down with a sexually transmitted disease, get heavily into drugs, and did the minimum amount of work required to graduate, Mrs. Estrada was willing to turn a blind eye. In nine months Maria would finish high school, get a job, and would move in with two of her older female cousins who had their own apartment in Carpinteria. Latino girls didn't stay at home with their families until they were married anymore, especially antsy girls like Maria. Mrs. Estrada wasn't unhappy with that prospect.

But when Maria failed to show up at school the next day—the social services worker called, checking up on her—and didn't come home again that night, there was enough cause for alarm that Mrs. Estrada, a divorced woman who had raised Maria on her own, was sufficiently worried that she called the police and filed a missing-persons report. Because Maria had been gone for less than two days, was over eighteen (which made her ineligible for an Amber Alert), and had a history of casualness in her schedule, the officer who took down the information didn't give the call a high priority. He promised Mrs. Estrada that a detective would get on it in the morning, but that in all likelihood Maria would turn up soon.

Although she was still worried after she talked to the cop, Mrs. Estrada was inclined to agree with him. She knew that her daughter was a tramp, and figured that Maria had probably found some jerk with money to shack up with for a few days. She would have a line of bullshit all prepared when she finally waltzed back home, and they would dance around the subject, and Maria would promise to stay in touch better, and they'd sweep the trouble under the rug, same as they always did.

Kate Blanchard stared at the notes on her computer screen. The words were blurring together; she shook her head to clear the cobwebs.

She was tired; recently, she seemed to be tired most of the time. She had nineteen active cases on her calendar. In addition, there were the two nights of law school, three hours each night, as well as her normal household chores. And of course, trying to spend time, not just sharing space, but real quality time, with Sophia.

Since their return from San Francisco, Sophia had adopted an attitude of sullen nonaggression toward both her mother and her school. She was up early without prompting in the morning, the day's clothing and accessories neatly laid out the night before. She talked to her mother about what was going on in her life—school, kids, her routine—without revealing anything personal, anything about her feelings. In the evenings she did her homework, watched television, talked to her sister on her cell phone. It felt to Kate like they were two strangers on a long ocean cruise who had been assigned to the same table for meals and had to exchange polite conversation.

She was trying her best to bridge the gulf between them. The day after they returned home from San Francisco she had dipped into her savings and bought Sophia a car from a mechanic she trusted. It was a twelve-year-old Volvo with high mileage, but it ran decently. Sophia hadn't shown much outward emotion when Kate handed her the keys—a quick hug and a "Thanks, Mom"— but she was thrilled to have it. She could come and go on her own now without having to worry about borrowing her mother's car. Sophia had already started putting her own personal touches on the old wagon—dried flowers woven around a bird's feather hung from the rearview mirror, and an Indian shawl she'd found in a local flea market covered the worn backseat.

"Hi, Mom."

Kate turned in surprise. She hadn't heard the front door open. "Hi there," she answered back.

Her office was on Anapamu Street, close to the courthouse, the central police station, and coincidentally, the high school. Last spring, Sophia would stop by after school and do her homework while she waited for Kate to drive her home. This was the first time this year she had come here after school.

Kate flushed with enjoyment from the unexpected visit. "How's school?" Not the most intimate of questions, but she was treading lightly these days.

"The usual crap. My last period class was cancelled, so I thought I'd come bug my mommy." Sophia tossed her backpack onto a chair. "You want to hear my latest news?"

Kate looked up from her computer screen. "Sure."

Sophia unsuccessfully tried to appear nonchalant. "I auditioned for the fall play."

"That's great!" Kate could feel the smile spreading across her face. "What is it?"

"*The Wizard of Oz*. It's not a musical. We're doing the original play, not the movie."

"What part did you try out for?" Kate asked eagerly.

Under her olive complexion, Sophia crimsoned slightly. "Dorothy. I won't get it," she said quickly. "There are too many girls who've been doing the plays at school since their freshman year. The drama coach has his policies—new kids never get leads. But I could get one of the other parts, like a munchkin."

Kate stood up and gave Sophia a hug, both for love and support. This was a good sign, Sophia's first positive move in a long time. Kate almost literally felt her shoulders lighten. "Have an upbeat attitude," she told Sophia. "Maybe the drama coach will think outside the box."

Sophia nodded. "Whatever happens, it'll be fun." She peered over her mother's shoulder at the computer screen. "Whatcha working on? Not that I'd understand, even if you explained it to me. God, Mom, the shit you have to deal with sometimes. I don't know how you do it."

That makes two of us, Kate thought. She had to find a way off this treadmill.

Sophia grabbed her backpack. "See you later. Do you have school tonight?"

"Afraid so," Kate said apologetically.

"No big deal," Sophia assured her. "You'll be home by nine. I'll wait to eat with you." She kissed her mother on the top of Kate's head. "You need new shampoo, Mom. I'll stop by the mall later and get you something that doesn't have a ton of chemicals."

She walked out the door, closing it behind her. Kate luxuriated for a moment in her daughter's lingering aura before getting back to her workload.

Keith Morton crisscrossed Rancho San Gennaro in his vintage Jeep Wrangler. He was beginning his biannual survey of the ranch. It would take weeks to cover the entire property, but that was all right, there was no hurry.

Keith was the ranch foreman. He and his wife, Esther, lived in a small house on the opposite side of the property from Juanita McCoy's house. Keith had the right personality for running a ranch—he loved rural life, he was patient, he was comfortable with his station in life. He was good at fixing almost anything that needed fixing on a ranch: machinery, fences, painting, plumbing, working with livestock. A good rider, and good with weapons.

Esther complemented his skills with her own—canning, gardening, animal husbandry. A childless couple in their mid-forties, they had been living and working on the ranch for over two decades; first Keith by himself, then Esther with him, after they got married. They were throwbacks to an earlier time, when a cowboy could have a life living on a ranch. Juanita was thankful to have them; not many people wanted this kind of life anymore.

Keith's Jeep maneuvered over the bumpy ground. As he came over a low rise, the ancestral ranch house came into sight in the distance, its west-facing windows reflecting the late afternoon sun. Off to the side, about half a mile from the house, he spied some turkey buzzards circling overhead, their small, ugly, naked red heads protruding from their bony shoulders. Keith hated buzzards. They were disgusting creatures, flying hyenas feasting on rotting meat. Usually when he saw a flock hovering like this, he would get a cold feeling in the pit of his stomach, because it almost always meant one of their calves had been killed by coyotes or wild dogs. Or a mountain lion. Five years ago, a rogue puma had gone marauding on the ranch, killing off two calves before he tracked it down and shot it. You were supposed to notify the state Bureau of Fish and Game if a predator killed your livestock, but nobody did. You killed them, then reported it. Maybe.

He stopped twenty yards from where the buzzards were clustered on the ground. Grabbing his shotgun from behind the seat, he got out and walked toward them. When he had halved the distance between his Jeep and the carrion-eaters, he fired a shot into the air. The sound reverberated across the hills. The buzzards flew up in a flurry of beating wings, cawing raucously, angry at having their meal disturbed.

He approached the spot where the birds had congregated—a low ravine, overgrown with thick mesquite brush. Thousands of flies, a black, living cloud, were swarming the area, their buzzing as loud as a chain saw. The stench filled his nostrils with a sharp, acrid smell that made his eyes tear.

What a mess, he thought in disgust, covering his mouth and nose with a hand to try to ward off the smell, which was overwhelmingly putrid. What was it? A deer? Another wild pig? Hopefully, not one of their livestock. He couldn't see it clearly; whatever they were feasting on was half-hidden under the clumps of dense brush.

Surmounting his revulsion, he walked a few steps closer. Using the barrel of his shotgun, he pushed the bushes aside to get a better look. For a few seconds, he stared at the remains, which were covered with writhing maggots, trying to figure out exactly what they were feasting on. Then he recoiled, violently.

"My God!" he blurted out, a hand going to his mouth to hold back the retching.

He sprinted back to the Jeep and grabbed his cell phone from the glove box. Fumbling with the buttons—they were small and his hands were shaking almost uncontrollably—he punched in 9-1-1.

All the entrances to the ranch were sealed off. Detectives from the county sheriff's department, led by head forensic detective Marlon Perdue, a twenty-year veteran, secured the remains. They also began a search of the area, on the chance that some evidence had been left behind by whoever had dumped the body; it was assumed that she (the victim was a woman—they could barely tell, the body was in such poor shape) hadn't gotten here on her own.

Perdue walked over to the old house, Keith Morton in tow. Impressive, Perdue thought. A real piece of history. He noticed that there were wrought-iron bars over the windows, and that the place, in general, appeared secure. He tried the front door—locked.

"Do you usually keep this locked up?" he asked Keith.

Keith nodded forcefully. "Hell, yes. There's a lot of valuable stuff in there. Impossible to replace."

Perdue looked the house over again for a moment, then walked back to where the remains were being handled. Overhead, helicopters from the tri-county area television stations circled like the vultures Keith Morton had found devouring the remains. A body discovered in the wild was always good television, the more grisly the better—this would be the lead story on tonight's local news. If it turned out that the yet-unidentified woman had not died from natural causes, or if she came from a

well-known family, or if one of several other juicy factors came
into play, so much the better, certainly for ratings. There was
already a good hook to this story, because of the location of
where the body had been found—Rancho San Gennaro was the
oldest operating ranch in the county, and the McCoy family was
one of its most socially prominent clans.

The corpse was placed in a body bag and put into a waiting
ambulance. Sirens blaring, lights flashing, the ambulance, escorted by a covey of motorcycle officers, headed toward Highway
154, which would lead them over the pass and into the city.

The remains were brought to the lab at Cottage Hospital, in
Santa Barbara. Peter Atchison, the county's pathologist, positioned the remains on the stainless-steel examination table. After
taking several photographs of the corpse, he snapped on a fresh
pair of latex gloves to begin the autopsy. I don't even need a saw
or knife, he thought with dark, grisly humor, I could almost do
this one with a spoon.

He turned on the tape recorder.

"These are the remains a woman who I would roughly cal-
culate to have been in her mid-teens to late twenties," he began.
"The amount of decomposition makes a more specific calculation
impossible. This ambiguity also applies to time of death, as the
high summer temperature has accelerated the normal pace of
decomposition. She seems to have been fully developed physically and sexually, but again, the remains are too poor to tell with
any certainty."

He began probing what remained of her torso. Almost immediately, he saw the reason for this corpse's demise. "Ah, damn it!"
he cried out involuntarily.

Marlon Perdue, who was witnessing the procedure, looked
up sharply. "What?" he asked, alerted to trouble by the tone of
Atchison's voice.

Atchison reached up to the supply shelf to get a sterile pair of tweezers. Using them as a spreader, he pointed to a small piece of metal in the chest cavity. "There."

Perdue bent over to get a closer look. "Shit on a stick," he exclaimed flatly.

As Atchison plucked out the foreign object and dropped it into a ziplock evidence bag, Perdue dialed the sheriff's direct emergency line. "Sheriff Griffin," a man's impatient voice came from the other end of the line.

"Marlon Perdue here, John," the detective said. "I've got preliminary results of the cause of death for the body we took from Rancho San Gennaro."

"What do you have?" the sheriff asked warily.

"Dr. Atchison found a bullet in the corpse," Perdue told his boss. "This victim was shot to death."

Atchison managed to lift a partial thumb print. It was sent to the state's regional Department of Justice forensic lab in Goleta. Within an hour, the cause of Maria Estrada's disappearance had been solved.

SPRAWLED OUT ON her sofa, Kate, exhausted from a long day's work, watched the youthful woman newscaster on the Channel 3 evening news. The reporter was in front of the county courthouse, a popular venue for television stand-ups. Behind her, reporters from other stations, some from as far away as Los Angeles and San Diego, were talking into their stations' cameras. Sunlight shone on the façade of the massive, Spanish-style courthouse; the report had been recorded earlier that day.

Sophia, busy with her homework at the kitchen table, looked up when she heard the reporter say "Maria Estrada." She turned away from her laptop and sat next to her mother.

A photograph of Maria from last year's high school yearbook came up on the TV screen. ". . . The missing girl was last seen eating lunch after school at a local taco stand," the reporter spoke into the camera.

The shot changed from the picture of Maria, a frozen smile on her face, to overhead helicopter footage of sheriff's investigators at the crime site. The camera zoomed in to the remains being placed into the body bag and followed the ambulance as it began driving away.

"Anyone with information about this case is urged to contact the county sheriff's department," the reporter said into the camera. An 800 number came up on the screen. Then the number faded out, and the reporter announced, "With us is Santa Barbara County sheriff John Griffin."

The camera widened to include the sheriff, a thin, middle-aged man in a western-cut business suit. "What can you tell us so far?" the reporter asked him. "Have you developed any leads? Are there any suspects?"

Griffin shook his head. "No one we wish to reveal at this time. We have some possible leads," he added with a deliberate vagueness. "When we have more substantial information, we will let the public know."

Meaning you don't have squat, Kate thought. The police don't go trolling their 800 number unless the cupboard is bare.

"There's speculation this killing may be drug-related," the announcer continued, gamely fishing for an angle.

"That's a possibility," Griffin replied, stubbornly noncommittal. "We're looking into it, along with other scenarios. Which is all I have to say for now." He walked out of the shot. The announcer turned to face the camera again. "That's it from here," she chirped. "Back to you in the studio, Arlene."

Kate hit the "off" button on her remote. "Did you know this girl?" she asked Sophia.

"Yes," Sophia answered, her eyes still on the blank screen. "I mean, I knew who she was. We didn't move in the same circles. She was more . . ." She hesitated.

"More what?" Kate asked with curiosity.

"Sociable," Sophia said charitably. "She wasn't into academics. We didn't have any classes together."

Sophia's description of Maria confirmed the rumors circulating around the courthouse—the dead girl screwed around. Her behavior would further complicate the sheriff's investigation; any man she had known might be a suspect. And there was the possible drug connection, which had to be taken seriously. Maria was related to Hector Torres, an activist in the Latino community who had been in the drug trade, years ago. He had supposedly gone straight, but you never knew. There was also the possibility the killer might be someone Maria had encountered the day she was killed; a transient who could be a thousand miles away by now.

This was going to be a hot case—that was a given. A high school girl with possible drug connections is murdered and the decomposed body is discovered on the property of one of the county's most distinguished families. All the elements for tabloid sensationalism.

Sophia got up. "I have this essay due tomorrow." She shuddered. "God, this is so horrible, mom! This girl was in my class. We breathed the same air."

Kate stood and hugged her. "I know." She pulled her daughter tighter. "I know, honey."

They held on to each other for a moment, then Sophia went back into the kitchen and hunched over her computer again. Kate looked after her. *That murdered girl could so easily have been my daughter,* she thought with a mother's gut-wrenching fearfulness.

Juanita McCoy ushered Louis Watson and Cindy Rebeck, the two veteran sheriff's detectives who had been assigned to head up the murder investigation, into her living room. They sat across from her as she slowly leafed through some eight-by-ten photos of Maria Estrada.

"I've never seen this girl," Juanita told them, after she carefully looked at the pictures. She handed them back to Rebeck. "I'm sorry." She sighed. "That poor child. Her family must be going through hell."

Rebeck, a tall, leggy blonde wearing a short skirt, a light cotton blouse, and low heels better suited for desk-jockeying than fieldwork, slid the pictures into a manila folder. She understood the old lady's tenderhearted attitude toward the victim's family, but she personally could never indulge in sympathy—she had a job to do, emotions got in the way.

"The security gate at the road-head?" she said. "That leads to the section of your property where the body was found? Do you keep it locked?" They had noticed the gate on the drive up.

Juanita nodded. "Yes, we do. We have concerns about theft, and vandalism. The original family homestead at the end of that road contains artifacts that are valuable and sentimental to our family. You don't want people coming onto your property that you don't know about," she said proprietarily.

"How many people normally come and go to that area?" Watson, a beefy man in his forties, asked.

"Only my foreman and his wife have unlimited access. They're my only full-time employees; everyone else who works on the ranch is seasonal, and they don't use that road."

Watson and Rebeck had already interviewed the Mortons. They didn't know anything, and they had solid alibis for the time frame when the girl had gone missing.

"Although if anybody wanted to get onto the ranch, they wouldn't find it very hard," Juanita continued. "The property is big, and remote. And there are ways to skirt around the gate," she added. "But the gate does help—some deterrent is better than none."

Watson made some notes. "You didn't see any suspicious activity for the days prior to the body being found?" he asked.

"No. It's usually quiet out here." Juanita bowed her head. "What a tragedy for her family," she said again.

Watson felt bad for Mrs. McCoy. This body had been discovered on her ranch, so now she was being dragged into the muck, even though the forensic detectives were almost positive that the murder had not been committed where the remains had been discovered. The preliminary investigation indicated that the girl had been killed somewhere else, then brought there. This was a remote location; a good place to dump a body you didn't want found. If the ranch foreman hadn't been out there surveying the property, the vultures and flies would have picked the corpse clean before it was discovered, and then it might never have been found. Regardless of where the girl had been killed, however, the body had turned up here. Mrs. McCoy was going to be in the limelight. Not something to wish on an older woman, particularly one of her stature in the community.

Juanita walked the detectives outside, shielding her eyes

against the high midday sun. "I hope you catch the killer soon," she said. "I don't like all these people tramping around out here."

"So do we," Watson answered tightly. "And we'll do our best to keep our incursions to a minimum. But we do have a murder to solve."

"I understand," Juanita answered. She went back inside, after promising to call them if she thought of anything that might be helpful.

"It's so pretty out here," Rebeck commented, looking past the barn to the pasture. "The authentic old Santa Barbara."

Watson, oblivious to the beauty around him, said darkly, "This is going to be a bitch."

"Tell me about it," Rebeck answered, her partner's morose objectivity bringing her down to earth with a thud. "We'd better come up with somebody who saw this *chiquita* the day she disappeared. She was a social butterfly, there have to be witnesses."

The detectives walked to their department-issue Crown Victoria. Watson slid in behind the wheel. He turned the ignition, but didn't put the car in gear. "There's one thing that doesn't compute."

"What?" Rebeck asked, as she fastened her seat belt.

"The gate on the road that leads there. If I'm trying to dump a body, I'm going to look for a place that's more accessible."

Rebeck nodded thoughtfully. "Maybe it wasn't locked that day. I'll bet they don't check on it that often."

"Anything's possible," Watson agreed glumly. He lightly banged on the steering wheel. "We'd better get lucky with a witness or we're going to be up shit's creek."

8

RIVA GARRISON, STEPPING out of the shower, glanced over at her husband, Luke, who was trimming his goatee with a battery-powered trimmer. "The gray's beginning to overtake the brown, big boy," she observed acutely, if not kindly. "You're starting to look like Willie Nelson."

"I'm not braiding my hair, if that's the direction you're pushing this conversation," he replied. "It isn't nearly long enough. And there aren't that many gray ones, comparatively." He squinted into the steamed-up mirror. "I'd say no more than ten percent."

It was six-thirty in the morning. Luke had already been out for his run. Now he stood naked in front of the mirror, a cup of coffee on the sink, peering at his foggy image.

Riva wrapped her own long, luxuriant, mink-brown hair in a towel and began drying off with another. "And aren't you about due for your annual eye exam?" she asked.

He rolled his eyes in mock-exasperation. "When did you start channeling Don Rickles?"

"Just stating the facts, counselor." She sat on the toilet lid and began drying off her legs. She nudged his bare tush with her toes. "Man turns fifty, it's like he becomes someone else. What is that?" she teased.

Three months ago, Luke had celebrated his fiftieth birthday. Riva had thrown a balls-out party for him. Everything was done up perfectly: she had a big tent erected in the backyard, where a caterer grilled New York steaks, baby back ribs, and Maine lobsters for two hundred of Luke's friends. Jack Daniel's, Johnnie Walker Black, and Veuve Clicquot were the house-pours. She also imported a killer blues band from L.A. It was a great bash: to quote John Lennon and Paul McCartney, "Everybody had a good time." Nobody thought about the flip side of that verse, "Everybody had a hard year."

Except Luke, who woke up the next morning with a raging hangover and the first gray hair in his beard. Since then, his goatee had become increasingly pewter in appearance. It was still mostly brown, but the tide was turning.

Not that he gave much of a shit; he wasn't a vain man. But it reminded him that life didn't go on forever. He had two young children and a wonderful wife. He wanted to hang around with them for a long time to come. The gray in his beard, the reading glasses he had started using a couple of years ago, the daily five-mile run that used to take thirty-eight minutes and now took forty-two; all signposts of this mortal coil we struggle through.

Well, that was a bit overreaching, he thought as he finished his beard-trimming and lathered shaving gel onto the rest of his face. No Hamlet he. *To be* was the only way for him, it always had been; *or not* was never an option.

That didn't mean he had to like the creeping grayness. Although a bit of distinction was a plus in the courtroom. If your hair grows to your shoulders, your goatee looks like it belongs on the face of a '50s tenor sax player, and you often don't wear a tie into court, you have to be a damn good, if not near-great barrister, to pull it off; and like the legendary Gerry Spence, who he saw occasionally around town and also famously didn't wear a tie, Luke was a great lawyer. Juries loved him, as did his clients.

It had been some journey, he thought, as he carefully shaved around his goatee, getting to the midcentury mark. Youngest District Attorney in the state at age thirty-four, gone from office (voluntarily, but under a cloud) before age forty, virtually retired by age forty-three, then a new life working the other side of the aisle as a criminal-defense lawyer by age forty-five. A real roller-

coaster of a ride. A wonderful wife, two healthy and bright children, work that he enjoyed (at least some of the time). Life was
good. Knock on wood.

Even with gray hairs and less-than-perfect vision to live with.

He answered Riva's jibe through the mirror. "He becomes a
fifty-year-old man, no more, no less," he stated, only the slightest
bit testy. "You don't need to be a rocket scientist to figure that out."

"And . . . ?" Dry now, she threw her towels into a hamper.

"And nothing. It's just a fact. A fact of life."

"And a benchmark."

He stared at her through the frosted glass. "What is the point
of this?" he asked, now a bit . . . petulant? Not a nice emotion.

She kissed him between the shoulder blades. "There is no
point. I'm teasing you, is all. Can't a wife tease her husband?"

"Not before seven in the morning."

"When else do we have time to ourselves?" she asked.

As if on cue, a high, shrill child's voice clamored: "Mommy!"

"Not for the rest of today, obviously," Luke answered.

Riva threw on a robe. "I'll be right down," she called back
equally loudly to their son. "And don't yell, you'll wake up your
sister."

Luke laughed. He put down his razor and reached into the
shower to turn on the spigots.

"Are you having breakfast with us this morning?" Riva asked
as he stepped in.

He shook his head. "I have a client coming in early."

"What about dinner? You haven't been home to eat with the
kids once this week."

He nodded—he was a notorious workaholic, but he was getting better. He didn't want to be an absentee father, like his own
had been before he had abandoned the family, when Luke was still
a kid. "I'll try. I'll definitely be home before bedtime," he promised.

"Mrs. McCoy, how are you?"

Juanita was in Luke's reception area, sitting erect and still like a bird on a wire. It was a few minutes before eight; she was his first appointment.

"I hope you don't mind that I came early," she said as she got up. "I was awake and I had nothing to do, so I just drove in."

"Of course not."

"Your associate was nice enough to get me some coffee," Juanita said, looking over at Margo Howells, Luke's stalwart paralegal and all-around girl Friday.

"Good." Luke smiled to himself. He liked that Juanita had called Margo his "associate," rather than "secretary." She was an old lady chronologically, but she was modern in the world.

He ushered Juanita into his office. "Hold everything," he instructed Margo, as he closed the door.

"To answer your question, I'm all right, personally," Juanita told him as she sat down. She carefully placed her coffee cup on the edge of his desk. "Distracted."

"I can imagine," he replied sympathetically, sitting down opposite her. "That must have been quite a shock, a murdered girl found on your property."

"It was," she agreed. "Horrible. That poor girl. And her mother." She shuddered. "Outliving a child is a parent's worst nightmare."

"I hope I never know." An older parent, Luke was over forty when the first one was born. A compartment in a far recess of his brain was reserved for worrying about them. Most of the time the drawer was closed, so that he didn't feel anxious about them consciously, but he knew it was always there. "So," he said, positioning a legal pad on his knee, "how can I help you today?"

"I need some legal advice."

Luke sat back, perplexed and a bit disturbed. When Mrs. McCoy had called and said she had an issue to discuss with him, he had cleared his calendar to fit her in right away. But there had been an unsettling itch as he wrote her name on his schedule. McCoy and Dixon, her late husband's law firm, handled her legal affairs. Why was she coming to him? Was she in some kind of

trouble she didn't want them to know about? Was there a criminal issue with that murdered girl? Henry's firm didn't do criminal
work.

"Two police detectives came by yesterday," Juanita said.
"They were trying to find out how that girl wound up on the
ranch, who might have put her there, was there anything I knew
that could help them." She hesitated for a moment, then spoke
again. "I told them I didn't know, *which I don't*," she said
emphatically. "But there was one thing I didn't tell them, because
I didn't remember it at the time. But now, thinking back, I realize
I didn't fully answer a question they asked me."

All right, Luke thought. Here's the reason she came to a criminal-defense lawyer. "Which was?" he prompted.

She adjusted her position on the chair. "They asked how
many people have access to that section of the ranch. And they
also mentioned the security gate on the road that leads to it. I
explained who comes and goes—hardly anyone—and then they
moved on to other questions."

She fidgeted some more; he picked up on it. Something was
stuck in her craw, and she was having a hard time coughing it up.
"What I didn't tell them," she said, "because I simply forgot, was
that there *had* been someone at the ranch, about the same time
the girl disappeared." She shifted around in her chair yet again.

This is uncharacteristic for her, Luke thought, because normally this woman was a rock. Something was really troubling her.
"Who was it?" he asked, his ballpoint poised over the yellow pad.

"My grandson, and a friend of his," she said with a nervous
catch in her throat. "They showed up the morning of the day the
police say the girl disappeared. They had been on the road for a
couple of weeks and they stopped by to see me before they went
back to college. In Tucson," she added with precision. "Steven—
my grandson—is a senior at the University of Arizona. So is his
friend. Tyler. Tyler Woodruff."

Luke hummed silently to himself. This was a wrinkle that
needed to be ironed smooth.

"The boys couldn't have known anything," Juanita continued, as if pleading a case that as yet didn't have any accusation attached to it, "because they weren't at the ranch during the day, except when I was there. They didn't return until later that night, and the police said the girl must have been abducted in the daytime."

Luke tilted back in his chair. He wanted to help her, but her personal feelings, particularly for a blood relative, weren't going to satisfy the sheriff and D.A. He needed facts. "Where were they, and how do you know?"

"In Santa Barbara," she answered. "They gave me a rundown of what they'd done, the next morning. They hooked up with some friends. I don't know what they did, exactly. Whatever college kids do, I assume. They got back late that night, I made them breakfast the next morning, and they took off. I haven't spoken to Steven since then," she concluded.

"Did they tell you who they were with? Any names you recall?"

She shook her head. "No. Just friends."

"Have you spoken to your grandson about this murder?" he asked her. "Does he know about it?"

Juanita shook her head. "No, I have not spoken to him." She raised a finger as she reconsidered. "I did mention in an e-mail I sent to my daughter-in-law—Steven's mother—that a body had been found on the ranch, but I didn't get into any particulars. Just that a body had been found on the property, of a local girl who had been shot. But no," she concluded, coming back to his question, "I haven't said anything to Steven about it."

"But he probably knows, if you told his mother."

"I suppose," Juanita agreed.

"And he hasn't communicated anything back to you about it. That he knows anything about it."

"No," she said. "He hasn't." She thought for a moment. "She may not have told him. Steven doesn't live at home, he shares an apartment with Tyler. I don't know how often he talks to his parents, but I doubt it's on a daily basis."

Luke put his pad and pen aside. "There's two separate areas

to be considered here," he said. "One is legal, the other's ethical."

She looked at him intently.

"The detectives didn't *specifically* ask you if your grandson or some other particular person was there, did they?"

Her eyes squinted as she attempted to recall exactly what was asked and answered. "No. They did ask who had access to opening that gate, I think. Maybe they didn't. I'm not sure."

"But you didn't deliberately mislead them, or lie, cover up, whatever."

"Absolutely not," she answered forcefully.

"Legally, I don't see that you have a problem," he told her. "The question we should ask ourselves is, what's the *ethical* position? I say this because of who you are in the community, your reputation, which is sterling, and also because a girl was killed, and a good citizen wants to help the police find out who did it. Does that make sense?"

"Of course."

"You personally didn't see anybody who could have been involved, right?" he asked.

"No. I didn't."

"But you don't know if your grandson and his friend did. They never mentioned anything."

"No," she answered again.

"So maybe they did."

Her face twitched with alarm. "And they *concealed* it? I can't imagine . . ."

"No, no, no," he said quickly, not wanting to frighten her anymore than she already was. "But they might have seen or heard something which meant nothing to them but would have value to the sheriff's investigators. Details that are meaningless if you're not looking for them."

Her face softened in relief. "I understand."

"Here's the deal, Steven: you and your pal Tyler are going to have to come here and talk to the police."

Before Luke called Steven McCoy in Tucson to tell him that he and Tyler Woodruff were going to have to return to Santa Barbara to be interviewed by sheriff's detectives about Maria Estrada's murder, he and Juanita McCoy had a brief meeting with Alex Gordon, the county D.A., who had once worked under him. After listening to Juanita's summation, Alex called Cindy Rebeck and Louis Watson and put them on the speaker box, so everybody could be part of the discussion.

The boys had to be interviewed—that was a given. They were potential material witnesses to the dumping of a murder victim. The question was where the detectives would interview them, Tucson or Santa Barbara. After a brief discussion, Alex and the cops, with Luke's concurrence, decided to bring the boys to Santa Barbara, rather than flying the detectives to Arizona. If something of value came out of their discussion, particularly regarding physical evidence, the boys would already be on the scene. The detectives would avoid having to make an extra trip, and they'd cut down on expenses.

Steven knew about the body being found on the ranch. His mother had called and told him, after she heard the grisly news from Juanita. He hadn't thought much about it one way or the other, except how it would affect his grandmother.

"But I don't know anything," he protested to Luke over the phone. "If I did, I would have called somebody back there. I'm just starting classes," he continued, "I'm up to my ass in work. Do I really have to come?" he asked. "Can't we do it over the telephone?"

"No, this can't be handled long-distance," Luke answered. "They have to question the two of you in person, Steven, if for no other reason than to cover their butts," he said candidly. "They can't risk some reporter finding out that you and Tyler were camped out on the property the same time the girl disappeared and they never talked to you about it, particularly if they haven't solved this case by then. Very bad publicity, which they do not want. They have thin skins, they bruise easily."

"So why can't they come out here and talk to us? Isn't that how it's usually done?"

"Sometimes," Luke agreed, "but this time they want you here, in case something sparks."

"But I already told you. We didn't see anything. It's going to be a waste of time," Steven complained.

"So be it," Luke answered. "It'll be less than twenty-four hours out of your life, that's not a big deal. You're doing it for your grandmother, okay? She's upset about all this, and I want to put the whole shebang behind us. So suck it up."

The caller on the other end of the line wouldn't identify herself. "I don't want to get involved," she said to the police dispatch operator. She had something to tell them about the girl who got murdered, Maria Estrada. "The day she disappeared? I saw her at Paseo Nuevo."

"What time was that?" the operator asked.

"Early afternoon."

"Did you see anyone with her?"

"Yeah, I did."

The operator grabbed a notepad and pen. "Did you recognize this person with Maria?"

"No, I don't know who it was," came the soft reply.

"Was it a man or a woman?"

"A guy."

"Could you tell how old he was, approximately?"

"I don't know," came the uncertain reply. "Her age, a little older?"

"What was his ethnicity? Asian, African-American, Latino, Anglo," the dispatcher rattled off.

"White."

"Tall, short, thin, heavy?"

"Pretty tall," the girl said. "Over six feet. On the thin side, but built good. His hair was like dirty-blond, you know? Kind of light brown."

The dispatcher began punching in the number to Detective Rebeck's cell phone. "Did he have any unusual features? Tattoos, visible scars?"

The voice on the other end paused. "I didn't see any scars or tattoos."

"Can you be more specific where you saw this fellow and Maria Estrada?" came the next question. "A restaurant, a store?"

"They were coming out of Elaine's," the caller said.

The jewelry store in the mall where kids got their ears pierced, the operator recalled. "Okay. Could you see where they went after that?"

Rebeck's line was busy. The dispatcher disconnected and started dialing Watson's.

"What is that sound?" the caller asked.

She had heard Watson's number being punched in. "Nothing, it's . . ."

"Are you trying to trace my call?" The voice on the other end sounded frightened.

Quickly: "No. That was just a time-code. So did you see . . ."

The line went dead.

Cindy Rebeck showed Maria's picture to two salesclerks at Elaine's Jewelry Store. Both young women recognized her immediately.

"She's in here all the time," the anorexic-looking one with purple-dyed hair told Rebeck. She laughed. "She's a total earring whore."

"What's her problem now?" the other, a sweet-faced redhead, asked. "She get caught shoplifting? I always keep my eye on her, for sure."

"She was murdered," Rebeck answered tersely. "Don't you ever watch the news or read a paper?"

Both women's mouths formed O's of shock. "That chick that was found at that ranch?" spike-hair exclaimed. "That was her?"

"Yes," Rebeck said grimly. "Do either of you remember her

being in here about a week or so ago, during the afternoon?"

"I do," the redhead volunteered. "I worked that day. She came in the middle of the afternoon, about three o'clock."

Rebeck took out her notepad and ballpoint. "Was she with a man?"

"She sure was," the salesgirl answered brightly. "He bought her a pair of earrings. Sapphire studs. I mean, not real sapphires, sapphire-colored, the stones." She grinned. "This wasn't Kobe Bryant–level buying."

Stay calm, girl, Rebeck told herself. This could be the break they desperately needed. "Do you recall how the man paid?" she asked carefully. "Did he use a credit card?" *Dear God, she thought, could it be this simple?*

The girl immediately shook her head. "Cash. I remember, 'cause I had to break a hundred. We don't get many hundred-dollar bills in here. It's like he did it to impress her, you know?"

It had been a shot. "Was she impressed?" Rebeck asked flatly.

"I guess. I was," the girl said with a laugh.

"Can you describe him? Height, weight, hair color, eyes? Anything you can remember."

"Early twenties, I'd guess? A UCSB type, you know?" She paused, recalling a quick transaction that had occurred over a week ago. "Tall, on the thin side, but built nice. Dirty-blond hair. Your basic surfer dude is how I'd describe him."

The salesgirl's description matched the anonymous caller's, which meant the odds were better than decent that this unidentified John Doe was Maria's killer. Rebeck scribbled the information down. "Is there anything else you remember about them?" Hopefully: "Did they talk about where they were going?"

The salesgirl shook her head again. "Not a word. She put the earrings on, gave him a big fat smooch, and they went their merry way."

9

LUKE PICKED STEVEN and Tyler up at the Santa Barbara airport and drove them to the sheriff's compound. Juanita would come for them when the questioning was over and drive them to the ranch, where they'd spend the night before going back to Tucson the following morning.

"Is there anything we should look out for?" Tyler asked. He was nervous. His only encounters with the police had been for speeding, making too much noise at parties, the usual college high jinks. Steven, on the other hand, seemed loose and relaxed.

Luke shook his head. "Just tell the truth and you'll be fine," he counseled them as he dropped them off at the front door.

Cindy Rebeck had to brace herself against the corner of her desk when Steven, followed by Tyler, ambled into the cramped cubicle she shared with Louis Watson. My God, she thought with an involuntary shiver, he's a virtual match to the description, from his dark-blond hair to the soles of his Tevas, of the unknown man who had been the last person seen with Maria Estrada while she was still alive; although he was more handsome than she had expected. She could see girls going for this boy in a heartbeat. Girls like Maria Estrada. She glanced over at Watson, who nodded back: he had noticed the similarities, too.

There are a thousand boys at UCSB who fit this description, she reminded herself. Still, the coincidence was unnerving.

"We're going to do this in the conference room," Rebeck said, after they introduced themselves. "Roomier in there." The conference room was set up for audio- and videotaping. The cops wouldn't tell the boys they were being taped—it wasn't legally required. The department's position, like that of most police departments, was that they would adhere to the letter of the law, but not beyond it.

"Can we get something to drink?" Steven asked. He had downed a bottle of water on the drive in from the airport, but he still had dry-mouth from the airplane.

"Sure. What do you want?" Watson asked.

"Coke?"

"Two?" Watson looked at Tyler, who nodded.

They sat at a long, bare metal table, the boys on one side, the detectives facing them. The detectives had positioned the boys so they would be clearly seen by the hidden video camera.

After IDing themselves, the boys, the time, date, and place, Rebeck said, "What we need for you to do is recapitulate your entire day, in as much detail as possible, from when you arrived at Mrs. McCoy's ranch until you left the following morning. You with me?"

The boys nodded in agreement.

"You got there what time?" she began.

"Around noon," Tyler answered.

"A little before," Steven corrected him. "Closer to eleven."

Watson looked from Steven to Tyler. "Which was it?" he asked.

"Yeah, that sounds right," Tyler agreed, deferring to Steven. "Eleven."

Watson wrote the time down on his notepad. "At eleven o'clock in the morning"—he was being as specific as possible for the tape-recording—"you drove onto the property. Where were you earlier that day?"

"Cambria," Steven answered. "We camped out at Moonstone Beach. We got up early in the morning and drove straight down."

That could be easily verified, Watson thought as he made another notation. "You called your grandmother to let her know you were on your way?" he asked Steven. "Your cell phone, pay phone?"

"Neither," Steven answered. "I didn't know she'd be there, at the old house. It's not like she goes over there every day, she doesn't live there. It was a fluke she was there when we showed up."

"So the gate was open," Rebeck said, more to herself than to the boys. So much for the ranch's so-called tight security. She started to write the information in her notepad.

Tyler spoke up. "No, it was closed."

Her hand froze in midair. "Closed? Do you mean locked?"

"Yes," Steven confirmed.

The detectives, now confused, looked at each other, then at the boys again. "How did you get in, if it was locked?" Rebeck asked Steven.

"I know the combination," he told her matter-of-factly. "I've been going there all my life."

Rebeck took a moment to calm herself. This was a fuckup on her and Watson's part, she thought in self-anger. They should have anticipated that. It cast a new and potentially unsettling light on their investigation.

Pull it together, she admonished herself. "You drove in, and then what?" she continued.

Overlapping each other with mild, inconsequential corrections, the boys recounted their brief, happy encounter with Juanita, the discussion about sleeping at the old house, their plans to have breakfast with Juanita the next morning. "Then we drove into Santa Barbara," Steven concluded.

"And you locked the gate behind you when you left?" Watson asked.

"Yes," Tyler answered.

"No," Steven said simultaneously.

Rebeck sat back. This was getting worse; or maybe, much better. "Which was it?" she asked them. "Locked or open?"

"It was open," Tyler said sheepishly, glancing over at Steven, who was scowling.

"You're sure?" Rebeck asked him, openly skeptical.

He nodded. He looked over at Steven again, then away. "At the time, I thought we had locked it, because Mrs. McCoy had been real concerned about telling us to, so that was stuck in my mind. But when we came back at night after dinner, it was unlocked, and bozo here reminded me he'd forgotten to lock it up behind us, and not to tell his grandmother how he'd screwed up, so she wouldn't get upset with him. So yes, we left it open," he petered out.

Yet another unexpected turn, Rebeck thought to herself. Some routine questioning this was turning out to be. If the gate had been left unlocked, anyone could have gotten onto the property.

"You drove into town," Watson said, keeping the flow going. "Straight into Santa Barbara, no stops along the way?"

"That's right," Steven said. Tyler nodded in agreement.

"Where did you go?"

"We stopped for lunch at a Mexican place near the high school, then we drove over to the mall on State Street," Steven told him. "Paseo Nuevo, it's called?"

If Rebeck's pen had been a pencil, it would have snapped in two. "Paseo Nuevo?" she said, echoing Steven.

"Yes," he confirmed. "The one with California Pizza Kitchen."

"I know where it is," she said. "I want to make sure that was the location." *The last place Maria Estrada was seen alive.*

"Yes, we were at the mall," Steven repeated. "Isn't that where everybody winds up sooner or later? There or the beach?"

"I don't know," she answered. "I'm buried here most of the time. Or out solving crimes," she added, forcing a tight smile.

"Which I'll bet you're good at," he said, smiling back.

Is he flirting with me, she thought, partly astonished and partly unnerved. She looked over at her partner, who raised a bemused eyebrow.

Turning away from Watson, Rebeck put the thought out of her head and redirected her focus. This was all a lark to Steven, she thought with a rush of anger. A girl was dead, her decomposed body found close to where the boys had slept, and he thinks it's a joke.

Then she cautioned herself: back off. You're reading too much into this. Their attitude wasn't that unusual or callous. They're young, she reminded herself. They don't get it yet, that life can be a bitch and there's too much ugliness in the world.

"So now you're at Paseo Nuevo," Watson said, moving the questioning back on track. He took Maria's picture out of a folder and laid it in front of them. "Did you see her? Any chance at all?" He slid it closer to them. "Look closely. This is important."

The boys studied the photo carefully. Tyler was the first to look up. "I didn't see this girl," he said, almost apologetically. "I'm sorry, but I don't recognize her at all."

Steven was intent on the photo. "What about you?" Watson asked him.

Steven turned his face to the detectives. "No." He slid the picture back across the table. "I never saw her."

It was a shot, Watson thought. You have to take them, no matter how long they might be. "Okay. So how long were you there, what did you do, where did you go after that?" he continued.

"Which one of us?" Tyler asked.

Watson looked at him in confusion. "What do you mean, which one of you?"

"We split up."

They took a break, ostensibly so everyone could stretch their legs, go to the bathroom, get some fresh air. Rebeck and Watson huddled in their cubicle. "How do you want to play this?" she asked him. Every instinct in her, tuned by twelve years on the job, was humming.

Watson, too, was off-balance from this new disclosure. "We've got to question them separately, see if there's a hole in either one's story big enough to drive the case through." He shook his head. "Man, I did not expect anything like this."

Rebeck pulled at a piece of dry skin on her lip. Rummaging in her purse for her ChapStick, she said, "Do we need to Mirandize them?" Finding the tube, she ran it over her mouth.

Watson considered the implications. "I think we can go a little longer without technically crossing the line," he decided. "I don't want to scare them so they clam up, and I don't want them crying for a lawyer. Definitely not Luke Garrison."

Rebeck pressed a tissue to her lips to blot the salve. "Just thinking of implicating Juanita McCoy's grandson in this murder scares the shit out of me. We'd better be super careful. Careers have been blown over less."

"He had access," Watson reminded her. "No small thing."

"*If* the gate was locked, which they said it wasn't," she rebutted.

"Woodruff claimed it was, until McCoy changed his mind for him," Watson countered doggedly. "Maybe his memory was better than McCoy's." He sat down heavily on the edge of his desk. "Or maybe the McCoy kid is lying."

"Please, let's not go there, not yet, anyway," she implored.

"You're right," he agreed. "Not yet."

They flipped a coin. Rebeck got Steven. "Keep your legs crossed," Watson teased her. She turned away from him and went to fetch Steven.

Interview with Tyler Woodruff. Conducted by Detective Louis Watson, Santa Barbara County Sheriff's Department. Audio- and videotaped (hidden camera and recorder).

Q. (Watson): You drove straight to the Paseo Nuevo mall from the ranch, is that correct?

A. (Woodruff): That's right.

Q.: Once you were there, what did you do? Try to remember as many specifics as possible.

A.: We went into a couple of stores. Brookstone, the Discovery Store. Didn't buy anything. What else? Nothing, really, until I met my friend Serena.

Q: Who is Serena? What is her last name?

A.: Hopkins. A girl I went to high school with in L.A. She goes to UCSB.

Q.: Was this a planned meeting? How did you get in touch with each other?

A.: It was accidental. She was in the mall and she spotted me.

Q.: Okay. What happened?

A.: We talked for a little bit. I introduced her to Steven. Then she and I took off.

Q.: Without Steven McCoy.

A.: Right. She offered to hook him up with a friend of hers, but he didn't go for it. We'd been together for almost two weeks, we needed a couple hours' break from each other.

Q.: What time was this? Try to remember as accurately as you can.

A.: (*after a pause*) I'd say two. Between two, two-thirty.

Q.: What did you and this Serena do? Where did you go?

A.: We drove down to the beach. Near the harbor. We rented bikes . . .

Q.: (*interrupting*) Whose car did you take? Hers or yours?

A.: Hers.

Q.: And whose car were you and Steven using, his or yours?

A.: His.

Q.: What make?

A.: A Nissan Pathfinder.

Q: Color?

A: It's blue. Dark blue, like navy.

Q.: Okay. So you and Serena Hopkins did what again?

A.: We rented bikes and rode along the bike path. From the

Bird Refuge to a parking lot near City College, I don't know what that area's called.

Q.: (*answering for him*) West Beach. For how long?

A.: About an hour. We stopped a couple of times.

Q.: Then what?

A.: We drove to her apartment. It's in Goleta. She shares it with three other girls.

Q.: What did you do there?

A.: Not much. Hung out. Had a few beers. Watched some TV.

Q.: Just you and her? Was anyone else there?

A.: Mostly it was just us. One of her roommates stopped in for a little while, but she didn't hang around.

Q.: She was giving the two of you privacy?

A.: (*subject hesitates before answering*) You could put it that way.

Q.: How long were you in Goleta with Serena Hopkins?

A.: Till about six-thirty.

Q.: Then what did you do?

A.: She drove me back to the mall and dropped me off.

Q.: What time did you and she part company?

A.: About seven. A few minutes before. Me and Steven had said we'd meet back there at seven.

Q.: And at that point you and he got together again.

A.: Yeah. (*There is a moment's hesitation*) Not right away.

Q.: Not right away?

A.: Steven wasn't there when I got there.

Q.: When did he show up?

A.: About an hour later.

Q.: So that would be eight o'clock?

A.: Right.

Q.: Did Steven say where he was?

A.: At a movie. He lost track of time.

Q.: (*There is a pause on the tape. Sound of papers being shuffled.*) So between two or two-thirty in the afternoon, and eight o'clock at night, you and Steven McCoy had no contact with each other. Is that correct?

A.: Yes.

Q.: What happened once the two of you got together?

A.: We had dinner at Brophy's Restaurant, down by the wharf. Then we drove back to the ranch.

Q.: (*Another pause, more shuffling of papers*) Now when you got there, the security gate at the entrance to the property was unlocked. You're positive about that?

A.: Yes. Unlocked.

Q.: And you were surprised, because you thought it had been locked. That was what you remembered.

A.: (*after a lengthy pause*) At first, yeah, but then Steven reminded me that he'd forgotten to lock it when we left earlier.

Q.: But your initial reaction was that he had locked it when you left earlier. Is that correct?

A.: (*another pause*) Yes.

Q.: All right. Go ahead. What then?

A.: We parked near the old house. We went inside, but it was dark, so we couldn't see much. There's no electricity in the house.

Q.: Remind me again. Did you sleep inside the house?

A.: No, outside. We only spent a few minutes inside, since it was too dark to see much inside.

Q.: (*Pause*) Very important now: did you see anything, hear anything, any unusual noises, any vehicles coming or going, any voices? Footsteps? Anything at all, during the time you were on the property.

A.: (*firmly*) Not a thing. If anybody came or went while we were there, I don't know anything about it. We were sleeping, but if someone did come by, I'm sure we would have heard it.

Leaving the boys to cool their heels in their respective interview rooms, Watson and Rebeck huddled together in their cramped office. He filled her in on his interrogation of Tyler, then she told him about hers, with Steven.

After Steven and Tyler split up, he had hung around the mall—he couldn't specify exactly how long—then he had driven to Butterfly Beach, where he parked on Channel Road near the Biltmore Hotel. He sunbathed, swam, jogged as far as Miramar Beach and back, then laid down and worked on his tan again. He was alone the entire time.

"He didn't talk to *anyone*?" Watson asked. "That seems odd."

"According to him, not a soul," Rebeck answered. "Which felt strange to me, too, because this boy—man—is definitely tuned into women." She hesitated. "There were times during my questioning when I felt like he was mentally undressing me," she confessed, feeling embarrassed. She didn't want to give her partner any ammunition for teasing, but Steven's attitude had been too obvious to ignore. His sexual magnetism, and his awareness of it, had been apparent to her almost from the beginning of their conversation. She had actually been concerned that he was going to hit on her. To her relief, he hadn't.

"I could see he was doing that earlier," Watson said. "You didn't seem all that put off by it," he added, maintaining a poker face.

"No comment," Rebeck told him. She felt her cheeks redden.

"Just an observation," Watson teased her dryly. "The point being, there are plenty of women who would go for that. Especially young ones."

Like Maria Estrada. He didn't have to spell it out—they both understood that clearly.

Rebeck continued her recitation. After Steven left the beach he came back into town, where he popped into Kris & Jerry's Bar off State Street and drank a couple of draft Anchor Steams. He hadn't talked to anyone in the bar. He thought the bartender was a woman, but again, he couldn't remember for sure.

"That should be easy enough to check out," Watson said. "If the bartender was a woman, she'd remember him."

"For his sake, let's hope so," Rebeck said.

Watson nodded slowly. "I hear you."

After he left the bar, Steven went back to the mall and took in a movie: *Collateral*, with Tom Cruise.

"That's definitely checkable," Watson said.

"But he had to think a minute to remember it," Rebeck retorted. "The marquee's right there, front and center, anybody passing by would notice it. I asked him about it, trying to get some information you wouldn't know if you hadn't seen it."

"Clever. And?"

"He was fuzzy with most of the details. Hit man comes to L.A. Jamie Foxx was in it. He remembered it was directed by the same director who did *The Insider*, all of which he could have read about in a review."

"Or he could have seen it some other time," Watson said.

"That's true," Rebeck agreed. "At any rate, when he got out of the movie it was eight o'clock, and he met up with Woodruff," she concluded, folding up her notebook.

The rest of his story matched Woodruff's. The gate had been left unlocked. They hadn't seen or heard anything back at the ranch.

"What now?" Watson asked.

"Let's call the girl the Woodruff kid was with," Rebeck decided. "If she corroborates, Woodruff's clear."

"What about McCoy?"

Rebeck's forehead wrinkled. "Five, six hours alone? Plenty of time to meet Maria Estrada, drive up to the ranch, kill her, drive back. In his dark-blue Pathfinder." She grimaced. "You never have a good alibi when you need one."

"You think he needs one?"

She pondered the question. "Let's eliminate whatever elements we can, then see what's left."

Tyler had programmed Serena's number into his cell phone, so Watson was able to reach her easily. He explained that the police were questioning everyone who had been at the location where the recently murdered girl was found.

Serena substantiated Tyler's account of their afternoon
together, then asked nervously, "Is Tyler in trouble?"

"No," Watson answered. *Now that you've cleared him.*
"This is purely routine."

"Good," the girl's tinny voice replied. "Tyler wouldn't hurt
anyone."

We're all capable of violence under the right conditions, even
the Pope, Watson thought, but didn't express. This girl didn't
need to share in his acquired cynicism about human nature.
"That's nice to know," he said. "Thanks for your time."

He hung up. "Woodruff checks out," he told Rebeck. "The
girl alibied him, airtight."

"Which still leaves McCoy." She ticked the incriminating
points off on her fingers. "Five or six hours unaccounted for by
any corroborating witnesses, knowledge of a remote location
where the body was discovered, color and make of his car, the
combination to the lock . . ."

Watson nodded. "A lot of coincidences. But let's get real. We
don't have anything substantial enough to hold him on. His
stonewalling is annoying, but it isn't criminal." He picked at a
cuticle. "We're going to have to cut them loose. If this was some
lame off the street I'd hang onto him for another day, sweat him
a little, because there certainly are holes in his story. But the
grandson of Juanita McCoy? Not in this man's lifetime. Unless
the order comes down from above."

Marlon Perdue, the forensic investigator who worked with the
coroner, pulled up to a stop in front of the old ranch house. Keith
Morton was already there, waiting for him. Perdue got out of his
car and stretched his legs. It was a good forty-five-minute drive
out here from his office in Santa Barbara, and his back had been
acting up. He needed to see a chiropractor, and start working out
on a regular basis. If he could ever make the time.

"Hello again," he called out in greeting. Morton had been
here when they had taken the body away. They hadn't spoken

again until yesterday, when Perdue called and asked that he be allowed to look inside the house.

"Thanks for doing this," he said to Morton.

The foreman nodded curtly.

Perdue grabbed his equipment case from the backseat of the car. It was hot out here, at least fifteen or twenty degrees warmer than in town, where the ocean breeze served as a natural coolant. He took off his sports coat, folded it neatly, and laid it across the driver's seat. He had stashed his automatic in the trunk of the car before coming out; if he didn't need to show his weapon, he preferred not to. "Is the door open?" he asked.

"I unlocked it after you called," Keith confirmed. He leaned against his pickup. "What are you looking for in there?"

"Evidence."

Morton frowned. "I thought the girl was killed somewhere else. That's what the news reported the sheriff said."

"She wasn't killed where you *found* her," Perdue replied, correcting him. "We don't know where she was killed." He looked around. "Has anyone been inside this place since the body was discovered?"

Morton shook his head. "I've been keeping an eye out since the body was found. If someone has been here since then, I'd know it."

That was helpful. If there was any evidence in the house, the chances it hadn't been contaminated would be better. He walked across the gravel to the front door. "Do you want me to come in with you?" Morton called after him.

"No. The fewer people inside, the better. I'll call you if I need you."

"I'll be here," Morton said laconically. He leaned back against his truck and pulled his hat over his eyes.

Perdue took a set of sterile latex gloves from his briefcase, snapped them over his hands, and turned the front doorknob. With a faint groan of hinges, the heavy door creaked open.

The house was cool and dark. Carefully walking across the

room, Perdue pulled back the heavy curtains. Shafts of sunlight filtered in through the high, dirty windows. What a fascinating old place, he thought, as he looked around. This is living history, better than a museum. He would love to come back on a non-official basis, when he could browse the library, look at the paintings with unhurried appreciation, and enjoy the essence of the place.

The living room was still. Dust mites hovered in the somnolent air. Talk to me, Perdue said to himself. Do you have a tale to tell?

On the far wall next to the walk-in fireplace he noticed the gun cases. He walked over and casually tried one of the handles.

The door swung open. Surprised that it wasn't locked, he looked inside at the rows of rifles, shotguns, and handguns. These are ancient, he thought, going back as far as the Civil War, from the looks of some of the rifles. Beautiful pieces, as pretty as sculpture.

He bent over to get a closer look. Then he straightened up, walked to the front door, and flung it open. "Could you come in here a minute?" he called out to Morton.

Keith pushed off from the side of his truck, where he'd been half-dozing. As he reached the front door, Perdue tore open another package of sterile gloves. "Put these on, please," he said, as he handed them to Keith.

Keith pulled the gloves over his large, knotted hands. He followed Perdue inside. Perdue led him to the gun cabinet.

"Do you normally keep this locked?" Perdue asked.

"Of course," Keith answered. He was clearly upset. "That collection's worth a fortune. It's insured for over a million dollars."

"When was the last time it was unlocked, to your knowledge?"

Keith shook his head. "I have no idea." He thought for a moment. "There was a charity benefit out here six months ago, for the rodeo association. Mrs. McCoy might have shown some of the pieces to them. There's some major gun collectors in that bunch. You'd have to ask her."

Perdue squatted down on his haunches. "That revolver," he said, pointing. "It looks out of place."

"You're right," Keith agreed. "It should be here." He pointed to another row in the cabinet, where several period handguns were laid out symmetrically. There was an empty space where one was conspicuously missing.

Perdue took out a tissue and lifted the revolver from the cabinet. Carefully, he laid it down and took his evidence notebook out of his briefcase. Thumbing through the pages, he scanned the section detailing the bullet that had been removed from the victim's body. "What caliber would you say this shoots?" he asked Keith.

Keith looked closely at the revolver. "It's a 1913 Colt six-shot, so I'd say a .38 WCF."

Perdue had an encyclopedic knowledge of guns and ammunition—it was an essential part of his job. A .38 WCF (Winchester Centerfire) cartridge, which was no longer commonly used, had a different bullet-weight than a regular .38; to an expert, it was an easy bullet to identify. The bullet Dr. Atchison had extracted from the victim's heart had been a .38 WCF.

He reached into his briefcase again and took out an evidence bag. "I'm taking this with me," he told Keith. "I'll give you a receipt."

Keith stared at the old revolver, his face registering shock. "You think this could be what killed her? Christ, I don't think any of these have been fired for years. I didn't know any of them were even loaded."

Gingerly, Perdue picked the gun up, put it in the bag, and placed it in his briefcase. "Maybe it wasn't. But we're sure as hell going to find out."

10

ALEX GORDON, A legitimate four-handicap, laced a long draw down the left side of the fairway on the par-five sixth hole at La Cumbre Country Club. If you hit a long-enough drive you could cut the corner. The ball would run down thirty yards to the bottom of the hill, leaving a long iron or fairway wood to the green—a good chance for a birdie.

Alex birdied number six every three or four rounds. It was one of his money holes. His normal Saturday afternoon group made every kind of bet under the sun. Nassaus, automatic presses, sand saves, low number of putts, holing out from off the green. Whatever they could think of. The stakes were low—nobody won or lost more than fifty dollars a round—but it made the game more fun, gave it an extra edge.

It was a great day for golf. Warm but not too hot, dry, hardly any wind. After the rest of his foursome teed off (he had the honors, he'd birdied five, a short par three) he walked to his ball, which had settled nicely in the left-center of the fairway. Unlike most of the men he played with, Alex didn't ride a cart. He believed walking was more legitimate, more like the game was meant to be played, the way Hogan and Bobby Jones had played it. He was thirty-eight years old, and fit—he worked out five days a week. When he was sixty-five or seventy, after they'd put him out to pasture, maybe he'd start riding.

His Titleist Pro V-1 had found a perfect landing: a flat lie and a clear shot to the green, two hundred and fifteen yards away. A hard three-iron or easy five-wood. As usual, his was the longest drive by a good thirty yards—he was the only one with a legitimate shot to get home in two. He was already licking his chops.

His cell phone rang.

"Oh, man, would you give us a break?" Chip Simmons cried out. "Turn that piece of shit off. It's Saturday, for Christ's sakes."

Bringing your cell phone to the course was bad form; Alex knew that. He didn't like keeping his on, but he had to. Being a D.A. was like being a doctor; you were always on call.

"Sorry," he apologized. He walked away from the others, so he wouldn't disturb them. He looked at the display, then stabbed the *On* button. "This is Alex," he announced, keeping his voice low.

He listened for a moment, then whistled low through his teeth. "Has the kid been read his rights yet?" After a few more seconds: "Damn straight, John. Have them do it right away, I don't want this bollixed up on a Miranda violation before we're even out of the gate, in case this actually turns out to have legs. I'll be at your shop as soon as I can."

He hung up and walked back to his ball. "Everybody else hit?" he asked.

The others nodded. "You're up," Chip told him.

Alex reached into his bag and pulled out his five-wood. Standing over his ball, he looked toward the green. He set his feet, waggled a couple of times, and let fly.

The ball arced high into the air, a sweet floating fade. It hit front-center of the green and rolled to within ten feet of the pin. He had a bona fide chance at eagle.

He put the head cover back on his club and slid the club into his bag. "Putt out for me," he told Chip. "I have to go to the office."

Steven and Tyler were waiting in the sheriff's conference room. Someone had brought in sandwiches and Cokes for lunch. A television set was on, tuned to a college football game.

Rebeck came in and closed the door behind her. The boys stirred themselves. "What's going on?" Steven asked her.

"It won't be much longer," she told them, dancing around the question. She opened the door. "Would you mind waiting outside with my partner?" she said to Tyler. "I need to talk to your friend. Alone."

The boys exchanged looks—*what's this all about?* Tyler shrugged. He hoisted himself to his feet.

"See you in a minute," he told Steven.

Steven slouched into the cushions. He was getting antsy, but also, although he didn't want to show it to these cops, he was getting angry. He and Tyler had flown out here on their own time, told the cops everything they knew, which basically was nothing, and now they were being diddled around. "What do you want now?" he asked Rebeck.

Rebeck took a laminated card out of her badge case. "You have the right to remain silent," she recited in a flat monotone. "Anything you say can and will be used against you in a court of law. You have the right to speak to an attorney, and to have an attorney present at any questioning. If you cannot afford a lawyer, one will be provided for you at government expense."

Luke Garrison, in a pair of grass-stained shorts and a baggy T-shirt he'd been wearing while spreading compost over his wife's flower garden, barged into the lobby of the sheriff's compound. John Griffin and Alex Gordon, who was still in his golf shirt and slacks, were waiting for him.

"Where is he?" Luke demanded harshly.

"In my conference room," Griffin answered.

Luke turned to Alex. "What's going on, Alex? These boys come out here of their own free will to do you a favor, and now you're holding them? What's this about?"

Alex put up a placating hand. "Calm down, Luke."

Luke brushed aside the conciliatory gesture. "Don't jerk me around, Alex, you read them their Miranda rights. These kids must be scared out of their gourds. What are you doing?" he demanded again.

"The detectives read *McCoy* his rights," Griffin said, correcting Luke's assumption. He paused. "It wasn't necessary for Woodruff. He'll be on a plane back to Arizona within the hour."

"And Steven?"

"We're holding him." Before Luke could start protesting again, Alex added, "We read him his rights to protect him, Luke. We *want* his lawyer in on this."

"In on what?" Luke railed. What rabbit hole were they going down? "Is Steven McCoy being accused of something? What kind of idiocy is going on here?"

"We think we've found the gun that killed the girl," Alex told him, looking over at Griffin, who nodded solemnly.

That was a staggering piece of information. As a former prosecutor, Luke knew how important a piece of evidence that would be. "Where?" he asked. "But anyway, what does that have to do with Steven McCoy?"

"Inside that old house, where they camped out."

The picture was coming clear now—alarmingly so. "That doesn't mean Steven had anything to do with the killing." Luke caught himself up. "What do you mean, *think*? Have you found it or haven't you? Don't play games with me, Alex. I was the guy who recruited you fresh out of law school, remember?"

Alex regarded Luke calmly, but inside, he was churning. Luke had been his first boss, when he was the county D.A. Their relationship had changed considerably over the years, but there was still a strong emotional undercurrent. Luke was the alpha dog, and always would be.

"Yes, Luke, I certainly do," he answered. "And I'll always be thankful to you for doing it." He took a fortifying breath. "Which is why we're handling this so carefully. We aren't certain if the gun that was found on the premises is the murder weapon. We're testing it now. But there's a good chance it is, given the caliber of the bullet and some other technical stuff." He paused. "But if it is, we have to look at McCoy as a suspect. He had access to that property, which almost no one else does. The only

other people that we know of are the foreman, who has a clear
alibi for the time frame when the abduction and murder took
place, and Mrs. McCoy. You think Juanita McCoy did it?" he
asked bitingly.

"Don't be an asshole, Alex," Luke said testily. This was no
joke now.

"My point exactly," Alex retorted.

"This is utter bullshit," Luke protested. "Steven McCoy had
nothing to do with that murder. For God's sakes, man, I know
you want a suspect, but you're really grasping here, and it could
bite you in the ass, big-time."

"I hope you're right, Luke," Alex said levelly. "Indicting the
grandson of Juanita McCoy for murder is the last thing anybody
in this county wants to do, believe me. Christ, if anyone would
know that it's you, you sat in the hot seat, you know how intense
the pressure can be."

Luke didn't want to hear about their problems. Protecting his
client was all he cared about. Although technically he wasn't
Steven's lawyer yet, he would be if Steven was indicted for Maria
Estrada's murder. This was Juanita and Henry McCoy's grandson. No one in this county could say no to Juanita McCoy; certainly not him.

"But so far, you don't know if the gun you found is the murder weapon," he told Alex.

"We don't, you're right," Alex agreed readily. "And if it isn't,
good for him. But if it is . . ."

No one spoke for a moment. The implication needed no
voice.

"I haven't gone anywhere with this yet," Alex said, "except
to protect McCoy as best I could so far and make sure his lawyer
was involved. He's sitting back there, drinking a Coke, watching
USC play football on television." He paused. "But I want something from you, in return for my white-glove handling."

"What?" Luke asked suspiciously.

"I want to fingerprint him and take photos." He hesitated

momentarily as he saw the look of anger cross Luke's face. "Don't force me to do it the hard way, Luke," he warned his former boss. "Because I will if I have to."

This is a textbook example of being between a rock and a hard place, Luke thought. "Steven McCoy will comply voluntarily," he told the District Attorney and the sheriff.

The crime lab in Goleta dusted the revolver for fingerprints. Three sets were recovered. A comparison with Maria Estrada's thumbprint from her driver's license was a match to one of them, conclusive proof that the victim had touched the gun.

After the fingerprint tests were complete, Dana Wiseman, the lab's bullet expert, test-fired the revolver. He shot three .38 short bullets, identical to the one Dr. Atchison had taken from Maria's heart, into a six foot by three foot stainless-steel tank filled with water. Then he measured the test bullets against the evidence bullet.

The old gun had left very specific and unique markings. The bullets matched. It was a eureka moment—they had found the murder weapon. Now they had to try to find out who the other prints belonged to.

The police photographer took front and side head shots of Steven. Then he was sent downstairs to the fingerprint section, where a full set of his prints were taken and transferred to a computer. The entire process took less than fifteen minutes. Steven was brought back upstairs and released to Luke, who drove him to his office, a few blocks away.

Steven seemed to be more upset at the way he was being treated than worried about why. "What the hell's going on?" he asked Luke, as Luke escorted him into his office. "Where's Tyler? What are they doing with him?" he asked, concerned for his friend.

"Tyler's on his way back to Arizona."

Steven seemed genuinely perplexed. "So why aren't I?"

During the time it took to photograph and fingerprint Steven,

Alex Gordon had given Luke a broad-strokes account of the sheriff's investigation and the detectives' Q and A's with Steven and
Tyler. Luke had to admit (to himself, not to Alex) that Steven's
story wasn't promising; parts of it were potentially very damning.

"Because there are holes in the account you gave the police
about what you did on the day the murdered girl disappeared,
that have put you under suspicion," Luke told him. "The cops
want to check them out further, before they send you home."

Steven's attitude changed immediately. There was no ambiguity in it now—he was scared. "You're joking, right?" he asked
incredulously.

"I wish I was."

"What kind of holes?"

"Whether the security gate was locked or unlocked when you
guys left to go to town, for instance."

"Fuck," Steven blurted out. "Tyler said he thought it was
locked, right?"

"He vacillated. Also, there are several hours where your time
is unaccounted for, which is always a red flag to a cop. And most
importantly, they may have found the gun that was used to kill
the girl."

He was watching Steven closely as he passed on this information. Steven wasn't showing any guilt, just fear. Luke took that
as a positive sign. Or at least, a hopeful one.

"Where did they find it?" Steven asked. "And anyway, what
would that have to do with me?"

"In the old ranch house."

"And they think that . . ." Steven tailed off. "It's not that old
revolver, is it?"

Luke stared at him in bewilderment. "How do you know
about that?" he asked nervously. Jesus Christ, he thought, what
kind of Pandora's box are we opening?

Steven started pacing the room in agitation. "When I was
showing Tyler around that night I saw this old revolver from my
grandparents' gun collection lying on the floor. I knew it

shouldn't be out in the open, but I didn't know where it belonged. It was too dark to see very well, so I picked it up and stuck it back in the gun case where I could fit it in."

Luke groaned. "You picked up a gun near where a murder victim was found and you didn't tell anyone?" This kid was his own worst enemy. "Why not?" he asked in exasperation.

"I didn't know it was any kind of murder weapon," Steven protested. "It was just a gun sitting there."

"But you knew later! Why didn't you say anything once you heard?"

Steven looked down at the floor. "I didn't connect it. I didn't even think about it."

For a moment Luke couldn't speak, he felt so impotent at this sudden blast of bad news. "I have to call the D.A. and try to explain this to him," he finally said, reaching for the phone. "This is very bad news for you, Steven, I'm not going to sugar-coat it. If it is the gun that killed her, your fingerprints will be all over it."

There was a knock on the door. Juanita McCoy hurried in. Luke had called her from the sheriff's office, while Steven was being fingerprinted. She looked at her grandson. "Oh, Steven," she cried out, her voice heavy with worry. "My God, what's happening?"

Steven stood up. "I'm in trouble, Grandma." His voice was quivering.

Juanita hugged him protectively. Turning to Luke, she asked, "What in the world is going on here? Is he?"

Luke nodded. "Yes, I'm afraid he is."

"Why?" she asked in bewilderment.

"They found an old gun at the ranch house they think killed the girl," Steven said. "It was sitting out when Tyler and I came back that night. I put it back in the gun case, because I knew it shouldn't be lying around."

"Which will connect him to the murder, if the gun matches," Luke told her.

Juanita frowned. "This gun. Was it an old Colt revolver?"

"I don't know," Luke answered. "Why should that matter?" She sat down with a thud. "Because I took it out of the gun cabinet, the morning Steven arrived."

Luke's head snapped up so fast he cricked his neck. "What did you say?"

"That gun Steven found and put back in the case? That old revolver?" Her look to Steven was one of utter remorse. "I was by myself, and I heard a car coming up the road. My foreman wasn't around, and the gate was locked, so nobody should have been able to get up there." Her eyes tightened shut, as if she was trying to will the episode to have never happened. "You hear about these terrible things happening nowadays. Which, of course, did to that poor girl." She turned to Luke. "I took the gun out of the gun cabinet. I wasn't planning to use it, I didn't even think it was loaded, it hadn't been fired for years. I wanted to scare off whoever was trespassing." She fell back in a heap. "Then I saw who it was." She turned to Steven. "You. I put it down and came outside, and forgot all about it." Her hands were trembling in her lap. "Does that make any difference?"

"It might," Luke answered cautiously. This confirmed Steven's account of how he had come across the gun inside the house—that he hadn't taken it out of the case, but found it where his grandmother had inadvertently left it. No one would question Juanita McCoy's word.

Still, something felt off. "Where did you put the gun?" he asked Juanita.

"On a side table, near the front window," she answered. "Why?"

"You didn't drop it on the floor?"

"Heavens, no!" she answered. "Drop a weapon? It could go off, or it could be damaged. No one with a wit of sense would drop a gun," she insisted. "Why do you ask?"

Steven answered the question. "I found the gun lying on the floor," he told her.

"Which means whoever used it panicked and dropped it,

right there," Luke concluded. "Someone who doesn't know anything about handling guns." He picked up the phone and punched in Alex Gordon's cell number. "Alex? I have some vital news about that gun."

"So do I," Alex came back from the other end of the line. "It's the murder weapon. The lab confirmed it. I was about to call you." He paused. "McCoy's fingerprints are all over it."

Luke covered the mouthpiece. "The gun is a match," he told Steven and Juanita. "And, of course, your prints are on it, Steven."

Steven sat down next to Juanita. They held on to each other like two survivors of a shipwreck clinging to a life raft.

Luke spoke to Alex over the phone again. "I understand. But there's an explanation." He repeated what Steven and Juanita had told him. "You must see the significance, Alex," he said ardently. "It's a horrible coincidence, but it explains why the prints are on the gun."

As he listened to the senior D.A.'s reply, Luke's face began to cloud over. He shook his head, back and forth. "Yes, I understand," he replied. "Have it your way. For now."

He slammed the phone down in disgust. "In essence, the D.A.'s answer is, 'So what?' Instead of taking the gun out, you found it lying there. The point is, the bullets matched, and your prints are on it. They just got the word from the crime lab. So are the victim's, by the way, which makes things worse. That gun is the murder weapon—no ifs, ands, or buts." He braced himself against his desk. "The detectives will be here any minute to arrest you."

Juanita moaned, and curled into a ball. Steven wrapped a protective arm around her thin shoulder. "It's going to be okay, Grandma. I didn't kill her." He looked at Luke. "Can you come with me?"

It's times like this when you hate your job, Luke thought. "Not now. After you're booked, I'll be allowed to see you."

"When will that be?"

"Later tonight or tomorrow morning, hopefully."

"I'll have to stay in jail tonight?" Steven asked, his voice rising in a tremolo.

"Yes, unfortunately." There was no easy way to explain this. "You're going to be in jail for a few days, until we can enter a plea. This is a murder case, Steven. It isn't going to go away fast."

Steven fell back, his arms splayed out to the sides. "Jesus Christ. How did this happen?"

There are only two answers to that question, Luke thought grimly. Either you're the unlucky victim of a series of terrible circumstances, or you did it. There were times when he had to be painfully blunt with a client. This wasn't one of them.

There was a knock on the door. Luke stood up, then helped Steven to his feet as Rebeck and Watson took a few steps into the room. They both avoided looking at Juanita.

Rebeck, her eyes ablaze, did the honors. "Steven McCoy, we are arresting you on the charge of murder, under section 187 of the California Penal Code."

Steven started to collapse. Luke held on to him to keep him upright. Juanita, hunched over on the couch, was utterly distraught. This is the kind of stress that can kill an elderly person, Luke worried, as he looked over at her. She was a tough old bird, but this was an experience way beyond what anyone could ever be prepared for.

Watson cuffed Steven's hands behind his back. Luke was at Steven's side as the detectives led Steven outside.

As soon as they opened the front door, they were blinded by a wall of television lights. An unruly posse of camera operators jostled with each other for position, boom-mikes swung overhead, TV reporters carrying hand microphones pushed toward them like Pickett's troops charging Cemetery Ridge. The reporters started yelling on top of each other, a blizzard of sound.

"When did you decide . . ." "Is the charge going to be first-degree murder? . . ." "What's his name . . ." On and on, a babble of controlled hysteria.

Luke helped Watson and Rebeck rush Steven through the throng to the waiting car. Watson pulled the back door open and pushed Steven inside, cradling his head against the doorjamb. Rebeck ran around to the driver's side, rudely pushing aside a microphone that had been thrust in her face. "No comment," she called out. "The sheriff will issue a statement later."

Watson jumped into the passenger seat. The unwieldy sedan fishtailed down the street as it headed for the freeway on its way to the county jail.

Fucking chickenshit cops, Luke thought in anger, as he watched the car disappear around a corner. They had deliberately leaked Steven's arrest, to make their sorry asses look good. Down the line, Alex Gordon would pay a healthy tribute for this.

He needed to calm this circus down, if only by a fraction. "My client has fully cooperated with the authorities," he said into the cluster of microphones. "I am confident that when this all shakes out they will release him, because there is no irrefutable evidence against him." He deliberated for a moment, then decided to fire a shot across the bow. "The sheriff's department has been under incredible stress to make an arrest in the Estrada case, even though no one knows whether her killing was deliberate, accidental, or a dozen possibilities in between. While I'm not saying the police were pressured into making a premature and improper arrest, in a case as important as this one there should be a strong preponderance of evidence before anyone rushes to judgment."

He stopped. They could draw their own conclusions—and they would. "That's all I have to say—for now."

11

KATE DRAGGED HERSELF through the front door of her Westside bungalow. It was a few minutes after nine. She had spent most of the day with Luke Garrison, going over preparations for Steven McCoy's booking and arraignment. She did the PI work on Luke's serious cases; this one was going to be particularly grueling, because of who was involved: a murdered Chicano girl and a young, handsome Anglo defendant. That Steven was from one of the county's most prominent families was additional gasoline thrown on the fire. It wouldn't be a national story like the Michael Jackson circus, but locally it would be as important. Starting tomorrow, this case would take precedence over everything else on her schedule.

She tossed her purse and carry-bag onto the couch and collapsed in a heap. "A drink," she moaned. "My kingdom for a vodka and tonic."

Sophia, dug in at the dining-room table, sheets of scratch paper scattered about, looked over at her mother with a complete lack of sympathy. "I suck at calculus, Mom," she whined. "Why did you make me take AP instead of regular?"

"Because challenges nourish the soul," Kate responded. "And I didn't make you take anything. I suggested it."

"Strongly suggested."

"You'll do fine," Kate said, dismissing the complaint. Last week's nemesis had been AP physics. Sophia would get A's in both. "What did you have for dinner?"

"I didn't."

"Weren't you hungry? There's still leftover chicken in the refrigerator, isn't there?"

"I didn't feel like chicken. We had chicken twice already this week."

Kate kicked off her shoes. "What do you want on your pizza?"

"Green peppers and mushrooms. What are you going to have?"

Kate punched in the phone number for Rusty's Pizza Parlor. "Just cheese, I guess. No heavy toppings."

"Watching your weight again?" Sophia teased her.

Kate whacked a thigh. "Yeah, right. As you can see, I'm making great progress." She recited their order, telephone number, and address over the phone. "Half an hour," she said as she hung up. "How much more work do you have?"

"A couple hours, at least. I've still got to write a paper for English after this."

Kate padded into the kitchen. She took the vodka bottle and a handful of ice cubes from the freezer. Dumping them into a tall glass, she twisted open a bottle of tonic. "Do you want anything to drink?" she called out.

"Do we have any champagne?"

"What?"

Sophia came to the kitchen door. "You know. That bubbly stuff that goes up your nose."

"I know what it does. Since when do you drink champagne, or any booze? Especially on a school night."

Sophia's smile split her face. "When I get a part in the school play."

Kate almost dropped her glass. "Is it a good part?" she asked. Please God, she thought, not a munchkin or some other doofus background character.

Sophia was beaming. "The best."

"Dorothy? You got *Dorothy*?" Kate was overjoyed. "That's wonderful!"

"No, I didn't get Dorothy," Sophia said, scrunching her eyes like she had cut into an onion. "Dorothy's totally boring. She's this goody little girl with her goody little dog who dances down the yellow brick road butting into everybody's business. There's no future in Dorothy, Mom. Judy Garland wound up a pill junkie."

"Then what?"

"Heh heh hey, my lovely," Sophia croaked, pitching her voice an octave lower. "What unpleasant surprises I have in store for you." Switching back to her own voice, she sang out: "The Wicked Witch of the West! She's the arch villain, Mom. The baddie's always the best part."

"That's great," Kate enthused. This was the most animation Sophia had shown since she'd moved down here. "But unfortunately, I don't have any champagne. You'll have to settle for a Diet Coke." She opened the refrigerator and took out a cold can. "Do you want a glass?"

"I'll drink it straight." Sophia cracked the top and licked off the foam. "Are you going to be working on that murder case, Mom?" she asked. "The girl from my school?"

Kate, caught off-guard, hesitated before answering. "What do you know about it?" she asked nervously, bothered both by the tone of the question and how it came out of her daughter's mouth.

"It's all everyone in school is talking about. It was on the six o'clock news. Luke Garrison was talking about it. He's the lawyer for that McCoy guy, isn't he?"

"Yes," Kate answered heavily. That's where this was coming from—Sophia knew she did Luke's PI work. It was logical she would assume her mother would be involved in this. Logical, and upsetting.

"So are you going to be working on this, Mom?" Sophia asked again.

Kate suppressed a sigh. "Yes," she answered. "I am."

Sophia took a sip of Coke. "So what happens if you work on

it for awhile and you realize he really did it? Would you keep working on it?"

Kate reeled. This had never come up before—it was uncharted waters between them. "Yes, I would," she said gravely. "That's my job. It's not up to me to make judgments. That's why we have juries."

"But if you knew, for sure," Sophia persisted.

Kate tried to explain: "Even with the most airtight case you can never know for absolutely, positively sure. And there are always extenuating circumstances. It's never completely black and white."

Sophia shook her head in strong, almost violent disagreement. "Sometimes you do know, Mom. I think that sometimes, you have to." She stared at her mother intently. "What if it had been me, Mom? Would you still defend him?" She gathered up her work. "I'm going to study in my room. Call me when the pizza gets here."

PART II

12

"WHAT IS THE charge?"

Alex Gordon answered for the prosecution. "Murder in the first degree. Reserve the right to add extenuating circumstances."

A copy of the complaint had been delivered to Luke's office earlier that morning, so he knew what was coming. Still, hearing the charge out loud was crushing. He put a supportive hand on Steven's shoulder as they stood behind the defense table.

The judge turned and looked at Steven. "How do you plead?"

In a low but firm voice, as Luke had instructed him, Steven McCoy answered, "Not guilty, your honor."

Superior Courtroom #3, where the arraignment was being held, was sparsely occupied; this was only the beginning of the process. The next step would be the bail hearing, which would take place in a few days, after Steven had been evaluated regarding his potential flight risk, and danger to the community. Luke wasn't worried about a negative finding on the danger issue. But if the report found that Steven might run after posting bail, that would be harder to overcome. Alex Gordon would fight granting bail, and fight it hard.

A few days after that the preliminary hearing would be held, at which time the prosecution would show enough evidence to bind Steven over for trial. Luke knew that was a foregone conclusion. They had plenty of evidence. He had gotten lots of convictions with less evidence than Alex had already.

Finally, after all that warm-up, there would be a new arraignment, at which time the trial date would be set. Then the real work would begin.

Luke was wearing a Brooks Brothers blue blazer, button-down white shirt, dark slacks, and a Yale tie he'd won in a poker game. For him, this outfit was almost formal attire. A serious charge required a serious, somber look. His client was in jail garb—standard-issue blue jail top and pants, and scruffy shower slippers. Behind them, seated in the first row, were Kate Blanchard, his paralegal Margo, Juanita McCoy, and a middle-aged couple Luke assumed were Steven's parents. He hadn't met them yet—they had flown in last night, from Tucson. After this hearing was over—a matter of only a few minutes—and Steven was taken back to the jail, Luke would sit down with them and explain what they could expect over the next several months. He wasn't looking forward to it; he wouldn't be painting a pretty picture. Already, they had the shell-shocked look on their faces of people who had just been in a horrific car wreck and didn't know if they had survived or not.

Across from him, on the other side of the aisle, Alex Gordon stood tall, his eyes straight ahead on the judge. Next to Alex, standing equally erect, although almost a foot shorter, was one of the department's senior deputy D.A.'s, a barracuda named Elise Hobson. Elise was a career prosecutor, who had worked under Luke when he was the District Attorney. She was a couple of years younger than Luke, and she held her age well, arising at four-thirty in the morning to hit the weights, the treadmill, and the StairMaster. She had been married and divorced twice, once fresh out of law school and again a few years later, and had long ago publicly sworn off commitment—her determined, liberated single lifestyle was a running, friendly joke among her friends. Which didn't mean that she discovered, in middle age, that she was a closet lesbian; she was simply against attachments, they didn't work for her. She didn't even own a cat, she so valued her independence.

She had no problem with men, as friends or sexual partners,

and she had the capacity for surprising tenderness. After Luke's painful divorce from Polly, his first wife, he and Elise had spent a long weekend together in Big Sur. It had been an excellent seventy-two hours—Elise was a good lover, fierce and funny, and pleasurable company the rest of the time. But they didn't take it any further. He was her boss, recently recovering from the devastation of his failed marriage, and they both knew there wouldn't be anything between them in the long-term. But that seventy-two hours had been therapeutic for him, at a time when he had been in dire need of stroking and all-around TLC.

It was only after he had blown off his career, left town with his tail between his legs, met Riva, got married, and moved back down to Santa Barbara, that Elise confided, one night at Intermezzo when they bumped into each other over drinks, that he was the only man for a long time that she had given thought to getting serious about, and that she had been saddened and a bit wounded that their relationship hadn't gone any further. It had meant more to her than he had realized. Her candid admission had unnerved him, because he had used her, had assumed she knew he was using her, and was doing it to help him, no strings or feelings attached. He had been wrapped up in his own feelings then, not aware of anyone else's.

They were still cordial with each other, but they were no longer friends. She prosecuted people, he defended them. They'd had some intense battles in the local courtrooms. He had won more than his share of them, which didn't sit well with her—that tough, competitive nature of hers took defeat poorly. And the undercurrent of their brief but intense encounter hung over them, a mist no one but them could feel.

He glanced over at her and Alex. Both were deliberately avoiding looking at him. Behind them, two rows deep, were some of the policemen and others who had brought *State* v. *McCoy* to this point. And behind them sat the family of the murdered girl, Maria Estrada. A sad-looking woman dressed in traditional Mexican mourning black was undoubtedly the victim's mother.

There were some young adults, probably siblings or cousins, and a man a decade younger than Luke, who sat erect on the wooden bench, slightly apart from the others, his eyes burning holes into Steven's back.

Luke knew the man, Hector Torres, from way back. Torres was a charismatic figure in the Latino community. He owned a plumbing supply shop, and was also a partner in a popular Chicano bar on the Westside. He was a former member of the Mexican Mafia, and had done a couple years in prison on drug-trafficking charges. Since his release from Soledad, fifteen years ago, he had stayed out of trouble, although local law enforcement continued to keep tabs on him. He was also, surprisingly for a man of his background, well-educated—he had finished junior college in prison, and got his bachelor's degree in business from Cal State Northridge after his release.

Torres was the patriarch of his large family; Maria Estrada's mother was one of his sisters. He was fiercely loyal to his family—it was common knowledge that if anything happened to any of them he would take care of the problem, no matter what it was or what steps needed to be taken to do it.

Luke looked at Torres until Torres was compelled to return his stare. The two men held each other's eyes for a moment, until Luke, satisfied he had made the connection, turned back to face the judge. Hector Torres, he thought: shit. Let's hope he doesn't become part of an already dicey situation.

"When will you be ready to come back for the bail hearing?" the judge asked Alex.

"Two or three days, your honor. It shouldn't take long."

Luke jumped in. "We request the earliest possible preliminary hearing, your honor."

The judge, a retired appellate court judge pinch-hitting for Judge Allison, who was on vacation this week, turned to the prosecution side. "How's that with you?" he asked.

Alex conferred with Elise, the two whispering back and forth for a moment. He turned back to the judge. "We could do it seven to ten days after the bail hearing."

"Excuse me?"

Alex and Elise turned and finally looked at Luke.

"It could be done in forty-eight hours, your honor," Luke said. He was anticipating that Steven would be denied bail at the initial hearing. He wanted to hurry the process along after that, so bail could finally be set and Steven could get out of jail. "The District Attorney's office has always had a good record of moving things along. I don't understand the delay this time."

Alex scowled. "The court has up to ten days, your honor. Let's not forget, this is a murder trial."

As if anyone would forget for a nanosecond, Luke thought with rancor. Alex was throwing down the gauntlet early; he would have to respond with equal force, all the way down the line.

The judge looked from one side of the aisle to the other. "The preliminary hearing will be a week after the bail hearing," he decided, satisfying neither side. "You are counsel for the defense, Mr. Garrison?" he asked Luke.

"Yes, sir."

The judge turned to Alex. "Who's going to be prosecuting from your office?"

"I am, your honor. With Ms. Hobson."

The judge's face registered mild surprise. D.A.'s rarely tried cases; they had a department to run, scores of lawyers and hundreds of cases to oversee. "You are?" he asked, wanting to make sure he was hearing Alex correctly.

"Yes, I am," Alex answered firmly. "With Ms. Hobson, as I stated."

Luke and Steven sat in the small attorney-client holding room adjacent to the courtroom. Luke made a quick appraisal of his client. Steven's face had a day-old stubble, and his hair was matted from not being washed, but he didn't look terrible. He did, however, look very scared. His eyes darted around furtively, first at Luke, then taking in the room, then back at Luke.

"How much longer am I going to be in here?" he asked. His voice was thin and sounded like rust.

"I'll run you through the entire drill," Luke told him. "But first, how are you doing?"

"How do you think?" Steven answered in irritation. "I hate it in here. This is like . . . how did this happen?"

You were arrested for murder, Luke thought. With more than enough evidence to support the charges. "Have there been any intimidation or threats?" he asked. "Are the jailers treating you okay?"

Steven shook his head no to the first question. "I'm okay. They've got me in isolation. They watch me every second, even when I take a dump. It's better being by myself," he admitted. "I don't want to be around the guys I see in here, they're crazy, most of them. And most of them seem used to it, I guess they've been in here before."

Luke explained to Steven that he would be held in custody, at least until the bail hearing.

"So then I'll be able to get out?" Steven asked hopefully.

"If the judge grants it." He couldn't let Steven's expectations exceed reality; as his lawyer, he had to deal with the situation responsibly, which meant being straight with him.

Steven looked at him quizzically. "Why wouldn't he?"

"Because you're charged with murder. The District Attorney is going to make the argument that you're a candidate to jump bail, flee the country, go into hiding. It'll depend on whether the judge agrees with him, and how persuasive I can be to convince him you're not a threat if you're not in jail, and that you'll show up for your hearings and especially the trial."

Steven went white. "Jesus Christ. I might be in jail for months?"

Luke didn't pull his punch. "It could be a year. You don't rush murder trials. If it means you're in custody for a few extra months, as opposed to going to trial before we're absolutely, completely prepared, you're going to do the time."

"Like Robert Blake," Steven said in a flat monotone. "Or O.J."

"Don't put yourself in that category, emotionally," Luke cautioned him. "This is a murder trial, but it's not the same. You won't be under the intense media microscope like they were. It's critical that you stay positive, for your mental wellness, and for us to put on the best defense. You can't be hangdog, Steven. I know that's hard to hear, but you have to suck it up."

Steven stared at him. "I'll try," he said flatly.

"That's all I can ask for. I'll see you every day, and you can have other visitors. I assume those were your parents, sitting with your grandmother?"

Steven nodded. "They're totally freaked out."

With good cause, Luke thought. "I'll arrange for them to meet with you, after I talk to them."

He stood up. A sheriff's deputy opened the door. "You're going back to jail now," he told Steven. "Your parents will see you there."

They shook hands.

"Stay strong," Luke admonished Steven. The deputy cuffed Steven and fitted a set of irons to his legs. Steven, shuffling awkwardly in his restraints, was led to an outside door, where he was placed in a sheriff's vehicle for the trip back to the jail, four miles down Highway 101, at the sheriff's complex.

Luke and Kate met Steven's parents back at Luke's office. Juanita made the introductions. They shook hands solemnly all around. Steven's father, Garrett, was a rangy man, about his son's height but forty pounds heavier, with a soft gut. Laurie, his wife, was of average size, wiry-thin. Her black, curly hair was feathered-cut tight against her skull.

"I can't tell you how sorry I am about this," Luke told them.

"As am I," Kate seconded.

"Thank you," Garrett muttered. Laurie didn't speak; she shook her head and stared at the tile floor.

They sat down at Luke's conference table. Kate noticed that Laurie McCoy made sure she didn't sit next to her mother-in-law. The woman is an outsider in this family, she immediately intuited. Intimidated by Juanita, and resentful of it.

"Let me lay out the timetable for you, the first part," Luke began. He took a folder out of his hand-tooled leather briefcase, a gift from Riva. "As you heard in court, there will be a bail hearing in a few days. The preliminary hearing will be a week after that," he told them. "Formal charges will be presented, and we'll request bail."

"So then he'll get out, at least?" Laurie asked hopefully.

"Not necessarily," Luke cautioned. "This is a capital case. There's a possibility bail won't be granted at all. I'm sure the District Attorney will fight it," he said, repeating what he had told Steven. It didn't sound any better the second time around.

"Why?" Laurie cried.

"Because the state takes the position that an accused murderer shouldn't be out on the street. And there have been recent situations where the defendant jumped bail and fled the country. It left egg on everyone's face, particularly the judge's. So bail has become an iffy situation in a crime of this seriousness, you need to know that going in."

As Kate listened to Luke explain the problem she could see both parents deflate, as if they were tires that had sprung slow leaks. She leaned forward, her hand touching Laurie's across the table. "Even so, there's still a good possibility Steven will get bail at some point," she said, trying to sound optimistic. She turned to Luke, who nodded in muted agreement. "It will be high, but because Mrs. McCoy is one of our leading citizens, I think the judge will go for it. With stringent restrictions," she added.

"Like what?" Laurie asked fearfully.

"I'm almost positive Steven won't be able to leave Santa Barbara County," Luke said. "At least that."

"But what about college?" Laurie asked in alarm. "He's a senior. He's graduating this spring. He's applying to medical school." Her voice was rising in near-hysteria. "He's on the volleyball team. He's their best striker, he was all PAC-Ten last year."

"Not now, he isn't," Luke told her frankly. Sometimes you had to deliver the news in a manner that left no room for argument.

"Jesus," Garrett muttered. "It seems pretty damn arbitrary."

"This is a murder case, Mr. McCoy," Luke reminded him. "It doesn't get any more serious than this."

"What else?" Laurie asked impatiently. "What other restrictions?"

"Steven will be confined to a specific area and he'll have to report in every day. It's basically house arrest, but it's better than sitting in jail for a year, which is what usually happens, since most defendants can't make bail at the level that's going to be set."

The parents looked at each other with concern. "How much bail are we talking about?" Garrett asked nervously.

"It could be a million dollars," Luke answered. "Robert Blake was set at two million down in Los Angeles, Michael Jackson at three, right here, for a lesser charge." He looked at the parents sympathetically. "District Attorneys across the country are fighting bail for serious crimes, no matter how high it's set. And in the current political climate they're getting their way," he added in personal distaste.

Garrett groaned out loud. "A million dollars? That's a hundred thousand dollars to a bondsman?"

"Cash," Luke confirmed. "Plus collateral. To cover the rest of the bond, in case the defendant jumps."

"Like what?" Laurie fretted.

"Money from savings accounts, stocks, disposable property. Whatever you have of value."

"Like our house?" she asked, even more worried.

"Yes," Luke said, "if it's worth that much."

The two parents exchanged a worried look. "How much is

this going to cost, in total?" Garrett asked. "Assuming that you're Steven's lawyer all the way through," he added.

Luke was prepared for this. Discussing price was the most unpleasant part of the job, so it had to be gotten out of the way as soon as possible, without ambiguity.

"At least two hundred thousand dollars," he answered. "It could be significantly more, depending on several factors—investigation time, bringing in expert witnesses, a host of possibilities. There are dozens of elements that come into play when you're building a defense, particularly in a crime of this seriousness." He splayed his hands on top of the table. "I'll require a seventy-five-thousand-dollar retainer as soon as possible."

Garrett visually recoiled. His mouth made some mewing sounds before any actual words came out. "That's a lot of cash to raise on short notice, on top of the bail," he bleated. "We'll have to . . ."

"I'll post Steven's bail, and put up the collateral. And I'll pay the legal fees as well. All of them."

They all turned to Juanita, who had been sitting on the sidelines, taking everything in.

"Mother . . ." Garrett started to protest, once he found his voice.

She put up a restraining hand. "I have the money, and I own the property to cover it," she said in a tone of voice that foreclosed argument. "The murder happened on this ranch. I'm responsible, even though Steven didn't do it."

"I . . ." Garrett started to protest, but then looked at his wife, and dropped any opposition he might have mustered. "All right, Mother," he said, his voice registering both resignation and relief. "If that's what you want."

"It's settled, then," Juanita declared briskly.

The McCoys didn't stick around after the decision as to who would pay their bills was made. Juanita went home, and Steven's parents went to the jail to see their son. Luke would present a detailed plan for Steven's defense when he knew more about everything, particularly after he'd had time to talk to Steven, in depth. Until then, they would all have to cope as best they could.

"What do you want me to do first?" Kate asked Luke when they were alone.

"We should try to find a credible alibi witness for Steven. Someone who saw Steven and interacted with him long enough to remember him, and will swear to it."

Kate gave him a dubious stare. "Don't you think he would have told us, if there was one?" she asked reasonably.

"You'd think so," Luke agreed, "but one thing I've learned over the years, memory is unpredictable. You'd be amazed at what you don't remember, even important stuff, and the reverse, the stupid crap that stays in your memory bank forever, and what doesn't. Song lyrics, shopping lists, the street you crossed on your way to grade school can be embedded in your brain forever, but for a million dollars you can't remember what you had for dinner last Wednesday night. Look," he continued, "I know it's a long shot, but it can't hurt to try. We don't have a hell of a lot else to work with yet. I'll have Steven fill out a detailed questionnaire, but there will be empty spaces, there always are." He rapped her lightly on the shoulder. "As usual, you're going to have to fill them in."

They took a few minutes to coordinate their calendars for the rest of the week. "This is going to mess my schedule up but good," Kate told Luke candidly. "I wasn't expecting something this heavy to come up right now."

"So you'll juggle it, same as you always do," he responded, as he leafed through his phone messages. "I didn't go looking for this, either, but shit happens."

"I know, but it's worse than usual this time."

The distressful tone of her voice captured his attention. "Because of your daughter?" he intuited.

Kate nodded. "My workload is already more than I want,

plus I've got law school two nights a week and Saturday mornings, but yes, it's really about Sophia. I basically forced her to give up her senior year in high school up north, with all her friends and activities, so we could have one good year together before she left for college. And I'm not putting in the time with her."

"Do you want me to get someone else? I'll understand if you do."

She paced the floor. "This feels like a loser, Luke. I want everyone to have the best defense team possible, but I also want to see justice done. I can't help but think that if the circumstances had been only a little different, Maria Estrada could have been my daughter. Which Sophia has strongly pointed out to me," she added. "She has enough problems in her life right now without being the daughter of the woman who's trying to get a murderer off, which is what the kids in her school will be thinking. And saying."

"You think Steven's guilty," Luke said flatly. "You're pretty convinced."

"Aren't you?" Kate responded. She never liked prejudging a case, but she also believed it was important to be honest about the cards you've been dealt, regardless of the sermon she had preached to her daughter. You did better work if your vision was uncluttered with sympathy or self-deception. "Look at what we know so far. It's brutal."

Luke leaned back, his head cupped in his hands. "All the more reason why he needs a kick-ass defense."

"I know," she answered irritably. He wasn't letting her off the hook. "But you can't feel good about this. His fingerprints are on the murder weapon, for God's sake!"

"This is true. And he has a reason why."

"And a jury's going to believe that?" she bit off in irritation. "If that's the best we can do, Luke, you'd better start thinking about pleading him out."

Luke shook his head. "There won't be any pleas on this one. Alex won't go for anything less than murder one. I'm in this from now till the Second Coming, Kate. But you don't have to be, you really don't. You have legitimate reasons to bail." He paused. "I'm not even sure I want you on it, if this is how you feel."

That stung. "My feelings don't affect how I do my job. You know me better than that. I'm always professional, to the core."

"Yes, you are," he responded, "but everyone has their breaking point, and you sound like you're close to yours."

"It's not that. It's . . ." She picked up her purse. "I need to talk to my daughter about this. I'll let you know in a couple of days."

Luke walked her to the door. "Fair enough. But if you're in, Kate, you're in all the way. Agreed?"

She nodded solemnly. "Agreed. All, or nothing at all."

13

KATE AND SOPHIA started their hike up Cold Springs Canyon Trail at daybreak, to avoid the heat that by midmorning would grab the hills in a tight fist. Sophia, wearing a new pair of Lowa hiking boots that Kate had recently bought for her as an enticement to get outside more, bounded up the trail like a young mountain goat. Kate tried to keep up with her daughter's energetic pace, but soon fell back to a more comfortable tempo. The race goes not to the swift but to the determined, she doggedly repeated, almost as a mantra, while simultaneously admonishing herself to start working out again regularly.

The trail rose steadily into the Santa Ynez mountains. Far below, slivers of Santa Barbara could be glimpsed through the thick stands of sycamore, oak, bay laurel, and willows that covered the hillsides. The houses on the Riviera, clustered along winding, narrow roads above the city, reminiscent of ancient villages in Italy and Greece, threw off pale glitter of early morning light from their white walls and tile roofs, while further below, along the harbor, a series of boats were heading out of the breakwater on their way to the Channel Islands, or for day-sails up and down the coast.

They crossed Cold Springs Creek, bone dry after six months without a drop of rain. In the distance, a lone bird lazily rode the thermals. Kate took her binoculars out of her daypack to see if she could identify it. Her former lover, Cecil Shugrue, a winemaker in the Santa Ynez Valley, had indoctrinated her into the pleasures of wildlife watching. Now, whenever she went hiking, she carried binoculars and a Santa Barbara County birder's guide in her daypack. Four years after they'd broken up she still thought about Cecil when she went on a hike like this or drank a glass of locally produced Pinot Noir.

The bird was a red-tailed hawk, common in the area, particularly in the foothills. It rode the draft like a surfer taking a gentle wave, its wings almost motionless as it glided across the sky. Over in the valley Kate had seen dozens of them, along with Golden Eagles, other types of hawks, several varieties of owls. Predator birds.

The skin on her left heel was beginning to get irritated. Her boots were old and worn-down. She should have bought herself a new pair when she'd bought Sophia's, but she was trying to economize, and she hadn't wanted to share the moment, she wanted Sophia to have it to herself. A small thing, buying a pair of boots, but every distinction she could bring to Sophia's life was important. They helped assuage the guilt feelings.

Sophia doubled back to rejoin her. "There's a flat shady spot around the corner up ahead," she informed Kate solicitously. "We can rest there."

A bit defensively: "I'm not tired."

"You're not moving very fast."

"I'm enjoying my surroundings," Kate said, turning her head to the right and then to the left as if to emphasize her point. "It's not a race."

"I know that," Sophia said cheerfully. "But there's so much cool stuff to see. We don't want to get bogged down."

"We have all day." It was Saturday. The first Saturday Kate hadn't worked or gone to law school in months. It was a liberating feeling, to be doing something you wanted to do rather than a task you were supposed to do.

"It'll be too hot later on. That's why you wanted to get started so early," Sophia reminded her.

"Well, yes," Kate admitted. She smiled. "I'll try harder."

"Mom," Sophia said, exasperated. "I'm not criticizing."

"I know. It's me bemoaning my woeful state of conditioning."

They came to a small, grassy knoll where the trail temporarily leveled off, and rested on a flat slab of limestone that was bathed in dappled sunlight. Patches of shade abated some of the heat that was beating down from the already warming sky. Stands of scrawny, bent live oaks, their roots burrowed into the dry, powdery ground, formed ragged sentinel-rows on both sides of the trail.

They drank water and shared an energy bar. Kate applied more sunscreen to her face and neck, then passed the tube to Sophia, who dutifully did the same. You'll thank me thirty years from now, Kate thought, when your friends are getting precancers cut from their faces and you aren't. She hadn't worn suntan lotion as a kid; her mother didn't know from that stuff. She'd had to learn about that on her own, through trial and sometimes painful error. Like the way much of her life had gone. She wanted her daughters to benefit from her advice and experience, even when they rebelled against it, or ignored it altogether.

Her exposed heel, once she had pulled off her shoe and sock, was red but not yet blistered. She rubbed aloe vera salve into it, then laid a strip of moleskin over the sore spot.

"You need new boots, Mom," Sophia observed. "These are shot."

"It's on my list."

"Which means you'll buy a new pair in maybe five years?"

"When I get around to it."

"Knowing you, that won't be for a while, if ever. You hardly ever do anything for yourself."

"I do what I need to do," Kate responded defensively.

"Only the basics, and not even them sometimes. When was the last time you had a professional pedicure? Or a facial?" She took Kate's bare hot foot in her hand. "Look at this. What man wants to get in bed with a woman who doesn't take care of her feet? It's like not shaving under your arms."

"Who I sleep with is none of your business," Kate said,

embarrassed at her daughter's openly commenting about her sexuality, which had been virtually comatose since Sophia had moved in with her; a conscious choice, but one that was beginning to chafe. "And you have friends who don't shave," she added. "Don't you?" She looked at her foot. The polish on her toes was peeling. She had been a bit negligent about stuff like that lately. Too many things to do and not enough time.

"No," Sophia answered firmly. "That's sixties hippie stuff. The earth mother deal, now very passé, in case you hadn't heard. You're a professional, Mom, you can't look like a flower child."

"I shave under my arms and my legs," Kate protested. "Anyway, what are we talking about that for? Look around you. It's beautiful here. We don't need to dissect my personal hygiene. Not now."

Sophia sat back. "Agreed. But you're getting a pedicure, this week. My treat."

"Okay, okay." Kate pulled her sock back on, then the boot, which she laced up tightly to guard against further friction. "And I can pay for my own, but thanks for the offer."

They laid back on the rock and felt the sun on their faces. A warm, comforting feeling.

"Hey, Mom?"

"What, honey?"

"How come we're here today?"

Kate propped herself up on an elbow. "What's wrong? I thought you liked getting away from the city."

"I do, Mom. I'd rather be here than in town any day. Well, most days."

"Then what?"

"School."

"School? It's Saturday."

"*Your* school," Sophia clarified. "You have class on Saturday. Was it cancelled?"

Kate pushed some strands of damp hair off her forehead. "No, it wasn't cancelled. I didn't feel like going today."

"Is that okay?" Sophia asked, concerned. "Don't they get upset?"

Kate took another swallow from her water bottle. "I can miss one class. It's introductory, since the semester just started. I'm ahead of most of the people there, because of my background."

"And because you're smarter than they are, and you study harder."

Kate smiled. "Maybe. I'm getting through it, that's all I care about." She paused. "I'm thinking of taking this semester off."

Sophia stared at her in surprise. "Why? You've been working toward your law degree for almost three years now. You're practically finished."

"I'm not quitting," Kate assured her. "It's one semester. I can start up again . . . later," she said with a dismissive wave of her hand. "People do it all the time in this school. It's flexible that way, it's set up for working people like me."

"But why would you want to take off now?" Sophia persisted.

"So I can be with you more."

Sophia stared at her. Her face reddened. "Mom . . ."

"It is not a big deal," Kate said in a rush. "The school will be there, it isn't going away. But you are. This is your last year of high school. You moved here to be with me. I have a lot on my plate, so if I can clear some of it off, I want to."

Sophia took a deep breath. "Thanks, Mom," she said, after she had regained her composure. "I really appreciate that."

"I'm not doing it because I have to," Kate assured her. "I'm being selfish, really. I *want* to spend time with you. You're my daughter, what's more important than us being together?"

"Well . . . nothing, I guess." Sophia paused. "It's not going to be all the time though, is it?"

Kate laughed. "I'm not going to hijack your social life, don't worry about that. If I don't see you because you're with your friends, that's fine, that's the way it's supposed to be. But when you do want me around I want to be there, when I can. My not going to law school for a semester or two will give us the chance to spend more time together." She swept in their surroundings with a wave of her arm. "Like now."

"Well, if you're sure that's what you want . . ."

"It's exactly what I want."

Sophia smiled. "Okay, then. Me, too." She looked around at the stands of alder and sycamore that rose above them. "It's so beautiful up here. It reminds me of Cecil's place."

"Yes, it does," Kate said wistfully. "Not as lush as this, but still beautiful."

Sophia looked up at the trail, switchbacking higher into the hills. "His vineyard isn't far from where the girl was killed, is it."

Kate nodded. "They're fairly close to each other, that's right."

Sophia looked thoughtful. "Are you still working on the case?"

Kate looked at her sideways. "I'm not sure," she answered slowly. "I haven't decided yet."

Sophia looked at her in surprise. "I thought you already had."

"I may change my mind."

"Why?"

"Because . . ." The answer felt like a hairball in her throat. "Of how you feel about it."

Sophia recoiled. "What are you talking about?" she asked, both frightened and upset. "What does how I feel have to do with it?"

"A lot, to me," Kate answered. "You told me that if Steven McCoy was really guilty, I shouldn't help defend him."

Sophia exhaled heavily. "Well, is he?"

"I don't know," Kate answered, recalling her accusatory conversation with Luke about this very issue. "But like I told you, it wouldn't matter if he was. I'm going to give every client my best effort," she said, feeling the guilt of her own judgmental stance. "There are too many lawyers and PIs out there who phone it in if they think they have a loser case. I don't ever want to be one of them."

Sophia sat back down heavily. "I don't want to make this

decision, Mom." She sighed; more a groan. "This is too heavy to lay on me."

Kate sat next to her. "It's not that. It's that I care about your feelings. How it's going to affect your life." This wasn't going well. "And it's not like Steven McCoy won't have a good defense if I'm not involved. Luke Garrison can find another detective, it's really not that big a deal."

"Still . . . it's what you do."

Kate shook her head dismissively. "I've been wanting to cut back anyway. It's about timing, that's the problem. I have to tell Luke I'm in or I'm out. Because if I am, I can't quit, it would screw things up. I'm a professional in my work. I pride myself on that, Sophia." She took her daughter's hand. "But I can walk away from this. I absolutely can."

"I don't want you to do that," Sophia said. "It's just that . . ." She stopped.

"What?" Kate prodded.

"What if it turns out that he really is guilty? That you find out, for sure. And then what if he gets off? It's like, how could you . . ." She stopped.

"Live with it?"

Sophia nodded.

"It would be hard. But it would be worse if I knew he was innocent and was convicted." She paused. "Look at me, Sophia. Look at me."

Slowly, Sophia turned to her.

"It isn't the case that matters, any particular case. It's how the law, at least in theory, levels the field, makes everybody equal. Everybody deserves a fair trial and a good defense. That's one of the reasons we're the country we are, despite our warts."

"A fair trial? You mean like O. J. Simpson's?" Sophia rejoined. "What was fair about that? He bought his verdict."

"It's an imperfect system," Kate agreed. "It's badly abused sometimes." Like everyone she knew who wasn't black, she had been outraged over how Johnnie Cochran had gamed the system.

"But the alternatives are worse, believe me. I've been in third-world countries where the justice system is no system. At least we have a chance for justice, and most of the time, a decent chance."

Sophia looked at her. "It's not my decision, Mom. It's yours." She picked up her pack. "Whatever you decide, it's going to be okay between us." She laughed. "Like I care about what the kids in my school think. They don't even know who I am, I'm just someone who blew in for a few months and will blow right out again." She slung the pack over her shoulder. "Anyway, you can't bail out on Luke. He's counting on you."

"So you can live with my being on this?" Kate asked with trepidation.

"Yes." Sophia started walking up the trail. Kate picked up her pack and scurried after her. Sophia stopped and turned back. "Besides, the trial's not going to be for months. Not until spring."

"Yes," Kate answered. "A trial of this importance takes a long time before it gets to court."

"So by then, I'll be graduated, and who cares after that?"

They began climbing again. The heat from sun baked their backs as they made their way up the trail.

14

. . . .

IT WAS AFTER four in the afternoon by the time Luke was able to clear his other pending cases and get to the jail to see Steven. It was their second meeting since Steven's arraignment. The first time, Luke had gone over procedure—what, where, when. How to act in here, particularly if he was placed in the general population. The dos and don'ts of dealing with his jailers. Survivor 101.

Steven was showing the psychological effects of his confinement. He seemed listless, almost as if he were on downers. They were in the room reserved for lawyer-client meetings; the only room in the jail, Luke knew, that wasn't bugged. The space was Spartan—a metal table bolted to the floor and a few battered metal chairs. The floor was concrete, the walls chipped plaster. The paint on the walls was a dirty off-white; the floor was puke-neutral, deeply scuffed. There was one small window opposite the thick steel door. The double-pane glass was bulletproof, covered with heavy-gauge mesh. The door, thick steel, was also reinforced.

Luke knew this room intimately—he had met with dozens of clients in here. The room never changed; it was always depressing. If he ever went back to the other side of the aisle (on a scale of slim to none . . .), his first order of business would be to slap a fresh coat of paint on the entire place. Something with color in it, so that you didn't feel like you were in a Siberian gulag. This wasn't prison, a warehouse for long-term convicts. This was a county jail, housing short-timers who had committed minor offenses, and men who hadn't yet been convicted of any crime. Innocent men, technically. Like Steven McCoy.

"How are you?"

"Shitty. How else would I be?"

"Are you being treated okay?"

"Nobody's hassling me, if that's what you mean. I'm still in isolation."

"Are you eating okay?"

A half head-shake accompanied a shrug. "I eat enough so I won't be hungry. The food sucks, it's all starches. In Mexico at least they let you bring in your own food."

You don't want to be in a Mexican jail, Luke thought. You don't know how good you have it in here. "Hopefully, that will change tomorrow," he said, trying to sound more positive than he felt.

"You mean when I get bail?"

"Yes, if you get bail," Luke answered evenly.

Steven picked up on the difference between the certain *when* and the uncertain *if*. "So that's still a possibility?" he asked, his voice wavering. "Not getting bail?"

"Yes," Luke answered. "Which I've already explained. This is a murder case," he repeated, yet again. "Bail is often denied in murder cases, especially the first time it's requested. But if it is denied tomorrow we can take another crack when we can make a credible case for it."

Steven looked down at the floor. His body sagged. "Is there anything we can do to improve the odds?"

Luke leaned closer to him across the table. "That's one of the reasons I'm here." He reached into his briefcase and took out the questionnaire he had given Steven to fill out. "You need to help me here, my friend. Help me help you, you get it?" He placed the document on the table, slid it over to Steven. "You didn't fill this out the way I asked you to."

Steven's expression as he looked at the form was one of incomprehension. "What didn't I do?"

"You didn't fill it out in any detail." Luke leafed through the list. "You were at Butterfly Beach, but where? Next to the Coral Casino, or down by where the road turns up to the Music Academy? What side of Channel Drive did you park your Pathfinder on? Details like that." He flipped over a page. "You had a couple of beers at Kris & Jerry's Bar. Describe whoever you saw and whatever you did, in as much detail as you can, down to the brand of beer you drank." He sat back. "And so forth."

Steven stared at him. "What's the point of what kind of beer I drank? I wasn't drunk, if that's what you mean. Or where I was at the beach, or any of that? I don't get it."

This was a bright kid, supposedly. Honors student, on his way to being a doctor. He wasn't showing that now. Or maybe he wasn't connecting the dots because he was psychologically and emotionally in shock. "You were in several public places . . . so you say."

Steven nodded. "Yes."

"But you don't remember anyone from any of them."

Steven shook his head. "I was on cruise control, you know what I mean?"

Luke did know. He had done that himself, after the divorce from Polly. Up in Mendocino County, where he had run with his tail tucked between his legs, he would go for days, weeks, in a fog. So he understood Steven's blank frame of mind on that day. But that didn't help this situation, it made it worse. They needed to connect some dots.

"Here's why these things could be important. *You* don't remember anyone, but someone might remember *you*. The more you can be specific, the more there's a chance we can find whoever that might be. Because if we can locate someone who clearly remembers you from that afternoon, you have an alibi, and we could all go home happy campers. *Now* do you understand?" he asked again.

Steven nodded slowly. "So you want me to go over this again?" he asked, looking at the form.

"Yes, and fast. I'll send somebody for it tomorrow morning,

first thing. Put in everything you can think of, no matter how irrelevant you might think it is. Don't filter." He stood up. They had done enough for one day. "One more thing. Take care of your personal hygiene. If they don't let you shower every day, give yourself a sponge bath in your sink. Shave. Use deodorant. Brush your teeth." He grabbed Steven's forearm in a tight clasp. "This is going to be a long journey, Steven. You have to stay strong."

Steven looked at him forlornly. "That's easy for you to say, Mr. Garrison. You're not the one who's in here."

"Bail is denied. The preliminary hearing is scheduled one week from today. At that time you can bring up your request again," Judge Stanley Allison told Luke.

"Thank you, your honor," Luke answered dutifully. He looked across the aisle to the prosecution table. Alex Gordon looked back at him for a moment, then turned away. Elise Hobson maintained her rigid composure—she didn't so much as steal a glance at him. "We will definitely do that," Luke told the judge, as much to plant a burr under Alex's hide as for the record.

He sat down next to Steven. He could feel Steven shivering under his jail jumpsuit. "Don't get too upset about this," he whispered into Steven's ear. "I expected it to happen this go-around. We'll do better next week."

Steven nodded; then he slumped back in his chair.

"Stay strong," Luke urged him. "We'll get you out." He gave Steven a reassuring squeeze on the forearm. He wished he felt as confident as he said he was.

A courtroom deputy touched Steven on the shoulder. Steven shuffled to his feet. The deputy cuffed Steven and led him out of the courtroom.

Luke stood and walked to the back of the courtroom, where Kate sat with Juanita McCoy. Steven's parents weren't present—they had called last night and told Luke they couldn't handle the tension. They would come for the following session. Luke had been surprised, but not shocked. They were fighting their own emotional battles over this, particularly their guilt about what they might have done to prevent it, like every parent does when their child becomes involved in a tragedy.

He didn't want to think about the eight-hundred-pound gorilla in the room—that Steven's parents might really believe their son murdered Maria Estrada, and were beginning to emotionally distance themselves from him. Luke had seen that in a few other situations similar to this one. It was heartbreaking for everyone.

Given the grim circumstances, Juanita McCoy looked relatively composed. Luke sat down next to her. "I'm sorry, Mrs. McCoy," he said. "It was a gutless call, but we were anticipating it, as I told you. We should have better luck at the next hearing."

"In a week?" she asked.

"Yes."

"That poor boy," she said. "How he must be suffering." She squeezed Kate's hand. "Is there anything I can do?"

Luke told her the same thing he'd said to her grandson: "Stay strong."

Kate swung into Kris & Jerry's Bar, which was tucked into an alley a block off State Street, the city's main drag. The bar was frequented more by locals than tourists, which was how the owners wanted it. The décor was a jumbled mixture of Trader Vic–style Tiki bar and Greenwich Village bistro, circa 1968. Kris, one of the owners, was a prominent land-use lawyer who spent most of his vacations in Hawaii, where he consumed copious quantities of mai tais and other tropical drinks; thus the Tiki-bar angle. Everyone in town was his friend, which made for a solid, steady clientele. The other owner, Jerry, a television and commercial director, had been a jazz and folk buff in the Village in the mid-'60s, where he grooved on the sounds of Miles Davis, John Coltrane, and Sonny Rollins; so the faux-homage to the White Horse was his contribution.

Over the decade that the two friends had owned the place the disparate styles had softened and blended into each other, so that now it was a comfortable, laid-back drinking spot for the over-thirty crowd. Most of the regulars were professionals—lawyers, architects, businessmen of both sexes. Layabouts and goofballs were strongly encouraged to skedaddle.

It was early, a few minutes after four. A couple of middle-aged men, who looked like real-estate agents, had established a beachhead in a booth near the back, drinking the first martinis of the afternoon. Other than that, the bar was empty, except for the female bartender and a waitress, both of whom looked to be in their late twenties or early thirties. They were California beach-style attractive, the kind of women men will order the extra drink from and then leave a big tip. They wore identical Tommy Bahama shirts in a tropical pattern, fitted black slacks, and open-toed black slides. They had good pedicures, Kate noticed, which reminded her to get one herself before her daughter ragged on her about that again.

Not the place where you'd think a twenty-one-year-old would choose to knock back a few, Kate thought, as she dropped onto a barstool. There were a slew of college bars on lower State for people his age. And this one, being off the beaten track, wasn't that easy to find. So if Steven had been in here the chance that someone might remember him was better than zero, which were the results she had gotten at the other places on Steven's list.

It had been a frustrating beginning. She had talked with employees from the Coral Casino, the private swimming club at the beach where Steven had laid out in the sun and then swam. Nobody had a clue about him, which was what she expected. Ditto the Biltmore, the posh hotel across the street. This was her last stop of the day before she went back to her office and dove into the rest of her work.

"Vodka tonic, double lime," she told the bartender, as a cock-tail napkin was placed in front of her.

"Coming at you."

She watched the woman make her drink. Crisp, no wasted motion. When the libation was placed in front of her she took a nourishing sip. Perfect. And it was billable.

"Ask you a question?" She reached into her soft attaché case and pulled out the file with Steven's picture in it. It was a good likeness. He looked like a unique human being, not a generic composite.

The bartender came over. "What's up?" she asked.

Kate slid the picture across the bar. "Any chance you've ever seen him in here?" she asked. "Take your time."

The bartender looked at the picture for a moment. She nodded. "I remember him. He goes to college."

If Kate had wings, she would have flown up to the ceiling. "That's right, he does," she said. "Do you remember anything else about him?"

The bartender smiled. "He was a cutie. I remember that."

My God, did we strike gold, Kate thought? She took out a notepad and pen. "What else do you recall?"

"He was casually on the make. Not offensively or anything," the woman added quickly. "I was throwing off a welcoming vibe, too. I have ten years on him, but if it works for Demi Moore, why not?"

Why hadn't Steven mentioned this, Kate thought? This was an attractive woman, he had to have remembered flirting with her.

And then it hit her. The woman had been doing the flirting. Steven had been polite, but not in touch. He was in his own space, he wasn't picking up on the signs. The woman had been reading the tea leaves wrong. How easily single women deceive ourselves. She could relate to that.

"Can we get specific about a few things?" she asked the woman.

"Like what?" Not cagey, exactly, but protective.

"You and he didn't get together outside of here, did you?"

The bartender shook her head. "No. He claimed he had a

prior commitment. I thought he'd be back the next day and we'd pick up where we'd left off, but I never saw him again. Men," she sighed.

"He had school the next day," Kate explained. "So—can we lock down when he was in here? Around four or five o'clock, right?"

The bartender frowned. "Four or five? No. It was eleven or twelve."

Kate almost fell off her barstool. She grabbed the edge to keep her balance. "Twelve at night?" she sputtered.

The bartender nodded. "We aren't open in the morning. Four at night till one in the morning, those are our middle of the week hours. Two on the weekends. Anyway, what's this about going back to school? He was on winter break, he wasn't due back for two weeks." With some rancor: "So he claimed."

"So it wasn't September 14 that you saw him in here?"

"This September? A few weeks ago?"

"Yes."

The bartender shook her head with certainty. "If he had been in here then, I would have remembered it."

"He hosed us."

Kate was thoroughly pissed off. Two days of shit-detail work and it had come to a blatant lie.

"Maybe not. She might not have been on that day. Or she came on after he left. Or maybe he got the bars confused. I'll ask him about it."

It was after seven o'clock. They were in Luke's office, a few blocks from hers. She had walked over after she had finished the pile of work she'd been neglecting.

Kate stood up. "I promised my daughter we'd eat dinner together, unless I had an emergency. Which this is not," she stated emphatically.

Luke got up, too. "I'll walk out with you."

The low sun was casting long shadows across the asphalt as

they walked to their cars, which were parked next to each other in his lot. Luke was looking forward to a cold beer, a dip in the pool with his wife and children, steaks on the barbeque. A shot of single-malt scotch to go with the beer.

He thought about the barmaid's story. Regardless of Steven's actual innocence or guilt, he would represent him as best he could. But if Steven was deliberately lying to him, that turned the equation upside down. He could live with a client holding back damaging information; they all did that. But to outright lie, that was unacceptable. They would get straight on that issue, first thing in the morning.

Kate's thoughts, as she opened her car door and tossed her purse onto the passenger seat, weren't about whether or not Steven McCoy had lied. She was thinking about herself, and her involvement in the case. She had committed to it, and she always honored a commitment. But there were boundaries. She could live with helping to defend a guilty man. The system didn't work otherwise. But she didn't want to be part of a grand deception— that they would come to believe that Steven was innocent, or at least that he wasn't guilty beyond a reasonable doubt, work their tails off to get him acquitted, only to learn, too late, that he was really guilty and that he'd been lying to them all along. Those were the kinds of cases that drove lawyers and investigators to drink, to ulcers, to dropping out.

She had been on the fence about this case. She had finally decided to take it because Sophia had given her blessing, and because she felt guilty about not standing with Luke. But the combination of her gut-feeling that Steven had killed that girl, combined with the emotional proximity of the situation to her own child, was a rock in her stomach.

She should have jumped off the train when she had the chance. Now it was too late. She was on for the ride.

15

JUANITA TOOK A Valium before she went to bed, but it didn't help. She hadn't had a decent night's sleep since Steven was arrested. Her mind was racing. What must it be like to be in jail? Terrifying for someone like Steven, who had never been in serious trouble in his life.

The weight of her complicity in that girl's murder, and Steven's being accused of it, lay on her heart like a crushing stone. The old revolver. It all came back to that. Why in the world had she taken it out of the gun cabinet? So what if somebody had come onto her property? What was she going to do, actually shoot them? She hadn't even thought it was loaded. That was one of the miseries of getting old—fearfulness. Her grandson might spend the rest of his life in prison because she had allowed her irrational fear to overwhelm her common sense.

She was going to fix that. How she would do it, she didn't know. But somehow, she was going to atone for her mistake.

Once again, Luke met with Steven in the holding room at the jail. Steven looked about the same as the last time Luke had seen him. At least he isn't looking any worse, Luke thought. He had to remind himself to cut Steven some slack. The kid—he was a man, but he was still young, and in here he looked younger than he did in the free world—was up against a situation he had no preparation for, and he hadn't figured out how to cope with it yet. But that didn't mean he was going to lighten up on getting at the truth, whatever that was in the moment. That wouldn't help either of them.

He tossed the latest questionnaire on the table. "This isn't much better than the last one," he said.

Steven stared at the pages. "I did the best I could. I'm blanking on a lot of it. It's like . . ." He threw up his hands.

"That's a damn shame," Luke told him, "because your amnesia is hurting you, man. And another thing." He rapped his knuckles on the pages. "Your so-called sojourn in Kris & Jerry's, before the movie? We have a gold-plated witness who said you weren't there. What's your answer to that, pal?"

Steven looked at him with bewilderment. "What witness are you talking about? Someone who *didn't* see me there? That's like saying I was a ghost."

"Cut the bullshit, Steven," Luke said harshly. "Kate Blanchard checked your story out with the bartender who was on duty that afternoon. She remembered you, from a year ago, and she flatly denied that you were in there that day." He sat back. "What gives?"

Steven slowly shook his head in denial. "I don't remember who served me, I've already told you that. And what's this about a year ago?"

"The bartender said you were in there over your Christmas break, and that you chatted her up. She remembered it enough to remember that you weren't there on September 14," Luke told him.

This time Steven's head-shake was emphatic. "No way, man," he protested strongly. "Look. I don't remember who served me. I don't remember who served me last Christmas, either." He tried to smile, but his face wouldn't hold the effort. "I flirt with lots of women. Everybody does in bars. But I don't remember who that was, or even if it happened." He tilted back in his chair. "If some woman is carrying a misguided flame for me, that's her problem."

Luke regarded him carefully. "So you're sticking to your story. You were in Kris & Jerry's on the fourteenth."

"Absolutely."

Luke exhaled heavily. "Okay. I have to go with your word," Luke told his client. I hope it doesn't blow us up, he thought.

He sat back. "Let's get down to the important business. Your preliminary hearing is set for the day after tomorrow. The prosecution is going to lay out the minimum they need to get an indictment. Your fingerprints on the gun are going to be enough to bind you over for trial." He shuffled Steven's papers back into his briefcase. "I want to waive our rights to a preliminary hearing and request that we go directly to trial. It'll speed up the bail hearing, and frankly, Steven, the prosecution's going to get that indictment. A monkey could get you charged on the evidence they have, and these people aren't monkeys, they're sharp." He smiled tightly. "They should be. I trained most of them. But I need you to agree to waive that hearing."

Steven felt his throat tightening. "You mean admit I did it?" he managed to croak out.

Luke shook his head. "You're not admitting guilt. But you are agreeing that there's enough evidence to go to trial." He fixed his look at Steven. "The press is going to be all over this. Larry King, Geraldo, all the talk-show ghouls. I want to give them as little as possible." He leaned forward. "You need to trust me on this, Steven. On everything."

Steven nodded slowly. "If that's what you think, then you should do it." He stood up. "I hope it's the right thing."

Luke spent an hour on the phone twisting Alex Gordon's arm, until Alex reluctantly agreed to waive the preliminary hearing. "But we are going to be fighting bail, in any amount. I want you to know that," Alex told him.

"I wouldn't expect any less," Luke rejoined. Before Alex could renege on their agreement, he added, "I would do the same, if I was in your shoes."

"See you at the hearing," Alex told him curtly.

"See you," Luke began to answer, until he realized that Alex had already hung up and he was talking to himself.

Kate drove through the gate, which had been left open for her, and started up the narrow, bumpy road. She had never been to Rancho San Gennaro before. She knew that Mrs. McCoy opened up this section of the old ranch a few times a year for various charitable functions, but as she didn't move in those circles, she had never had occasion to come here. Until now.

She was here because she needed to see where the killing happened. Judging by Steven's testimony (regardless of whether or not he was the one who fired the gun), it was almost certain that it had taken place inside the old house. She would also check out where the body had been found; how far it was from the house, how difficult it would have been to move the body there, how it would have been hidden, and so forth.

Once she was actually at the location, a picture would start to form. After years of doing this work, that was almost always how it happened. The location would talk to her. The trick was knowing how to listen.

A three-decades-old Mercedes was parked near the house. As Kate approached, the front door of the house opened, and Juanita came out. Kate parked her car next to the Mercedes. "Hello, Mrs. McCoy," she called.

Juanita smiled as she approached. "Welcome to the family *casa*, our humble abode."

Kate looked at the old place. This woman's humble abode would be anyone else's dream-fantasy. An honest-to-God American ranch house, right out of an old John Wayne movie. Except this one was real.

As she was getting her bearings, the passenger-side door of her car opened, and Sophia scampered out. She looked around, wide-eyed. "This is so *cool*," she gushed.

Kate put an arm over Sophia's shoulder. "This is my daughter Sophia, Mrs. McCoy. I hope you don't mind that I brought her. This is take-your-daughter-to-work week," she joked. "Sophia, this is Mrs. McCoy, the owner."

"I'm delighted," Juanita said warmly. "I'm very glad to meet you, Sophia." She smiled. "And please call me Juanita. Both of you."

She led them inside. The heavy window curtains had been raised, so the light was decent. Kate looked around. "Is that the gun case where the . . ." She paused—she didn't want to say "murder weapon" in front of her daughter.

"Yes," answered Juanita. "That's where it was." She pointed to a small side table next to a Queen Anne chair that was covered in a dark, heavy brocade. "And that is the table I put it on."

Kate walked over to the table. She stood there for a moment, her eyes closed, trying to visualize the scene. Two people. Maria and her killer. She fought not to let Steven's image come into her mental picture, but it was difficult. Who had picked up the gun? Whichever one felt threatened. Probably Maria—she was the victim. But it could have been the person who was with her. Maybe he—again, she had to fight not to see Steven here, in her mind's eye—had felt like he was under attack.

Another scenario, which no one, neither Luke, the cops, or the District Attorney's office, had yet thought of, suddenly came to her. There could have been more than two people here. The assumption was that this was a boy-girl tryst gone wrong. What if it wasn't? What if, after Maria had left the earring shop with a boy, whoever he was, she had hooked up with a different group of people? Or maybe that boy was involved, but with some others.

Maria Estrada was Hector Torres' niece. Hector had been off the books for a long time, but there were always rumors. Wouldn't that be an out-of-the-blue stunner, if this was drug-related? That it wasn't a random killing, but part of something bigger? Which would mean Maria wouldn't have been a passive victim, but would have been at least partially responsible for her own death.

Kate didn't want to think badly of anyone, particularly a girl who had been murdered. But she had a client who had been charged with murdering her, and she wanted to get him off anyway she could, as long as it was legal. She would discuss these ideas with Luke later today, after she finished up here and she and Sophia went back to town.

She slowly made her way through the house, room by room, making notes in one of the small reporter's notebooks she always carried. Had the police gone over this entire place? Or had they become so enraptured when they found the gun that they didn't look for any other possibilities? Cops loved to develop a theory, have it confirmed, and then exclude any alternatives. She'd had that mind-set when she was on the Oakland PD. Most of the time, the theory held up. But not always.

She looked out one of the living-room windows into the side-yard, where Sophia and Juanita were down on their hands and knees, their faces inches off the loamy ground, digging in the soil. The two of them were practically head to head. Juanita was talking and Sophia was listening intently, her head bobbing up and down as she took in the knowledge Juanita was dispensing. They seem so at ease with each other, Kate thought, almost with a pang of jealousy.

She reached into her purse and took out her digital camera, another tool of the trade. The window made a perfect frame. She took the picture.

Kate stood where the ranch foreman had found the remains. It was a good place to hide a body. The area was a massive bramble of bushes, like the Br'er Rabbit's briar patch. Whoever had dumped the body here hadn't been so unnerved by the killing that he couldn't think clearly enough to get rid of the evidence. Or if one of her other theories turned out to be what really happened, he, or they, wouldn't have been flustered at all.

In any case, this had been a good hiding place. If the foreman hadn't been riding by that day, the body would never have been found.

She looked toward the house. Even though it was only half a mile away, carrying a hundred and forty pounds of dead weight to this spot wouldn't have been easy. Whoever did it was strong.

Steven McCoy was a tall, rangy boy. He could have carried the dead girl here, especially if he had to.

She took some more pictures.

Sophia and Juanita were sitting on an old wooden swing under the gazebo when Kate came back to the house. They were laughing about something. Juanita put a grandmotherly hand on Sophia's. They looked as if they had known each other forever.

They looked up as Kate approached. "Did you get everything you needed?" Juanita asked.

"For this time. I might want to come back later. Thank you for being so gracious."

"Anything I can do to help Steven, of course I will."

"We have to get going, kiddo," Kate said to Sophia. "Did you have fun?"

"Lots. Juanita has a stable at her house, Mom. She keeps horses in it. Can we go see them?"

She had a ton of work overflowing her desk. "We've already taken a lot of Mrs. McCoy's time. I'm sure she has other things to do."

"The one thing I have plenty of is time," Juanita said. Her eyes were almost twinkling as she and Sophia exchanged a conspiratorial glance.

Kate looked at her daughter. She hadn't seen her this happy since she had moved to Santa Barbara. "Okay," she agreed cheerfully.

The stable was dark and cool. Sophia and Juanita were in front of the stall that quartered Juanita's mare. The mare nuzzled Sophia's hand.

Kate stood apart from Juanita and her daughter. She didn't need to be here, but she was glad she was.

Juanita handed Sophia a quarter of an apple. "Give her this. She loves them. You'll be her new best friend."

Sophia held the apple in the palm of her hand. The mare slurped it up, sucking on Sophia's fingers. Sophia giggled.

"Have you ridden?" Juanita asked her.

"At camp, one summer," Sophia responded. She made a face. "It wasn't really riding. We sat on horses and walked around a ring in a circle, with a counselor leading us."

"That's the way you start." Juanita said. "Would you like a riding lesson?"

"Sure," Sophia answered eagerly. "When?"

Juanita reached for a bridle. "No time like the present."

Sophia and Juanita stood in the riding ring. Sophia had exchanged her flops for a pair of worn boots. A riding helmet, covered with brown felt, sat atop her head. The horse she was going to ride, a large roan, already saddled and bridled, stood by docilely as Juanita held the reins. Kate was outside the ring, watching. She had her camera ready.

"This old boy is named Pecos," Juanita said, rubbing the horse's nose. "He's about twenty now, and he's the perfect horse to start on, nice and mellow. Go ahead, make friends with him."

Sophia put a tentative hand on the horse's shoulder.

"Nice and firm," Juanita instructed her. "Tell him he's a good horsey."

"Good horsey," Sophia said, rubbing the old horse's flank. "Good boy."

Juanita took one of Sophia's hands in hers. "You don't need gloves for now, but let's see how you and I match. Put your hand on mine."

Sophia touched her palm to Juanita's.

"Close enough," Juanita said. She reached into her back pocket and dug out a pair of worn leather gloves. "Try these on."

Sophia pulled the gloves onto her hands. They felt like silk. She flexed the fingers.

"How's the fit? Nice and snug, but not too tight?"

"They feel good," Sophia said. "These are really nice gloves."

"These were mine, when I was your age." Juanita ran a hand over them. "You can use them whenever you come here."

There was a low mounting block in the center of the ring. Juanita led the horse to it. Sophia hugged her shoulder.

"Get up on the block," Juanita told her. "I'll hand you the reins. Take them in your hand and grab the saddle horn. Stick the ball of your left foot in the stirrup and help yourself up by pulling on the horn, then swing over. Pecos will stand nice and steady for you. Watch me."

As if she were a jockey, Juanita mounted the old horse. Then she swung her right leg over and slid off. "Now you do it," she told Sophia.

Sophia climbed up onto the block. She took the reins in her hand as Juanita had told her. She grabbed hold of the saddle, slipped her left foot into the stirrup, pushed herself up, and was sitting pretty.

Forty-five minutes later, when Sophia's first riding lesson was over, she had not only walked her horse by herself, but had stopped, started, and turned him in a circle. Before they were halfway done, Kate had shot an entire roll of film.

Sophia followed Juanita's instructions for taking off the horse's saddle, blanket, and bridle. She watched as Juanita coiled the bridle and mounted it on a hook on the wall. Then she did it herself, getting it perfect the first time. She brushed the old horse down, cleaned his hooves as Juanita showed her, and filled his water bucket.

"Good job," Juanita said as they left the stable and walked over to Kate, who was waiting outside in the shade. "Any time your mother can bring you out here I'll give you more lessons. You'll be a good rider lickety-split."

"I have my own car," Sophia said with proud authority.

Juanita smiled. "Then you don't have to wait on mom. Call to make sure I'm here, so you don't waste your time. Tomorrow, if you want."

"I have play practice tomorrow," Sophia said, almost apologetically. "But I can come on Saturday."

"Saturday it is, then." She looked over at Kate. "If that's all right with your mother."

Kate's smile was so broad it almost hurt. "That's fine with me," she said. "Perfectly fine."

16

"YOU'RE LOOKING PARTICULARLY sharp this morning," Riva told Luke, as he stood at the island in the kitchen. He was reading the L.A. *Times* Sports section and drinking a cup of coffee. "The great Luke Garrison must be nervous," she teased him. It was barely sunup, but Luke had been awake for almost an hour. After a hard run through the hills around his house, he'd shaved, showered, and put on his number-one court outfit, a dark gray Oxford suit with a subtle blue pinstripe. It was a holdover from his D.A. days. He wanted to look extra-sharp this morning, and solidly pro-establishment.

"I'm concerned," he admitted. "We drew Judge Yberra for the bail hearing. He's tough on bail. And he's been hearing footsteps."

"Because the victim was a Latina, and so is he."

Luke nodded. Riva had good instincts, and she was tough. She had lived with a drug dealer before they'd gotten together; she'd had to be strong to survive in that world.

"Yberra's up for re-election next year," he told her. "He doesn't want to piss off a big chunk of the electorate, particularly his core. And Alex is fighting it like a demon."

"For the same reason?"

"Partly. He wants to look tough on crime, and he wants to make a statement. You've got these poor Latino and black kids in jail waiting on their trials because they can't make bail, even if it's only a few grand. Along comes a privileged white one who can write a big check. So you decide he's going to play the game with the same equipment." He tried his coffee. It was hot—he blew on the rim. "I can't fault Alex. I don't like the way the field is tilted, either. And if Steven McCoy really is guilty . . ."

"Is he?" she interjected.

"I don't know. It doesn't matter, at least not yet. But if he is, or if he thinks he's going to get convicted, he might take off. You can wrap electronic bracelets on every limb of his body, but if he wants to bolt, he'll figure out how to do it."

He tried his coffee. It was drinkable now. "And if he did manage to get out of the county," he said, "it would be hell to pay getting him back. When you have a potential death case, which this could be, most countries won't extradite. Neither Yberra or Alex Gordon wants to be the dumb ass who let a murder suspect get away. Hasta la vista career, baby."

"You'll figure something out," she told him supportively. "If you can't pull it off, ain't nobody can."

As they sat at the defense table waiting for Judge Yberra's appearance, Luke looked around the courtroom. On the prosecution side of the aisle, Maria's family had taken up their posts in the first two rows. Behind them were several girls and a few boys, Maria's age. Friends who had come in support of the family, Luke assumed. Hector Torres was also among the spectators. Maria's uncle sat apart from the others, his eyes locked onto Steven's back. Luke could almost feel the heat from Hector's intensity.

On their side, the representation was sparse. Kate Blanchard, a few reporters, and the McCoys, Juanita and Steven's parents. They sat in a tight cluster behind the railing that separated the actors from the audience.

"All rise."

Judge Yberra, a stocky man in his fifties, sporting a luxurious salt-and-pepper mustache, strode into the court and up to the bench. He nodded to both sets of attorneys, first Alex and Elise, then Luke. Sitting down, he looked at the open folder in front of him.

"*People* v. *McCoy*," he read aloud. He set the file aside. "Since both parties have agreed to waive the preliminary hearing and bind the defendant over for trial, this hearing is about request for bail. Are you prepared to proceed?" he asked the prosecution.

"We are, your honor." Elise was going to do the honors today.

Luke stood at the defense table. "Request defendant be released on his own recognizance, pending arraignment and trial."

Elise popped up like Carl Lewis leaving the starting blocks. "That's preposterous, your honor! This defendant shouldn't be granted bail under any circumstances, particularly not on a get-out-of-jail-free card."

"I see that's your position," Yberra said, glancing again at the material on his podium. "I should warn you that if bail is granted, it's going to be high," he told Luke sternly.

That's encouraging, Luke thought. At least the door was open now. "How much, your honor?"

"Well, Michael Jackson's bail was three million dollars, and he was charged with a lesser offense in this county," Yberra said.

Luke's jaw almost dropped. He had thrown that number at Steven's parents to make them understand how serious this was, but he would never have expected an amount remotely that high. Michael Jackson was one of the most famous people on the planet, and a multimillionaire. His Santa Barbara County ranch alone was worth over forty million dollars. Luke had been out of the local loop for awhile, but he didn't think that bail for over a million dollars had ever been set for a regular person in the county.

"That's if I grant it," Yberra said. He turned back to Elise. "Make your case for denial."

So I can agree with it, Luke thought with anger, his earlier optimism fading away. This was a prime example of why judges should be appointed, not elected. All those aggrieved people sitting behind the prosecution's table were potential voters.

Elise ticked off the reasons why Steven McCoy should not be

granted bail. The flight risk, first and foremost. Steven was a poster boy for that. He had money and motive. And there was another factor, she added mysteriously. An extenuating circumstance that might be added to the murder charge, which could elevate the charge from life without parole to execution.

"We aren't prepared to add that charge yet, your honor," Elise said, standing tall in her four-inch heels. "But it's going to be one of the first things we will get into once the trial date is set and all the charges are formally filed. You can certainly deny bail until then."

It has to be rape, Luke thought. He had been worried about that—now, even though it wasn't yet stated, it hung over their heads like a huge, menacing thundercloud.

In California, murder by itself isn't enough to warrant the death penalty. Another crime has to have been committed along with the murder. Armed robbery is often the case. Kidnapping. Killing a police officer also qualifies, which Luke had never agreed with, even though he was a former prosecutor. Why was a cop's life more important than a civilian's? A policeman knew that being in harm's way was part of the job.

It was all about politics, and an institution that was way too sensitive and insular. A kid gets gunned down in south-central L.A., his mother cries. A cop gets killed, the funeral parade of uniformed policemen is five miles long.

If Steven had raped Maria Estrada, his DNA would show up. DNA was the gold standard now. If Steven's DNA was found in the victim, Luke wouldn't be trying to win an acquittal; he would be fighting for a sentence of life without parole, rather than the death penalty. It would be an uphill battle.

Yberra seemed to be in agreement with Elise. "Your argument sounds reasonable." He turned to Luke. "Another week or two shouldn't be that much of a hardship, should it, Mr. Garrison?"

Luke was still standing. "It isn't about time, your honor," he said. He walked a few steps closer to the bench. "Let me remind the court, and my colleagues across the aisle as well, that Mr.

McCoy voluntarily returned to Santa Barbara when he was requested to do so by Mr. Gordon. Would a flight risk have done that? If he was going to run, your honor, he would have done it then. But he didn't, and he won't now."

Yberra sat back. "There's a point there," he conceded. Back to the prosecutors: "What about that?"

Elise shook her head in strong disagreement. "McCoy wasn't a suspect then. He thought he was going to waltz through a beauty contest and skip on home. That isn't the situation now. He is going to be tried for first-degree murder."

Yberra nodded as if giving the matter his grave attention. "I'm inclined to go with the prosecution on this one, counselor," he said to Luke. "One or two more weeks to sort this out isn't going to make that much of a difference."

Luke nodded tightly. There are times to fight a judge, and times not to. This wasn't the time to waste a bullet. He leaned over to Steven. "It's going to be another week," he whispered. "This judge is too scared to do the right thing."

Steven covered his face with his hands. "Where would I run to?" he whispered back.

Luke had no answer.

"I'm going to deny bail at this time," Yberra announced. "You can reinstate your request at the arraignment next week," he said to Luke. He prepared to gavel the session closed.

"May I say something, Alberto?"

Yberra looked up at the woman in the back of the room who had called him by his first name—a major breach of protocol in a courtroom. But he couldn't call this woman on that. She was too important.

"Yes, Mrs. McCoy?" He didn't want to sound deferential, but he couldn't help himself.

Juanita came forward until she was at the railing, behind her grandson. "It's always been Juanita, Judge Yberra," she said with a thin smile, "but we should be formal here, I agree." She put a hand on Steven's shoulder. "This is my grandson."

"I know that," Yberra answered uncomfortably.

"Do you think a grandson of mine would run away?"

Yberra almost swallowed his tongue. He turned toward Alex Gordon as if for guidance. Both Alex and Elise were rigidly at attention, deliberately not looking at Juanita. Alex's hands, gripping the tabletop, were almost white from pressure.

"My grandson will not run away," Juanita promised Yberra. "I will be responsible for him." She locked eyes with the judge. "Is my word not good enough for you, Judge Yberra?"

"Your word is good with me anywhere and at any time, Juanita," Yberra said tightly. He looked at Alex and Elise, as if to say, "This is a force too strong for me to resist."

"And please," Juanita pressed on. "Three million dollars? You would think Steven was O. J. Simpson or Ted Bundy. Be reasonable, judge. Be fair. Especially since I'm putting up my own money," she added sharply.

"Five hundred thousand dollars," Yberra said tightly. Anything less and he'd be pilloried. He slammed his gavel down. "Formal arraignment this coming Tuesday. Court is adjourned."

Luke clapped Steven on the back. "Congratulations," he told his stunned client. "You're out. They'll keep you in a holding cell for a couple of hours, until we do the paperwork." He looked back at Juanita, who had retreated to the rear of the courtroom with Kate and Steven's parents. Kate grinned as she gave Luke a quick thumbs-up. "You owe your grandmother big-time, Steven," Luke said. "Don't make her regret what she did for you."

"I won't," Steven promised. "I'll do everything right from now on."

As he prepared to leave, Luke glanced back at Maria's family. Hector Torres was having an animated conversation with Maria's mother, his sister. As Luke headed out, he and Hector locked eyes for a moment. Hector's look, and the stark emotion behind it, was pure venom.

17

AFTER HIS KIDS were born Luke stopped collecting, restoring, and riding classic motorcycles. His wife had been a hard-core biker mama, but now she was a mother of two small children. And he was their father, hopefully for a long time. After months of cajoling and pleading from Riva, he gave in. His days of riding against the wind were over. Marriage is, among other things, a series of negotiated compromises. This one hurt more than most, but he'd had his decades of hard riding. Maybe when the kids were grown and he was a doddering geezer he'd ride on two wheels again.

At the time he stopped, he owned a 1953 Vincent Black Shadow, a pre-war Indian, a 1974 Harley-Davidson Electra Glide, plus a couple of Italian motorcycles for when speed, rather than style, was of the essence. He sold the Indian and Harley and the Ducatis, but he put the Vincent in storage. Someday his son might want it. He'd never sell it, because he would never be able to find another one. Black Shadows were as rare as Stradivarius violins. It had been the miracle of a lifetime when he had found this one, and even more extraordinary that the owner was willing to sell it to him. He wouldn't get that lucky a second time. Some people collect incredible bottles of wine they never open, others buy great works of art no one ever sees. He owned a legendary motorcycle he might never ride again.

But he was still a committed gearhead, so he switched to classic muscle cars of the '60s and early '70s: Dodge Challengers, Pontiac GTOs and Grand Ams, Chevy Camaros. They were some of the greatest automobiles America had ever produced. Songs had been written about them, as well as doctoral theses discoursing on what the GTO and its brethren—Dodge Chargers, Chevy Camaros, Shelby Mustangs, and the like—symbolized: the mystique and romance of the rugged American frontier spirit. All of which boiled down to the unalloyed fact that they were testosterone monsters. He knew the handling was heavy, they got terrible gas mileage, and they were an affront to the environment: but they flew off the line, the air conditioners cooled the inside down to meat-locker temperatures, and you could catch rubber not only in first gear but in second as well, if you knew how to pop the clutch ever so delicately.

Luke had recently finished rebuilding this car, a Fontaine-blue '66 Pontiac GTO coupe. He had spent over ten thousand dollars restoring this tribute to the American assembly-line worker to its original, pristine condition, albeit with a few more dependable components, like modern wiring and hoses, a radiator that didn't boil over in traffic, and a modern sound system. He could blow out eardrums for two blocks in any direction.

He still preferred two wheels to four, but these cars were buff. They were the envy of every car freak in Santa Barbara, particularly the Latinos. At car shows they would cluster around his wheels like workers around the queen bee, checking it *out*!

Someday, his son might drive this wonderful dinosaur. Or his daughter.

The highway flowed under the GTO's oversized tires. He and Kate Blanchard were driving to Juanita's ranch to prep Steven McCoy. The formal arraignment was two days away.

He had brought Kate with him to hand-hold Juanita McCoy. The old woman had been a rock, but she needed to be stroked. She had written a check to the court for $50,000 to post Steven's bail, and had signed off a portion of her property as collateral for the rest of the $500,000. And unless Steven's bail was revoked, she would be responsible for him from now until the trial.

Kate leaned back in the low passenger bucket seat, watching the trees whiz by. Off in the distance, halfway up a low hill, she saw a herd of cows grazing on the sparse brown grass. They moved slowly in the oppressive heat. She was glad for the old car's hefty air-conditioning—the rush of cold air up her bare legs felt good. Her legs were too pale; she had hardly any sun this year, too much work. This weekend she'd hit the beach. Maybe Sophia would come with her. They were spending more time together. She hoped that would last.

She ran a hand over the tightly woven seat fabric. She had never ridden in this car. "I don't see you as the NASCAR type," she said to Luke. "More like a Porsche driver, or a hot Beemer."

"They're fine machines," he agreed. "But everybody drives them. Hope Ranch housewives, Montecito au pairs." He patted the leather-wrapped steering wheel. "I can work on this myself. You can't do that with modern cars, all the computers and space-age gunk they have." He smiled, a slight upturn of the lips. "This brings back memories of the cars the cool guys in my neighborhood drove when I was a kid. Which I could never afford."

"Where'd you grow up, east L.A.?" Kate asked jokingly.

"The east San Fernando Valley. Same difference."

"Seriously?"

"Uh huh. It wasn't all Chicano then, there were still pockets of blue-collar whites in Tijunga and Sunland." He swerved around a dead possum that lay smeared across the center of the road, the heavy car nosing down on its front-end shocks before it straightened up again. "My old man bailed when I was pretty young, so we had to scuffle. My mother was a working woman. That little bungalow off Vineland Avenue was the best she could do for my sisters and me, and let me tell you, we were damn grateful for it."

"But you went to UCSB. Stanford Law School."

"On scholarship." He grinned at her. "What, you thought I was born a child of the patrician class? I had to work damn hard to achieve my effortless savoir faire."

Our backgrounds aren't that dissimilar, Kate thought with surprise, as she looked out the window at the low rolling hills festooned with burnt-out mustard grass and scrawny live oaks that jutted out of the ground at weird angles. She had always liked and admired Luke, but now, learning stuff about his past she'd never known, she liked him even more. Too bad he was married; plus she really liked his wife.

Trash that thought right now, she warned herself. Fantasizing about married men can lead to appalling consequences, like getting involved with them. There were still a few good men out there who weren't attached. She had been with one, not too long ago. That she wasn't with him now was on her, not him. When it came to relationships it was still more comfortable for her to live in the dreamworld than the real one. Someday she'd get past that. She hoped.

Since Kate couldn't be in the house when Luke and Steven talked about the case, because she wasn't covered by the attorney-client privilege, she and Juanita took a walk around the property. Juanita wore an old straw cowboy hat against the glare of the afternoon sun. Kate had on a jauntily decorated visor from last year's Summer Solstice parade. It was her favorite parade of the year, the only one that didn't take itself too seriously.

"How are you doing?" she asked Juanita. The old woman seemed to be in good spirits, considering all the dirt that had been thrown on her.

"Better than I expected," Juanita replied candidly. "Steven has been very helpful and cooperative. Although I know he's going through hell. Who wouldn't be?"

Kate nodded silently. Who wouldn't be, indeed?

"Is there a chance he'll have to go back into the jail, once he is formally arraigned?" Juanita asked. "The D.A. seems hell-bent on making that happen."

"You should ask Luke about that," Kate answered cautiously.

"If it happens, Steven will survive," Juanita said, surprisingly blunt. "He's made of strong material. Although it would be crummy. Spiteful. My husband was a lawyer. I'm sure you know that,

everyone knew Henry, or knew of him, although he didn't practice the brand of law you get involved with." She plucked a piece
of honeysuckle off a low vine and chewed on it. "He was establishment through and through—we were members of the Valley
Club, you don't get more establishment than that—but he always
had a deep suspicion of the coercive power of the state. He wasn't
a right-winger, but he was sort of a Barry Goldwater libertarian
when it came to the government having too much power."

She spat out the honeysuckle. "Is your daughter coming here
again?" she asked, changing the topic. "She could be a good rider
with practice."

Kate hesitated before answering. Sophia was excited about
learning to ride. But the situation had changed. A boy was living
here who was going on trial for the murder of a girl who had been
Sophia's age. Steven was Luke's, and by extension, her client, but
that didn't mean she was comfortable with her daughter being
around him.

"I don't know," she answered evasively. "She's been pretty
busy. I'm sure she'll call you."

Juanita smiled. "I hope she will." She gave Kate a reassuring
pat on the arm. "She would be in safe hands with me."

Luke and Steven sat across from each other at Juanita's kitchen
table. "You look like you've gotten a lot of sun since you've been
here," Luke observed.

Steven grinned. "My grandmother has me working in her
garden. With this wind, the weeds are humongous. My back's
killing me, but it's worth it. The vegetables are great. And she
cooks a mean tri-tip. This is the best I've ever eaten in my life. A
shitload better than that crap they feed you in jail." His face
darkened. "Am I going to have to go back in there? Grandma and
I have been talking about it."

"It will depend on whether the D.A. has anything else up his
sleeve, besides the straight murder charge," Luke answered.

"Like what?"

There was no point in pussyfooting around. "If they add rape to the murder, there's a strong chance your bail will be revoked, because it would make this a potential capital case. Do you understand what that means?"

"I could be electrocuted?" Steven asked, his voice suddenly shaking.

"It's lethal injection now, but yes, if you were found guilty of murder and rape, it could happen."

Steven stared at Luke in shock. "I never saw this girl. I didn't kill her, and I sure as hell didn't rape her." He thought for a moment. "How could they prove that, anyway?"

Luke explained to Steven that if he and Maria had intercourse, even if it was consensual, his DNA would be present in her body, unless he used a condom.

"I know that," Steven said. "I'm pre-med," he reminded Luke. "Or was," he added morosely.

"But we still can't claim you and she had consensual sex, with or without a condom, because our argument is that you never saw her. So I'm going to put it to you one more time, Steven. You never met Maria Estrada. You never laid eyes on her."

"No," Steven answered. "Never."

"You never had sex with her."

"No."

"And you didn't kill her."

"Absolutely not."

Luke sat back. "Okay, then. We're pleading innocent, all the way."

"I *am* innocent," Steven replied hotly. "Listen. Can they force me to take a DNA test? Jack off into a bottle or something?"

"They'd take a sample of your blood," Luke answered, "which they can and will do. Very shortly after your arraignment."

"In a couple of days."

"Yes."

Steven let that information percolate for a moment. "What if they *don't* find my DNA in her?" he asked. "They won't have a case, right? They'll have to let me go."

Luke shook his head. "You didn't have to rape her to have killed her. Your fingerprints are on the murder weapon, Steven. So were hers. You both handled that gun. That's clear-cut."

"But without that DNA, they can't go for the death penalty," Steven argued doggedly. "And if it wasn't there that would be good for me, wouldn't it? Help my chances? Cast doubt on the rest of their case?"

"It could," Luke answered guardedly.

"Then I want to take a DNA test. Can we ask for it first, instead of waiting for them to make me?"

Luke was rocked. This would be like diving into a quarry without knowing how deep the water was. A positive DNA test might not be legal proof of murder, but for real-world purposes, it would seal a guilty verdict.

"Think hard, man. You really want to do this?" he asked Steven. "And for God's sake, please be absolutely truthful. You did not have sex with this girl."

"I never saw her. I never was with her. So there was no way I could have had sex with her."

Now that the preliminary skirmishes were over, a permanent judge, Fred Martindale, had been assigned to the case. Steven was scheduled to appear in his courtroom tomorrow to face the formal charges. Then the show would really begin.

Luke was waiting outside Judge Martindale's chambers when Elise Hobson, who had been alerted to his request for a pre-arraignment meeting only an hour earlier, came storming in. She was alone.

"What's going on, Luke?" she asked her former lover and boss. She was clearly pissed off. There was no love in her attitude toward Luke now. "What game are you playing today?"

"Where's El Jefe?" he countered, sparring with her. He loved to get under Elise's skin. It was so easy, like dangling a piece of yarn just out of the reach of a kitten. She should learn to play it cool. But that would never happen. She wasn't wired that way. She only had one speed.

"Santa Maria," she answered. "He's tied up in north county all day. He isn't happy about your calling this meeting on short notice, Luke," she fumed. "He wants to be in on everything."

Luke knew that Alex Gordon was a control freak who hated surprises. "What's the matter?" he needled Elise, "you can't make any decisions on your own?"

Elise was close to blowing—he could read the signs. "Don't be an asshole," she spat back. "I have as much authority as I need. So let's be adults about this. Why are we here? Is this another one of your half-assed forays into the unknown?"

Before Luke could come back with a pithy remark that would squash her like a bug, the door to the judge's office opened. His secretary, a cheerful matron who had known Luke for almost two decades, came out. "It's nice to see you again, Luke," she said cheerfully. With less brio: "Hello, Ms. Hobson. The judge will see you now."

"Nice to see you, too, Eunice, as always," Luke replied. He motioned with a cavalier sweep of his arm. "Ladies first," he said, winking at Elise. "And as to your question: in a minute, you're going to know why."

Ruddy-faced, white-haired Fred Martindale was elegant in his robes. But his court was dark today, so at the moment he was in shirtsleeves. He had been eating lunch—the remains of a chicken salad sandwich were on his desk. He looked at the document in his hand.

"Have you seen this?" he asked Elise.

"She hasn't, your honor," Luke answered quickly, before his counterpart could react. "I just finished it an hour ago. I wanted to make sure you got it immediately, since you have to rule on it quickly." He took a copy of the document out of his briefcase and handed it to Elise. She read the top sheet.

"Motion for DNA analysis? What the hell is this?"

Ignoring her, Luke turned to Martindale. "The arraignment is tomorrow. My client is going to be indicted for first-degree murder. At the bail hearing, the prosecution said they might bring additional charges that could elevate this to a possible death-penalty case." He brandished the motion in his hand. "There's nothing to justify that except adding rape to the charge. And the only way they can make that stick is if the coroner can extract sperm from the victim's body and match it to my client's DNA."

"Wait a minute," Elise interjected angrily. "We haven't brought rape into the picture. This is a murder case, your honor. I don't know what the hell Luke's driving at."

"Bail, your honor," Luke answered. "The prosecution does not want my client out on bail. They fought it at the bail hearing, and they've promised to bring the issue up again. If they can attach a rape charge to the murder, they can appeal for his bail to be revoked under the so-called 'threat to the community' clause." He brandished his copy of the motion in Elise's face. "My client didn't kill Maria Estrada. He never laid eyes on her. Which means he couldn't have raped her. He wants to be tested so we can take that charge off the table."

The motion was only a few pages long. Martindale flipped through it quickly. "Did the coroner get any sperm from the victim?" he asked Elise.

"Yes, your honor," she answered.

Hands laced behind his head, Martindale rocked back in his chair. "Were you going to bring it in?" he asked.

Elise was grim-faced. "We want the option," she admitted.

"Then better sooner than later." Martindale got to his feet. "Your motion is accepted," he told Luke.

"Thank you, your honor. We would like to have it done as soon as possible. And we'd like the results before the arraignment."

"So would I," Martindale said. "Find out from the coroner how long it will take to match McCoy's blood to their samples," he instructed Elise. "If it's only a few days, we'll postpone the arraignment." He turned to Luke. "You know the old saying, pal: be careful what you wish for."

"I hear you, judge."

Did he ever. Glancing at Elise, who was making notes on his motion, he thought to himself, she's in the catbird seat. If, incredibly, Steven was lying about this, the prosecution could phone it in. And if there was no DNA match, Steven was still going on trial for murder, and she and Alex still had a great case.

18

REBECK AND WATSON picked Steven up the following morning and drove him to the lab at Cottage Hospital in Santa Barbara to have his blood drawn. Although it was hot out, Rebeck wore a pantsuit. She didn't want Steven looking at her bare legs. When he was just a naughty boy flirting with her, it was acceptable to feel an illicit thrill from his attention. But that was before his arrest. He was a murderer now. She didn't have to wait for the trial and verdict, she was sure of it. One of her cardinal rules was that you don't play games with criminals. It does occur—cops are human—but the fallout is always terrible. She had heard stories of women officers (it was always women) who had fallen in love with convicts. Their careers, their entire lives had been ruined. She wouldn't allow that to happen to her.

Steven barely glanced at the detectives as they placed him in the backseat of their Crown Victoria. They drove him over the pass and into the city. Watson went into the lab with Steven and stood guard while the blood samples were taken. Then they drove him back to the ranch.

The testing was completed in less than forty-eight hours. Judge Martindale had postponed the arraignment and convened a special hearing. The session was closed, so there was no one present except the necessary court officials, Luke, Alex Gordon, and Elise Hobson.

Dr. Atchison, the county pathologist, was on the stand. Judge Martindale would do the questioning. On both sides of the aisle, the lawyers were at attention. Luke was usually a cool customer, but he was sweating bullets now.

"When you did the autopsy you were able to extract semen from the victim's body, is that right?" Martindale asked Dr. Atchison.

Atchison nodded. "Yes."

"From her vaginal area?"

"Yes," Atchison answered again. He looked up. "Her rectum had also been penetrated, although we didn't get semen from it."

Jesus, Luke thought. That would really inflame a jury.

"Did you compare it to the blood sample taken from the defendant?"

"We tried to."

Luke perked up. Across the aisle, he saw Alex frown.

"*Tried*? Meaning what?" Martindale asked.

"The body was in an advanced state of decomposition," Atchison explained. "It had been outside for several days during the hottest time of the year. So although we were able to get some sperm samples from it . . . excuse me, her . . . they were of poor quality."

"Were you able to get a match?"

Atchison shook his head. "Not one I could testify to."

Luke sagged back in his chair like a puppet whose strings had been cut. Next to him, Steven broke into a smile for the first time that he had been in a courtroom, while at the prosecution table, Alex was shaking his head, either in disagreement or frustration, Luke couldn't tell. Probably both.

Martindale made a note to himself. "The charge of rape is excluded from this trial. Arraignment tomorrow morning, as scheduled." He looked out at Luke and the prosecutors. "Unless there are questions from any of you, we're finished for today."

Alex got up. "No questions, your honor," he said heavily. "We'll be ready tomorrow morning."

As he sat down, Luke rose. "I have a question."

"What is it?" Martindale asked.

"You say you got DNA from sperm samples taken from the victim, but they weren't good enough to match up with my client's, is that right, Dr. Atchison?"

"That's correct."

"Well, let me ask you this. Could you tell if the samples came from more than one person?"

Atchison nodded. "Yes, we could tell that."

"And did they?"

Again, the pathologist nodded. "They did."

"Could you tell how many?"

"Not with absolute sureness," Atchison answered. "But I would make an educated guess that there were at least three separate DNA strands."

Luke made a show of taking that in. Then he asked, "Are you saying that at least three different men had sex with Maria Estrada shortly before she was killed, Dr. Atchison?"

Alex was on his feet. "Objection, your honor," he called out, clearly disturbed by where this was going. "You have already eliminated rape from this trial, your honor. The victim's sexual history is therefore irrelevant."

Martindale thought for a moment. "Overruled," he said. "We're not at trial here. I'll decide later if this information can be used. You can answer the question," he told Atchison.

Atchison nodded. "Again, I wouldn't swear under oath to how many partners she may have had," he said. "But if you want my professional opinion, the answer is that she was sexually active with at least three men in the days leading up to her death."

"Would it be a correct assumption to make that she and her sexual partners didn't practice safe sex?" Luke continued. "You wouldn't get DNA samples from semen if condoms had been used, would you?"

This time it was Elise who sprang up to her feet, but before she could yell out her objection, Atchison was already answering. "That's correct. Proper use of a condom would not leave semen."

Luke looked over at the prosecution table. Alex was writhing in anger. This was information he didn't want to hear. Everyone knew Maria Estrada wasn't Mother Teresa, but for an eighteen-year-old girl to have had multiple sexual partners, particularly without taking precautions against AIDS or other communicable diseases, was terrible news for them. Until this morning, their case had been almost bulletproof. Now there was a crack in the wall. Juries didn't think well of young girls who fucked around and had anal sex to boot, even if they had been murdered and abandoned.

"For the record, we object to this line of questioning," Elise said.

"Objection is sustained this time," Martindale said. "We've heard enough of this for now."

Luke sat back. It didn't matter—he had gotten what he needed.

Atchison detailed more unflattering information about Maria. Traces of Tetrahydrocannabinol (THC), the active ingredient in marijuana, had been detected in her tissue. So she was probably high at the time of her death. He was still testing for other drugs.

Luke had his defense now, certainly an important part of it. He would put the victim on trial. It wasn't a strategy he liked to use, because she wouldn't be able to defend herself. She would be violated yet again; this time it would be her family and her reputation that would take the assault. But given the volume of evidence against Steven McCoy, he didn't feel he had a choice. His job was to pry a *Not Guilty* verdict from twelve jurors. Questions of morality and ethics would have to be left to others.

PART III

19

NOBODY WHO HAD known Maria Estrada was willing to talk
about her (so they told Kate, when she approached them), but
most of them did, anyway. Gossip is so seductive, she thought
wryly. Why else is *People* magazine so popular?

Everyone who did talk about Maria began by itemizing her
many virtues—how sweet she was, what a generous friend,
always there for someone in need, didn't take no crap from no
one, the usual laudatory bullshit that acclaims the deceased in far
rosier terms than were ever used about them when they were
alive. But then tendrils of schadenfreude would start to seep
under the cracks, which reminded her of a quote that defined
what being a detective was all about—No one gossips about
other people's secret virtues. So-called friends of Maria recalled
the times Maria had stolen a boy from a girl who thought she and
Maria were friends. Not because Maria really liked the boy, but
because she could. Then, in a few weeks (sometimes it only took
a couple of days), she would dump the chump, and blithely move
on, leaving two broken kids in her wake. Or she would pit two
boys, friends, against each other, doling out sexual favors to both
(by almost all accounts, Kate discovered, sex for Maria Estrada
was as easy and natural as brushing her teeth), telling each (in
sworn secrecy) that he was the one, she was only seeing the other
so as not to hurt his feelings. Or some equally lame lie. And then
she'd drop them both, and two boys who might have been friends
going all the way back to T-ball no longer even spoke to each

other. Or they got into public fights, even while they knew they'd been used.

Sometimes there was money involved—not straight-out payments, she wasn't a whore, but favors, gifts. Drugs, jewelry (like the earrings that had been bought for her the afternoon she was killed), clothing. If you had dope, she was there to party. Partying was what she did best. She could party longer and harder than anyone her age.

What seemed to drive Maria, more than anything, was the power that came from being the queen bee. But that had been waning. Girls who had been less mature in tenth and eleventh grade had caught up to her. They didn't need to get warm in the fringes of her limelight—they found out they could create their own. She was still a force. But she wasn't going anywhere, and everyone knew it. She was destined to be one of those kids who peaked in high school and never reached those glamorous heights again. The kind of fading star who, ten years later, people would look at and say, "What did we ever see in her?"; or even worse, "What a shame."

Despite the cattiness, though, the consensus amongst the chatterers was that Steven McCoy, the guy the cops had in jail, was the killer. Everyone knew about Maria and the unknown boy who had bought her a pair of earrings at the mall; a boy who matched Steven's description. The earrings had been found with the body, like totems from the tomb of an Egyptian princess. The foregone conclusion was that McCoy had bought her the earrings, and then had killed her.

Exactly why he had killed Maria, no one knew. Sex, drugs, or both. Maria commonly had drugs, or could get them easily, although she wasn't a dealer, or even a mule. But her family had a history with drugs. Or maybe it was something else altogether.

"Everybody always assumes the worst," one particularly blunt girl said to Kate, as they stood outside a video store. "Nobody'll say it, but it's like she got what she deserved, you know what I mean? Like what was she doing with this guy? It's like that girl who accused Kobe Bryant of raping her. What was she doing sneaking into his room if she didn't want to fuck him?"

The school was her next stop. The vice-principal was reluctant to help, until Kate mentioned that Maria's teachers could talk to her informally or do so under the threat of subpoena. That got the administrator's attention.

Maria's teachers didn't mind talking to Kate. But although most of them didn't bother to conceal their antipathy toward their former student, even though she was dead, they couldn't shed any light on who might have killed her, if it wasn't the boy already in custody.

After she was finished with the teachers, Kate talked to more friends of Maria's, kids she hadn't questioned yet. Mostly it was the same old nothing; but just when she was about to give it up and move on, a nugget fell from the pan. A girl remembered seeing Maria at lunchtime on the day she disappeared. She was going into Chico's, a taco stand on Milpas Street that was a block from the school. The girl told Kate that Maria and her girl-gang ate there regularly. Maybe someone there would remember if she was with anyone suspicious, other than Steven McCoy.

"How come you didn't tell anyone about this before?" Kate asked.

The girl shrugged. "No one asked me."

That made sense. The cops had their killer. They didn't need—didn't want—any information that might imply that they were wrong.

Kate gave the girl her card. "If you can think of anything else, give me a call," she requested.

The girl glanced at the card. "Blanchard? Are you Sophia Blanchard's mom?"

Kate had discussed the case a few times with Sophia. Sophia had demonstrated no inclination to pursue the discussion, so they had let it go. She didn't want Sophia pulled into this, but she couldn't escape the question.

"Yes," she answered.

The girl smiled. "She's a nice kid. Tell her hi for me."

"Thanks," Kate said to the girl. She felt a surge of gratitude from the offhanded remark. "I will."

It was the middle of the afternoon, so there were only a few customers at Chico's Mexican Restaurant and Take Out. The counterman, a short, stocky Latino with Mayan features, remembered Maria immediately.

"She was always trying to watch her weight, so she usually ordered a tostada and a Diet Coke. But sometimes she'd fall off the wagon," he said with a gap-toothed smile, "and get an enchilada combo, or tamales. I thought her body was excellent," he added. He wiped a spot of grease off the counter. "These young girls worry too much about their booties. A man doesn't want a stick. You want some meat on those bones. Like J. Lo."

"Do you remember if she was here the day she disappeared?" Kate asked him.

He nodded. "Yeah, she was. I remember hearing about her later and thinking I might have served her last meal to her. She ate light that day," he recalled, "chicken tostada and iced tea." He shook his head in regret. "Pretty damn sad."

"It was," Kate agreed. "Was she with anyone?"

"Not when she came, but later."

A blip on the radar. "What happened later?"

"It was crowded, and Maria was at a table by herself. These two boys had their food and were looking around for a place to sit down. There weren't any empty tables, so they asked if they could sit with her, and they did."

"Did you know them?" Kate asked. "Did Maria?"

He shook his head. "I didn't, and I don't think she did, either. I hadn't seen them here before. I figured they were college kids, they looked older than high school."

"Were they Anglo, Latino, Asian, what?"

He laughed. "They were definitely not *hermanos*. Blond surfer dudes."

"Did you notice anything that went on between the boys and Maria? Did they talk to each other?"

He shook his head. "I wasn't paying close attention. It was busy. We do a big lunch business."

You paid closer attention than you're willing to admit, that she knew. "After they finished eating, did you notice what they did, Maria and these boys? Did they leave together?"

He shook his head. "She left first. Then them."

"How much after?"

"Not long. Maybe a couple minutes."

Kate nodded. "Thanks for your help." She started to leave; then, seemingly as an afterthought, she turned back to him. "If I showed you some pictures, do you think you could recognize them if they were the boys who were with Maria that day?" she asked.

He shrugged uncomfortably. "I don't know."

She was already opening her bag. "It'll only take a minute."

He looked at her with suspicion. "I guess not," he agreed reluctantly.

She took a pair of eight-by-ten photos of Steven and Tyler out of her purse and laid them on the counter. The counterman stared at them. After a moment's hesitation, he tapped his finger on Steven's picture.

"This could be one. Kind of looks like one of them." He turned to the picture of Tyler. "This one, no. He doesn't look like the other one."

"Are you sure?"

The counterman was losing patience with this. "Hey, it was a busy time, and I only saw them for a couple minutes, like I said," he told her. "But this one"—he pointed to Tyler's picture again— "I don't think so."

Kate was flush with excitement. "We know the boys were together earlier in the day. So if one isn't Tyler, the other one couldn't be Steven."

"Because some taco slinger says so?" Luke challenged her. He felt compelled to play devil's advocate—from experience he knew that photo ID's were notoriously undependable. "Find me a jury that'll be swayed by that and I'll treat you to a vacation in Paris. And I guarantee you, if we ever put that guy on the stand, Alex Gordon would blow him away in ten seconds flat."

"I think it's good stuff," Kate argued stubbornly. "You're the one who keeps saying it must have been someone else. Now I give you this on a silver platter and you shit on it. Jesus, what else can I do?"

"Hey, I'm not saying you didn't do good," he mollified her. "But this isn't much."

"It's better than nothing. Isn't there some way you can find out where Steven and Tyler were then? Can't you ask Steven?"

"Yes, and I will," Luke answered. "Except anything he says is automatically tainted. But we can try another angle." He punched his intercom. "Margo, do you have an Arizona phone number for Tyler Woodruff? I think there's one in our files."

"I'll see," came the filtered reply.

They waited a moment while the number was located. Luke jotted it down, picked up the phone, and dialed. A few seconds went by, then he said, "Tyler?" He paused, then gave Kate a thumbs-up. "This is Luke Garrison, Steven McCoy's lawyer." He listened to the other end for a moment. "He's out on bail, at his grandmother's ranch. He's not allowed to talk to you, that's why your call didn't go through." He glanced at Kate. "Listen, Tyler, I have a couple of questions for you. I'm here with my private investigator, Kate Blanchard. I'm going to put you on the speaker, so she can listen in."

He punched up the speaker phone. "Hi, Tyler," Kate said.

"Hi," came back the echoing reply.

"So, Tyler," Luke said, "I want to go back to the morning you and Steven got to Santa Barbara. After you and Steven left the ranch you drove into town and had lunch, right?"

Kate looked at Luke with concern. She didn't recall any mention about the boys eating lunch.

To her surprise, Tyler answered, "Yeah, we did."

"Mexican food?"

Another "Yes."

Now Kate stared at Luke in astonishment. "Are you clairvoyant?" she whispered.

He grinned. "Just lucky," he whispered back. "Mexican food is usually the choice of guys their age. Now for the million-dollar question." He talked into the speaker again. "You went to a joint near Santa Barbara High called . . ." He waited a moment, as if recalling a thought, or checking a note. "Chico's, right?"

"Chico's?" Tyler said. He sounded confused. "We didn't eat at any place called Chico's."

"Where did you eat, then?" Luke asked. "I thought Steven said it was near the high school." Both he and Kate were leaning toward the speaker box, as if close proximity would make Tyler's answers more legitimate.

"At a taco stand called La Super Rica," Tyler answered, his voice hollow in transmittal. "Steven was raving about it on the drive down. It's a tradition for him to have lunch there whenever he's in Santa Barbara."

Luke smiled. One for their side; finally. "So La Super Rica is where you guys ate lunch, not Chico's? You're sure."

"Yes," came the muffled reply.

"About when? Twelve, one o'clock?"

"One sounds about right. After that we went over to the mall, and I met Serena. Anyway, why do you want to know about this Chico's place?"

"Just clearing my records," Luke answered. "That does it. Thanks for the time. We'll be talking again before the trial." He punched off the connection.

Kate sat back. She felt relieved and vindicated. She had passed the devil's advocate test. And Steven was a little bit farther from conviction—she hoped. For the first time, she was beginning to think that Luke was right, that Steven might be innocent.

"Satisfied now?" she asked.

"It's better than nothing," Luke allowed, "but it's no silver bullet."

"It sounds pretty damn convincing to me," she protested. "If they were at La Super Rica when Maria was at Chico's, they couldn't have been the boys who met her there."

"If Woodruff's telling the truth."

"You think he's lying?" she asked in disbelief.

"He could be. If they did meet Maria, he'd have good reason to cover Steven's butt. I'll come at Steven sideways on it, see if he gives the same answer." He leaned back. "But it might not matter anyway."

"How could it not?"

Luke ticked off the reasons on his fingers. "One: Maria Estrada shares her lunch table with two boys. Two: Who aren't Steven and Tyler, if we take your man at Chico's word that Tyler's picture wasn't a match. Three: Maria leaves. The guy at Chico's said they didn't leave together, right? She and those boys left separately."

"Yes."

"Maria goes to the mall. She meets another fellow, who's been identified as looking like Steven. Mr. Big-Spender buys her a pair of earrings to entice her to go somewhere with him, a reasonable person could infer." He tapped a finger on his desk for emphasis. "We've got her and Steven in the mall at about the same time. That's dead certain now. So they could have met there regardless of who she was with at Chico's. Not outside the realm of possibility, is it?"

"I suppose not," Kate answered sullenly.

"Hey, lighten up," he told her. "You did good. It's possible there's another set of boys in play now. Maybe Steven has a doppelganger. We'll definitely start working on that. But . . ." He raised his finger in warning. "Steven's afternoon is still unaccounted for, he had access to the ranch, knew the combination to the lock on the gate, and both their prints are on the murder weapon. Those are the elements we're up against. All the other stuff is noise."

A minute ago Kate had been high. Now she was deflated again. "So now what?"

"We need to keep coming up with these contradictions and alternatives. If there are enough of them, we can establish enough doubt that a jury will be squeamish about convicting Steven." He church-steepled his long fingers. "Or we can find the real killer." With a wry smile, he added, "If he exists."

20

KATE HAD BEEN awake early enough to hear the papers, the *News-Press* and the L.A. *Times*, hit the front door. That was about six, six-thirty. She lay in bed, naked under a sheet, debating whether to get up, make coffee, and leisurely read the papers, or to lie in bed and meditate for a few minutes. She had closed her eyes for a moment to think about which choice to make, and then it was a quarter after eight. She had fallen back asleep.

There was rattling going on in the kitchen. She threw on her robe and padded out in her bare feet. Sophia was at the counter, drinking a cup of coffee and eating a toasted onion bagel spread with almond butter. She was already dressed for the day, in jeans, a Radiohead T-shirt, and running shoes.

"Hey, Mommy. I made coffee."

Kate was still feeling the sleepiness melt from her body. "That's good. So what's on your agenda? You're up early."

Sophia bit into her bagel. "Riding lesson," she said around her chewing.

"Riding lesson?" Kate repeated. Her brain was still fuzzy from sleep.

"With Mrs. McCoy. We talked about it, remember?"

The fog cleared. "At her ranch?"

"Well, yeah. That's where the horses are."

Kate crossed to the cabinet above the drain board, took a mug out, shuffled over to the coffeemaker, and poured herself a cup. She took a carton of milk out of the refrigerator, topped up the mug, and sat down on one of the stools alongside the island.

"You didn't say anything about going out there." She could feel her heart all of a sudden, fluttering inside her chest.

"Sorry," Sophia answered casually. "Thought I did. She and I talked about it on the phone, day before yesterday."

"I . . ." Damn, Kate thought. How am I going to approach this? She took a sip of coffee to stall for a moment. "You know her grandson is living on the ranch?"

Sophia nodded. "You told me. She bailed him out, right?"

"Yes." Now what? "I don't know if he's allowed to see other people. Besides his grandmother and ranch people. And his parents." She sounded ludicrous, a babbling idiot. "And his lawyer."

Sophia looked at her as if she were talking in an unknown language. "Why? He's innocent, right? Isn't that what you believe?"

"Well, what I believe . . ."

"He's innocent until proven guilty. Right?"

Kate took a deep breath. "Right."

"So what's the problem, Mom? I'm not going to be hanging around with him or anything. What are you worried about?"

About my irrational fears as a mother. Which someday, when you're a mother yourself, you'll understand.

"Nothing," she declared, trying to sound totally positive and comfortable with this. "I'm not worried about anything." Juanita McCoy would never let harm befall Sophia. Of that, she was certain. She forced a smile. "Have a great time. Say hello to Mrs. McCoy for me."

Sophia had her lesson in the little riding ring next to the stable. When it was over, she and Juanita went into the house and drank Arnold Palmers. Juanita spiced the drinks with fresh mint from her spice garden. Sophia had been curious to see Steven McCoy in the flesh, but he was nowhere in sight.

"It's a beautiful day," Juanita observed, looking out the window to the foothills. "Not too hot, for a change. Why don't we go on a picnic? Unless you have to get back."

Sophia shook her head. "I don't have to be back any particular time."

Juanita fixed egg-salad sandwiches on whole-grain bread. She wrapped them in Saran Wrap and made up a picnic basket of the sandwiches, homemade potato salad, ripe peaches from one of her peach trees, and a large water bottle. Putting on large straw hats for protection against the sun, they went back outside, mounted their horses, and rode off toward the foothills.

Sophia sat tall in her saddle, as Juanita had taught her. After climbing a gentle plateau, which led them high enough so that they could see Lake Cachuma, the county's main water source, which glistened in the midday sun, they headed into a section that was denser with growth—stubby, crooked trees, mostly native oaks, and thorny native bushes. Juanita led them up a trail that wound through the area. They rode single file, Juanita leading, Sophia close behind. The horses skillfully picked their way over the hard terrain. Then the area cleared, and they were in open country again.

It's so beautiful, Sophia thought, so stark and compelling. The loudest sound was the wind coming down from the hills. Overhead, large birds glided in the thermals, like she'd seen when she went hiking with her mother in the hills above Santa Barbara. There were more of them here—hawks, eagles, buzzards. Wild turkeys, the toms big as goats, their red cocks standing up on their heads like greased-up pompadours, attended to by smaller, less colorful hens, could be seen among the dense clumps of bushes. And there were mule deer, dozens of them in packs, running along the brown burnt-grass mesas. The deer weren't skittish until the horses got close to them; then they bounded away in long, loping strides.

They rode side by side now, walking easily. "Breathe in deeply," Juanita instructed Sophia. "The aromas are as engaging as the sights."

Sophia inhaled through her nostrils. She could smell sage, rosemary, other sharp, almost overpowering odors she didn't recognize. "This is awesome," she said. "Thank you for bringing me."

"Thank you for coming," Juanita replied. With the slightest tinge of sadness, she added, "It's been a long while since I had as nice a companion as you to share these spaces with."

Sophia flushed from the compliment.

They crested a ridge and headed down into a deep meadow, now dry grass from lack of rain. Off in the distance, two men were working on a fence, stringing barbed wire onto posts. Near them, a group of cows were grazing.

"That's my foreman, Keith Morton, and my grandson, Steven," Juanita explained. "Let's ride down and say hello."

They made their way toward where the two men were working. As they approached, the men heard them and looked in their direction. The taller one, who had his shirt off, waved.

Juanita waved back. "That's Steven."

The boy who's been arrested for murder, Sophia thought. She felt her skin tingle.

They rode to the men and stopped when they were a few feet away. The older man, the foreman, was wearing a short-sleeved western-style shirt with snap buttons, jeans, and worn boots. A straw cowboy hat was perched low on his head. His tool belt hung low over his hips. Steven, Juanita's grandson, was in khaki cargo shorts and running shoes. His T-shirt was slung over the fence. He was hatless. His lean, muscular body glistened with sweat.

"How's it going?" Juanita asked.

"Going okay," Keith answered. He tipped his head toward Steven. "He's a capable worker. Easier with two sets of hands."

Steven smiled. He looked from his grandmother to Sophia.

"This is Sophia Blanchard," Juanita said, making introductions. "This is my foreman, Keith Morton, and my grandson, Steven McCoy."

Keith muttered a low "Hello." Steven looked Sophia full in the face and said, "Hey."

"Hello," Sophia answered to both of them. She didn't want to stare at Steven, but it was hard not to. He was hot, and not from being out in the sun. If Brad Pitt had a younger brother, he'd look just like this boy, she thought.

"Sophia's mother is a detective working on your case," Juanita told Steven.

"I know," he answered, still smiling.

Sophia looked off, so that she didn't have to face Steven dead-on. There was an intensity coming off him that was both compelling and scary. She could see how a high school girl would go for this boy in a heartbeat. Or any girl, even a grown woman.

"Do you come out here a lot?" Steven asked her. He had his gaze fixed on her.

"I'm giving Sophia riding lessons," Juanita informed him. "She's a natural," she said pridefully of her student.

"I'll bet you are," he said to Sophia. "You look like it, how you sit your horse."

Sophia could feel herself blushing under her hat. "I'm just starting out," she said quietly.

"It's a good place to learn," he told her. "And a good teacher to learn from. She taught me, back when I could barely climb up onto a saddle."

Juanita smiled at the memory. "You were a good student, too."

Steven grinned back at her, then looked at Sophia again. "I could go riding with you, when you come up here again."

Sophia felt her muscles tightening all up and down her body.

"Sophia's my private riding partner," Juanita said, deflecting Steven's attempt at ingratiating himself. "You have your own stuff to take care of. Which keeps you busy enough."

"You're right," he answered. The smile faded, but he kept his eyes trained on Sophia.

"Don't work too hard," Juanita told her foreman and grandson.

"We're almost done," Keith told her.

"Good," Juanita said. "I'll see you later. Come on, Sophia."

"Nice to meet you," Steven called to Sophia.

Sophia nodded without replying out loud. Juanita turned her horse to ride away. Sophia followed. The old woman and the young girl rode back up into the hills, where they could find a pretty patch of grass, get off their horses, lay out in the shade, and enjoy their lunch.

Later that afternoon, a girl who was about eighteen or nineteen went through the metal detector at the sheriff's compound and walked up to the reception desk.

"Can I help you?" the duty office asked. He was a uniformed sergeant. He was sitting at a desk, copying some field reports into a computer.

"I want to talk to somebody who's working on that murder case," she told him. "Maria Estrada."

He looked her over. She was wearing jeans, a top that showed four inches of chubby belly, and flops—the standard uniform. Light brown hair cut Jennifer Aniston–style, nondescript figure, a slouch in her posture. Why can't teenage girls stand up straight, he thought? He had two at home, he was an expert on the subject. He got up and walked over to her. "What about?" he asked.

"To tell them something. That might be important."

They already had their suspect and a bulletproof case against him, from what he knew. But if this girl had fresh information, they should find out what it was.

"Detectives Rebeck and Watson are the leads," he told her. "Let me see if I can page them. Have a seat."

She sat down on a plastic chair that was against the far wall, crossed one leg over the other, and jiggled the flop on her foot. She didn't seem concerned or nervous about being in the sheriff's office.

The sergeant spoke on the phone for a moment. He hung up and looked at her over the counter. "I contacted Detective Rebeck. She'll be here in a few minutes."

The girl nodded. "Can I use the bathroom?" she asked.

A female sheriff's deputy led her down the hallway to the

ladies' room. When she came out, the deputy brought her back to the desk area. A few minutes later, Cindy Rebeck, wearing a mid-thigh skirt, low heels, and a linen blazer, came in the door. She walked over to the girl and introduced herself. "You want to talk about the Maria Estrada murder?" she asked. "Is there something you know about it?"

"Yes," the girl answered to both questions.

Rebeck led her through the complex to the detective's area. They sat down in her small office. "What do you want to tell me?" Rebeck asked. She had been on her way out to the valley, to a wine tasting in Los Olivos. She hoped this wouldn't take long.

The girl's story only took a few minutes. Rebeck sat up straight, listening intently. When the girl was finished, Rebeck grabbed her cell phone and dialed.

"It's me," she said. "Good thing I caught you in. We just got a nice juicy plum dumped in our laps. Get here as soon as you can, and bring Tyler Woodruff's interview with you." She hung up. "My partner is on his way in," she told the girl. "I'd like him to hear this. And we will want to take a formal statement from you."

A few more minutes passed. Rebeck and the girl sat in Rebeck's office. A couple of detectives stuck their heads in the door to see what was up, but Rebeck shooed them away.

Watson came shuffling in. He was dressed as usual, Joe Friday–style. "Sorry," he apologized perfunctorily. "There was a fender bender on 101." He had Tyler Woodruff's transcript in his hand. "What's up?"

The girl told him what she had told Rebeck: she had seen Maria Estrada and a boy walking out of Paseo Nuevo. His arm was around her shoulder, and they were smiling at each other. They crossed Chapala Street, and got into his car.

"You're positive it was Maria," Rebeck said. She had asked this question already, and gotten an affirmative answer, but she wanted Watson to hear it from the source.

"Yes," the girl said firmly. "It was her."

Watson eyeballed the girl. She didn't seem to have an agenda, but you never know. "Why didn't you come forward with this information earlier?" he asked her.

The girl shrugged. "I wasn't thinking that much about it. Then I saw something on the news the other day about Maria being in the mall that day, and I remembered. So I thought I should tell somebody."

"Okay," Watson said. He took Steven's picture out of his file and laid it on the desk in front of the girl. He was walking a fine line by doing this—it could be construed as improperly influencing the witness—but he decided that with everything else they had, he could get away with it. "Is this the boy she was with?" he asked.

The girl stared at the picture. "It looks like him," she said, after staring at the photo for a few moments. "He had his back to me mostly, and I didn't know him. I knew Maria, that's how come I know it was her. I think it's him, but I'm not sure," she said apologetically.

"That's all right," Rebeck assured her.

Watson put Steven's picture back into the file. "This car they got into. What kind was it?" he asked.

"An SUV."

"What make?" Watson continued, as he thumbed through the interview.

She scrunched up her eyes, thinking. "I'm not sure. I don't know cars that good."

"But you definitely saw them get in."

"Yes."

"Then what?"

"They drove away. Up Chapala."

"Which leads to Carillo, which leads to the freeway," Rebeck noted, her voice rising in excitement. "Which leads to Highway 154."

He nodded. "What about the color?"

"It was dark. Dark gray, or blue," she answered.

Watson scanned the transcript until he found what he was looking for. He read out loud. "Question, me: Whose car were you and Steven using, his or yours? Answer, Woodruff: His. Question: What make? Answer: A Nissan Pathfinder. Question: Color? Answer: It's blue. Dark blue, like navy."

He looked up. Rebeck was smiling, a gotcha shit-eating grin. Watson smiled, too, although not as broadly.

The girl looked from one cop to the other. "Is that all right?" she asked. "Does that help you?"

Rebeck put a reassuring hand on the girl's forearm. "Yes," she answered warmly. "It certainly does."

They wrote down the girl's information. After she left, Rebeck let out a whoop. "Is that icing on the cake, or what?"

"If it stands up," Watson said, immediately raining on her parade.

"You think she's lying?" Rebeck asked with incredulity.

"I don't know," he answered evenly. That was one thing about him—he was never too up or too down. A good quality in a cop.

Rebeck hated getting crapped on, but her partner was right—they had to be careful not to be blinded by their own euphoria. "Why would she?"

"Who knows? Publicity, wanting to be part of something important." Watson looked at the notes he'd made of the girl's statement. "It's public info that Maria was in the mall, and finding out what kind of car McCoy drove wouldn't be hard to do." He tapped his fingers on the notes. "Her reason for not coming to us with this until now doesn't feel completely legit, either."

Rebeck recoiled visibly. "Are you saying she might be a setup?"

"It isn't likely," Watson answered carefully, "but it could be."

"Who would do that?"

"Whoever wants to nail McCoy's coffin shut." He paused. "Or deflect attention from anyone else."

She stared at him, hard. "We have our killer."

"I think so, too," he agreed. "But we'd better not blind ourselves to other possibilities. We sure as shit don't want this to
blow up in our faces. "

Luke spread the pile of burning coals across the grate of his barbeque. The mesquite had burned down to a fine whiteness. He
was cooking tri-tips. They would take about an hour. Riva had
recently gotten him a gas barbeque at Home Depot that had every
bell and whistle under the sun, but he preferred grilling over
charcoal when he had the time, particularly when he was cooking for a lot of people, chuck-wagon style. The taste of food
cooked over real charcoal was always better than gas. Gas was
fine during the week, when he was late getting home from the
office and wanted to fast-cook steaks, chicken breasts, or halibut,
but today he was taking life slow and mellow.

It was Saturday, late afternoon. From their house's vantage
point on the Riviera, the city below them lay bathed in warm,
long-shadow sunlight. This was the last full weekend until the
end of daylight saving time, which marked the official closure of
outdoor-cooking season.

A couple dozen people (and their kids) had been invited over;
they had been drifting in for the past half hour. Everyone was
clustering on the spacious deck, eating guacamole and boiled-in-
beer shrimp, drinking beer and wine (lemonade for the kids),
waiting until it was time to dig into the roast, potato salad,
coleslaw, and rice. It was a motley bunch—a few old lawyer buddies and their wives/husbands, a lesbian couple he had known
since his prosecution days (one of them was a lawyer he partnered
up with occasionally), and a bunch of newer friends, parents of
kids who went to school with their kids. That's what their social
life revolved around now—their children. Everyone Luke knew
who had small kids was in the same boat, which suited him fine.
He'd never been happier.

Kate Blanchard drifted over to the grill. One hand was
wrapped around the neck of a cold Sierra Nevada, the other

held a paper plate loaded up with chips and dip.

"Good-looking tips," she commented of the slabs of beef on the grill. She chugged down some beer. "If you get tired of lawyering you could become a caterer."

Luke smiled at her. "Exchange one unhappy set of clients for another? No, thanks."

"Need any help?" she volunteered.

"Naw, I'm okay. The hard part's all done now." He looked past her. "Did you bring a date?"

She shook her head. "I'm single tonight. Unless my daughter shows up later."

Luke pushed the tri-tips around on the grill to keep them from sticking to the hot metal. "Where is she?"

"Taking a riding lesson," Kate answered. "At Juanita McCoy's ranch. Juanita's teaching her how to be an authentic Santa Barbara cowgirl."

Luke's eyebrows raised. "She's out there on the ranch? Where Steven McCoy's staying?"

Kate nodded. "Uh huh."

"You're cool with that?"

"Not completely. But I don't like to tell her how to run her life. She's a pretty independent girl. And she has her head screwed on right most of the time, knock wood."

Luke frowned. "Even so, I don't think that's a good idea," he said.

"Are you worried about her?" Kate asked. He had pushed her alarm button, the one she had fought earlier to suppress.

"No," he answered. "I'm thinking more about Steven, about him being around a girl who's the same age as the one he's accused of killing. The press or the D.A. gets hold of that, it could make our lives messier." He started flipping the hunks of meat over. "Which we don't need, we're messed up enough with this case already." He took a hit off his beer. "Why don't you go hang with Riva?" he suggested. "She was saying the other day how she'd like to see you more often."

"Me, too," Kate said. She knocked her beer bottle against his. "Cook 'em good, partner."

She walked over to Riva, who was sitting at a wrought-iron table with her two-year-old daughter perched on her knee. Riva smiled as Kate sat down next to her.

"How are you?" Riva asked warmly. "Long time no see."

"It's been hectic." Kate dipped some guacamole onto a chip and offered it up to little Claire. "Is it okay?" she asked.

"Sure."

The girl had her mother's dark, exotic looks. She opened her mouth like a sightless baby bird, and Kate slipped the chip in. God, how long had it been since one of hers was this tiny, she thought? The days go slow, but the years fly by.

Riva leaned back in her chair, catching the dying rays on her face. "It's such a nice day," she said dreamily. "I'm glad you could come."

"Me, too."

"No man tonight?" Riva asked.

"No man," Kate answered.

For a long time, not having a man in her life felt good, liberating. She had made some bad choices in that area, and she needed space to regroup and rejuvenate. But that was getting old. She wasn't looking for love, or even a hot romance, but it would be nice to get laid. She couldn't remember the last time she had gone this long without sex.

She looked over at Riva, whose little girl was cuddling up against her. She has it made, Kate thought with a pang of jealousy. Luke was one of the good guys, a true prize. Once in a while, when she lay in bed at night bringing herself off with her fingers, she conjured him up. It was always satisfying.

But that was all that would happen with Luke—a solitary, nighttime fantasy. She'd had affairs with married men and had not regretted them, nor had she felt any guilt, either for herself or for their wives. She was certain that human beings were not naturally monogamous. They stayed faithful to their mates because of social pressures and fear of discovery. And occasionally, as seemed to be the case with Luke and Riva, because of love and knowing that nothing out there was any better, or even as good.

She didn't sleep with married men anymore, though. Not because of them, but because of her. She had decided that if she had sex with a man she wanted the possibility of something more—a relationship. Not that one might happen, but that it could, that there was the chance. Unfortunately, she hadn't met any single men who turned her on. There weren't that many around who qualified, and she didn't have the time to pursue them, should one arise. Maybe there was a surprise around the next corner—that would be nice—but she had reconciled herself to being alone and celibate until next year, when Sophia was at college.

That was another thing. She didn't want Sophia to wake up and find a strange man coming out of her mother's bedroom. There had been instances of that in the past. It had always felt dirty.

"I wish I knew someone to fix you up with," Riva said, breaking into her imaginings. "But I don't know any decent men around here except the fathers of Buck and Claire's playmates, and they're all attached. None of them are your type, anyway."

"Thanks, but I'm not in the market right now anyway," Kate told her. "I don't have time for a hot new romance."

"But if one were to drop into your lap," Riva teased her.

"I'd try not to fumble it."

She drank the rest of her beer. It was warm. She got up and helped herself to another one from the Igloo. If she wound up drinking too much she would take a cab home and get her car in the morning. Even without a partner, she was going to have fun tonight.

Sophia showed up as Luke was slicing the tri-tip. Her face and arms were bronzed from being out in the sun. "Hey," she said, giving her mother a peck on the cheek as she got in line to fill a plate. "Smells good."

"You got here in the nick of time," Kate told her. "Have you been at the ranch all day? You're three shades darker. You remembered to put plenty of lotion on, didn't you?"

Sophia nodded. "It was glorious out there, Mom. Just like in the western movies, but a million times better. And yes, I was slathered in SPF 30, don't worry. Juanita made sure of that. She's been putting sunscreen on for fifty years, even before they found out the sun was bad for you. It's why she hardly has any wrinkles, even though she's old."

They carried their food to one of the tables, sitting down next to Riva, who was cutting up a piece of meat for Claire. "She's a smart cookie," Kate agreed. "So how did the lesson go?"

"Super," Sophia beamed. "Juanita says I'm a natural."

"So you've told me. Both of you."

"I'm going out again next weekend. I love it out there."

Luke plunked down next to Riva. He had made up plates of food for both of them. "Where's the Buckmeister?" he asked.

"With his buddies," she said, pointing with her fork to a table across from them, where half a dozen boys, aged six to ten, were chowing down. "Fraternity row."

"Ah so," he said, smiling. God, how fast they grow up, he thought. He looked at Sophia. It couldn't have been too many years ago that she was his son's age. Now she was a woman. "Glad you could make it," he told her. "Your mom says you've been out at the McCoy ranch, taking horseback-riding lessons."

"Yes, I have," she answered.

"I'll bet Mrs. McCoy's a good teacher." He cut into his tri-tip.

"She's really good. I've learned so much in such a short time."

Luke asked the question Kate had wanted to ask but had been afraid to. "Did you see Steven McCoy out there?"

Sophia nodded. "He was out in one of the pastures, helping Juanita's foreman fix a fence. We talked to them."

"You talked to him?" Kate blurted out.

Sophia looked at her with puzzlement. "Yeah, Mom. It would've been rude not to, wouldn't it?"

"So you and Juanita McCoy rode right up to them and had a conversation?" Luke asked, keeping his tone light, the question almost a throwaway.

"Yes." Sophia took a bite of tri-tip. "This is delicious, Mr. Garrison."

"Thanks. And it's Luke, to you. For how long?"

"Did we talk? I don't know. A couple of minutes, I guess." Sophia looked at her mother. "Is there something wrong?"

Kate thought for a moment. "It's not about right or wrong, Sophia," she said carefully. This was a potential minefield. "It's about appearances."

"Because he's been accused of murder?"

Luke answered for Kate. "Yes."

"But he didn't do it." Sophia looked from Luke to her mother. "Isn't that right? So why shouldn't I be able to talk to him?"

Kate had no answer. She turned to Luke.

Luke skirted Sophia's question. "It would be better if you didn't have any contact at all with Steven McCoy, for his own good. He needs to not only be completely clean, he needs to *appear* that he is. I'm not going to go into his bail conditions with you, but they're tight. If the police went out there, which they can and will do without notice, and saw him with you or any girl, even if there were other people around, it would look bad for him."

Sophia stared at him. "That's stupid."

"It is," Luke agreed. "But that's how it is."

Sophia pushed away from the table. "I'm not going to stop taking riding lessons, Mom," she told Kate stubbornly. "You can't make me."

"I don't want you to stop," Kate said. She felt miserable about this. "I want you to use common sense, though. You can take riding lessons from Juanita without having anything to do with Steven." She took Sophia's hand. "Come on. Eat your food. Let's have a good time. We'll deal with this later."

"So I can keep going?" Sophia asked. She wanted to nail this down.

Luke smiled at her. "Of course you can. Like your mother says—use discretion. You wouldn't want him to get into any more trouble than he already has, would you?"

"No," Sophia answered. She thought back to the feeling that had come upon her like a fast-rising fever when she saw Steven out in the field, his shirt off, his body tight and gleaming with sweat like a young, oiled god. She didn't want to get him into any more trouble. She didn't want to get herself into trouble, either.

"I wouldn't want to," she told Luke and her mother. What she actually didn't want, she left unsaid.

Luke drove out to the ranch Monday morning. He sat at Juanita McCoy's kitchen table with her and Steven.

"I'll make this short, sweet, and clear," he told them. There was no smile in his voice, as there usually was when he talked to Juanita. "You need to stay clear of Sophia Blanchard or any girl, or any woman, who comes out here," he said, staring at Steven. "No exceptions. Is that understood?"

Steven looked back at him with flat eyes. "What about the lady cop who comes out here to check up on me? Her, too?"

"Don't get cute on me," Luke shot back at him. "I'm not in the mood. Anyone other than cops or other officials who have business with you."

Steven didn't break eye contact. "Why am I being treated like a leper?" he complained. "I didn't do anything. Isn't it bad enough that I'm going on trial for a murder I didn't commit, that I'm missing my senior year of college, that I'm probably fucked from ever going to med school, even when I'm acquitted? What about *my* rights?"

Luke was annoyed that Steven had used the word "fuck" around his grandmother. "You're out on bail," he told Steven testily. "That's a major right which you don't seem to appreciate. If it wasn't for your grandmother you'd be sitting in the county jail picking lint out of your belly button, so stop bitching and get your head straight. You do what I tell you, when I tell you, and how I tell you. End of discussion. Are we copacetic about that?"

"Yes," Steven answered frostily. "We're copacetic. Like in a Clint Eastwood movie, right? Your way or the highway." He stood up. "I've got work to do with Keith."

He walked out of the kitchen. The door slammed behind him. Juanita shook her head. "I apologize for Steven's rude behavior, and his potty mouth. I'm sorry about this. He's under a lot of strain."

"I know that," Luke told her, "but he needs an attitude transplant, and he needs it right now. If he comes into the courtroom with that chip on his shoulder, we could have the best case in the world and we'd still lose." He leaned in toward her. "I'm going to be straight with you, Mrs. McCoy. We don't have the best case in the world. You're a smart woman, I'm sure you've figured that out by now. I'm running as fast as I can, but I'm not making a hell of a lot of headway. So he's got to get with the program. Which means he has to stay clear of everyone who comes here. Especially Sophia. I could lose my detective over this, Kate Blanchard was really steamed about it. She's a hundred percent professional, but she's also a mother."

Juanita nodded somberly. "I understand."

"And you have to do your part."

She looked up in surprise. "What else should I do?"

"Your ranch is how big, fifteen thousand acres?"

"Eighteen thousand," she corrected him.

"So in all this eighteen thousand acres, you couldn't find enough space to ride around with Sophia Blanchard without running into Steven?"

Juanita flushed. "I wanted to see how Steven was doing," she told him. Her voice quivered with contrition. "I wasn't thinking. I apologize."

Luke was sure no one talked to Juanita McCoy as bluntly as he had just done, but he needed her to understand how important this was. "Okay," he said, backing off. "No harm, no foul. Sophia really likes you, and she loves learning to ride. I don't want to have to take that away from her."

"I like her, too," Juanita said. "She's special. I don't want to do anything to hurt her, or to hurt Steven's chances, either. I'll keep them separated from each other any time she's out here. They won't even see each other," she promised.

Sophia and a girl Kate hadn't met were lounging on the couch, watching television, when Kate came in. It was a few minutes after seven. When Kate knew Sophia was going to be home for dinner she tried to finish work by six, but today had been particularly busy. Luke wasn't the only lawyer she worked for, and although none of the other cases she was currently involved with were as dire, they still needed to be taken care of. Two of them were going to court next week—a drug situation with teenagers, and a tough custody battle. Both had needed her immediate attention.

The girls looked up as Kate closed the door and started leafing through the mail. "Hey, Mom," Sophia called.

"Hi." A few bills, mostly throwaways. Nothing that needed to be read immediately. She came into the living room. "What're you up to?" She looked at the set. VH1 was on, an Avril Lavigne video. She plopped down into the easy chair that was catty-corner to the couch.

"Nothing," Sophia answered. "We're on break from play rehearsal, so we came here. We're heating up a pizza in the oven. It'll be ready in a few minutes. There's plenty, if you want some."

"Maybe," Kate said. She needed to cut down on the carbs, but pizza sounded good.

"Mom, this is Tina," Sophia said. "Tina, this is my mom."

The other girl stood up. "It is nice to meet you, Mrs. Blanchard," she said formally in a high, soft, Spanish-accented voice.

"Thank you," Kate replied. She looked the girl over. Pretty, with delicate features. Less robust than her own child. "You're in the play, too?"

"Tina's on the tech squad," Sophia explained. "She's too shy to make a fool of herself in front of six hundred people, like me. Or too smart."

The girl blushed.

"I'm sure it's the latter," Kate said. "It's nice to meet you, Tina."

"This is Tina's first year at school, same as me," Sophia said. "We're making our own club up. We're going to call it the Outcasts. Or maybe the Under the Radars. The Invisibles is a contender, too."

It hurt to hear comments like that from Sophia, even when spoken in jest, because she knew the joking was for self-preservation. Sophia was doing better socially, but coming to a new school for your senior year could never be a happy situation. Knowing another girl who was in the same boat had to be of some comfort.

"Where did you go before?" she asked the girl.

"Locke," Tina answered. "It's in Los Angeles."

Kate knew L.A. well enough to know that Locke High School was in south-central, in a very tough area. That part of the city had been totally black for decades, but more recently it had become increasingly Latino. It was a hotbed of gang activity, a tough place to survive in. This girl is stronger than she looks, she thought.

"Do you like it here in Santa Barbara?" she asked.

The girl nodded. "Too many guns in Los Angeles. Too much killing."

Amen to that, Kate said silently to herself.

The timer went off in the kitchen. "Calorie time," Sophia called out, getting up from the couch. "You gonna join us, Mom?"

"I'm not hungry yet. Maybe I'll have a slice later," Kate said. They ate at the kitchen table. The girls washed their pizza down with Cokes. Kate joined them with a glass of chardonnay. When they were finished, the girls cleaned their plates and loaded them in the dishwasher.

Sophia grabbed her purse and keys. "We're gonna be really late tonight, Mom, we've got full dress rehearsal in two weeks and we're pathetically behind. So don't wait up. I don't want to come home and find you asleep in front of the TV again, okay?"

"Yes, ma'am," Kate answered.

"I'm serious. I don't want to feel guilty that I've got to get home so my mommy won't get worried."

"All right already," Kate surrendered. "It was nice to meet you, Tina. I'll see you again, I'm sure," she told Sophia's new friend.

Tina glanced at Sophia. "It was nice to meet you, too, Mrs. Blanchard."

Mrs. Blanchard. Kate didn't like being called that. She had only kept the name "Blanchard" because it was the girls' name. Usually when someone called her Mrs. Blanchard, she would immediately correct them: "It's Kate." Or in the rare formal situation, she'd allow a "Ms." But with this girl she would let it slide. She understood that Tina came from a culture which mandated respect for adults, and frowned on easy informality.

"Don't wait up," Sophia firmly reminded her again.

Maybe Sophia was hooking up with a boy after rehearsal, Kate thought with a sudden epiphany. Not the worst thing that could happen. Her daughter wasn't a flake—any boy she got involved with would be acceptable, and safe.

Kate smiled. "I promise."

21

················

THE FIRE STARTED midday, high up in the tinder-dry Los Padres National Forest. By nightfall it had jumped the initial fire lines and was burning out of control, threatening several small towns in the Santa Ynez Valley, hundreds of homes, and thousands of acres of prime agricultural, recreational, and commercial property.

Every fire department within a hundred-mile radius joined forces to fight the fire. From all over the state, rangers from the forest service were flown and trucked in and were immediately thrown into the battle. Convict work-crews from Santa Barbara, Ventura, and San Luis Obispo counties were pulled from the honor farms and brought to the front lines to cut firebreaks, working alongside the professionals.

Within twenty-four hours after the fire started, over two thousand people were trying to stop it. They were pissing into the wind. Unless the weather changed radically—the wind dying down and shifting, the temperature dropping, some other freakish and unlikely act of nature—the fire was going to burn until it got to where there was nothing it could feed on. Maybe the area around Lake Cachuma, the huge county reservoir, or the Rancho San Marcos golf course, three hundred acres of grass and sand, would slow it down. The worst-case scenario, which had to be seriously considered, was that it wouldn't be stopped until it reached the Pacific Ocean.

Andy Cassidy's fire department F-150 lurched to a stop outside Juanita McCoy's house. Andy was an assistant county fire chief in charge of the Santa Ynez region, the headquarters for the valley's fire department. He was bone-tired; he had been up all night fighting the fire, on the front line of attack. He needed to get back to the station and grab a couple of hours of badly needed sleep before he headed out again. But first he had to try to persuade old Mrs. McCoy to leave her ranch.

She stood outside her front door, staring at him with determination. "I'm not going anywhere," she told him in a firm voice. "Not yet, anyway."

"Mrs. McCoy . . ."

"The fire's at least twenty miles from here."

"And moving damn fast," he said in a frustrated tone of voice. "It could reach the edge of your property by tonight. Earlier, if the winds pick up like they've started doing."

"The edge of the property's a long ways away," she said, her eyes turning to the east, where plumes of dark smoke rose in the distance against the rust-red sky. "There's a good chance it won't reach this far."

He'd known this wasn't going to be easy. He wished this evacuation had been mandatory, instead of voluntary. By the time the county legally insisted that she and the few other holdouts like her had to leave, everyone would be too busy trying to hold the fire back to assist the stragglers in getting out. That's how lives were lost. Mrs. McCoy was an important person in the county, practically an icon. Leaving her to her own devices was stupid and dangerous. But short of hog-tieing her and carrying her off, he didn't know what else he could do.

"And what about the old ranch house?" she asked him. "What's going to be done to protect it?"

"We'll do everything we can," he vowed. He was well aware that the house was an historic landmark. Not as significant as one of the original Missions, like La Purisima, but still very important. "If the fire starts really threatening that section, we'll dig a wide trench to stop it. Bring in the water planes if we have to."

"The 1990 fire jumped the highway," she reminded him,

scoffing at his promise. "Six lanes, like nothing. If this one's that strong it'll jump any measly, last-minute firebreak you can cut. And if you dump five tons of water from a plane on that old house, the force could flatten it." She shook her head. "I'm not ready to leave. Not yet."

There was nothing more he could do. "I'll check in with you later," he said. "If I can. Don't be stupid about this, Mrs. McCoy," he implored her. "No house is worth your life."

He could see by the tightening around her eyes that he had spoken out of line. "Mrs. McCoy," he said, trying to be conciliatory, "get your people to take whatever valuable stuff they can out of that house, but please, don't risk your life over it. What good would that do?"

"I can take care of myself, and my property," she told him firmly. "You'd better get some sleep, Andy," she admonished him. "You're out on your feet."

Kate Blanchard, working at her office, had the radio on to the all-news station. They were broadcasting live updates of the fire every fifteen minutes. It sounded very grim.

She had not talked to Juanita McCoy since this time yesterday, when she'd called to find out how dangerous the situation was, and to fret to Juanita for her and Steven's safety. Juanita had been determinedly upbeat, insisting that the fire was not going to affect them directly. She and Steven were absolutely safe, she had assured Kate, when Kate urged her to evacuate. If the wind changed direction and they were in any peril, of course she would leave. But that wasn't necessary yet.

The phone call hadn't been assuring; in fact, the opposite. Juanita was blinding herself to the dangers, Kate knew, because of her devotion to her land. Somebody ought to go out there and pull her off the place forcefully, she thought with a growing sense of anxiety. Not her, though. That wasn't her job. She had felt stymied and frustrated by her inability to do anything.

Sophia came in and flopped down in the chair next to her

desk. Kate glanced at her watch. It was lunchtime. Sophia had a free period after lunch on Tuesdays and Thursdays, so she had an hour and a half before she had to be back on campus.

"Have you eaten yet?" she asked Sophia. "Do you want to grab something?"

"I guess." Sophia cocked her head toward the radio. "Anything new?"

"No," Kate answered. "Everything's still out of control."

"Have you talked to Mrs. McCoy today?" Sophia asked. She was clearly worried.

Kate shook her head. "Phone lines are down. Only essential calls are being routed through. Cells are down, too."

"I wish we could go up there and help," Sophia lamented.

"I know you do. But there's nothing we could do, and all the roads are closed."

Over the past two weekends, Sophia had taken three riding lessons with Juanita. After the formal lessons, they rode all over the ranch property, for hours and hours. Keeping her promise, Juanita made sure to keep Sophia away from any contact with Steven.

In the afternoons, when they were finished riding, Sophia worked alongside Juanita, in her garden. The summer vegetables were about finished, and there was a ton of picking, canning, and freezing to be done. For a girl who had always lived in a city and had never had any taste of rural life, it was an exhilarating experience. Last weekend she had come home with a huge bag of produce from the garden—tomatoes, squash, corn, two varieties of melons, and enough pole beans to feed them for a month.

"The winter garden goes in in November," she told her mother authoritatively. "Kale, spinach, lettuce. Turnips. It's fun, Mom, you should come out with me."

"That would be nice," Kate had answered. She wouldn't, though. Not because she didn't like to; she enjoyed getting her hands dirty, seeing things grow that you had nurtured. But Sophia was developing a special relationship with Juanita McCoy, and she didn't want to intrude.

"I hope they're okay up there," Sophia said, her voice laden with concern. "She and Steven."

Steven McCoy. That was another dilemma. If Juanita did evacuate, where would he go? According to the bail requirements, he had to reside with her. But if she had no residence, where would that leave him?

Kate wondered if Luke had thought about that. Later on, after Sophia went back to school, she'd remind him to think about it.

"Let's get lunch," she told her daughter. "I'm starving."

Juanita McCoy paced in her kitchen as she listened to the ongoing reports on the police band. It didn't matter where they were trying to stop the fire, or even slow it down—it was relentlessly pushing the fire brigades back. As she looked out her windows she could see, two or three times an hour, the fire planes overhead on their way toward the center of the blaze, dipping low as they approached the heart of it, releasing their loads of retardant, then banking away and heading back to the airport to be reloaded. In their wake the fire would subside for a few moments, then roar back to life and move relentlessly on.

Despite Andy Cassidy's attempt at pacifying her, she knew that the firefighters weren't going to save the old building that had been the cornerstone of the family's property for five generations. Every ounce of their effort would be consumed with trying to keep the fire from burning all the way over the pass, into the city of Santa Barbara.

Juanita, Steven, and Keith Morton stood at the edge of the old ranch-house lawn. Steven, wearing a T-shirt, jeans, rough-out leather cowboy boots, and a battered felt ten-gallon hat that had belonged to his grandfather, was trying to comfort her dog, who was skittish and jumpy. With an animal's sixth sense she knew that danger was approaching.

Juanita had tried to talk Steven into evacuating when the fire department had pressed her again, this morning. He had dug his heels in.

"Where would I go?" he challenged her. "Back to jail? I'll take my chances here. Besides, I'm not going to leave you here by yourself."

She had tried to reason with him. She was an old lady who had lived a full life. If the worst possibility happened, she would move on to a higher world, with no regrets. But he was a young man, on the cusp of beginning his life.

He had refused. She had put herself on the line for him. He had to stand with her now.

She didn't argue. She was scared for him—she was scared for herself and Keith, of course, but they lived here, this was their life. She believed they had no choice, which Steven did. In her heart, though, she was proud he had decided to stay. The blood force had skipped her children, sadly, but it was alive in her grandson.

The large water tank was forty yards from the old house, at the edge of the gravel road. The ranch wells automatically filled it whenever the water level dropped more than ten feet from the top.

To their east, the fire had taken over the sky. Flames could be seen coming over the hills at the north of her property. It was coming like a glacier, as unstoppable and inevitable.

"How much water do we have in the holding tank?" Juanita asked Keith Morton.

"Eight thousand gallons," he told her. "Full to the brim. I topped it off last night."

"The pumps are primed, ready to go?"

"Yes, ma'am." He was calm, cowboy-laconic. "Got plenty of fuel, too. We could run 'em four or five hours if we had to."

"It'll be half an hour or less, one way or the other," she said, a hand sheltering her eyes as she peered at the fire. "We'll save it, or we won't," she told him stoically.

He didn't reply; none was necessary.

"It's just the three of us now," she told him. That was her principal worry—that even if they had enough water, and enough water pressure, two of them fighting this massive inferno might not be enough to hold it off.

Over the past day and a half, Keith and Steven had rounded up the cattle, loading them and the ranch horses into trucks that had been driven to safety in Paso Robles, a hundred miles north. And earlier in the day Juanita had sent Esther, Keith's wife, into Lompoc, which was out of the fire's path. Esther had protested, but Juanita had insisted. There was no reason to put a life in danger that didn't need to be. Before Esther left, they had loaded up her truck with the photo albums, silverware, some of the rare old books, and a few of the special paintings; whatever they could fit in.

Juanita went inside the old house and turned on the battery-powered police radio she'd brought with her from her own place. As she listened, she heard one fire chief tell another, in a dismal tone of voice, that a convict crew was being trucked over to help the forest rangers who were even now on the edge of her property (she could tell from the coordinates he was reciting), trying to cut backfire trenches. Their hangdog inflections told her they weren't making any progress. The fire was marching right at her.

By now, Andy Cassidy and everyone else would have assumed she had left the ranch. He wouldn't come by to check up on her again, nor would anyone else. They had to think she was doing the right thing, which was that she wouldn't put her life on the line for material stuff, regardless of its value.

She still could. When she was gone, all that would be left to signify her time on earth would be a few pounds of ash. Why should a building, or books, old furniture or old paintings, be any different, any more valuable?

There was no logical answer. Only one of continuity, and remembrance.

"We have a few hours before we have to make our decision,"

she told Keith suddenly. "You and Steven wait here for me."

"Where are you going?" he asked her, alarmed.

She sidestepped the question. "I'll be back fast, one way or the other. If it unexpectedly blows up in your face, get out," she ordered him sternly. "And make sure he goes with you," she said, pointing over at Steven. "Don't be heroes," she admonished them. "It's highly overrated."

The inmates on the crew that was trying to set up a firebreak at the crest of the hills that marked the northern boundary of Rancho San Gennaro were tired, sweaty, filthy. They had been working the fire lines for over ten hours without a break, and they were getting mutinous. Although volunteering for this perilous duty was to their benefit—their sentences in the county jail would be shortened—that didn't mean they should be worked like pack animals. The professional firefighters who had been cutting breaks alongside them had been relieved by a fresh crew two hours ago. Where the hell was their relief?

Their supervisor, a fire department lieutenant who was trained in using convict labor, was as angry as his troops. He didn't like being out here in this treacherous, isolated location with a bunch of pissed-off jailbirds. Even though the men weren't violent criminals—they were mostly honor farm detainees serving sentences of less than a year—they were still bad citizens with crappy attitudes and chips on their shoulders. Any slight could tick them off, which was usually the reason they wound up in jail in the first place. Dealing with authority, which was paramount here, was hard for them to handle.

He turned and looked down the hill as the sound of a Honda all-wheel-drive ATV broke through the rumble-noise of the approaching fire. As he and the convict crew stopped working to watch in surprise, the off-road buggy charged up the hill, bouncing off low rocks and scrub brush, and skidding to a stop in front of them.

The rider, who was on the small side, jumped off the bike and approached them. As the rider got closer, he took off his full-visor helmet.

The rider was a woman. An old woman, wearing a silver braid halfway down her back. "Who's in charge here?" she demanded.

"I am," the lieutenant said, stepping forward. He was a local man from the valley, so he recognized her immediately. "What in God's name are you doing up here, Mrs. McCoy?"

"This is my property, Hollis," she answered. She knew all the firemen by face and name. She threw them a big barbeque on the ranch every year, to thank them for the work they did for the community.

"I know, but weren't you evacuated already?" he asked. He couldn't believe this old woman had ridden all the way up here, right to the fire's edge.

"No, and I'm not going to be," she said fiercely. She looked at the weary, dirty men. "What are you doing here?"

"Trying to cut a firebreak, so we can save some of *your* property," he told her, not concealing the annoyance in his voice. "You shouldn't be up here, Mrs. McCoy," he said in irritation. "It's dangerous as hell. You need to go back down. Immediately."

She shook her head. "There's nothing up here worth saving, and that fire looks too strong for you to stop it here anyway. They've got you boys on a fool's errand."

"No shit," one of the inmates within hearing distance muttered under his breath.

"Where are your trucks?" she asked the fireman.

"What?"

"Your trucks," she repeated testily. "You didn't hike all the way up here. How'd you get here?"

He pointed down the hill, where two Army-style all-wheel-drive convoy trucks were obscured in a low arroyo.

"Get your men and their equipment in those trucks and follow me down the hill," she ordered him.

He stood there, slack-jawed.

"Come on!" she said loudly, "there's hardly any time left!"

"I can't do that," he stammered. "We have our assignment here."

"To remind you, *here* is on *my* property," she told him with a steely firmness. "You need to help me on another part of the property. Where you can do some actual good." She stood in front of him with her fists on her skinny hips. "You don't want me complaining to Chief Jackson that you wouldn't help save a California historic landmark when you had the chance, just because some dumb jerk told you to be one place instead of another."

John Jackson was the county fire chief, the deputy's boss. Jackson was well-known for not suffering fools gladly, or at all. And Mrs. McCoy was a big cheese around here. Being on the wrong side of the two of them was not a smart idea.

Seeing him still wavering, she promised, "I'll cover for you if anyone questions it."

That was good enough for him. If technically breaking orders would appease these men up here, and more importantly, mollify her, he would stand behind that. "Grab your gear and load up!" he yelled to the inmates. "We're moving out of here."

Juanita bumped and skidded across the ranch on her ATV, riding it like a half-broken mustang as she sped down the uneven terrain. The inmates sat on the hard truck beds as they lurched after her along the dry broken ground, their backs pressed against the sidewalls for traction, holding on as best they could, cursing a blue streak about the crazy old lady who had bullied their supervisor into allowing them to be recruited for some private purpose of her own as easily as a school principal intimidated a petrified third-grader.

Juanita rode up to the ranch house in a cloud of dust, the trucks following in her wake. "I found us some help!" she yelled at Keith, smiling triumphantly. "Start them bushwhacking as much scrub as they can," she barked at Hollis. "A few of you, help my foreman set up the pumps."

The inmates were whipped, but she reenergized them with a zealot's manic gusto. They could feel the blast-furnace heat of the oncoming fire as they cut a firebreak a hundred yards around the house in all directions, denuding the landscape of every tree, bush, and flowering plant that had grown and flourished there, some for centuries. It's only trees, Juanita thought as she watched the ragged band of workers decimate the foliage. Wood and leaves, old gnarled roots. It's going to burn down anyway, and new growth will emerge from the phoenix. But the house is irreplaceable. The fear of losing it animated her to keep her captive crew working.

They stood in a ragged line between the house and the incoming fire. The pumps had been hooked up to the water tank. Juanita stood next to Hollis, intently watching the inexorable onslaught of the fire.

"When do we start the pumps?" she asked him, bouncing nervously from one foot to the other as she fought to keep her emotions under control.

"As late as possible," he answered calmly, his professional eye trained on the fire. "You've got plenty of water, but it's going to go faster than you realize, with all these pumps pulling at the same time. We don't want to waste the wet-down, because the heat will dry it out fast, once we start hosing the place down."

The plan was basic deterrence: they would wait until the last possible moment, then wet down the house and surroundings. If the ground was wet enough, the fire should divert around them. But that didn't always happen, Hollis had explained. A fire of this intensity could flow right over wet ground, creating its own wind to force it forward, at the same time sucking the ground and the air dry, nullifying their effort and leaving everything in its path scorched, including them.

Hollis would know pretty quickly if that were the case. If that happened, they would have to bail out really fast. He had his trucks lined up on the road that led from the house to the highway, and behind them, the ranch foreman's truck. If he gave the order, they would abandon the fight and hightail it out of here, no hesitation. Mrs. McCoy had agreed to that before he'd allowed his men to start working. He was in charge now; she had to follow his orders. He wasn't going to have her death, or anyone's death, on his hands.

The fire was an eighth of a mile from them. "Start the pumps!" Hollis called out.

All four pumps engaged with a roar of ignition. Three of them would wet the grounds down in a 360-degree circle, making sure every inch of the perimeter was thoroughly doused. The fourth pump had been hoisted to the roof of the house, which would get its own drenching.

Two hundred yards. Closing fast.

"Now!" Hollis yelled.

The pumps unleashed torrents of water in long, powerful arcs. In less than thirty seconds the entire radius for a hundred yards in every direction was soaked, the ground turning to mud, the house dripping water from its eaves. The trucks, too, were wet down, to keep them from exploding if the fire reached them.

"Keep it coming!" Hollis hollered.

The water from the hoses pummeled the ground with the explosive power of a hydroelectric dam. Juanita was rigid with fearful anticipation as she watched the flames coming at them like a huge ocean wave. My God, she thought, this must be what it's like in Hell, for real. She could feel the intense, expanding heat of the fire—not only from the fire itself, but from the potent wind it was creating, that was blowing sheets of flame toward them. The accompanying smoke was intense, black, churning toxic clouds. The firefighters had stripped down and doused their shirts with water from the hoses, pushing them to their faces as masks against the smoke. The wind blew sideways sheets of water back onto them, soaking them to the skin through their clothing.

Juanita held a soaked towel to her face, her eyes peering over the top, watching the fire coming at them. Even though she was wet to her bones her skin felt dry and brittle, like the desiccation from a fever.

It's too strong, she thought miserably, her eyes tearing from the smoke and heat. It's going to overwhelm us. Any second now, Hollis would order them to retreat.

The fire reached the cleared perimeter. For a moment it seemed to hesitate, as if it were a living creature testing unfamiliar and treacherous terrain. The forward flames shot skywards, accompanied by three-hundred-foot-high billows of noxious smoke. The sound from the burning was deafening, a freight train roaring through her ears.

"Keep hosing down the house!" Hollis screamed above the din. *"We're holding it! Son of a bitch, we're holding it!"*

A hundred yards in front of them, the relentless drive of the fire was in momentary suspension. The flames rose higher, as if building energy to leap across the bare, soaked ground and turn whatever was in its path to ash. Then, like the Old Testament Moses parting the Red Sea, it broke.

"Keep it coming! Keep it coming!" Hollis' voice was hoarse from yelling. He spun to Keith, who was standing on the ladder that climbed up the side of the holding tank. "How much left?"

"Almost half the tank!" Keith yelled back in jubilation.

"Keep it coming!" Hollis cried out yet again.

The flames surged around them like a lava river flowing from an erupting volcano. They stood in the eye of the storm as the fire roared by, devouring everything in its path except Juanita McCoy's ancestral home.

22

STEVEN WAS MISSING.

It was a couple of hours before Juanita realized he was gone. After the blaze had swept by them, leaving a small island of live vegetation surrounded by a sea of burnt devastation, everyone had been too numb to think clearly. Then Hollis rounded up his work crew (he counted noses to make sure none of them were unaccounted for), and took off to go fight the fire again.

When it was clear that the fire had moved on, Juanita took her dog and went back to her own house to assay the damage. She instructed Keith to go up into the property and make a preliminary estimate of how big a mess the fire had left behind.

Miraculously, her house and the outlying buildings were still standing. In anticipation of such a catastrophe, she'd had Keith cut a quarter-mile-wide swath around the house, stable, and outbuildings at the beginning of the summer. So although the fire had burned right to the edge of the cut, it had been turned away by lack of fuel to burn.

She poured herself a healthy shot of Patron tequila (she rarely drank, but if ever an occasion called for a stiff one, this was it), and said a prayer of thanksgiving. Mother Nature had looked kindly on her today. She felt truly blessed. The smooth agave felt good going down. It calmed her nerves.

She punched in Keith's cell number. There was a rumbling of static, but the reception was functional enough for them to hear each other. "How is it there?" he asked her.

"Still standing, miraculously," she told him, raising her voice to be heard over the static. "How about where you are? Where are you, anyway?"

"Up in Indian Ridge Canyon. That fire burnt a hell of a lot of your timber down, Mrs. McCoy. Scorched a damn bit of good pasture, too."

"That's all right," she answered. "It'll grow back. Nothing that can't be replaced by time. You didn't see any loose animals out there, did you?"

"None of ours. Although I'm sure some deer were trapped, unless they crossed Highway 38 and got to ground around the lake that the fire didn't hit. We won't know for weeks." He paused. "God was smiling on us today."

"I didn't know you believed in God, Keith."

"I don't. But that don't mean He don't believe in me."

She laughed. "Come on back down. You need to go out to Lompoc to collect your wife. I hope your own house made it."

"Six of one, half a dozen of the other," he answered stoically. It wasn't his property. "Esther got out her precious keepsakes. If we have to, we can put up a double-wide until you can build us a new one."

The static was getting worse. She could barely hear him now. "Drop Steven off here on your way to Lompoc," she requested, raising her voice so she could be heard. "He can't leave the property."

For a moment, there was no sound. She thought the connection had been broken. "Keith?" she asked. "Are you still there?"

He came back on. "I thought Steven was with you."

Her throat constricted. "No, he isn't." A vein started pulsing in her temple. "When was the last time you saw him?"

"I don't remember," he answered, the static almost drowning out his voice. "After the fire passed us . . . I thought."

Juanita shut her eyes, trying to recall the scene. They had all been celebrating when they realized they had turned away the inferno. She was sure Steven was there with them, whooping and hollering it up with all the rest. It had been so chaotic, and at the same time, so draining.

"He must still be back at the old house," she said, trying to force conviction into her voice.

"I'll go back and check," he told her over the bad connection. "I'll meet you there."

Steven wasn't there. There was no sign of him anywhere.

Juanita stood in the middle of the gravel driveway. Around her, in every direction, the effects of the fire were devastatingly manifest. All the old grapevines, the fruit trees, the arbors—gone. In a few places, a charred remain of a tree or bush stuck out of the black ground like a wounded sentry standing watch over a bloody battlefield. The ground was still hot—heat waves shimmied in the now-still air. Here and there, an ember glowed on the ruined earth. Tendrils of smoke drifted up from the burning, and the smell of burnt vegetation was heavy in her nostrils.

Keith pulled up in his truck and got out. "Anything?" he asked.

She shook her head. "No."

"Where do you think . . . ?" He stopped.

"I don't know. I don't know what to do about this," she said.

"He was here with us when the fire passed by," Keith said. "I remember that clearly."

"I do, too," she agreed. She looked around. "So then . . ." She tailed off.

He put voice to what she had been thinking: "Are you going to call the police?"

"I don't know," she replied. "I mean, I don't know if I want to do that yet."

Keith spread an arm. "Well, he ain't here. I guess we should go back to your place and look around there some more."

Juanita's ATV was gone.

"Are you sure you parked it back by the stable?" Keith asked her. Steven's problems with the law were none of his business, but he had to ask. Ordinarily, he didn't probe into Mrs. McCoy's personal affairs, but she had wrangled him into this. And he knew what a toll this situation with her grandson was taking on her.

"Yes, I'm sure," Juanita answered. She was starting to get a headache. "This is all messed up," she moaned. She shook her head to clear the cobwebs. "I need to think about what might have happened to Steven. And what I'm supposed to do about it."

That evening, a little after seven, Luke got the call at home. "Mrs. McCoy!" he exclaimed. "How are you up there? We've all been worried." He glanced over at Riva, who was hovering anxiously near the phone.

There had been no communication with anyone in the valley for the past two days, since the phone lines had gone down. Not being able to find out what was going on up there had everyone freaked out.

Juanita, sitting at her kitchen table, looked out the window at the empty barn and the silent fields. "I'm all right," she said. She was tired and she sounded like it. "We managed to save our property, including the old house."

"That's wonderful!" Luke cried out. He gave Riva a thumbs-up. "The fire didn't come to your property? I thought you were right in the path."

"We were," she said. "But we staved it off."

"You stayed and fought it?" *What in the world?*

"I'll tell you all about it later, when I see you," she said. "That's not why I called."

"Okay," he said slowly. "As long as you're safe, that's all that matters."

He liked this old lady. The more he knew her, the more he cared for, and admired her. She was full of gumption. And she was soulful. Standing up for her grandson, when it was clear that his own parents weren't going to be able to, had been a true act of love and devotion. And courage. Not every seventy-six-year-old, living out in the country on her own, would have been willing to take on such a difficult assignment.

"Yes," she affirmed. "I'm safe."

There was a lull. Luke filled the void. "You had a reason for calling," he reminded her. "What is it?"

Her hand that was holding the phone was shaking. She propped her elbow on the table to steady it. "I can't find Steven."

Oh, fuck, Luke thought. "When was the last time you saw him?"

"This afternoon. About six hours ago."

"Where was he?"

"With me. He was helping me fight the fire. He was right there with me and the firefighters, shoulder to shoulder."

This will be some tale to hear, Luke thought. But that wasn't the issue now. "And then what?"

"I don't know. It was a madhouse out there. We fought off the fire that was coming right for the old ranch house. Right for it!" She took a deep breath to calm herself. "Afterwards, everyone was at their wit's end. It was very emotional, let me tell you."

"And where was Steven in all this?" he asked, nudging her back on track.

"Well, like I said, he was with me," she answered. "And then, he wasn't. I thought he had gone with my foreman back into the property, to start seeing how much damage the fire had caused. Because by then the fire had burned its way through whatever part of the ranch it was going to burn. Do you understand?" she asked. She was talking rapidly, her mouth barely able to keep up with her brain.

"More or less," Luke answered. This was too confusing without knowing where all the pieces of the puzzle were. He would have to get filled in on that. But first, there was this problem.

Riva, standing near him, mouthed "What is it?"

"Trouble," he mouthed back. Into the phone: "So you have no idea of where he might have gotten to."

"Not a clue." Her voice rose in pitch again. "That fire is raging all over," she cried out. "He could be in danger."

Or dead, Luke thought. That was chilling. "It'll be all right," he said. He sounded more optimistic than he felt. "If he does show up, call me immediately, no matter what time it is."

"I will," she promised.

Another thought: "Have the police been checking up on Steven? Do they know he's missing?"

"No," she answered. "They haven't been in touch since the fire started."

That's one good thing, Luke thought. He could finesse this until tomorrow, or maybe longer. Everyone's attention was on the fire; the whereabouts of a kid out on bail, even for murder, was on the back burner. And Steven had been checking in with his handlers every day, so there was no reason for suspicion. Not yet.

"I'll come see you early tomorrow morning," he told her. "Do you have someone up there to be with?"

"I'm all right," she reassured him. "It's my grandson I'm worried about."

Luke picked Kate up at seven the following morning. He had asked her to come with him. She had a calming influence on Juanita McCoy. That might come in handy, because this meeting wasn't going to be pleasant.

They were at the ranch by eight. There was little traffic going in their direction—the stoppages and congestion caused by the fire had eased, now that it had moved away from the immediate area.

Juanita sat them down at her kitchen table, offered them strong coffee and homemade boysenberry strudel, and told them the saga of how she saved her family's ancestral home.

They listened in astonishment as they bit into the strudel, which was delicious. "That's incredible," Luke said. "You're an amazing woman, Juanita."

"Truly amazing," Kate seconded with a mouthful of light,

flaky pastry. Was there anything this woman couldn't do? She felt blessed that Sophia had Juanita as a grandmotherly role model. She hoped that when this was all over, they would be able to maintain their relationship. That would hinge on what happened with Steven, both now and in the future.

"I did what I had to do," Juanita said modestly. "In hindsight, I suppose it was crazy. I wasn't thinking, it was pure reaction."

"Well, congratulations," Luke said. "You're probably the only person in the valley who's going to have a happy ending from any of this."

"If Steven shows up," she said, bringing them back to earth with a thud.

Kate sighed. "No word yet?" she asked.

"Nothing. I'm so worried about him. He could be injured." She hesitated. "He could be dead." She covered her face with her hands, which were shaking.

Luke pushed his coffee and cake to the side. This was not the time for tea and sympathy. "Mrs. McCoy." He took her hands in his. "I don't think he's injured. And I don't think he's dead." He made her look at him. "I think he's gone."

She looked confused. "He's missing, of course I know that."

He shook his head. "Not missing." He glanced at Kate before saying the condemning word again: "Gone."

"You mean on purpose?"

Luke nodded. "If your vehicle was here I'd have a different feeling about this. Who else would have taken it, except Steven?"

"I don't know," Juanita answered. "Nobody, I guess. Do you think he might have run away?" she asked them.

"I don't know what to think," Luke answered. "All I know is, he isn't here, and that ATV is missing. I'm not going to pussyfoot around, Juanita. This is bad news. Have the authorities tried to contact him, since we talked last night?"

"No."

"Well, that's one thing in our favor," he said. "For now. Because pretty soon, they're going to. And if he isn't here to talk to them, he's in it up to his neck."

"What should we do?"

"I don't know," he answered. She had been in denial, common in circumstances like this. The reality is too fraught to face, so you don't, you emotionally bury it. "We can't go to the police about this," he told her, as Kate nodded in agreement. "We have to stay low to the ground for as long as we can. We're going to have to hope he shows up before they try to contact him again."

He stood up. "I'm in a ticklish position here. As an officer of the court, I'm required to obey the law, even if it means going against the interests of my client. By rights, I should let the sheriff's office know Steven isn't where the stipulations of his bail say he has to be. If it gets out that I knew he was gone and that I hadn't reported it, I could be sanctioned. I could even have my license to practice law suspended. Kate could lose her license, too."

"I'm sorry," Juanita told both of them, shaking her head in misery. "I should have paid more attention to where he was."

Luke put a comforting hand on her shoulder. "You have no blame in this. It's on him, all of it. He knew what was required, and he's blown it off."

"If he took off," she said, still holding out hope that Steven's disappearance could be explained in an acceptable manner.

Luke finished his coffee and motioned to Kate to do the same. "We're going back to town. Call me if you hear anything. If the police do call, stall them and then let me know, immediately. Use the fire as an excuse if you have to." He shook his head in frustration. "I didn't tell you that, by the way. I wasn't even here this morning, and I haven't heard from you that Steven's flown the coop. We'll deal with all of that later—if we have to."

Luke was in a sour mood as he pushed the GTO over the pass on the drive back to Santa Barbara.

"I can't believe what an idiot Steven is," he fumed, down-shifting as they careened through a hairpin curve. "What could he be thinking?"

"You're sure he's skipped," Kate said, pushing her feet against the floorboards to keep from sliding out of her seat. She, too, had a pit in her stomach over this.

"What other reason could there be?"

"I don't know," she answered. "There could be a plausible reason," she said, with little conviction.

"What?" he asked impatiently. "Come on, Kate."

"Hey, don't yell at me. I'm just a fly on the wall."

"Sorry. And you're not, you're in this as deeply as any of us." Luke rolled through another turn. "If you have a good explanation, I sure would like to hear it."

She thought about that. "What if he thought they were being evacuated and he went to a shelter voluntarily, assuming Juanita would be there."

"And when he found out she wasn't, he didn't get in touch with her? No."

"Okay. Well, what if he took off with the fire crew and is fighting the fire somewhere else."

He looked at her like she was nuts. "Why would he do that?"

"To pay them back for helping save the old house?"

Luke laughed mirthlessly. "So now he's an altruist? That'll be the day."

She slumped in her bucket seat. "I tried."

"None of it washes. The missing ATV proves he took off."

She knew he was right. "But why would he, knowing it makes him look even more guilty than he already does?"

"Sheer panic. Everything becomes magnified, even survival. Like how they could all have died in that fire. A rational person could claim that Juanita was reckless, and put lives in danger."

"She said she had an escape exit," Kate reminded him. "The fire chief was there."

"Exits get blocked. And you know how she is, she's an immovable force, impossible to stand up to."

Kate smiled. "Tell me about it."

"What I've worried about all along is that even if *he* knows he's innocent, when no one else does, and most everyone thinks the opposite . . ."

"He submitted to the DNA test voluntarily," she reminded him.

"This is true. But the case against him is strong, and he knows it."

They crested the final curve before coming back into the city. "So what can we do?" Kate asked.

"Hope he turns up alive. With a great excuse."

The call from Alex Gordon came after lunch. "We've been trying to reach Steven McCoy up at that ranch, but we're having a hard time getting through."

"Maybe their lines are down," Luke answered. "There is a fire raging in their neighborhood, in case you haven't been watching the news."

"The fire passed by there yesterday, wiseass," Alex said. "And their place was saved, in case you didn't know," he added, throwing Luke's sarcasm back in his face.

"Who told you that?" Luke asked, feigning ignorance of the situation.

"The fire chief. That old lady commandeered an entire squad of firefighters to save her place. They're going to be telling the story in the forest service for decades. She's a feisty one, that Juanita McCoy." His voice turned somber again. "Seriously, Luke, we need to be in contact with Steven McCoy. The detectives running this case are getting antsy. And so am I." Before hanging up, he added, "Nobody wins if I have to go see the judge about this."

Juanita came outside as she heard the detectives' car pull up in front of her house. It was late in the afternoon—the sun was in her face. She shielded her eyes as she stared at Watson and Rebeck.

"Hello," she said pleasantly. She kept her voice neutral. "How are you today?"

Watson knew that Rebeck, impatient, would cut right to the chase, so he jumped in first. "We're okay, thanks," he replied. He looked out into her property. "I hear you survived the fire. Better than most of your neighbors."

"We were lucky," she told them. "Divine providence, perhaps. I don't know about how others have fared, I've been busy here. And the phones were down until a short time ago."

"Is that why Steven hasn't been checking in?" Rebeck interjected.

Juanita frowned. "How could he?"

"Right," Watson said. Her answer was obvious, and it made them look like bullies. This was a nice old lady, and a powerful one. He didn't want to get into a pissing contest with her. "Which is how come we drove up here." He took a step toward the house. "Is he inside?"

Juanita shifted, blocking him. "No," she replied. "He isn't."

Enough with the song and dance, Rebeck decided. "Where is he?" she asked harshly.

"Out there." Juanita made a vague sweeping gesture with her arm.

"Out there where?" Rebeck pressed.

Juanita stared at her for a moment. "I don't know, precisely," she answered. "It's a big property. He's checking for damage. He's been gone since early this morning. Why? Is there a problem?"

"We want to know where he is," Rebeck persisted. "We need to document him being here, in the flesh. See him, or talk to him."

"Umm." Juanita thought for a moment. "I don't know how I can help you this precise moment, because as I said . . ."

"He's out there somewhere, I know." Rebeck finished. She was in full ill-humor now. "Don't you have a way of contacting your people? Walkie-talkies or something?"

"Of course we do," Juanita answered, the tone of her voice

insinuating that the question was an insult. "Unfortunately, they aren't functioning now. We used up all the batteries fighting the fire. My foreman is picking up fresh ones when he goes into Los Olivos tomorrow," she lied easily.

Rebeck shifted her weight from one foot to the other. When was she going to stop wearing heels on assignments like this? As soon as they got back she was going to throw a pair of running shoes in the trunk for such contingencies. Looking good is important, but if your feet hurt, you can't concentrate.

Watson looked at his watch. It was almost six. In less than an hour, it would be dark. "What time will Steven be rolling in?" he asked. "He can't do anything out there after dark, can he?"

"No," Juanita said.

"So pretty soon, huh?" he asked optimistically. He didn't want this to go south. That would fuck things up royally, for everyone.

"Unless he decides to stay out there," Juanita told them.

The detectives looked at each other. Was she shining them on? It felt like it.

"Why would he?" Watson asked.

"So he won't waste hours riding in and out," she explained. "It is a big ranch. Sometimes he stays out overnight." She looked from one detective to the other. "There's nothing wrong with that, is there? He is still physically on the ranch. I thought that's what the bail agreement said. That he was confined to the ranch, unless given permission to leave. But it didn't say where on the ranch, did it?" She made as if to turn away. "Should I go inside and read it over? I'm sure I understood it, but maybe I was mistaken. Do either of you happen to know?" she asked with an air of benign innocence.

"It doesn't say exactly where on your ranch," Watson admitted. That had been a fuckup. They should have confined him to a more specific area, rather than allowing him to roam at will over dozens of square miles, most of it rugged and hard to get to.

He eyeballed the high sign to Rebeck. "There's no use us

hanging around here," he said. "But . . ." He raised a cautionary finger. "We must be in touch with him by tomorrow morning, Mrs. McCoy. Without fail. Or he'll be in a lot more trouble than he already is."

Rebeck, driving away, saw Juanita in her rearview mirror. The old lady was staring at them. As they drove out of sight, she raised her hand in salute.

"She's bullshitting us," Rebeck declared. She was badly pissed off.

"You're not prepared to give her the benefit of the doubt?"

Rebeck brayed laughter. "No fucking way. She knew exactly what to say to be inside the letter of the law. Cunning old bitch."

"So?"

"It's the D.A.'s call. He's going to have to go to the judge. Judge Yberra's going to be shitting wooden nickels. He put his ass on the line for that old lady. He's going to look like a fool if that kid flaked."

Watson nodded in agreement. "It'll be hell to pay, all around." He groaned. "We're all going to look like assholes if this kid's slipped us."

Luke got the word that night, at his house.

"If Steven McCoy doesn't present by nine tomorrow morning, either in person or via a verifiable phone call, he will be officially proclaimed to be a bail-jumper," Alex told him. "And when we catch the little fuck, Luke—which we will, they all turn up in the end—he can turn the lights out. Because the party will be over."

Kate threw clothing and toiletries into an overnight bag. "I'm going out to Mrs. McCoy's ranch," she told Sophia. "You'll be okay by yourself, won't you? It's just for tonight. If you want, you can stay at the Garrisons'."

Sophia was friendly with Luke and Riva. She was their main

babysitter. They paid top dollar, fifteen an hour. Working for them was fun, because she really liked their kids and the money paid for her gasoline and other expenses that her allowance didn't cover.

"Why are you going up there?" she asked Kate. "It's after ten at night, Mom."

"Moral support," Kate answered. "There's a crisis. I don't like her being alone."

"It's Steven, isn't it. Did he run away?"

"I don't know," Kate answered tersely. "We can't find him."

"Maybe he got hurt," Sophia said logically. "Trying to help."

Kate shook her head. "He didn't." She zipped her bag shut. "So which? Here, or the Garrisons?"

"I'm coming with you."

"No you are not," Kate answered immediately. "You have school tomorrow. The ranch isn't a place for you to be now."

Sophia stood her ground. "I can miss a day, I've had perfect attendance this year. Juanita's more my friend than yours," she said stalwartly.

Kate smiled at her. This was a good kid she had raised, almost in spite of herself. "All right. Get your stuff. We have to go, now."

It was after midnight, but no one was sleeping. The three women were hunkered down in Juanita's living room. All the lights were on, as if the brightness might attract Steven, like a candle attracts a moth.

Sophia and Juanita were trying to play Scrabble, but it was a listless attempt. This is like attending a wake, Kate thought, as she watched them plunk their squares down on the board. Which in a fashion, it was. Steven McCoy wasn't officially dead yet, but in her mind she could hear the nails being pounded into his metaphorical coffin. Even though she was depressed about this looming catastrophe, she was glad she had come out here, and she was also happy that Sophia had insisted that she come, too. Leaving Juanita to deal with this misery by herself would have been heartless. And it was a condition of the job. Juanita was paying through the nose for their help. This wasn't a 9–5 gig, it had become 24/7, both professionally and personally.

But she would be here even if she wasn't getting paid. This was about a burgeoning friendship, particularly between an old lady and a young girl. Friends help friends. They were friends now.

The Scrabble game ended. Kate looked at the serpentined board. "Who won?"

"She did," both Juanita and Sophia said simultaneously. They looked at each other, and laughed. "We weren't keeping score," Sophia said. "It doesn't matter who wins or loses." She stretched and yawned, sprawling back on the couch.

"Why don't you go to sleep?" Juanita suggested. "The couch in my office is a foldout. I can make it up for you."

"Why don't you both go to sleep?" Kate told her. "We can do this in shifts. I'm not tired yet, so I can take the first watch."

Juanita shook her head. "I'll sleep when this is over. However it turns out." She stood and stretched her lower back. "I'm going to put a pot of coffee on. Does anyone besides me want some?"

Mother and daughter both said "Aye." Juanita went into the kitchen. Sophia came over and flopped down next to Kate.

"What's going to happen when morning comes?" she asked quietly, so she wouldn't be overheard.

"If Steven hasn't shown up?"

Sophia nodded.

"Luke Garrison will call the District Attorney and report that Steven is missing. Then he'll officially be a fugitive from justice, his bail will be revoked, and he'll be a wanted man." She shuddered. "Then it's a question of waiting, until he's found."

"Dead or alive?"

Kate jerked around to look at Sophia. "That's harsh."

Sophia shook her head as if to say, "Not harsh enough." "I don't feel sorry for him at all," she proclaimed. "I feel bad for Juanita, what he's put her through. She doesn't deserve this."

"No," Kate agreed. "No one does."

"But her especially," Sophia said insistently. "She went out on such a limb for him." She made an angry face. "He's so selfish."

Juanita came back into the living room. "Coffee will be a minute. Does anyone want anything to eat?"

"No, thanks," Kate said. "Sit down, Juanita. You don't have to be the hostess."

Juanita turned and looked out the big front window, into the darkness. "Oh, Steven," she lamented. "Where are you?"

The light was diffused in the shiny window glass. At first it was two small pinpricks in the dark, then it grew as it approached, two shimmering mirages.

Kate sat up with a jerk. Sprawled out on the couches, Sophia and Juanita were sleeping heavily. The lights were off in the living room—a single fixture remained on in the kitchen.

When did we fall asleep, Kate wondered? And who turned the lights off? Was it me? She couldn't remember.

She looked at her watch. 4:20. The depths of night, when in the city even the all-night prowlers, the drunks and the predators and the street low-life were tucked away in their holes. Out here, though, where on a clear night the sky was alive with a million stars, there was an entire nighttime society: owls, coyotes (who never sleep), burrowing vermin, nocturnal hunters and gatherers. Or human predators, looking for an easy, out-of-the-way mark. Like an old lady living alone.

She slipped her shoes on. Her automatic was in her purse. She took it out and flipped the safety off. Then she moved to the side of the window, so she could look out, but not be seen by someone looking in.

The vehicle parked in front of the house. The lights were doused, and the engine stopped running.

Kate looked behind her. Juanita, too, had heard the sound. She looked at Kate. "Who is it?" she asked.

"I don't know," Kate answered quietly. She leaned over and looked outside again.

For a moment, all was still. Then Steven McCoy stepped off of his grandmother's ATV. He walked around to the other side and helped a woman get down. The woman, who looked like she was in her early to mid-thirties, moved very slowly, limb by limb, like a deck chair unfolding. Normally she would have been attractive in a Katharine Hepburn sort of way, but even in the dim light Kate could see that she looked awful now, as if she had been through a brutal ordeal. The woman said something to Steven, who gave her a reassuring hug.

They walked to the back of the ATV. They leaned down and together lifted something out of the back, as if picking up a load of firewood.

"Who is it?" Juanita asked again. She got up and came toward Kate.

"Steven," Kate told her. "And a woman."

"Oh, thank God," Juanita said in thanksgiving. She started for the front door.

Kate put a restraining hand on her arm. "Wait," she said cautiously. She tucked the gun away in her jeans, so it couldn't be seen.

They stared out the window. Steven and the woman were assisting a man, who looked to be a few years older than the woman. His arms were draped over their shoulders. He hung almost limp, like a scarecrow. Kate could see that one of his pant legs had been cut off almost to the crotch, and that a makeshift splint had been secured around the bare leg, from above the knee to the ankle. There was clotted blood on the leg, and on the splint.

Carefully, Steven and the woman carried the invalid toward the kitchen door. Before they could reach it, Juanita rushed over and flung it open.

"Steven!" she cried out. "Thank God."

Steven McCoy looked like death warmed over, but his companions looked even worse. "You need to call 911," he said. His voice was low and hoarse. "His leg is broken, and he's lost a lot of blood."

Gingerly, they helped the man with the broken leg onto a kitchen chair. "We need water," Steven said. "We haven't had any for over a day."

Sophia, rubbing sleep from her eyes, drifted into the kitchen. She looked at the unknown man and woman, then at Steven. "Where were you?" she asked. "You had everyone scared stiff. Especially your grandmother."

Steven tried to smile, but he couldn't pull it off. "It's a long story. I'll tell you after the paramedics come. Right now, I just want a drink of water."

The ambulance was there in less than half an hour. "You're lucky you're alive, man," the lead paramedic told the injured man, who had lapsed into semiconsciousness. "Whoever splinted your leg and stopped the bleeding saved your hide."

"Him," the woman told them, pointing a dirty, shaking finger at Steven. There was a slender gold wedding band on her ring finger. "Our savior." She reached out and grabbed Steven's hand. She held it tightly, like it was a life preserver.

"You know your stuff," the paramedic complimented Steven.

"I did what I could," Steven said wearily. His modesty was real; Kate could hear the lack of ego in his voice. Her attitude toward him was turning 180 degrees, yet again.

The paramedics strapped the injured man to a board and carried him out to their ambulance. Steven and the woman trailed them. The female paramedic jumped into the driver's seat. The other two loaded the injured man into the back.

"Either of you coming?" the lead paramedic asked. "You can ride in back with him."

"Me," the woman said.

"Good idea. You need to see a doctor, too." He looked Steven over. "What about you?"

"I'm all right," Steven said, declining the offer. "I need to stay here."

"Suit yourself. If you feel bad later," the paramedic cautioned, "call up right away. That's why we're here." He stuck out his hand. "If you ever want a job doing this, get in touch. We can always use good people."

"Thanks," Steven answered. "I appreciate that."

The paramedics climbed into the back of the ambulance. The woman hugged Steven. "Thank you," she said softly. "You'll be here?"

"I'm not going anywhere," he told her.

"I'll come see you. Maybe tomorrow. If that's all right."

"Sure." He gently disengaged from her. "You need to go."

She nodded. Then she leaned forward on her toes and kissed him on the mouth.

"I'll see you tomorrow," she promised.

"See you."

She got into the back. One of the paramedics closed the door. They drove off.

Kate, Sophia, and Juanita had been watching from the kitchen doorway. Steven came into the house. "I'm bushed," he said. "And I need a shower."

Sophia was standing next to him. "What happened?" she asked.

"I'll tell you after my shower." He crossed the room to the refrigerator and opened it. "I know I'm not allowed to drink, but is anyone going to bust me if I have a beer?" he asked, staring at Kate.

No one answered; they didn't have to. He took out a Sierra Nevada, twisted the cap off, and swallowed half of it down in one long gulp. Then he walked out, heading for the bathroom.

Juanita collapsed into a chair. "Thank God," she said. "Thank God."

This is going to be some story, Kate thought, with the smallest trace of cynicism. And when that woman comes back to see him, she's going to fuck the marrow out of him, married or not.

Six o'clock. Still dark out, but dawn was coming. Kate dialed Luke's home number. He answered on the first ring.

"Sorry if I woke you, but I had to," she told him unapologetically.

"I was up," he said. "What's going on?"

"Hold onto your hat. Steven McCoy turned up."

"*Whoa!*" His voice boomed into her ear. "How about that! Where are you?"

"At the ranch. I came out last night, so Juanita wouldn't be alone."

"That was kind of you."

"It was necessary."

"Well, good for you, either way. So he came back on his own? When?"

"About an hour and a half ago. And yes, it was voluntary."

"That's a relief," Luke said. "This would have been an absolute disaster."

"I know. It's been a long night here."

"So where was he?" Luke asked impatiently.

Kate could feel his antsiness over the line. There was a certain delicious perversion at hearing it, because he was almost never ruffled. "What did he say?" Luke peppered her.

"Easy, boy. He's taking a shower. When he comes out he's going to tell us everything." She smiled to herself. "He's going to be a hero."

"You're shitting me!" This was getting crazier and crazier. "Why?"

"I won't know until I hear it from him," she said. "But I know enough to feel it could be a real boost for us."

"I'll be there in forty-five minutes," Luke said. "Wait for me, so we can hear it together."

"Okay, but hurry up. I have Sophia with me, and I need to get her back so she can go to school." Before she hung up, she also told him, "If his story is half as interesting as I think it's going to be, you're going to carpet-bomb the papers and TV. This could be quite a coup for us."

Steven, refreshed from his shower and a breakfast of his grandmother's blueberry pancakes and scrambled eggs, got comfortable on one of the living room couches. He finished his coffee, put
the cup down, and told his story:

After we beat back the fire at the old house, I came back here.
Grandma and Keith were still at the old house. I was on this
super-energy high from what we had done, but I was bone-tired,
too, so I thought I'd take a nap. I was about to lie down when I
remembered this couple me and Keith had met a couple of days
before the fire started, up at the northeast section of the ranch.
They were camping in the Los Padres National Forest, where it
butts up against our boundary line. They asked if they could
camp on the property for a few days. There's a meadow up there
that's the perfect campsite.

If it was up to me, I would have let them. They were experi-
enced campers, so I knew they'd be careful about fire and haul-
ing their shit out. But Keith wouldn't, because nobody can be on
the property, it's ranch policy. You let one person do it, then
where do you draw the line? Which I can understand, especially
after what I'm going through now.

So they thanked us and said "Sure, no big deal," but I knew
as soon as me and Keith left they would come over onto the prop-
erty. I would if I was them, it's a real nice spot, and they would
have figured we wouldn't be back for a few days, so why not?

Anyway, now I was back here, and I realized that if they had
camped there, they might have been in the path of the fire. Which
freaked me out, thinking they could be trapped up there. So with-
out thinking, I jumped into grandma's ATV and took off. I fig-
ured they would either have gotten out ahead of the fire—that's
what I was hoping I would find, nothing—or they would need
help getting out. Either way, I assumed I'd be there and back in
four or five hours.

Well, I found them. They hadn't been able to get out because
Al—that's the guy—had fallen the day before and broken his leg.

Their cell phone battery had run down, so they couldn't call for help. Then the fire started, and their exit was cut off. They were able to retreat back into a section of the forest the fire had passed by, which was the only saving grace about their situation.

But they were stuck, because they couldn't hardly move, with his leg as bad as it was. He wanted her to leave him and try to hike out to get help, but she was afraid to leave him by himself, and she didn't know what direction to go in, she was afraid she would wander around and get lost. So when I showed up it was like a gift from God. That's how Willa—that's the woman's name—described it. She told me I was a gift from God. Which made me feel good, but I had to get them out to really qualify.

The first thing I did was tourniquet his leg to slow down the bleeding, and then I splinted it the best I could. That took a couple of hours. He was in awful pain, and I didn't have anything to give him for it. But I managed to patch him up good enough so he could be moved. We got loaded up, and we were about to leave.

And that's when we really got screwed. The wind shifted and blew the fire back into the path I had taken to get there. Which was the only way to drive out. So we were trapped.

It was surreal, like a cosmic joke, except there was nothing funny about it. The fire was blocking our way out, but in the other direction, it was clear. I could see all the way down to a road, maybe ten miles away. If Al could have walked, we could have been out of there in seven or eight hours. But because he couldn't, we were stuck. So we had to wait where we were until the fire burned out. I kept thinking a fire crew would come to put it out, but no one did. I guess they knew the fire would burn itself out and that there wasn't any danger to people. They couldn't have thought anyone was up there.

The last day was especially hard. We had no food, and then we ran out of water. It was hot, and Al was getting worse, he was hallucinating some of the time. It was almost to the point where me and Willa were either going to have to leave him and hike out

and hope he'd survive until we could get help back to him, or I'd
have to chance driving back down and trying to break through
the fire. Which I didn't think would work.

Then yesterday afternoon the wind changed again. I could see
the fire was dying where we needed to go. I kept watching, hop-
ing the wind wouldn't turn back again. Finally, we got lucky—it
didn't. By about ten, I could see that it had burned out. So Willa
and I strapped Al onto the back of the Honda, and came down.
I was still afraid we might hit a place where we couldn't get
through, but we made it.

Steven sat back. He was tired, and he was drained from reliving
his ordeal.

"That is so incredible!" Sophia blurted out.

Juanita was crying softly. She covered her face with her
hands. Kate put a comforting arm around her.

Luke looked at Steven in open admiration. "That woman was
right," he said. "You were a real gift to them."

Steven shrugged. "I did what I could. Anyone would have."

"I disagree, but we don't need to argue about that," Luke
said. "Let me ask you, though—how were you able to splint this
fellow, stop his bleeding, keep him alive?"

"I'm pre-med, and I've been an assistant paramedic in Tucson
for the past two summers," Steven said. "So I know that kind of
emergency care."

A piece of Steven's story jogged Luke's brain. "You said their
cell phone wasn't working, but why didn't you call for help?" he
asked. "Didn't you have your cell phone with you?"

"I'm not allowed to have it. It's a condition of my bail. You
should know that," he reminded Luke. "You signed off on it.
Besides, I would have been screwed if I had called in."

"Why?" Kate asked.

"Because I was off the ranch. Which is another restriction—I
can't leave this place." He ran his hands through his long hair.
"To be honest, I was torn about hoping someone would find us,"

he admitted. "I was worried about Al, but if we had been rescued they would have found out I was in violation. So in a perverse way I was glad I didn't have a phone, because I would have had to give myself up. I'm happy I helped them out, but I'm no angel. I sure as hell don't want to go back to jail."

Everyone stared at him. The idea that he would have been sent back to jail for risking his life to rescue these people chilled them.

Steven stretched and yawned. "I'm beat. I need to get some sleep."

"You deserve it," Juanita said. "And you are an angel," she said protectively. "You would have given yourself up, I know that about you."

"I don't know," he answered. "But it doesn't matter."

Juanita couldn't let this lie. She turned to Luke. "They wouldn't have revoked Steven's bail for that, would they?" she asked in disbelief. "For rescuing those people?"

"I would like to say of course not, but they might have," Luke answered. "There's a lot of passion about this case. Luckily, we don't have to worry about that now. I'm going to call the D.A.'s office and let them know you're here, that they can call or come see you to verify that." He stood up and shook Steven's hand. "You did good, man. You deserve an attaboy."

Kate and Sophia also got up. "We're leaving, too" Kate said. "Congratulations, Steven."

"Thanks." He glanced at Sophia, who was trying to avoid looking directly at him. "What about you?" he asked her in a teasing tone of voice. "Aren't you going to tell me what a great guy I am, too?"

She blushed. "You are." She turned to her mother. "I'll wait at the car." She rushed out. Steven watched her go, a bemused smile on his face.

Kate watched their interplay with mixed emotions. She was less fearful about Steven than she had been, and more convinced (although there was still doubt) that he hadn't killed Maria

Estrada. But even if he was totally exonerated, would she want her daughter to get involved with him? Sophia was still a girl. This was a man, in every sense of the word.

If it came up, she'd deal with it. She hoped it wouldn't.

Steven had a question for Luke. "I'm not allowed to have visitors, but Willa wants to see me tomorrow. Will she be allowed to?"

Luke thought about the proper response. "There's nothing that says she can't come see your grandmother. If you happen to be here, that's how it goes. I would prefer not to know," he added.

Steven winked at him. "You won't." He stretched once more, and left the room.

Kate and Luke walked outside. Sophia was waiting by Kate's car. "Pretty heavy stuff," Kate commented. "Are you going to use it?"

"Does a bear shit in the woods?" He smiled wolfishly. "This ranch is going to be crawling with the press by tonight."

Kate smiled back. "One for our side. Nice, for a change."

"Too bad the trial isn't in a week," he said. "We'd have great momentum. This is going to help, although I don't think any of it is going to be allowed in at trial. Still, it's better than a poke in the eye with a sharp stick." He opened the door to his car. "I'll have to find jurors with long memories."

23

BY MIDMORNING, LUKE'S office had leaked the story. The details were on the Internet before lunch, and he had to stop taking phone calls about it. By midafternoon, the parking lot at Cottage Hospital, where Al Destifano was recovering nicely, was jammed with remote television trucks and reporters from as far away as San Diego and San Francisco.

Both Al and Willa gave impassioned interviews about Steven's generosity, selflessness, and nobility. Willa in particular, now cleaned up and made up (after the mud and fatigue of her ordeal was scrubbed off she turned out to be a strikingly attractive woman), was especially passionate about Steven's heroism.

The only part of their narrative that wasn't true was where they had been found (Luke made sure they got their stories straight about that). They admitted, very sheepishly, that they had trespassed onto the ranch to camp out, and that Steven had found them inside the property line. So not only was he a hero, he was a law-abiding one.

Alex Gordon tried to talk the press into staying away from the ranch, citing security issues. When that didn't wash he went to court and asked for an emergency injunction, which was immediately and rudely rebuffed—the judge wasn't going to get near that hot potato.

Luke orchestrated Steven's interview process with the brio of a symphony conductor. Steven, standing in front of the barrage of cameras and reporters, his back to the sun-dappled hills of his grandmother's ranch, hair washed, beard shaved, looked like a

combination of dreamboat surfer and choir boy. He answered all
the questions with the proper mixture of self-effacement and
bulldog resolve. Partway through the proceedings, Juanita, playing the part of the old-fashioned grande dame, joined him on
camera. They were a striking couple—California's rich history
standing next to its bright future. That Steven was from Arizona,
and that he was out on bail on a murder charge, was hardly mentioned.

Standing to the side as he watched his client perform with the
cool but aw-shucks assurance of a movie star (Jimmy Stewart
came to mind), Luke knew that in a few days this cloud of euphoria would pass. Steven would still be confined to the ranch, he
would go to trial, and he would have an uphill battle. The trial
was months away, unfortunately. It was going to be hard to sustain this positive energy. News has a short shelf life, he knew—he
had been down this road before, with other clients in highly pub-
licized situations. Today's hero is tomorrow's footnote.

But for this brief moment in time, he was going to milk
Steven's heroics for all they were worth. A lot of this bullshit, he
thought, as he watched the reporters jockeying for position, was
over-the-top hype, the media's insatiable appetite for anything
sensational. But the core of the story—a man putting his own life
on the line to save that of others—was real. If there was any
enduring value in this, it would be whether the state had the
stomach and cold-blooded logic to convict such a man.

A blast of dry heat hit Kate as she walked out of the American
West terminal in Tucson. Even though it was late October, the
temperature was pushing ninety. Taking a moment to catch her
breath, she pulled her rolling suitcase to the car-rental pickup
stop and waited for the shuttle that would take her to the Hertz
lot. She was going to be here for two days; three, max. Sophia
could handle being on her own for a few days. If she got lonely
or nervous, she could bunk with the Garrisons.

It had been two weeks since Steven McCoy's dramatic rescue

effort and the media frenzy that followed. Luke had squeezed a week's worth of publicity out of it. Then it died down, and things were back to normal.

Kate was here to do basic detective work. She intended to interview any friend of Steven's who would meet with her. Steven had given her some names, and she had gotten a list from Tyler as well.

Luke wasn't going to call Tyler as a defense witness—there was nothing Tyler could testify to that would help Steven in the specific circumstances they were dealing with. But Tyler was going to be there, as a prosecution witness. He was on Alex Gordon's list, and Elise Hobson had already interviewed him over the phone. Later on, when the trial date was closer, Elaine or Alex would meet with Tyler and give him a good working-over; that was a given.

Not putting Tyler on the defense list had been a calculated decision on Luke's part. If he brought Tyler in as a defense witness, the prosecution's cross-examination would be bare-knuckled; but as their witness, they had to treat him more gently. Luke would still get a good crack at him, and by following the prosecution, he would have a better chance of turning Tyler's testimony to their advantage, or at least neutralizing it.

Kate threw her bag into the trunk of her rental car and drove into the city, where she had booked a room at a Marriott that was near the university. Most of the people on her list were students and lived in the neighborhood. She would see as many of them as she could today. Tomorrow morning after breakfast she would meet with Tyler and go over his story with him in detail, to make sure there were no new surprises. Then she would finish the rest of her interviews. She had set aside an additional day for follow-ups or appointments that had to be rescheduled.

Sophia danced around her living room, drinking from a glass of orange juice laced with vodka. Tina, a slice of Hawaiian-style pizza in one hand and a drink like Sophia's in the other, laughed along with her. She was almost faint-headed with laughter. This was her second drink; the vodka was definitely taking its toll. But so what? Tomorrow was Saturday. She didn't have to get up early for school. And she wouldn't have to face her parents, with their stern, suffocating, scared-stiff protection. She felt as if a demon had taken over her brain and was turning her into someone else, someone happy and carefree. This is the most fun I've had since I moved here, she thought. This is really what it's like to be an American.

Sophia flopped down on the couch next to her. "Is that a hoot or what?" she said, pointing to the television, where a DVD of *Legally Blonde* was playing. They had rented it from the nearby video store. It was a stupid movie, but Reese Witherspoon was so cute, and so pushy. And her clothes were cool, in a retro way that was almost new, it was so old.

"That's what I want to do someday," Tina said, looking at the screen.

"Be an actress?" Sophia laughed. "You're scared to death of performing. That's why you're on the tech crew, instead of being in the play."

Tina shook her head. "Not an actress. A lawyer." She looked away, embarrassed. "A college graduate."

"So why wouldn't you? You can do the work. Have you taken the college boards yet?"

Tina shook her head. "No. I haven't let myself think about it."

"Well, you should," Sophia said encouragingly. "You need to sign up soon, though. Latinos have an edge in getting into good schools," she told Tina knowledgeably. "I'm taking them again next month—I need to bring my math scores up. We could study for them together," she offered.

"I don't know," Tina balked. "I'm not that good with English."

"You're fine. You could handle AP work." Sophia had been in the GATE program—Gifted and Talented Enrichment, the top academic rung in California—since elementary school. The kids in those classes were almost all Anglos and Asians. Hardly any

Latino kids were in GATE classes. There was a glass ceiling that Latinos butted their heads against when it came to academics.

"Plenty of kids in my classes aren't as smart as you," she assured Tina. "You could try to test in next semester," she suggested.

"It's the last semester," Tina replied with resignation. She had wanted to try to test in at the beginning of the year, but she had been too scared. She knew her place—it had been seared into her since she and her family had risked their lives to be smuggled into California from Mexico, seven years ago. They were working on getting their green cards, but they weren't legal yet, and the future for that was murky, especially after 9/11 and the backlash against foreigners, especially illegal ones. Don't rock the boat was her parents' mantra. Along with be as invisible as you can.

"That doesn't matter," Sophia told her. "If you scored high enough, they'd have to let you in. And that would help on your college aps."

"I'll think about it," Tina said, unconsciously falling into the soft voice she used when she was feeling insecure or threatened.

"I won't bug you about that now," Sophia promised her. "Tonight is our time, sister," she said with a smile. "This is fun, isn't it?"

Sitting in a nice home, drinking vodka and orange juice (she would have to be careful not to drink too much, she didn't have much experience with drinking), eating delivery pizza, and watching a video with a friend—that was definitely fun, Tina thought. Sophia had invited her to spend the night, after play practice. She had confided that her mother was out of town, so they could party down. Moderately, of course. Since neither knew any boys they were comfortable enough with to ask over, they could have fun together.

Tina had called her mother and wheedled permission to stay over at her friend Sophia's. She had to lie to get it, guaranteeing her mother that Sophia's parents (she added a father) would be there, that they would go to bed at a reasonable hour, and that she'd come home in the morning to do her weekend chores.

"Want to get stoned?" Sophia asked her.

"Aren't we already?" Tina giggled, holding up her glass.

"This is vodka. I mean pot."

Tina bit her lip. She had never tried marijuana. She was probably the only girl in the high school who hadn't, except for girls like her who came from overly strict families. "Do you have some?" she asked timorously.

Sophia laughed. "I've got a couple of joints stashed away. You do smoke, don't you?"

"A couple of times," Tina lied uneasily. "Not very often."

"It's just the two of us, and we're not going anywhere," Sophia cajoled. "There's a quart of Ben & Jerry's Half Baked in the freezer and a package of Newman's Oreos, for when we get the munchies. Come on," she begged. "I don't want to do it alone."

Tina felt safe with Sophia. One more new experience to try. "Okay."

The girls were high. Not ripped—the grass wasn't that good, but they had a fine buzz going. *Legally Blonde* was almost over. They lay on their stomachs in front of the couch and stared at the screen.

When the marijuana high initially hit her, Tina had a blast of first-timer's paranoia. But she fought off the panic attack, and once that went away she found herself in a mellow space. The grass, the drinks (they switched to straight O.J.), the ice cream and cookies, and the overall feeling of friendship, was something she hadn't experienced since she had moved here. For years, really. She had never had a real friend here, she had always kept people at arm's length. Sophia was her first friend. She felt very lucky.

"My mom's going to be a lawyer," Sophia said, nodding in the direction of the screen. "She's going to night law school. She'll be done in a couple of years."

Tina admired Sophia's mother. She was tough, independent,

and not scared of anything, it seemed—the opposite of her own mother. "What kind of work does she do now?" she asked as she ate some ice cream off the tip of her spoon.

"She's a private detective."

Tina knew there were women police officers, but detectives, like in the movies? *Chinatown*, with Jack Nicholson, was one of her favorite movies. He was her image of a private detective.

"She works with criminals?" she asked.

"Plenty of them," Sophia answered. "She's working on a big case now, that's why she isn't here. She's out of town, interviewing witnesses." She bit into a cookie. "You must have heard about it. The guy who's accused of killing Maria Estrada."

Tina shuddered. That was scary, knowing someone who was closely tied into that. She had been thinking about the killing almost every day since Maria's body had been found. She had been one of the last people who had seen her alive. Her and the two boys she and Maria had been with after lunch that day.

The boy who had been arrested was named Steven McCoy. He was the one who had rescued the campers during the fire. She remembered that from television. His picture had been in the *News-Press*, too. She had cut it out and looked at it closely. He looked like the boy Maria had been with, but not really. Like they could be brothers, but not twins.

She knew she should have gone to the police and told them about what had happened with her and Maria. That's what a good citizen would do. She wanted to be a citizen, and a good one. But she couldn't; not then, and not now. Her family was in this country illegally. They could be deported, sent back to Guatemala. Her father had a job. She was going to graduate from high school. In her dreams, even go to college. She couldn't jeopardize that.

Besides, according to the newspaper, the police had plenty of evidence against McCoy. So even if he wasn't the one who had been with them, he could still have killed her. She didn't want to see an innocent man get convicted of murder, but it wasn't her decision. She was nobody. The police wouldn't even listen to her.

One thing she knew for sure—you can't trust the police. Her father had drilled that into her. After they were citizens, as good as anyone else in this country, then you could. Maybe. Her parents had a profound fear of the police. In their country, the police were as bad as the outlaws. The only difference was that one wore a badge and had authority, the other didn't.

Still, the events of that day had been eating at her like a worm in her stomach. She was desperate to talk to someone about it. Sophia would be a good one to do it with. She could pretend she knew someone who knew something, and was asking on behalf of this imaginary friend.

"If your mother is working for this man, she must think he is innocent," she ventured.

Sophia shook her head. "It doesn't work that way. Everyone deserves a good defense, guilty or innocent. That's up to juries to decide."

She was repeating what her mother had told her. She was her mother's daughter, no matter how hard she tried not to be.

"So she thinks he is guilty?" Tina asked. That would take a lot of the pressure off, if someone working for this man thought he was the murderer, but was doing her job anyway, because in America everyone had a right to a fair trial.

"She doesn't know," Sophia answered. "But the more we get to know him, the more we think he isn't."

"We?" Tina asked in surprise and alarm. "You know him, too?"

Sophia nodded. "I ride horses up at the ranch with his grandmother. She's a friend of mine and my mom's. I've seen him a bunch of times." She could feel a blush coming on. "He is really cute. Definitely hot."

Tina sat back. She could feel the marijuana paranoia coming back. "Have you . . ."

Sophia stared at her open-mouthed. "God, no! Are you kidding? I don't get near him, it isn't allowed. But I would," she confessed. "When this trial is over, if he gets off, which he should, I really do think he's innocent, and Luke Garrison, his lawyer, who my mom works for, is the best there is." She laid back against the couch cushion. "But he wouldn't. I'm like a kid sister to him. He's way beyond me."

That's where you're wrong, Tina knew. If he could have sex with you, he would. Like the boys she and Maria had been with. They were also in college, older, experienced. At least more than she was—Maria had been as experienced as a grown woman, to hear the stories about her. But the boys hadn't known that. They were out to have sex with girls, and they didn't care about their history. They didn't care about anything, except to have pleasure.

She knew that Sophia knew that. She was saying that Steven McCoy wasn't interested in her to protect her feelings, in case she tried to get friendly with him and he rejected her.

Tina needed to find out more about Steven McCoy. She also needed to talk to someone about what had happened with her and Maria that day. She didn't know anyone else she could talk about it with, except Sophia. Her mother would tell her to talk to the priest, but she had stopped going to confession years ago. Priests were no better than police. All those allegations about molestation proved that. She remembered sitting on a priest's lap at a fiesta when she was ten, when they still lived out in the countryside in Guatemala. He had touched her legs and her bottom under her thin dress. She had been scared to go to church for months after that. And once they had come to California, she had given up on religion. She still went to church when she couldn't avoid it, because she didn't want to get into a fight with her parents, but it meant nothing. It was like watching a movie. It wasn't real to her anymore.

Tonight was not the time to talk to Sophia about something this important. She felt too uptight—from the marijuana, the vodka, and from being in a house that not only wasn't her own, but belonged to someone—Sophia's mother—who would pounce on her if she ever found out about Tina being with Maria and those boys. But sometime in the future she would open up to Sophia, if she could figure out how to keep herself and her family safe. The weight on her, of what she knew, had become too hard to keep to herself forever.

It was late, after eleven. Kate had dinner alone, and now she was back in her hotel room. Earlier, she had tried to call Sophia, but didn't get an answer, which wasn't unexpected. It was Friday night. Sophia would be out with friends. She was more at ease now socially. That was good.

Out of the dozens of people she had talked to about Steven, not one had a bad word to say about him. Guys on the volleyball team, different girls he had dated, students in his classes, teachers. He was a good guy, a good friend, fun to be with, but not a slacker—he was serious about where he was going in life. A leader. No way would he murder anyone. That was the unanimous consensus.

One surprise to Kate was that for a man as attractive as Steven, his relationships with women seemed clouded in mystery. One girl, who was striking and was up-front about how much she had liked Steven, hypothesized that he had a secret lover, and saw other women when she wasn't available. A woman who lived out of town, maybe. Or more likely, this girl conjectured, the unknown woman was married. The relationship had to be clandestine. She had no basis for thinking this, she told Kate, it had been an instinctive judgment. Or perhaps it was hurt feelings talking.

She mulled over today's interviews. Generally, people Steven's age led transparent lives. They were too young to be guarded. But Steven was an exception. He was friendly and warm, but he definitely kept his own counsel. His almost willful lack of cooperation about what he had done on the day Maria Estrada was killed was evidence of that. Which supported the notion that he had a secret life he didn't want anyone, not even his best friends, to know about.

Kate had breakfast with Steven's parents in the hotel dining room. Garrett and Laurie seemed ill at ease with her. Or perhaps, she thought, giving them the benefit of the doubt, they were worried about Steven, and seeing her reinforced their fears.

"It seems strange for a parent to say this," Laurie told her, as she tortured a croissant into crumbs, "but Steven's been a mystery to us from the time he was in high school." She crimsoned slightly. "Not a mystery, exactly. We know our son, and we know he's a good person. That's not in question. But it's like . . ." She groped for the right terminology.

"He's self-sufficient," Garrett said, filling the void. "He doesn't like to be dependent on anyone. Never has, from the time he was small. He always wanted to be in charge of himself. He takes after my mother that way. Even when . . ."

"Steven's very bright," Laurie said, overlapping her husband. "Did you know he got into Stanford?"

Kate shook her head. "No." By now she knew that any mention of Juanita sat poorly with Laurie, who would immediately turn the conversation in another direction.

"Oh, yes," Laurie said proudly. "They were hot after him."

This woman sets my teeth on edge, Kate thought. There was nothing she liked about Steven's mother, and almost nothing about his father, either. But she had a job to do. She couldn't let personal feelings get in the way. Luckily for Steven, he was a throwback to his grandmother. At least in some respects.

Laurie's tone had cued Kate that she was expected to ask the obvious. "Why didn't he go to Stanford?" she inquired.

"Arizona gave him a full ride," Garrett answered. "For volleyball, but he could have gone on academic scholarship, too," he added with a parent's prideful boastfulness. "Stanford only had a quarter-scholarship available, volleyball can't compete with football and basketball. But we didn't care," he added quickly, "we were prepared to pay for Stanford." He glanced over at his wife, whose face looked like it was set in concrete. "But Steven didn't want that," Garrett continued. "He wanted to do it on his own."

"He didn't want to be beholden to us," Laurie chimed in yet again. "That's how he put it to us. Eighteen years old, and he doesn't want to be beholden to his parents."

Steven was good at pulling the rug out from peoples' expectations, Kate thought, even when they didn't want him to. He may not have known he was doing that, but that was the result. That could also be the reason his father and mother weren't as supportive of him in his time of need as would be expected. He had divorced himself from needing them, and now they didn't know how to be there for him.

She thought yet again of her relationship with her daughters. So far from perfect. It was getting stronger with Sophia, but with Wanda, no matter how much they loved each other, there would always be that chasm. Wanda had paid for her own education with scholarships, grants, and loans. She had never complained about the mountain of debt she had taken on, but it was there, in her face. She'd be paying off her student loans into her forties.

Sophia would be in that situation too, unfortunately. Another reason for Kate to finish law school and get in a position to make real money, better than she could ever do as a PI.

That was in the future. She had to deal with now. "Did Steven ever talk about his . . ." She hesitated.

"What?" Laurie asked impatiently.

". . . Love life."

Laurie jerked back. Garrett shifted uncomfortably in his chair.

"Not in any detail," Laurie said cautiously. "We knew some of the girls he dated. He brought some home occasionally. Generally, he didn't keep us up on that. Why do you want to know about that?"

Jesus, what planet were these people living on? "He's accused of killing a woman," Kate answered, biting her tongue to stop the acid drip. "If there is, or was, a special woman in his life, it would be very helpful to talk to her."

Laurie glanced at Garrett. "Not recently," she said with a shake of her head. "Not for some time," she added reluctantly. The croissant in front of her was confetti now. She pushed the plate away as if the sight of it repulsed her. "His friends would know better than we do about those parts of his life," she said tightly. "You should ask them."

A feeling of boisterous anticipation was in the air: Arizona was hosting USC in a critical PAC-10 game. Except for the traditional shoot-out with Arizona State, this was the most important football game of the year. The Wildcats had been a PAC-10 doormat for years, but this year the team had finally come together and was on the verge of breaking into the AP top twenty-five poll for the first time in over a decade. They were only a game behind Southern Cal in the conference standings, so a win today would catapult them into the running for the Rose Bowl, or at least a prestigious lesser bowl.

The campus was packed with fans, almost none of them students. Tailgating parties had sprouted all over the parking lot and out in the adjacent streets. Even before noon, the current time, the level of alcohol consumption was copious. Everyone seemed to have a margarita or a beer in their hands. The smells and smokes of the portable barbeque grills drifted in the air. Impromptu games of touch football were breaking out all over the area. Unbridled revelry was the order of the day.

This looks like fun, Kate thought, as she elbowed her way through the crowds past the stadium toward the library, where she was going to meet with Tyler Woodruff. She had never been to a football game in her life. Wanda had dated a boy in high school who was a member of the basketball team, but she didn't think Wanda had gone to his games. If she had, she'd never talked to Kate about it. She'd been too busy with her own stuff.

Kate had never been taken with men's team sports. Too much

unbridled testosterone. But right at this moment, weaving her way through the throngs of happy fans, she felt left out, as if these thousands of people, and millions like them all over the county— all over the world—had something she didn't. Something in common to root for, agonize over, argue about. A great feeling of community.

Tyler was sitting on the steps in front of the library, waiting for her. He stood up as she approached. "It's a zoo out there," he commented with a smile. "It's been crazy here for three days."

"I didn't realize," she said. "Is the football team good this year?"

"Better than usual," he answered. "It's SC weekend, that's why it's such a wild scene."

"Are you going to win?"

He laughed. "Do you believe in miracles?"

"Not usually. But sometimes I pray for them." Like for your friend Steven's defense.

"If we beat them, it's going to be a true miracle," he said. "But they do happen."

She glanced at her watch. "Are you going to the game?" she asked.

"Naw. I'd rather play than watch. And we've got volleyball practice this afternoon. I'll probably go to the Arizona State game at the end of the season. That's the one that really counts for us." He turned toward the entrance. "We can talk in the library. It'll be quiet."

She followed him up the stairs and into the building. After they passed through the metal detectors, Tyler signed her in. They went to a section in the stacks where there was a small area for sitting and reading. There was no one else there, so they could talk comfortably without disturbing anyone.

Kate took Tyler's file out of her bag and opened it up on the table between them. "Has the District Attorney's office been talking to you?" she asked.

The friendly smile faded from his face. "Yes."

"Did you tell them anything I don't already know?"

"I don't think so. They went over the interview with me again. You've read it, haven't you?"

"Yes, several times. Luke Garrison has it memorized, practically," she told him with a tight smile. "I have some different questions for you."

"Okay."

She picked up the legal pad she'd jotted her questions on and looked at it. "What did Steven do in Santa Barbara he hasn't told us about?" she asked bluntly. "Where was he, or who did he see that he's keeping a secret?"

Tyler flinched. "What do you mean?"

She stared at him. "Something happened that afternoon that he doesn't want anyone to know about. It was so important, or so reflective on him in a negative way, that he's holding it in, even at the expense of possibly being convicted of murder. We don't know what it could be, but there's something, I'm convinced of it. You don't get lost for that amount of time with no accounting, the way he's told us."

Tyler was visibly uncomfortable. "I don't know what you're talking about."

"For real?" She tapped the legal pad with a fingernail. "This is not the time for coyness anymore, Tyler. His life is at stake."

Tyler shook his head. "I don't know what to say. Do you want me to lie?" he asked plaintively.

She held her stare for a moment longer. "So from the time you went off with . . ." She looked at her notes.

"Serena Hopkins," he prompted her.

"Serena, right. From the time you and she left Steven, until he showed up outside the movie theater that night, you don't know anything about what he did."

He started at her blankly. "Only what he told the cops."

"He didn't say anything to you later? Something in confidence?"

"No. He didn't say anything."

She recalled the conversation she'd had the day before with the girl who had speculated that Steven was involved with a married woman. If anyone knew about that, it would be Tyler. She mentally crossed her fingers.

"You know the girls Steven's dated here, don't you?" she asked him.

"Most of them," he answered cautiously.

"Was one of them married? Or in a relationship that Steven and she would need to protect?"

Tyler's eyes widened. "Are you serious?"

Kate nodded. "One of his former girlfriends thought it was a possibility." An idea suddenly came to her. "Could this woman have known you two were going to be in Santa Barbara, and went there to meet him?"

"I don't . . ." he stammered.

"This is important, damn it!" Kate said fiercely. She felt like she was on to something. Her detective's gut. "If there is a woman out there Steven's protecting, Tyler, we have to know. This is no time for chivalry. Steven's life is at stake. I mean that."

He groaned. "There isn't," he told her. "At least, I don't know if there is. Which I think I would, we're pretty tight." He looked at her sadly. "I'm sorry."

Kate fell back against her chair. This was a dead end. She had hoped for a breakthrough, but it wasn't going to happen. She tried to read Tyler's body language. He seemed to be telling the truth. He wasn't covering for Steven. Too damn bad.

She picked up the pad and flipped through the pages. "The gun that Steven found in the house. That killed Maria Estrada. Steven says he picked it up that night and put it back in the gun case. Did you see him pick up that gun and put it away? *Actually* see him?"

Tyler looked away. "It was dark in the house. We were only inside for a few minutes. I couldn't see much. Steven knew his way around, so it would have been easy for him to do it."

"But you didn't actually see him pick the gun up and put it back in the gun case," she pressed.

A slow head-shake. "No."

A jury would hear that and believe that Steven had lied. Luke would have to work awfully hard to overcome that one.

She looked at the pad again. "The gate." This was the most important piece of the puzzle. "Initially, you told the police you thought it had been locked when you went to Santa Barbara."

He nodded.

"But then you remembered it hadn't been. Correct?"

Another nod.

"Because Steven insisted he had left it open."

"Yes."

"So you did leave it open, like Steven said."

"Yes," he answered slowly.

"You're sure of that."

He exhaled deeply. "I would say . . . yes."

You aren't sure of that at all, she thought, looking at him. He was miserable. All he wanted to do was protect his friend.

"You're going to be on the stand at Steven's trial, Tyler," she said. "You're going to be under oath. You're going to swear to tell the truth. Which you must do," she reminded him sternly.

"I know that."

"So tell me now. I'm the D.A., and I'm asking you that question. Do you swear the gate was open when you left that morning?"

The way Tyler shook his head it looked like it weighed a hundred pounds. "No. I can't swear that."

Kate tossed the pad onto the table. "Okay, Tyler," she said. "I'm not the D.A., and you're not under oath now. Tell me the truth, as best you can remember it. Was the gate open or locked?"

He looked at her.

"As best *you* can remember it," she repeated. "Not how Steven told you it was."

Tyler stared at the floor. "I thought it was locked. But I can't swear to it, either way."

You won't need to, Kate thought darkly as she walked back through the campus. Your ambivalence will be more than enough for the prosecution. And the jury.

The grounds were almost empty now. She could hear sixty thousand people in full roar as she passed by the stadium. Was a miracle happening in there, she wondered? There certainly weren't any happening for her.

Two buffed-out men were sitting in the hotel lobby as Kate entered. They were dressed in identical dark-blue sweatpants, muscle-style T-shirts with a small Tucson FD logo on the left nipple, and black Air Jordans. Their hair was neatly cut, not quite military-short. One sported a trim mustache. They got up and approached Kate.

"Mrs. Blanchard?" the mustached one inquired politely.

She winced. I must really be showing my age these days, she thought. Maybe I need a new hair color. Or a better workout regimen. Or a total makeover.

"Yes, I'm Kate Blanchard," she said, slightly wary.

"Todd Levine," the man said, extending his hand. "This is Barry Harper. We're the paramedics Steven McCoy worked under this summer. Our supervisor said you wanted to talk to us about Steven."

That explained the look. Cops and firemen (and apparently paramedics, who were associated with firemen) still wore mustaches.

"Thanks for coming," she told them. "I appreciate it."

Except for the three of them and an inattentive clerk behind the check-in counter, the lobby was empty. Everyone's at the game, she assumed. She noticed they both had beepers on their belts, so they were probably on call.

"I know you're busy. This won't take long," she promised.

They sat on couches in a quiet corner. The paramedics gave her their names, addresses, and telephone numbers, which she jotted down in her notepad. "Okay," she said, sitting back. Her notepad was balanced on a knee. "What can you tell me about Steven that I might not know and that would help his defense? I assume you have a positive attitude toward him," she added, smiling.

"Absolutely," said Levine, the one with the mustache. "He's tops in our book." He looked at Harper, who nodded in agreement.

"Fill me in," she said to them. "Describe his duties on the job. What kind of training he had. His interactions with people." She looked at her list of questions. "Any personal relationships he had with coworkers or others that you know about."

According to Levine and Harper, Steven McCoy was a gold-plated Boy Scout. A red-blooded, fun-loving guy, to be sure, but a damn good man, a rock-solid friend you'd want covering your back in a bar fight, or more importantly, someone you wanted next to you in their line of work, where instant decisions about life and death could literally spring up in your face, often in hostile and dicey surroundings.

"He's fearless," Levine said in admiration. He had been Steven's primary trainer, so he knew him better, particularly under pressure. "He'd charge into locations I wouldn't set foot in without an armed cop escorting me. Steven wouldn't hesitate— somebody was hurt, needed help, off he went."

"He's smart, that's a big part of why he's good," Harper chimed in. "He knows his procedures cold. Picked everything up immediately, never had to be shown twice. He's going to be a hell of an M.D. someday. I hope he goes into emergency room medicine, that's his calling. High octane, lots of pressure."

Levine had a worried look on his face. "Will this arrest prevent Steven from going to med school?" he asked Kate.

The question took her aback. They obviously didn't know, or understand, the seriousness of Steven's predicament. "Well, if he's convicted, he won't be going anywhere for the rest of his life," she said.

"But he won't be, will he?" Levine asked in disbelief. "You can't believe he's guilty . . . can you?"

"It doesn't matter what I believe. I'm not going to be sitting on the jury."

"Jesus!" Harper ejaculated. "How can this be? Is there any solid evidence against him, or is it mob hysteria?"

Kate looked at him quizzically. "Why would you think there's hysteria about this?"

Harper looked at Levine, who shook his head—in anger or resignation, Kate couldn't tell. "Never mind," he told her. "It won't matter."

She started to ask why it wouldn't matter, or what the *it* was he was referring to, but she decided to hold her fire. She could read body language well enough to know they wouldn't tell her, if there actually was anything to tell.

They recounted some of Steven's more courageous and colorful episodes from the summer. He had been a true stalwart, and a good friend. They were heartsick over this quagmire he had fallen into. And they were sure he was innocent.

Kate closed her notebook. "Thank you for your time, guys," she said. "You've been very helpful. We may want you to testify as character witnesses, or write letters to the court on Steven's behalf."

They assured her they would be happy to do either, or both.

As she was about to say goodbye she remembered the last item on her list. "Before you go. One more question. Was Steven seeing anyone in particular that you knew about? A special girlfriend, or . . ." She hesitated. She didn't want to start a rumor that could spread and become unmanageable and ugly. But not putting everything on the table wasn't an option anymore.

"Or?" Levine prompted.

"Could Steven have been in a relationship he had to keep secret?"

"A secret relationship?" Levine repeated.

"One that could put the other person in a compromising

position. Or Steven," she added. "Like with a married woman."

The two men exchanged what looked like significant glances.

"What did Steven say when you put that question to him?" Levine asked her.

"I haven't."

"You should," Levine said. "Because it's not our place to answer that. That's Steven's call. His alone."

It was after six by the time Kate's plane landed in Santa Barbara. She drove straight to Luke's office.

"How did it go?" he asked, once she was settled in with a cold Bohemia.

"Steven McCoy is a prince. He's trustworthy, loyal, helpful, friendly, courteous, kind, obedient, cheerful, brave, clean, and reverent. Did I leave anything out?"

"I don't know," he answered, laughing. "I was never in the scouts. Maybe thrifty?"

"That didn't come up." She took a hit off her beer. Man, she needed that.

"You didn't find any hidden bombs that could blow up in our face?"

She shook her head. "Actually, there were a couple."

He hadn't expected that answer. "What are they?"

"For openers, a part of what Tyler Woodruff is going to testify to."

"The gate?"

She nodded. "His best recollection is that it was locked when they left that morning."

"That's his final answer? He's going to testify to that?"

"He won't testify either way. But when Alex or Elise ask him which he thought it was, he's going to say he thought it was locked."

"But it could have been open. That's what's in his deposition."

"He's going to say locked," she rebutted stubbornly.

"I hear you," he said in an aggravated tone of voice. "You don't have to sound so goddamned gleeful about it."

"Just stating the facts, counselor."

That Tyler would testify that way wasn't a surprise, but it was a disappointment. Luke had hoped he would have changed his memory, but he hadn't, so they would live with it. He would have to figure a way to dilute it, without discrediting Tyler, who was firmly on Steven's side. "Okay, anything else?"

She told him about her meeting with the paramedics, and their reluctance to talk about Steven's love life, which she had intuited they knew something about.

"A secret woman?" he asked, following up her supposition. "Even if there was one, I don't know how we'd work it into our scenario."

"Unless she was in Santa Barbara and they got together secretly."

"You've brought that up before, but it doesn't make sense. The boys were planning on spending the day together. They only split up because Tyler's girlfriend showed up unexpectedly. Steven had no idea that was going to happen."

"I know," she said reluctantly.

"Then what is it? The other part of what you found out."

"This is going to sound judgmental, but it really isn't." She paused. "One of the paramedics was gay. He wasn't prancing around or anything, but he was definitely gay. The other one might have been, too. I don't know. But I'm sure about the one."

Luke hadn't seen that bombshell coming at all. "Are you telling me Steven McCoy is gay?"

"Why couldn't he be? It's never come up, but we need to consider that possibility."

Luke was dubious. "He's supposed to be such a heat-seeking missile toward women," he said.

"He's hot, for sure," Kate answered. "My daughter breaks out in a sweat when she's around him. Other women do, too.

Check out how Cindy Rebeck looks at him, the next time they're in the same place. She can hardly keep her tongue in her mouth."

"You just contradicted yourself," he pointed out.

"Not at all. How many women fell all over themselves over Greg Louganis or Rock Hudson?"

"Rock Hudson was gay?" Luke exclaimed in shock. "Are none of my childhood heroes sacred?"

She ignored his sarcasm. "Steven could be one of those people who are sexually comfortable with both men and women." She thought back to her meeting at the hotel. "I wouldn't be shocked to find out that this particular paramedic and Steven were lovers this summer."

Luke exhaled heavily. "What a mind fuck that would be."

"I know." She paused. "Are you going to ask him?"

Her question shook him off-stride, which rarely happened. "Ask Steven McCoy if he's homosexual, or bisexual?"

"Yes."

"I don't know," he answered cautiously. "That could be a minefield. And I'm not sure it matters."

"But it could," she argued strongly. "What if the reason Steven has been vague about where he was that afternoon is because he was in a sexual relationship with a man?"

The accusation—or supposition, or possibility—hung heavy between them.

"You know what I don't understand?" she continued. "If Steven is gay, or bisexual, why wouldn't he admit it, especially if it could give him an alibi, which he desperately needs. There's not that much stigma about being gay anymore."

Luke shook his head in rebuttal. "There isn't? Tell that to the Neanderthals who are pushing for a constitutional amendment against same-sex marriage."

"That's the religious right. I'm talking about normal people."

Kate had strong feelings about this issue. She'd had a strict fundamentalist Church of God upbringing, which from early

childhood had never appealed to her. Too narrow, too judgmental, too bleak. By the time she was thirteen she had quit going to
church, and she had never looked back. Her daughters had been
raised to be ethical and moral people. That was good enough for
her. They didn't need to go to church to know right from wrong.

"They are normal people," Luke corrected her. "Anyway,
that's not what the problem would be for Steven."

"What would it be, then?" she asked.

"Sports," he answered emphatically. "Steven's a first-class
athlete, almost an All-American in volleyball. Sports is one of the
most important parts of his life. In some fundamental ways, it
defines him. And that is the one area in American life where
homosexuality is still taboo."

"What about Martina Navratilova?" Kate countered. "Billie
Jean King? Babe Didrikson was one of the greatest athletes of the
century."

"They were women."

As a former jock, he knew about this from the inside.
Excepting figure skaters and gymnasts, being gay was unacceptable in the male sports world. "It's easier for women, they're
more accepting, and their sexuality doesn't define them like it
does for men," he explained.

"But there are out men athletes," she persisted. "I've read
about them."

"Only after their playing days are over. And for every indi-
vidual one who's had the guts to come out, there are a hundred
who haven't. The pressure's too great, there's too much social
stigma. He'd be ostracized from the people he's closest to.
Someday it'll be easier, but it isn't yet."

She slumped in her chair. "That's awful."

"So was segregation. And that's over now, at least officially."

A disturbing thought came to her mind. "Do you think Tyler
knows that Steven's gay, or bi?"

Luke shook his head forcefully. "You're jumping the gun,

Kate. We have no knowledge that Steven is anything other than one hundred percent straight. Don't jump slick with this," he cautioned her. "It's too explosive."

Kate was a tangle of nerves as she drove home. Maybe she was wrong. Just because Steven had worked with gay men didn't mean he was one.

It was the way the paramedics had reacted—Levine particularly—that had forced this feeling. There was something there, her instincts screamed that at her. And her gut was usually right.

She mentally added an item to her agenda: tomorrow, after she cleaned up her backload, she would put feelers out into Santa Barbara's gay community. Maybe someone would remember Steven from that day.

Going down that road would be dangerous, particularly if Steven resisted, which she assumed he would, since he had never said anything about his sexuality that would prompt such a perception. She would have to be careful how she handled this, because it could blow up in their faces. But she felt she had to, even though she hated the idea of outing someone who was resisting it. But if that turned out to be their only choice, she would do it. She would lean on Luke to push Steven, until he had to consent. It might ruin his reputation, but it might also be the only way to save him.

"OKAY, PEOPLE. YOU'VE tortured this enough for one night. That's a wrap."

The voice—a campy parody of dramatic weariness—was that of Mr. Dolan, who was directing *The Wizard of Oz*, the high school's fall/winter production. "Ten days till dress rehearsal and we're still not polished in act one, let alone the rest of it," he lamented. "To quote the bard, 'I fear for the fate of the republic.'"

"Wasn't it Abraham Lincoln who said that?" chirped one of the sophomore bit players. Everyone connected with the play, cast and crew, was on stage, awaiting instructions.

"This is drama, not U.S. history, Amos," Dolan rebuked the cheeky offender. "And who gives a flying bagel? You guys have not gotten with the program, and time is fleeting." He clapped his hands briskly. "I know tomorrow's Saturday . . ."

A chorus of groans rose up as one voice.

". . . but we need to tame this savage beast. I want to rehearse the poppy field scene tomorrow evening. I won't keep you long, I promise. Now get out of here, you nuts."

Outside, the kids started drifting away in small groups, heading for their cars and the street. Cassie Portsmouth, who was playing the Cowardly Lion, ran over to Sophia.

"Saturday night!" she bitched. "Can you believe that dork? What does he think, he owns us?"

Sophia laughed. "He does own us, until the play's over."

"He doesn't have to rub it in, though. Listen. Do you have an early curfew?"

Cassie was one of the kids Sophia had become friends with since she had started play rehearsal. Her social life had taken a strong uptick in the past month. She didn't moan about her old life up north as much anymore.

"I don't have a curfew," Sophia told her. "If I'm going to be out late I check in with my mom, but she's cool about it." Her mother treated her like an adult, another reason she was feeling better about her new life.

"Cool," Cassie said. "So you want to go to a party?"

"Where?"

"I.V. Some big party out at UCSB. There'll be a bunch of neat guys."

Meaning college boys instead of high school ones. Sophia wasn't impressed with most of the boys in her class; none of her friends were. They were still boys. She and the other senior girls were women.

"Sure," she replied. "I'm always up for a good party."

As Cassie started to talk to some other kids, Sophia noticed Tina hovering on the fringes of the group. Tina smiled when their eyes met.

"Hey, Cassie," Sophia called.

Cassie turned back to her.

"Can Tina come? We were going to hang out."

This wasn't true, but Sophia knew that Tina would appreciate being included. Unlike most of the Latinas in school, she was reaching out across ethnic boundaries for friends, Sophia being the main one so far. The two newcomers had been spending a lot of time together.

Cassie shrugged. "I guess." In a lower voice, she cautioned Sophia, "There aren't going to be many Chicanos. You think she'll be okay with that?"

"I don't think she cares," Sophia answered, "but I'll ask her."

Tina was more than agreeable—the alternative was going home and watching television with her family. Maybe she would meet a nice Latino boy. She didn't know any boys who went to college.

"I'll say I'm going to be with you," she told Sophia, as she dialed her number on Sophia's cell phone. Tina's mother had grudgingly accepted Tina's relationship with Sophia, who was a serious girl and a hard studier (so Tina told her mother). "I just won't tell them where."

Over the past month, Tina had been lying to her mother regularly about her out-of-school activities. She didn't like doing it, but she had no choice if she wanted any life of her own. Her mother was too strict. She didn't understand the difference between their old country and their new one.

"Yes, Mommy," she said in Spanish. "With Sophia. For the play. I may stay over with her, is that okay?" She listened for a moment, making a face for Sophia's benefit. "I will be careful, Mommy. I'll call you later."

She hung up and handed the phone back to Sophia. "You don't know how lucky you are, the freedom your mother gives you. It's like I'm still eight years old, living in a house with a tin roof."

Cassie handed Sophia a slip of paper. "Here's the address. My cell number's on there, in case you get lost. See you there."

"See you," Sophia answered. She and Tina hopped into her car and headed for the freeway.

The party house, which had been rented by half a dozen male UCSB students, was a couple blocks from the beach, so the ocean breezes and smells blew across the lawn and through the open doors and windows, where a hundred college kids and a couple dozen recruits from various local high schools were jammed up against each other. Outside, two kegs were going, and bottles of vodka and tequila were being passed around. Ditto cigarettes. Marijuana was being smoked as well, but not as openly—the local police were active cruisers in Isla Vista on the weekends.

Music blasted out of the sound system that was inside the house.

Sophia and Tina, outside on the lawn, were standing off to one side, taking in the scene. Sophia had been tempted to drink a beer, but she had chickened out and was having a Sprite, the same as Tina.

"Pretty cool, huh," Sophia said.

"I guess," Tina said unconvincingly. Tina was used to being around beer-drinking men—her father and his cronies drank beer all day long on the weekends—but not with boys her age, or just a little older. The scene here felt foreign and threatening to her. All these American kids, totally carefree. She thought she would have an anxiety attack if she didn't calm down inside.

"It's going to get crazy later on," Sophia told her. "UCSB is one of the top party schools in the country."

"Like how crazy?" Tina asked tensely. She wished she hadn't come. This wasn't comfortable to her. But she really liked Sophia and valued their friendship. As long as the two of them hung together, she'd be okay. Her worry was that Sophia would start talking to one of the boys and abandon her. Several boys had been looking over at them, but none had approached yet, fortunately.

Sophia checked out the college girls, for comparison. Some of them were showing a lot of skin, dressed in skimpy tube tops and shorts or short skirts. Others were dressed like her, in jeans and T-shirts. She didn't feel out of place. She had been to dozens of parties at Stanford with Wanda. This one wasn't any different, except the Stanford kids were tamer, not as eager to commit mayhem. She knew she was as attractive, pretty, sexy, however you wanted to say it, as most of the girls here. Still, she was on edge, not because she was socially uncomfortable, but rather from anticipation. A few boys in the high school had come on to her, but she hadn't met one she liked, and she was antsy about not having a boy in her life. These guys were older, more mature (although they weren't acting it now, but this was a party, you were supposed to let it hang out), and there was a better variety.

She was going to connect with a boy tonight. She could feel it. "Come on," she said, tugging at Tina's hand. "Let's mingle."

Reluctantly, Tina allowed Sophia to pull her into the middle of a group which included Cassie. Cassie was already partying hard—she knocked down a hit of Cuervo Gold and immediately filled her shot glass with more tequila, right up to the brim.

She held the bottle up to Sophia, who shook her head. "I drove," she reminded Cassie.

"You could cab home," Cassie suggested. "Or sleep it off here. That's what I'm going to do." She giggled. One of the boys standing next to her ran his hand along her ass, over her jeans. She playfully batted it away. He rested it on her hip, which she accepted.

"Having a good time?" Cassie asked Tina, who was shadowing Sophia like a glove.

"Uh huh," Tina answered. Every fiber in her body said otherwise.

Cassie put a friendly hand on Tina's arm. "Just go with the flow, you know?"

"Okay," Tina answered. The flow felt like a river that was carrying her toward a waterfall.

A nice-looking guy suddenly materialized on Sophia's shoulder. "Hi," he said to her. His smile was friendly, rather than leering.

She sized him up. Taller than her, cute, not an animal. More than acceptable. "Hi," she said back, smiling back.

"I've seen you around," he said easily. "Were you at last month's puke fest?"

She felt no need to lie. "No. I've never been here."

"That's okay. You are now, that's all that matters." He looked at the empty Sprite bottle in her hand. "What're you drinking?"

She shrugged nonchalantly. "Whatever." One drink wouldn't do any harm. She was going to be here for at least an hour. The effect would wear off before she got into her car.

He looked past her to Tina, who was almost rigid. "What about your friend? I'm Rory, by the way."

"Sophia," Sophia told him. "This is Tina."

"Pleasure, ladies. How's about a tequila sunrise?"

Tequila, but mostly orange juice. Tasty and weak. "Fine," she agreed.

"What about you?" he asked Tina.

"She'll have the same," Sophia said quickly, before Tina could object.

"Coming right up." He smiled and wagged a finger in their faces. "Don't go away."

He crossed the lawn to the bar. Tina leaned into Sophia.

"I don't want to drink alcohol," she protested in a whisper. "I'm already too tense."

"Relax. You don't have to drink it," Sophia told her. "Just stand there with it. One drink won't hurt, Tina. Trust me."

Rory brought their drinks back, and one for himself. "So tell me the story of your life," he said to Sophia as he passed them out.

She laughed. "Where do you want me to begin?"

Just like that, Tina was by herself. Sophia had danced away with Rory, leaving her to her own devices. Which were hopeless. She shouldn't have come, she thought for the umpteenth time. She should have said "no" to Sophia when she had been invited. It wasn't like Sophia was dying for her everlasting company. They were friends, and liked each other, but their real bond had been their otherness, and now that didn't apply to Sophia. The real reason she had been invited was because Sophia didn't want her to think she was leaving her out. Well, now she had, without a second thought.

She would have to gut it out. Move around the fringes and hang on until Sophia decided to leave. Maybe one of the other kids from class would decide to leave early, and she could hitch a ride. Fighting her shyness, she moved around the lawn, looking at faces, trying to find one that looked like it could be of her blood.

There weren't any. College was as segregated as high school.

She was thirsty, so she took a sip from her drink. It was sweet and cold. She couldn't taste the tequila, but she knew she would feel it later on. What she should do was get something to drink that didn't have alcohol in it. She didn't want to get high. That would raise her panic level even higher.

There was a carton of orange juice on the makeshift bar, near the doors leading into the house. She could top her drink up and cut the tequila. She walked over to the bar, and tipped some juice into her cup. Looking inside, she saw a table with food on it—chips, dip, cookies. Eating would help keep her head clear, too. She walked into the living room.

The noise level was higher in here. The music bounced off the walls, and the voices were pitched high to be heard over the music. She was getting a headache—from the noise, her own tension, and the pressure of being around so many people she didn't know, and felt awkward with.

Across the room, a bunch of college students were talking loudly to each other. One of them, a boy, raised his voice to make his point. Tina, startled, turned in his direction.

The boy wasn't looking at her, but she couldn't stop herself from staring at him. She looked at him intently for a few seconds—then she turned and rushed outside.

She was shaking, and her stomach was churning. For a moment she was afraid she would hurl, right onto the lawn in front of everyone. She fought off the urge, but she could taste the bile in her mouth.

It took her a few minutes to find Sophia, who was with Rory, at the edge of the lawn. Tina barged up to them. "I have to talk to you," she said breathlessly.

Sophia had just reached a sweet comfort zone with Rory. In a couple of minutes, she knew, he would lead her to some dark corner where they could make out without anyone seeing them. Her nerve endings were tingling with the prospect of it.

"Not now, okay?" This was totally annoying. What was wrong with Tina, had she gone blind suddenly?

"It can't wait," Tina said insistently. Her voice was almost tearing. "Please."

"I'll be at the bar," Rory said diplomatically.

Sophia watched him go with undisguised exasperation at being interrupted, then turned to Tina. "What is so important this exact moment?" she asked in irritation.

"I need to show you something. Somebody. Follow me."

"What . . ."

Tina cut Sophia off. Grabbing her by the arm, she led her to the French doors that separated the inside of the house from outside. The boy who had spooked her was standing in the same place he had been when she first saw him. He was talking loudly and earnestly with a girl who looked like Lisa Kudrow.

Tina pointed a trembling finger at him. "Do you see that boy?" she asked. "The one wearing the Big Dog T-shirt?"

Sophia peeked inside. "What about him?" She looked behind her, wanting to make sure Rory hadn't drifted away.

Tina's face was red, as if she was holding her breath. "I need to tell you something," she said. Her voice was shaking. "Something terrible."

"You have to promise that what I tell you will be a secret between us," Tina pleaded.

They had disappeared around the corner of the house. No one else was in sight or earshot.

"What is it?" Sophia asked, alarmed. "Is it about that boy?"

Tina nodded. "I've been holding this in for months. I've wanted to tell someone, but I couldn't. But I can't hold it in anymore. I have to tell someone." She stared hard at Sophia. "I'm going to tell you. But you have to promise me you'll keep it a secret. You have to."

Sophia almost recoiled from her friend's intensity. "O-kay," she said slowly. This was getting scary. "I promise. So what is it?"

Tina took a deep breath. "I was with Maria Estrada the day she disappeared. Me and two boys." She looked toward the house. "That boy I pointed out to you was one of the boys we were with."

Sophia felt the ground moving under her feet, as if an earthquake had suddenly erupted. "Are you boning me?" she croaked. "You were with her?"

Tina nodded. "I was. With him, and another boy.'

Sophia's jaw was hanging on her chest. "Are you sure?"

"I'm positive. I've had nightmares about it." Her lips were so dry she could barely speak. "I have to get out of here, before he sees me."

"You think he'd recognize you?"

Tina squeezed her eyes shut. "I'm sure he would."

This is awesome, Sophia thought. Her mother would freak when she heard this. "The other boy who was with you," she asked. "Was it Steven McCoy?"

Tina shook her head. She knew what Steven looked like, from television and newspapers. She had been devouring the story. "It wasn't him," she avowed. "He looked like him, but it was a different boy."

Rory tried not to show his irritation. "Why do you have to leave? We're just getting easy with each other."

"I can't help it," Sophia lamented. "My friend's sick. I have to take her home."

"Can't she take a cab?"

"It'll take too long." She tried to placate him. "It won't take long. I'll drop her and come right back. Wait for me, okay?"

He looked past her. "Do what you have to do."

Tina was scrunched up in a corner of the passenger seat. She was shaking like a wet dog. Sophia kept her eyes on the road. Even

though she'd only had one drink she didn't want to chance getting stopped by the cops, so she drove extra carefully. But she
could feel Tina, vibrating next to her.

By the time they got to the freeway, Tina had begun to calm
down. "Thank you for doing this," she said. "I hope I didn't mess
you up with that boy."

"No big deal," Sophia placated her. It was only a boy she'd
met at a party. This was much more important. "So are you going
to tell me what happened?"

The windows of Sophia's old Volvo were open. Tina stuck her
head out and took a deep gulp of air. The wind stung her face.
She left her head out for a few moments, like a dog savoring the
night smells. Then she slumped back, and stared out the window.

"I was by myself, having lunch at Chico's," she began. "It
was right after school started. I didn't know anyone. I was new in
town, and all I wanted was to get through the year and move on."

Just like me, Sophia thought. She had plenty of friends now,
so she didn't feel bad about that anymore. But Tina still did. Tina
was much more of an outsider, and always would be.

"Maria came over and introduced herself, and we talked for
a couple of minutes. At first I didn't know why she was being
friendly, but I was happy to talk to her. I knew that if we became
friends, I could have a good social life. Then she said she was with
these two boys, and she wanted me to pair up with her, so the
other boy would be with someone. That was the reason. Not
because she wanted to be my friend, but that she needed me. I
think she didn't want to get someone she knew into it, she wanted it to be a secret."

She moistened her dry lips. "Still, I went along. I wanted to
be with other kids, even if it was for the wrong reason. The boy
I was with called himself Billy. The one I saw back there at the
party. I don't think that's really his name. The other one, the one
with Maria, was Tom. I don't think that was his name, either.

"We drove up to the top of the Riviera. The boys had beer
and drugs, which was why Maria wanted to go with them. After

we got there, Maria and Tom went ahead of us down this trail, so they couldn't be seen. They were going to drink and do drugs and have sex. Billy and I lagged behind. We drank a beer and made out a little, but I wasn't going to do anything heavy with him. I didn't even know him, and I don't do that. I haven't, not yet. I sure wasn't going to do it with a boy I didn't know, the first time."

She breathed in heavily. "He was okay with me for awhile, but then he started to push me. He felt me up over my bra, then he tried to get his hand under it, then he tried to touch me through my panties, and I couldn't take it, I made him stop. Then I insisted that they had to take me back to town. Maria was really angry. I knew we weren't going to be friends after that. I figured she'd badmouth me all over school, but I couldn't help it."

She sighed sadly. "We drove back to town. They parked near Paseo Nuevo. I got out and walked toward Milpas. Maria went the other way, into the mall. And that was the last time I ever saw her." She slumped back in her seat, exhausted.

Sophia's heart was pounding. "Why didn't you tell anybody?" she asked. "This could be incredibly important."

Tina shook her head. "I couldn't."

"Why not?"

Tina looked at her with abject wretchedness. "My family is here illegally. Since 9/11, the government is really cracking down on undocumented people. If we were found out we could be deported overnight with the clothes on our backs and nothing else. Not our car, our furniture, the money in our savings account. Nothing we have worked so hard for." She buried her head in her hands. "I could not risk that."

"But there's a man in jail for a crime he didn't commit!" Sophia pleaded with her. "He could get the death penalty! You can't stay silent and let that happen."

Tina was in knots. Her body felt like it was full of cement. "I feel sorry for that boy." She fought to hold back the tears she could feel in her eyes. "But I cannot endanger my family's entire future, our lives. We are many. He is one." She stared at her hands. "Isn't his lawyer very good? And your mother? They can get him off anyway."

"Maybe they can, but maybe they can't," Sophia argued. "The case against Steven is really tight, according to my mom. But it might not be as strong if they knew about this. You have to tell them, Tina. *You have to!*"

Tina shook her head obdurately. "I can't. I'm sorry." She turned to Sophia. "And neither can you."

They approached the Milpas exit. Sophia slowed down and took the ramp down to the light. When it changed she took a left on Milpas and headed toward Tina's apartment on the east side.

They drove in silence through the dark streets. The houses and apartment buildings were small and old. Sophia pulled into an empty spot a few buildings down from where Tina lived.

Tina turned to her. "You promised me you wouldn't tell," she said fiercely. She stared into Sophia's eyes, so that Sophia had to look back at her. "Are you going to break your promise?"

"No," Sophia said softly. "I keep my promises. But you need to think hard about what you're doing, Tina. An innocent man could be sitting in jail. Saving your family isn't enough. You need to try and figure out how to save him, too."

The party was petering out by the time she got back. Almost everyone who was left had migrated inside. Rory was gone. Cassie, who was so high by now she could hardly stand up, told Sophia he'd left right after she did. Sophia didn't bother to ask if he left alone. She didn't want to know.

She fished a cold Evian out of a tub that was slushy with ice, unscrewed the top, and drank half of it down in one swallow. Her mind was racing from what Tina had told her.

Outside, at the edge of the property, a couple of boys were sharing a joint. One was the boy Tina had pointed out, the boy who had been with her and Maria.

Sophia could feel her heart starting to race as she watched him. He was teetering a bit, holding on to a plastic lawn chair for support. He and the other boy talked for a moment longer; then the one who wasn't "Bill" came back inside. Her quarry sat down heavily in the lawn chair.

Sophia waited until she was sure no one was going to join him. Then she fished a cold beer out of the cooler, twisted the top off, and went outside.

He was sprawled out, arms and legs akimbo. He looked more green behind the gills than stoned. Sophia dropped into the chair next to him. "You look like you could use a cold one, sailor," she said jauntily. She held the beer out to him.

He looked at her. "Do I know you?"

She smiled. "I don't know. Do you?" Then she laughed. "I'm Sophia. I'm a friend of Rory's."

He took the beer. "Thanks," he told her. He took a small sip. "Shit," he muttered. "Too much of a good thing is not always a good thing."

"You're young," she said cheerfully. "You'll recover." He hadn't told her who he was, so she outright asked him. "What's your name? Billy, is it?"

He stared at her slit-eyed. "You must be thinking of Billy Hall. But he doesn't look like me. I'm Jeremy."

"Which Jeremy?" she asked.

"Musgrove. Is there another Jeremy here?" He turned, as if someone else with his name would suddenly pop up behind him.

"Nice to meet you, Jeremy." She looked around. "This is a neat house. Do you live here?"

"Here?" He shook his head, then winced. "No. I live on the Mesa."

She glanced at her watch. It was late, after midnight. She had gotten what she needed, for now.

"Listen, Billy. I mean Jeremy. I've got to go. It was nice talking to you."

He looked over at her. It felt to her like he was checking her out. "Already?" he asked. There was a distinctive slur in his voice.

"'Fraid so." She fished in her purse for a pen and a scrap of paper. "If you want to call me, I wouldn't mind," she told him.

He smiled, a goofy, spacey smile. "Okay, fine."

She wrote her cell number and first name down and handed him the paper. He folded it and fumbled it into his back pocket.

"You're not going to lose it, are you?" she teased him. "I don't give my number out to just anyone."

"I believe you," he protested. He was attracted to her, she could feel it. It was a nice feeling, even if her motive for coming onto him wasn't clean. "Why don't you give me your number, in case you lose mine."

He nodded, as if that was a sage piece of advice. She handed him the pen and her notepad, and he scribbled his name and number on it. She looked at it to make sure it was legible. "Jeremy Musgrove. 555-0073."

"Check." He smiled again.

She put the paper in her purse. "Don't forget to call me." She shook a teasing finger in his face. "You're not a guy who says he will, but then he doesn't, are you?"

"No," he protested. He was cute, she thought. And not full of himself. A date with him wouldn't be so hard to take. "I'll call you tomorrow . . ." He caught himself. "In a couple of days."

"Hope so." She stood up. "Nice to meet you, Jeremy. And I'll see you again."

"You will," he promised. "For sure."

25

KATE HAD LUNCH with Dennis Cahill. He took her to the University Club. The food was passable and he could compare notes and exchange gossip with his friends, other middle-aged professionals. They both had Cobb salads and iced tea.

"Ten years ago, almost everyone would have a glass of chardonnay or a Bloody Mary with lunch," Dennis commented as he looked around the room. "Now they don't even open the bar at lunch anymore, except on Friday. Half the population is overweight, the other half is obsessively healthy. It's like politics. There's no middle ground anymore."

Dennis was Kate's closest gay (as opposed to lesbian) friend in Santa Barbara. He was one of the city's established estate lawyers. Like some other gays and lesbians she knew, Dennis came late to discovering his true sexual identity. He was married for twenty years before he finally came out, in his late forties. He had an ex-wife and two grown children, and after an awkward and hurtful interlude (his wife had been completely blindsided), he was on friendly terms with them again. He and his partner, a chiropractor named Wolfgang, even had Thanksgiving dinner with them (his wife had remarried, for which he was thankful). He considered himself blessed that he could have good relationships with his old life as well as his new one.

Between bites of salad, Kate explained her predicament.

"The thing that's killing us is Steven's disappearance for five hours on the afternoon the girl was last seen, which is the time frame when she was probably killed. His lack of cooperation is almost perverse, Dennis. It's as if he's hiding something."

"Like a sexual encounter," Dennis said, divining her intention.

"Yes."

Dennis put his fork down. "You think it could have been with a man?"

"Yes," she said again.

He picked at a piece of lettuce that was stuck in his teeth. "Have you asked him about this?"

"No. Luke's going to." She paused. "I expect the answer will be 'no.'"

He nodded, thinking. "You won't know until you do. But you're probably right. If he hasn't admitted it by now, given his dire circumstances, he isn't going to."

"That's what I'm afraid of," she admitted.

He forked up another mouthful and masticated slowly. "What makes you think this fellow is gay, anyway? Is he effeminate? Not that that's a true indicator. Some straight men are naturally fey." He winked. "And some gay men are as straight-looking as they come."

"No. It's not about his looks. He's very masculine. Very sexy to women. If he isn't all straight I'd think he would be bi. There's an androgynous appeal to him."

"Like Mick Jagger, when he was young."

"Yes," she answered. "Except he's very athletic. He's built like a young god. He has a real swagger, too."

"He sounds very . . . inviting," Dennis said with a smile. "A bit of rough trade, as the English say."

"But he's also very nice," Kate said. She didn't want to mischaracterize Steven, especially negatively. "Everyone who knows him says only good things about him."

Dennis sat back and looked at her carefully. "If this young man doesn't say he's gay, or that he has been attracted to men, why are you pursuing this?" he asked.

"Because we need something to explain his extreme reticence," she said. She hesitated. "And because I met a friend of his from where he lives who is definitely gay, and the unspoken seemed to be that there had been a sexual relationship."

"The unspoken," Dennis intoned gravely. "Of all the languages in the world, the most difficult to understand, and the easiest to misinterpret."

"Yes, I know. I don't like reading tea leaves. I prefer hard facts. But his trial date is approaching, and we're getting desperate."

Dennis nodded sympathetically. "From what I've read and heard, I can appreciate why." He put his fork down. "What do you want from me, Kate?" he asked her.

"To talk to your friends in the gay community and find out if any of them know him," she answered candidly. "Especially, if anyone saw him or was with him on that day."

Dennis looked at her questioningly. "This fellow is a generation removed from me," he reminded her. "Have you gone to the local gay clubs and bars and asked around? That might be more fruitful, pardon the dreadful pun."

"I'm going to," she said. "I wanted to touch base with you first. To make sure I don't fuck up my approach."

"You can't worry about that," he advised her. "You can only do your job. Breaking eggs is part of what you do, sometimes."

"I know, and I don't mind," she answered. "But in this circumstance, I don't want to open a Pandora's box that wasn't there in the first place."

Dennis finished his iced tea and held up the glass so the waiter could see that he wanted it refreshed. "Here's my advice, for what it's worth. Ask your client directly. If there is anything to your supposition, and he is willing to deal with it openly, then plunge ahead. Otherwise, drop it."

She was taken aback by his bluntness. "Just drop it?"

He nodded solemnly. "Yes. Because unless your client is cooperative, you can't win."

The waiter returned with a new glass of iced tea. Dennis took a long swallow. "I think you're on the wrong track," he told her. "But let's say there's something to it. Something he wants to keep secret, even in the face of the worst consequence possible. How in the world will you pry open that nut?"

"Find out who he was with, and persuade whoever it was to admit to it," she answered doggedly.

He shook his head. "That isn't going to happen. You'll be banging your head against a stone wall."

"I have a hard head," she replied. "I've banged up against a lot of walls with this head."

He smiled. "None this hard. If your client did have a sexual encounter with a man, that man would know about the situation, unless he was a transient, in which case you're really up the creek. But if it was somebody from here and he hasn't come forward, it means that for some reason—some good reason, given the importance of this—he can't. If he hasn't by now, he won't."

"Because he himself is closeted."

Dennis nodded. "He's married, he's socially prominent, he's a politician, a film star, something that will ruin him if he is openly gay. You remember Michael Huffington, don't you? Arianna's ex-husband?"

Michael Huffington was a former congressman from Santa Barbara county. A wealthy carpetbagger (his money was Texas oil), he had almost won a U.S. Senate seat in the mid-nineties through the sheer power of his wealth. His former wife, Arianna, had mutated over the past few years from right-wing provocateur to left-wing populist/gadfly and bête noire of the establishment.

"Yes. I voted for Feinstein," Kate said.

"As I assume you know, Huffington was a closeted gay man who came out after he lost the election. Probably the most liberating thing he ever did. But if he had come out before, he would have lost his base. Well, think of how that might apply to your situation."

She nodded. "I hear you."

"There's another issue," he went on, "which goes to the heart of this. If your client is gay—which I doubt, but let's say for the sake of argument that he is—and he hasn't admitted it, then even if he'd had a sexual partner who would normally corroborate the relationship, the partner won't do it. You don't out people who want to keep their sexuality private. It's unethical, and immoral. That's the kind of garbage *The National Enquirer* might spew, but not any decent man or woman I know."

Kate sat back, properly chastised. "I understand."

"Luke should put the question to this fellow directly, and if he denies it, that's it," Dennis said. "If you want to go to some of the gay bars and ask around, I'll give a list. But even if you got positive feedback, you'd have to be very careful," he warned her. "Some bottom-feeder might want to exploit the situation, and that would make matters even worse."

Sophia wasn't ready for her mother to know she had a date with a boy who could be a crucial witness in the Maria Estrada murder case, so she met Jeremy in front of the movie complex at Paseo Nuevo. The last place anyone saw Maria alive, she thought with irony. The "anyone" who might be this boy who was taking her to dinner and a movie, and who obviously liked her. He hadn't waited the socially cool three days to ask her out—he had called the next day.

They shared a salad and a pizza at Pascucci's around the corner, then bought tickets for a movie. It was a decent-enough comedy, but within fifteen minutes they had moved to the back row so they could make out. Jeremy was a good kisser, and he didn't push for anything more than feeling her breasts over her top.

After the movie ended, they bought ice cream cones at the hole-in-the-wall Ben & Jerry's. Sophia could see that Jeremy didn't know what to do next. She was too young for them to go to a bar, and he didn't seem to know what else they could do.

They sat on one of the wooden benches in the mall. "Is there something you want to say?" Sophia asked.

"Would you . . ." He stopped.

"Would I what?" she prompted. Come on, she thought. I'm the kid in high school. You're the experienced college guy.

". . . Like to come over to my place?" he mumbled.

This was going better than she could have hoped for. "The one on the Mesa?" she teased him.

"I only have one."

She sized him up (rather, she gave him the impression that she was sizing him up. She was already way ahead of him). "Okay," she said easily.

"You would?" He spoke as if he'd expected the answer to be "no."

"You'll have to bring me back here at a decent hour, my mom doesn't like me being out too late on a school night."

"No problem," he said quickly.

"Are we going to be alone?" she asked. "What about your roommates?" She didn't want to walk into a nest of horny college boys. She needed alone time with him, to work on him.

"We'll be alone," he told her. He didn't say anything about his roommates.

She finished her ice cream cone and licked the stickiness from her fingers. "Here are the ground rules. I'm not going to have sex with you," she told him firmly. "I'm not going to let you do anything more than what we did in the movies." She grinned. "But we can do as much of that as you want."

"That's okay," he said. "That's fine."

He's so eager, she thought. Like a puppy in a kennel. Pick me, pick me. She took his hand. "Come on, then," she said friskily. "Show me the famous Musgrove etchings."

Sophia was expecting the usual stucco apartment or small tract house with a bunch of students crammed in like a can of sardines. Instead, Jeremy lived in an upscale two-bedroom condo with a view of the ocean.

"Do you want something to drink?" he asked, as he closed the front door behind them.

"Okay," she answered, looking around in bewilderment. What gives here, she wondered?

"White wine okay? Or don't you drink?"

"I'll have a glass of wine, thanks," she answered.

These guys live better than me and Mom, she thought with surprise and a touch of envy as she checked out the place. The furnishings, while not inspired, were more expensive than normal student stuff. They looked like someone had gone to Restoration Hardware and the Pottery Barn and ordered whatever was needed. There were a few obligatory posters of rock groups and cult movies, but there were also some interesting, offbeat prints. There was also a large-screen high definition television in the corner of the living room, and a shelf stacked with tapes and DVDs.

Somebody who lives here has money, she thought. Could it be him, she wondered, as he got a bottle of white wine out of the refrigerator and screwed out the cork. Not that it would matter. She wasn't here for romance. Which was too bad—so far, he had been a nice guy.

He handed her a glass, and clinked his to it. "Cheers," he said.

"Cheers. Thank you."

She sipped her wine. It was good, better than the four-dollar Trader Joe's stuff her mother kept in the house. He definitely has taste.

"Where are the rest of your roommates?" she asked. She knew they would be in heavy make-out mode in a matter of minutes, and she didn't want someone coming in and finding her in an embarrassing situation.

He grimaced. "There aren't any."

She looked at him dubiously. "You live here by yourself?"

"It's a long story. I'll explain later." He took her hand. "You wanted to see my art collection. The best pieces are in the bedroom."

They lay on his bed, kissing feverishly. His hands roamed her back, her sides, his fingers caressing her breasts and nipples over her top and bra. But nothing more, as he had promised.

Sophia could feel his erection through his khakis as he ground against her leg. Most girls, she knew, would give the poor suffering bastard a blow job to put him out of his misery. At least a hand job. But she wasn't going to. She had set the rules and she was going to stick to them. She would go slow and steady and let nature take its course, if it was meant to. Plus she had her mission, the real reason she was here.

She wished she didn't have to use him. Later, if it turned out he wasn't involved in the murder, she could see him in a normal boy-girl way. He wouldn't even have to know he'd been used.

The condo's balcony had a nice view of the ocean and the Channel Islands. They lounged in deck chairs, their feet propped up on the railing. Jeremy was drinking Corona from the bottle. Sophia, wanting to keep her head straight, sipped a lemon Snapple.

"Want to smoke?" he asked her. He pulled a tightly rolled joint and a disposable lighter from his shirt pocket.

"No, but you go ahead," she told him. "Don't get too fucked up, you have to take me back to my car."

"I'll just take a couple of hits." He lit the joint and inhaled, holding the smoke, then letting it drift out of the sides of his mouth. No coughing, no gasping. An experienced doper. He took a swallow of beer to lubricate his throat.

Sophia looked out at the beach below them, the lights of the harbor, and the moonlight on the ocean. This was how she would like to live. Her mother made decent money, but they couldn't afford a place like this. Jeremy's family must be rich to pay for a condo this nice for a kid who was still in college.

"This is a great place," she enthused. "It must be expensive, especially since you live here by yourself."

"Yeah, it's pricey," Jeremy agreed laconically. He took another drag and pinched the blunt out with the tips of his fingers.

"How come you have two bedrooms, if it's just you?" she asked. She had looked into the other bedroom. It was fully furnished, but wasn't being used—it was too neat, nothing was out of place.

After not answering for a moment, he said, "I had a room-mate."

"Another guy?"

He nodded.

"What happened to him?"

He shook his head as if he didn't want to think about it. "He bailed out. Dropped out," he clarified.

"He was going to UCSB, too?" She didn't want her prying to be too obvious, but he didn't seem to be noticing.

He didn't answer her directly. Instead, he said, "It's all screwed up."

"What is?"

"Everything," he said darkly. "My life."

She stifled a laugh. "That's kind of dramatic, isn't it, Jeremy?"

His look at her was intense. "Not really."

She took on a look of sympathy. "Did someone die? The friend who was living here with you?"

"No, he didn't die. Nobody died," he said doggedly. "It's just . . ." He drank some more beer. "Forget it. You're right, it's not that terrible." He forced a smile. "Some date I turned out to be, huh? Mister doom and gloom."

"It was great until a minute ago," she said cheerfully. "Hey, I'm sorry I brought up whatever it was that ticked you off."

He shook his head. "It wasn't you," he told her. "It has nothing to do with you." He sighed. "Let's drop it, okay?"

"Sure." She went inside and got herself another Snapple out of the refrigerator. The contents were typical male student—lots of beer and other drinks, and almost no solid food. In the freezer (she checked) were stacks of frozen pizzas and Mexican foods—burritos, tamales, taquitos. Two bottles of vodka. All the basic college food groups.

She came back outside and sat down again, moving closer to him. "Your parents must be rich for you to afford to live in a place like this by yourself," she commented. "What kind of mogul is your dad?" she asked jokingly.

"I wish," he replied. "My old man works for county government in L.A., and my mom teaches school. We're barely middle-class. I'm here on scholarship."

"A brain." She was impressed. Scholarships to UCs were super-competitive.

"Or is it for sports?" He had a decent build, but he didn't carry himself like an athlete. And if he was a jock he wouldn't be living like this. This pad was too neat. She knew some athletes from Stanford, friends of her sister's. A jock's apartment was an animal house.

"Not sports," he confirmed. "I play club lacrosse, though."

"Cool. Maybe I'll come watch you sometime."

He looked at her. "You would?"

"Sure. I like lacrosse."

"There's a game next week. Can you come?"

"I'm in a play that opens in a couple of weeks, and we have a busy rehearsal schedule," she explained. "But if I'm available, I'd like to."

He stared at her. "You're awfully mature for a girl who's still in high school."

She felt a catch in her throat as she flashed to the years of Wanda and her living apart from her mother, and all the turmoil over her parents' divorce and her mother's downhill slide before she corrected herself. "I've had some tough times, like everyone else," she said. "I've had to take care of myself a lot."

Why are you telling him this, she thought, rebuking herself. You're here to find out about him, not the other way around. You don't want him to know about you.

"But nothing really heavy," she added. "I've got it pretty good." She thought about Tina, living in constant fear of being deported. Compared to people like Tina, she had it damn good. She swung the conversation back on course. "You were telling me how come you can afford to live in such fancy digs." She jumped in her seat. "Aha! I've got it. You're a dealer."

Jeremy recoiled. "Jesus, don't say shit like that!"

"I was kidding."

That was an overreaction to an obvious joke. Maybe she was onto something. Could Maria's killing be tied to drugs? She would ask her mother about that.

"It isn't funny," he declared hotly. "I've had friends who have been busted. And I'm not a dealer. For one thing, I'm too chickenshit. I couldn't handle the tension."

"Well, I'm glad to hear that," she said. "But anyway," she pressed him, "how do you pay for this place?"

"Peter pays for it."

"Who's Peter?"

"My roommate who jumped ship. His father pays for the whole thing."

She whistled low through her teeth. "Even though he's not here?"

Jeremy nodded. "His father signed the lease. When Peter decided to drop out this quarter his dad assured me he'd keep on paying. He knew I couldn't afford it."

"That was nice of him."

Jeremy nodded. "Peter's dad's a great guy." He frowned. "Peter doesn't treat him as good as he should."

"What do you mean?" she asked.

"He's just . . ." He waved off the rest of what he was going to say. "Let's say Peter can be self-consumed and leave it at that."

She looked at him. "You sound like you're angry with him."

He turned away. "Not really. You can't be angry with people for being who they are."

She let that go. Instead, she asked, "Why did he leave school? Was he doing poorly?"

Jeremy shook his head. "No. Classes had barely started." He sighed. "Peter was burned out and needed to take a quarter off. He's not the first one."

"So he'll be back after Christmas?" she asked.

"I guess," he answered. "I'll see him when I go home at Thanksgiving. See what his plans are." He drained his beer. "At least I don't have to worry about the rent. His father's paying for the whole year." He indicated with his arm. "This place costs more than my tuition and books."

"That must be a relief to you," she said.

"It is," he agreed. "Although I'm not doing very well this quarter. I have to keep a 3.0, or my scholarship's in danger. This is the first quarter I won't be dean's list," he lamented.

There's something weird going on here, Sophia thought. Something connected to Jeremy's having been with Maria Estrada that day, it had to be. Maybe—this was a real reach—he was connected with her getting killed. Or maybe his old roommate was.

Jeremy had freaked out when she had jokingly brought up the idea of his being involved with drugs. She had heard enough about Maria's family to know that before Steven was arrested the police and others had thought drugs could be part of why she was killed.

Whatever the reason, something very heavy was bothering Jeremy. Something deeper than his roommate flaking on him.

If Tina was right about what had happened that day, she now knew two people who had been with Maria Estrada on the day she disappeared. Two people who hadn't talked to the police about being with her. Tina had a reason to stay clear of the police. But what could Jeremy's be?

She needed to talk to her mother about this. "I need to be going," she said. "My mother will be getting antsy."

"Okay." He got up. "Listen. What we talked about, me not feeling good and that? It's no big deal. Sometimes school gets under your skin, you know?"

"Sure," she replied. "I get bummed all the time. I have to send my college aps in next month—talk about pressure! How come it isn't fun to be young all the time, like your parents keep telling you?"

"It never was, that's my theory," he answered. "They just

don't remember. Or they want you to find out that life's a bitch for yourself, like they had to."

She smiled at that. "It isn't always a bitch." She linked her arm in his.

"No," he agreed, smiling back. "Sometimes it's pretty damn good."

Kate was already asleep when Sophia got home. She'd left a note in the kitchen: "Have to be up and out early. Left you money for lunch. See you at dinner, unless you have play practice. Let me know. Love, Mom."

Sophia was impatient to tell her mother about Jeremy Musgrove, but it could wait until tomorrow. No one was going anywhere, and the trial was still months away. She watched *The Daily Show* and Leno's opening monologue, and went to bed.

26

LUKE DROVE RIVA'S BMW station wagon down the long access road to Juanita McCoy's house. The GTO hadn't been running smoothly for the past week, which was why he was using his wife's car. Over the weekend, he'd take the head off the engine block and put a new gasket on, and it would be good to go again. That was another nice thing about old cars—you could work on them yourself. You practically need a Ph.D. in physics and access to a million-dollar shop just to change the spark plugs on a modern car.

He parked in front of Juanita's house, got out of his car, stretched his legs, and looked around. God's country, he thought to himself, or an excellent facsimile. What would it be like to raise a family on a place like this—a throwback Norman Rockwell existence, yet less than an hour from downtown Santa Barbara. Financially, he didn't need to work anymore—he'd had some big scores over the past decade, and Riva was a frugal and savvy money manager. If he quit working today they'd be in good shape for the rest of their lives.

But he wasn't going to quit—he wasn't close to burning out. He loved the combat, the impact he had on people's lives, being in the mix. It might be a relief, though, to pull over into the slow lane in the other parts of his life.

Someday, they might do that. But not yet. Riva wouldn't want to live this far away from town while the kids were growing up. That's how she'd been living when he first met her, up in Mendocino County, the big house in the redwood forest. He was barely in the profession then; he had been on a self-imposed sab-batical, after his first wife had divorced him and his life was in shambles. Riva, too, had been in her own exile, and like him, had wanted nothing more than to cocoon. But once they connected, and brought each other out of the darkness, she was happy to rejoin civilization.

Life was better than ever. A smart man doesn't reinvent the wheel. Next summer they could rent a place out in the valley for the weekends, see how they liked it, without committing to any-thing permanent.

He looked at the hills surrounding him. There was something glorious about the silence, the majesty of size. He would talk to Riva about his idea, if they ever found time to be alone.

Juanita came out of the house. She had been cooking or bak-ing; an apron was tied around her waist. She smiled in greeting.

"Aren't you early?" she asked. "Steven said nine o'clock."

He glanced at his watch. 8:45. "There was hardly any traf-fic," he said.

"Come in. There's fresh coffee and cornbread muffins, hot out of the oven."

"Homemade muffins?" That would make the drive up here even more worthwhile.

"I wouldn't brag on them, but yes," she answered modestly.

He sat at the kitchen table while she poured him a cup of steaming coffee and set a plate of fresh muffins in front of him. He topped the coffee with half-and-half, sipped off the foam, and bit into a muffin.

"Delicious," he exclaimed, his mouth full.

She smiled. "Steven should be here in a few minutes. He was up early. Some work out on the range. He's becoming an honest-to-God rancher," she said pridefully. She paused for a moment. "Is there a reason you came to see him today?" she asked. "I mean, specifically?"

He nodded through his second mouthful of muffin. After he swallowed, he answered, "Yes."

"What about?"

"Sorry, Juanita, but I can't tell you. It's privileged, between Steven and me."

Her expression was one of doubt and annoyance about being shut out. "I'm his caretaker," she reminded Luke; not that he needed reminding.

"Doesn't matter," he told her. "I can't. If he wants to tell you later, that's up to him, not me."

Her lips formed a thin, tight line. "Is this more trouble?"

He shook his head. "Strategy, mostly. I can't say anything more."

She nodded. "I understand. I just want to make everything right."

"You're doing the best you can. He would be in a much worse situation if it wasn't for you."

"I know that," she said without false modesty. "That doesn't relieve the anxiety."

Luke started to offer some pithy cliché that would superficially placate her, but the high whine of a motorcycle engine cut through the air like the approach of a swarm of hornets. He looked out the window as Steven rode into sight. He cut the engine of the Honda ATV, dusted himself off, and came into the house.

"Good morning," he said to Luke. He kissed his grandmother on the cheek. "The north well pump's frozen up," he told her. "I'll help Keith fix it this afternoon. He went into Goleta to pick up the parts." He poured himself a cup of coffee and snagged two muffins off the plate.

"Do you want anything else?" Juanita asked him. "I could make you eggs."

"This'll do fine," he said, sitting down with them. He smiled at Luke as he buttered a muffin. "Nobody in the world can bake like this woman."

She waved a shy, girlish hand at him. "Anybody can make biscuits."

"Not that taste like these," he said. "You're the best."

Juanita almost blushed from the compliment. She got up and fussed with the coffee pot.

She acts as if she has a crush on him, Luke thought, as he watched their teasing bantering. Her own grandson.

That was the reason he was here this morning—Steven's sexual attractiveness, and how it could blow up in their faces. "Let's get down to business," he said to Steven. "Will you excuse us, Juanita?"

She took a sunhat off a hook that was set by the back door. "I'll be in the stable, if you need me."

"I'll check in with you before I leave," he promised her.

She walked out. Luke sipped his coffee. Steven polished off his first muffin and started on the second.

"You look damn fit," Luke commented. "Ranch life agrees with you."

He needed to amp up his own workout routine, he thought, as he looked at Steven. This kid made him look like a pussy. Granted, he was more than twice Steven's age, but he took pride in his fitness. Sitting across from him was live proof that he needed to push himself harder.

"There's nothing to do out here except work, and work out," Steven said. "I'm running seven miles a day, I'm down to a six-minute mile. A hundred push-ups, two hundred crunches. And working with Keith, he's like the Energizer bunny, he keeps on going and going and going." He got up and drew a glass of water from the tap. "And read. I'm reading some of the books in the old library. Dickens, guys like that. Stuff you don't read when you're in pre-med."

"That's one benefit of confinement. If you could call it that."

"It is," Steven agreed. Surprisingly, he wasn't showing hostility about his situation today. "I've had a lot of time to think about my life," he said. "Where it's been, and especially where it's going. I won't be the same person I was after the trial's over, that's for sure."

Meaning after you're acquitted, which you think is a fore-gone conclusion, Luke thought. Steven was either in deep denial, or he didn't want to let anyone see through the cracks in his facade.

He took the file that contained Kate's Tucson interviews out of his briefcase and set it on the table in front of him. Steven sat back down. "Have you come up with anything new?" he asked.

"Kate Blanchard was in Tucson, talking to friends of yours," Luke told him. He tapped the file. "People from college, kids you grew up with, people you worked with. They said you were the salt of the earth. Every one of them."

Steven smiled. "That was nice of them."

"You have a lot of people in your corner back there. A lot of people here, too," Luke added.

"Is that what you want to talk about?" Steven asked. He seemed puzzled.

Luke shook his head. "No."

"Then what?"

"We think you're holding out on us, Steven."

Steven looked startled. "What do you mean?"

"I don't know, specifically," Luke answered. "That's why I'm here. Not for the first time on this subject," he added.

"I don't get you," Steven said. "What would I be holding out on by now? What would I gain by not telling you everything I know?"

"That's a good question, which only you can answer." Maybe they were getting somewhere on this—finally. "Kate Blanchard and I have been doing this for a long time, Steven. We both have good instincts for what's real, and what isn't—what Hemingway famously called the bullshit detector. And our bullshit detectors tell us you haven't told us the whole truth yet."

Steven threw up his hands. "I can't believe you're still beating this dead horse."

Luke looked at him calmly. "Who were you with that after-noon?"

Steven shook his head. "I've told you. No one."

Luke leaned forward. "You're protecting someone, aren't you?"

"Like who?" Steven threw back at him.

"If I knew I wouldn't be asking, would I?" Luke answered. "Look, Steven," he continued, "I don't mean to be brusque. But we're losing the war. I need you to help me."

"I *am* helping. What do you want me to say? Do you want me to make something up?"

"No, of course not." Luke hesitated. "Is it a woman?"

"A woman?"

"A woman who can't afford to be associated with you publicly."

"Like what, a hooker? I've never paid for sex. I don't need to."

"A married woman."

Steven rocked in his chair. "Oh, mother. That's a good one. You think I might be willing to get convicted of murder to protect some married woman's honor?"

"It's been known to happen."

Steven shook his head. "I'm respectful of women, and I believe in keeping a confidence, but no way would I give up my life so some married lady doesn't get in trouble with her husband."

"Level with me, Steven," Luke implored. "You didn't have an affair with a married woman that you're covering up."

Steven shook his head forcefully. "I'm not saying I haven't fucked married chicks, but I wasn't boning one that afternoon." He grimaced. "I wish I had been. Then I'd have an alibi you'd believe."

"What about with a man?"

It took a second for the words to sink in—then Steven shot out of his chair. "Are you insane?" His face was beet-red. "Are you fucking out of your mind? You're accusing me of being with a man? Having sex with a man?"

"I'm asking. I have to cover all the bases."

"Well, the answer is *no*!" Steven shouted. He backed away from the table as if Luke was contagious with some infectious disease. "You think I'm *gay*?" he asked in disbelief.

"I don't think anything, Steven. I'm asking. I have to ask."

Steven's eyes went dead. "I am not gay. I do not fuck men. I do not let men fuck me, or suck me, or do anything sexual with me." He fell back against the kitchen counter. "Where the fuck did this bullshit come from? Did somebody in Tucson tell Kate Blanchard I was gay?"

Luke shook his head. "No. But there was an inference."

"From who?" Steven demanded.

"One of your coworkers. There was no accusation of anything," he reiterated. "It was more of an impression. Kate felt strongly enough about it that she thought we needed to pursue it. So I am."

Steven groaned. "Was it Levine?"

"Levine was one of the paramedics you worked with last summer?" Luke asked. He knew, but he wanted to hear it from Steven.

"Yes," Steven said grimly. "He was my trainer. I worked under him."

Maybe they had hit pay dirt, Luke thought. "What about him?"

Steven took a deep breath to gather himself. He sat down again. "After I finished my last shift on my last day of work, we went out for drinks. All the guys and women I'd worked with. It's intense, what we do, you form tight friendships. I was close to almost all of them, Levine included. He was like a big brother to me, because of being my trainer.

"I knew he was bent that way, but he'd never made a move on me," he continued. "I didn't give a shit, I'm not homophobic, I have gay friends. You do your thing, I'll do mine, we respect each other."

He drummed his fingers on the table. "We hit a bunch of bars, having a good old time, getting more and more shitfaced.

None of us were on call, so we didn't have to monitor how much we drank. Which was a copious amount. By the time the last group staggered out of the last bar, nobody was feeling any pain. None of us were in any shape to drive, so we grabbed a couple of cabs. Levine and me live in the same area, so we shared a cab. He was going to drop me off, then continue on to his place."

Steven stopped to refill his glass from the tap. He drank half of it down in one swallow, then continued.

"By the time we got to my apartment, I was blotto. I couldn't walk on my own, I could barely sit up in the cab. All I can remember is Levine getting me out of the cab and helping me to my apartment. We got into the apartment—he had to put his hands in my pants pocket to fish out the key—and I collapsed on the sofa. I share the apartment with Tyler, but he was off visiting his family, so we were alone.

"I just wanted to crash. I didn't give a shit about taking my clothes off or anything. I'd deal with it in the morning. Levine was standing there—I could hardly make him out, he was real fuzzy-looking, that's how drunk I was—and he's saying he'll put me to bed. I kind of mumbled thanks, but you don't need to, and then he's taking off my shoes, and my socks, and he's helping me out of my shirt. I'm lying there like a flounder, too drunk to stop him, and not figuring it out, what's going on. It's like my mother undressing me when I was a kid."

He paused again before continuing. "So then he pulled my pants off and I'm sitting there in nothing but my Jockeys, and he started to take them off, too, and I'm drunk as hell, I've never in my life been that drunk, but I knew what was going on. I grabbed his hand and pulled it off my shorts and told him he didn't need to do that, that was enough help. He stopped for a minute, and I'm thinking—don't forget, I'm bombed out of my gourd, I can't think for shit—that it's cool, he's going to leave. And then he leaned down, and he pulled them down to my knees, and he grabbed my cock, and he said, 'It's beautiful. I knew it would be.' Like he was talking about the *Mona Lisa* or something."

He ran his fingers through his hair, a nervous gesture. "I didn't know whether to shit or go blind. You know what I was thinking, in my totally inebriated state? That I didn't want to hurt his feelings. He was my friend, and I liked him. I knew he was gay, but he'd never made a move on me. But here I was, drunk, naked, and he couldn't resist the temptation."

Steven stopped again to drink more water. "I've never told anyone this," he said to Luke. "Not a soul."

"I'm your lawyer," Luke assured him. "Anything we talk about is privileged."

Steven breathed a sigh of relief. "That's good to know." He put his glass down.

"I knew what he was going to do—go down on me. One part of me thought, why not let him? It wouldn't mean anything, and he'd be happy. I was leaving the next day to go on the trip with Tyler, I didn't ever have to see Levine again. But the other half of me freaked. Getting sucked off by a man? I couldn't deal with it."

"So what did you do?" Luke asked.

"I kicked him in the face. Right in the nose. I broke his nose. The poor bastard started bleeding like a stuck pig. There was blood all over his shirt. He ran into the bathroom to get a towel. I pulled my shorts back up and put on my pants.

"He came back into the room with a towel covering his face. He took it away from his face, which was covered with his blood, and he said, 'I'm sorry. Can you forgive me?'

"We stared at each other for a couple of seconds. Then he turned and ran out. And that was the last time I saw him."

Luke felt as if the air had been sucked out of the kitchen. "You haven't heard from him since?"

"No." Steven looked away, toward the hills outside the window. "I've played sports all my life. The jock world is real harsh on gays—you're a former jock, you know about that. It's like if you're not ranting against homosexuals, your own masculinity gets called into question. You know what I'm talking about—if you really want to insult another athlete, you call him a faggot.

Yet at the same time, there's constant intimacy and nudity in the locker room."

He turned back, looking hard at Luke. "But there's a line, and you never cross it. I've played grab ass in the locker room—every athlete has. But it never, ever becomes sexual. That's one reason it freaked me out. But there was another one, that's even more important, because it was personal. I was a victim. If I had been a little more wasted, or if I wasn't a six-two, hundred-ninety-pound man in great shape, I wouldn't have been able to stop him."

He shuddered, thinking back on it. "And so was he, by the way: a victim. He never would have made that kind of play for me when we were sober; but drunk, he couldn't restrain himself." He shook his head sadly. "The poor bastard. He must have been as freaked the next morning as I was."

Quite a story, Luke thought. Telling it took some heavy cojones. "That's a compassionate way to look at it," he told Steven. "Personally, I'd have a hard time feeling sorry for someone who tried to assault me, no matter what the circumstances."

He gathered up his files. "I guess we can put that issue to bed. I'm glad we got it out in the open. But I'm going to say this again, Steven. If there's anything you haven't told us, don't hold back."

Steven shook his head forcefully. "There isn't."

"Fair enough." Luke put the files back in his briefcase and stood up. "I've wrung you out enough for one session. We'll talk again in a couple of days." He gave Steven a friendly tap on the shoulder. "Hang in there, man."

Steven's response was both blunt and cheerless. "Do I have a choice?"

Sophia disengaged from Jeremy and sat up on his bed. "Let's take a break," she said, fanning herself. "You're getting me awfully hot, Jeremy," she teased him.

"Maybe you should take off your blouse," he suggested, trying to sound cool and casual.

She made a face at him. "You know the rules," she reminded him. "This time, anyway," she added with a broad hint. Even though she wasn't very experienced, she knew enough about boys to know you keep something in reserve until you're sure you're ready to commit. To complicate matters, sooner or later he would know the real reason she had come on to him, and that would kill the romance, unless they were able to work past that. A dubious possibility. More likely, he'd be enraged with her for conning him. Which was why she was silently chastising herself for her lack of honesty.

But it couldn't be helped. She had a mission that was more important than Jeremy Musgrove's feelings. If, in the end, it was a misunderstanding, she would explain why she had done it. Until then, she was going to push this as hard as she could.

"Want something to drink?" he asked her.

"Okay. But no alcohol."

She had driven herself over to his apartment after play practice, and she didn't want to have anything on her breath, in case she got stopped on the way home. She wasn't old enough to drink legally, and she wasn't about to chance losing her license because of a beer or shot of tequila.

She pretended not to notice the erection straining his pants as he got up and went into the kitchen. He returned with a can of Bud Light for himself and a Coke for her. They sat on the bed with their backs to the headboard. She was wearing jeans. He ran his hand along her thigh.

"When is this play of yours?" he asked.

"Weekend after next. There's three performances—Friday and Saturday night, and Sunday afternoon."

"Can I come to one?" He sounded genuinely interested, rather than a canned response that might help him get into her pants.

She turned to him in surprise. "Sure. It's only a high school play, but I'd definitely like you to."

"Which one?"

"Any of them," she answered. "Maybe Saturday. I think that'll be the best. Get rid of opening night jitters."

Kate was coming Friday night. She wasn't ready to have her mother and her new boyfriend (okay, that was a stretch, but he was showing the signs of wanting to spend a lot of time with her) in the same space, especially if she wasn't around to monitor whatever conversations they might have about her. She absolutely didn't want him to know that her mother was a detective on the Maria Estrada murder case. That would freak him out, and would derail her scheme before she could get it rolling down the right track.

"A week from Saturday, then," he acknowledged. "I'll put it on my calendar."

"So how's school?" she asked him, deflecting the conversation back to her agenda. "Getting any better?"

"I'm getting through it," he answered dully. "Some days are better than others."

She leaned on her elbow and stared at him. "I think you're more bummed-out about your roommate bailing on you than you'll admit. I'll bet that's a big reason you're down."

He stared at her. "You're pretty wise for a girl who's still in high school," he said. The tone of his voice made his remark both a compliment and a puzzled observation.

She blushed. "Not very. I just know what it's like to lose a friend unexpectedly."

He nodded. "Yeah, well, you're right. It did bother me. Still does. I wanted a roommate. Now I'm off-campus and I'm living on my own."

"What was his reason?"

"He couldn't get some of the classes he wanted, which meant he wasn't going to be able to graduate on schedule. And there were personal reasons, too."

"Like what?" She kept her tone easy, so he wouldn't realize she was pumping him.

Either he didn't notice her pushiness, or he didn't want to call her on it. Or maybe he had been wanting to vent about this, and he'd finally found a sympathetic ear.

"Some trouble involving a girl." He took a hit off his beer. "I shouldn't talk about that," he said guardedly. "It isn't my business, and I don't know for sure."

"Boys have girl trouble, girls have boy trouble," Sophia agreed. "That's what screws the human race up ninety-nine percent of the time."

"Speaking from experience?" he asked. He was trying to keep it light, but she could hear the anxiety. The unasked questions: is there someone else out there other than me? Am I going to get dumped? Am I going to be hurt?

"Not personally," she answered. "I haven't gotten close enough to a boy yet to feel the pain of unrequited young love. But I'm sure I will someday, and I'm sure it'll hurt. It happens to everyone, doesn't it?"

"I hope not to you," he said sincerely.

You are such a sweet puppy dog, she thought. The perfect starter boyfriend.

She knew she could push him further. He was afraid of saying "no" to her. "So this girl who messed up your roommate's mind," she continued. "What's his name again?" He hadn't told her.

"Peter," he answered. "Peter Baumgartner."

"Peter, right. Was it a girl from school or a girl from home?"

"Neither one," he answered. "He met this girl, nothing much happened, and then things turned to shit."

"She dumped him?"

"She died."

Sophia gave out a low whistle. "What happened to her? Some kind of accident or something?" She hesitated. "Was he with her when . . ."

"She died?" Jeremy shook his head. "No. I don't know what happened to her," he continued. "All I know is she showed up dead, later on." He wrapped his arms around his legs, as if to form a protective shell. "He only met her once, for a couple of hours. I was with him, so I met her, too. It's one of those incredible things you hear about, but you never expect it could happen to you—being around someone who died. Someone young." He turned to her. "Like you."

She involuntarily jerked back from him. "Like me how?"

"She was your age." He paused. "I think she went to your high school."

Sophia inhaled and exhaled slowly. "You're not talking about the girl who was murdered this fall, are you? Maria Estrada was her name."

Jeremy licked his lips nervously. "I didn't know her name. I didn't even know about her dying until weeks later—I don't read the newspaper much or watch the local news. I'm still not completely sure."

"But your roommate must have known about it," Sophia pressed. "If her dying—being killed—caused him to leave school."

Jeremy shook his head obstinately. "It's not like that. It's not that simple," he insisted. "It's like all this shit was coming down on his head, and then this girl he'd met *one time* turns up dead . . ."

"The police say she was murdered," Sophia interrupted.

"Killed, murdered, how do they know?" he countered. "They weren't there, and dead women tell no tales. The point is, he had been with her just before she died. He was afraid of being connected to it."

"Do the police know about this?"

Jeremy shook his head. "No."

"Why not? Didn't you go to them? Did *he* go to them?"

"No," he answered obstinately.

"Why not?" she asked again. "It could be important."

"Or it could get us into a shitload of trouble for nothing. Hell, I'm not positive the girl that was found out on that ranch is the same girl we met. Who my friend met," he quickly readjusted.

"How could you get into trouble?" she pressed. "Do you

know anything about how she died? I mean, was killed?"

"No, I don't. But we were with her . . . he was," he correct-ed himself again. He wiped his face in his hands. "I shouldn't have told you this," he lamented. "I should have kept my mouth shut." He wheeled to face her. "Are you going to tell anyone about what I just told you?"

"Who would I tell?" she parried. Knowing full well who.

"The police. Who else?"

"But you didn't have anything to do with Maria getting killed." She paused. "Did he? I mean, does your roommate know anything about it?"

Jeremy looked away. "No. He doesn't." He looked back at her. "It's irrelevant now, which is why I didn't go to the police when I finally figured out who that girl might be. *Might be*, I want to be clear about that. I don't know for sure."

Yes, you do, she thought. You're perfectly clear about it. As clear as my friend Tina is. Who didn't go to the police, either.

"You should talk to somebody about this," she told him.

"Like who? I shouldn't have even told you. Shit," he groaned.

"I'm not going to tell anyone, if that's what you're worried about," she assured him. Which was a blatant lie, she couldn't wait to tell her mother. "But you could tell a lawyer. Lawyers are sworn to secrecy."

Jeremy stared at the ceiling. "Like I said, it doesn't matter anymore."

"Why doesn't it?"

"Because they found out who killed her," he explained. "Some guy from out of town. He's in jail now. He's going on trial in a few months. So there was no point in my—our—getting involved."

She sat cross-legged on the bed, facing him. "What if the police find out you and your roommate knew Maria?" she asked. "What if they found out you were with her right before she died? That will look like you're hiding something. What are you going to do then?"

He went ashen. "How are they going to know? You're not going to tell them, are you?" He looked like he was about to have a full-blown panic attack.

"No, I'm not going to tell the police. But what if somebody saw Maria and your roommate together?" she threw out, to see how he would react.

He started shaking. She had hit a nerve.

"Peter isn't connected with her being killed," he said stubbornly.

"Are you positive?" she challenged him.

"Yes," he insisted. "He had nothing to do with it. They have her killer, in jail." He got up. "I don't want to talk about this anymore. I've already said more than I should have." His grip was firm on her arm. "You're not going to tell anyone, are you? I can trust you, can't I, Sophia? Please tell me I can trust you."

Sophia looked into his eyes. "Yes, Jeremy. You can trust me to try to do the right thing."

"Mom!" Urgent whispering, even though there was no one else in the house. "Wake up, Mom!"

Kate came awake with a start. What time was it? She looked at the digital clock on the television cable box. 11:40.

"Hi, honey." She shook her head to clear the cobwebs. "I must have fallen asleep a few minutes ago." She distinctly remembered the weather report, which came on halfway through the eleven o'clock local news. Had she seen the sports, too? She didn't remember. "How was your evening?"

Sophia sat down next to her. "Mom, we need to talk."

27

LUKE, KATE, AND Sophia met in Luke's conference room. Sophia had called in sick (Kate did it for her), so she could take the morning off from school. The bombshell she had dropped on her mother last night had to be dealt with immediately. She could return after lunch, so she wouldn't miss play practice.

She recited her story to Luke, leaving out the names.

"Who's the friend who told you she had been with Maria and these boys?" Luke asked her, after she had finished.

"I can't tell you."

"Why not?"

"Because I promised her I wouldn't," Sophia said intransigently. She and Kate had danced around this last night for hours. She had given Tina her word that she wouldn't betray her, and she was going to stick to that, no matter what.

"You know, Sophia, I could subpoena you as a witness and take your testimony that way," Luke said. "Then you'd have to tell us, and at the same time it wouldn't be like you were giving up your friend."

Sophia shook her head doggedly. "I wouldn't do it, even under oath." She turned to Kate. "If you did that to me, I'd move out, Mom. I'd go back up north and live with Aunt Julie."

Her in-your-face statement—indictment—was so harsh, so unexpected, it took Kate's breath away. All these months of bonding, and her daughter would think of something that hurtful? She could feel her heart pounding away, somewhere in the vicinity of her knees.

"You can't," she threw back gamely. "You're still in high school."

"I'm over eighteen," Sophia countered. "I'm legally of age. I can do whatever I want. And live wherever I want."

Luke jumped in. "Ladies. Let's not get crazy, all right? No one's going to force you to do anything, Sophia. It was a suggestion, to help you get around what I know is a sincere moral dilemma for you."

Sophia took a deep breath. "Thank you." She looked at Kate, who was almost white, the color drained from her face. "I'm sorry, Mom. I didn't mean that, you know I didn't. I was just . . ."

"I know," Kate answered. She was sucking wind. For a moment she had actually thought she was going to faint. She looked at Sophia. "It's Tina, isn't it? She's the one who was with Maria and the boys."

Sophia stared at the floor.

Kate answered her own question. "I knew it. Why won't she talk to us?" she asks. "Was she . . ." She hesitated.

"She wasn't in on Maria getting killed, if that's what you're thinking," Sophia told her sharply. "Not a chance."

"Who's Tina?" Luke interjected.

"A friend of Sophia's from high school," Kate explained.

"Why can't she talk to us?" Luke asked Sophia. He glanced at Kate, then added, "Whatever you tell us is in confidence. We won't betray it. That's a promise."

Sophia ground her fists against her temples. "Oh, shit! I'll tell you why," she blurted out. "Because she's in this country illegally! Her whole family is. If she had to go to a trial and testify in public they could get busted and sent back."

"That's the reason, for real?"

Sophia nodded.

"Well, it's understandable," Luke said. "Which is why she didn't go to the police, I assume."

"Yes," Sophia answered. She had betrayed her friend. She felt absolutely miserable.

Kate took Sophia's hand. "Honey. We can figure some way out to help Tina, but she has to talk to us. It's vital."

"You can't talk to Tina, Mom. You can't!" Sophia said fiercely. "Didn't you hear what I've been telling you? I promised her I wouldn't tell anybody, not even you. Now I've broken my promise, but I'm not going to let *you* break it," she added, her voice shaking with moral intensity.

"Okay," Luke said calmly. "We hear you. Let's shelve this for now. What about this boy? What kind of promises did you make him?"

"The same," Sophia answered. She was disconsolate over this. There was nothing worse than betraying a confidence. Now she was betraying two. "That I wouldn't tell anyone." She looked at Luke. "He doesn't know my mom is working on the case. He's going to kill me when he finds out."

"You're using a figure of speech, I hope," he said. He leaned forward. "There's a point where protecting a friend, or keeping your word, runs up against the law, Sophia. Which may have happened in this case. Tina's situation is a gray area, but the boy's . . . what's his name?"

"Jeremy. Musgrove."

"Is clearly beyond any moral protection. He doesn't have Tina's problem with anything illegal, does he?"

Sophia shook her head. "No."

"He knew what had happened, but he didn't go to the police. What reason could he have had?"

"They were afraid of getting involved," Sophia said wearily. The more she thought about Jeremy's reason for not going to the police, the flimsier it sounded.

"The roommate who's gone missing. Do you know his name?" Luke asked.

Sophia nodded. She had committed it to memory. "Peter Baumgartner," she said in a hollow voice.

"He lives in L.A.?"

Another nod.

"You've started this ball rolling, so you're in this now, whether you want to be or not," Luke told her without pulling his punches. "But I don't want to see you get into any trouble because these friends of yours didn't do the right thing. For now, I'll hold off on the girl," he promised her. "If she has to testify at the trial, there's a way to grant her immunity so she won't have to fear that her family will be exposed." He tilted back in his chair, thinking. "Okay," he said, rocking forward again. "We've talked about this enough for now," he told Sophia. "Go back to school."

Sophia looked at Kate. "What about . . . ?"

"Everything you've told us stays in this room," Luke promised her, "until we figure out how to do this without hurting anyone more than we have to. But I want you to remember something, Sophia," he said gravely. "Steven McCoy has been accused of a crime that will send him to jail for the rest of his life if he's convicted. My duty is to defend him the best I can, which I am going to do. I understand your friends' concerns, although I think they're selfish and misguided, particularly this boy's. But for now, we'll keep this to ourselves." He squeezed her shoulder. "This is incredibly helpful. This could turn the tide for us."

"Thank you," she said wearily. "I have play practice after dinner again," she reminded Kate. "Less than a week to go. So it'll be a late night."

Kate stood up and hugged her. "You did the right thing, honey," she assured her daughter.

"I know, Mom," Sophia answered glumly. "But that doesn't make it feel any better."

After Sophia left, Luke and Kate stared at each other across his desk.

"This could be a total snipe hunt," Kate said hopefully. She so didn't want Sophia dragged into this case. "Do you believe his story? The motivation?"

"No," he answered flatly. "It's too glib, too rehearsed." He fiddled with a pencil. "I can understand why they kept this hidden. They thought they would come under suspicion, although they probably have credible alibis, or the boy wouldn't have spilled his guts to Sophia, no matter how besotted he is with her." He baton-twirled the pencil between his fingers. "Legally, of course, they didn't have to come forward, but as good citizens, they should have." He pondered their options for a moment. "No one else knows about this?"

"I can't believe this boy would have told anyone else," Kate assured him. "The boy only told Sophia because he's hung up on her, as you recognized."

She was going to blow her daughter's budding romance out of the water. Every time she thought they were making progress, up sprung another leak in the relationship. She didn't know how many more it could take before it sank. Witness how Sophia had almost come unglued a few minutes ago.

Luke grinned. "She was working her feminine wiles, huh? Did she learn that from you?"

"I wish. I've had more bad experiences with men than good ones. For sure, I haven't controlled the relationships most of the time." She shook her head regretfully. "And I've usually fucked up the good ones."

Luke gave her a funky look, but he didn't comment about how she'd just peeled off a scab. "Let's put these two that we know about on ice. They're not going anywhere. You need to check on the roommate. We have to find out what he was doing the afternoon of the killing." He shook his head in wonder. "Wouldn't it be unbelievable if your daughter wound up breaking this case for us."

28

THE PLAY WAS a roaring success. All the kids were terrific, but Sophia stole the show. Kate was admittedly biased, but anyone could see it. Sophia was a natural on stage; you couldn't take your eyes off her.

There were half a dozen curtain calls. Sophia's was the loudest and most raucous. While the adults were clapping loudly, the students, Sophia's classmates and kids from other classes, were chanting: *Sophia Rocks!*, as if she had scored the winning touchdown in the championship game. Sophia, standing on the stage with the other cast members, their arms around each other, her face shining with sweat, was radiant. Kate had never seen her so happy.

She waited outside the stage door with the rest of the parents, grandparents, brothers, sisters, and friends. Sophia was one of the last to come out. She was surrounded by friends—cast members, kids who had worked backstage, including Tina, other kids from school. Kate, suddenly the pushiest mother in the world, thrust her way through the throng to grab her daughter in a fierce embrace.

"You were so incredible!" She was practically screaming. "You were unbelievable!" She was bouncing up and down on the balls of her feet, she was so excited.

"Mom, calm down," Sophia implored her, glancing at her friends to see if her mother's out-of-control emotionality was rubbing off on her. Nobody seemed to be noticing, or if they did, they didn't think Kate's carrying on was a reason for her to be embarrassed. It's how parents act, they knew; all kids have to suffer through it.

A strange woman, apparently another mother, butted in on them. "You were wonderful," the woman gushed to Sophia. "You stole the show completely."

"Thank you, but I didn't," Sophia demurred. She didn't want to look like she was a prima donna, even if the raving wasn't of her doing. "Everybody was really good," she said, looking over and smiling at the girl who had played Dorothy, who was surrounded by her own entourage.

The woman ignored her. "Are you the mother?" she asked Kate. Before Kate could even nod "yes," let alone voice it, the woman continued, "She could have a career." She reached into her purse for a card, which she thrust into Kate's hand. "Call me," she commanded Kate. "I have a jillion friends in the business. This is a talent that must not go to waste." Turning to Sophia again: "This is the best high school performance I've ever seen. Thank you for such a special evening." She turned and disappeared into the throng.

"Who was *that*?" Kate asked, glancing at the card in her hand.

"Gloria Manning," Sophia answered. "Her daughter is Nicole. She's in tenth grade. She was one of the munchkins."

"Well, she was certainly taken with you," Kate said. "Like everyone else."

"Mom . . ."

Kate read out loud the inscription on the card. "Ivan Reitman Productions." The name jolted her. "*The* Ivan Reitman? *Ghostbusters*?"

"She's his line producer. Half the kids in the play have parents in the business. She says that to everyone, Mom."

In the business. Meaning movies and television; the only business in southern California, even as far from L.A. as Santa Barbara, that didn't have to be identified by what kind of business it was. As if it was the only business in the world that mattered. Which to those in it, it was.

"I'm sure she doesn't say that to everyone," she disagreed. "You don't have to be in the *business* to see how good you were."

Sophia rolled her eyes. "Mom, drop it."

"Okay," Kate said. "Excuse me for being a proud parent." She could feel tears welling in her eyes.

"Oh, Mom." Sophia hugged her. "You're such a softie."

Only about you and your sister, Kate thought. Which I balance out by being too harsh toward the rest of the world.

"Hello, Mrs. Blanchard," came a soft voice from behind her. She turned. "Hello, Tina."

"Did you like the play?" Tina asked shyly. "Sophia was very good, don't you think?"

"Yes, to both questions," Kate answered with a smile. She liked this girl. She hoped she wouldn't have to hurt her.

She could feel Sophia's eyes drilling into her. She turned away from Tina for a moment and looked at her daughter. Their eyes locked—then she gave the most imperceptible of nods. Her secret is safe, she was communicating. At least for now.

A horde of girls converged on Sophia, other kids from the show. They were all wound up. "Are you coming?" one of them cried out.

"Of course," Sophia answered. "We're going to a party at one of the kids' houses, in Montecito," she told Kate. She grinned. "His father's in the business, too."

"Okay." Kate had hoped they could have their own victory party, but that could wait. "We'll celebrate tomorrow night, or Sunday."

"Tomorrow?" Sophia asked. She seemed flustered. "Why are you coming tomorrow night?"

"I'm coming every night," Kate declared. "Tomorrow night and Sunday afternoon."

"But Mom . . ."

"I'm going to bring Luke and Riva Garrison with me tomorrow night," Kate went on, oblivious to her daughter's discomfort. "They'll love it, you know how much they care about you. And

I'm going to call Wanda, see if she can drive down for the Sunday show. She'll be so tickled to see you in this."

Wanda had always been the more celebrated of her girls. She was a star athlete and a standout student, the valedictorian of her high school class, magna cum laude at Stanford. This was a way to balance the scales between them. Wanda would be as proud of Sophia as she was.

"Mom . . ." She pulled Kate off to the side. "I don't want them coming tomorrow night. Or you, either."

Kate was hurt. "Why not?"

Sophia glanced around to see if anyone was eavesdropping on them, especially Tina. But nobody was paying them the least bit of attention, they were all in their own delirious worlds. "Jeremy's coming tomorrow night," she whispered.

"Jeremy? The boy who . . . ?"

Sophia nodded. "He doesn't know what you do. I don't want him to find out like that. He's going to freak out when he does. I need to pick the right time and place, so the whole world won't get splattered when he explodes."

Kate thought about how she should deal with this problem. "We could hang back," she suggested. "He wouldn't have to know we were there."

Sophia shook her head firmly. "No, Mom. Somebody's bound to point you out to him. Please."

Kate gave in. "Okay, I won't come tomorrow night. We'll all come on Sunday. Okay?"

Sophia was relieved. "Okay."

She turned to go. Kate stopped her. "I need to explain something, Sophia." She was deadly serious now. "Luke and I are going to talk to this boy. It's vitally important to us. I'll try my best to protect Tina, but there aren't any guarantees about that, either. But we'll do what we can to shield her, I promise you that."

Sophia stared at her with apprehension. "But Mom . . ."

"Don't forget, the reason you got together with Jeremy in the first place was to find out if he knew about Maria's killing," Kate said, overriding Sophia's objection before she could voice it. "And now you know that he does, from his own mouth. You started this," she again reminded Sophia. "We're incredibly grateful and lucky that you did, but you did, and we can't push the genie back into his bottle. So I'll respect your wishes about tomorrow night, but we are going to talk to him."

She gave Sophia a hug, which Sophia reluctantly endured. "Don't worry about hurting his feelings," she said, the protective mother hen again. "If he had done the right thing in the first place, it wouldn't be an issue. He's the one who has the moral problem, not you."

Sophia nodded. "I know, Mom. But still, I promised." She put on a brave smile. "I'll be okay with it. But don't come tomorrow night."

"I said I wouldn't, and I won't," Kate promised her. "Now go and enjoy your party. We'll have a celebration breakfast instead."

"I have a riding lesson with Juanita tomorrow. I'll be out of the house really early."

"I forgot." In truth, she hadn't forgotten—she didn't know about it. Sophia made her own schedule with Juanita now. "Give her my regards. Invite her to Sunday, too."

Sophia beamed. The better she knew Juanita, the more she liked her. It was like she had inherited a grandmother. She would love for Juanita to see her in the play, and she knew Juanita would love to see her in it.

"I'll do that," she promised.

The stable was dark and cool. It was a relief to be in here, after having been outside in the sun. It was late in autumn now, so the heat wasn't as bad as it had been in the months before, but it still got hot out here in the valley, even in the morning, when they customarily went riding.

Juanita was in the house, making their lunch. She had been thrilled at the invitation to come to the play. She hadn't been to a proper social function in Santa Barbara for over a year. Even though it was only a high school production on a Sunday afternoon, she was going to dress up fancy. Sophia deserved that respect, she'd declared, to Sophia's professed mortification. Although inwardly, she was pleased that Juanita took her seriously.

Sophia brushed and watered the horses and replenished their feed bags. Then she checked to see that the tack was wrapped and hung on the proper hooks. Satisfied that everything was in order, she sat on a low wooden bench and pulled off her riding boots, which she kept here. This was the only place she wore them. If she left them here, there was no chance she'd leave them home, by accident.

"Hello." The voice came from out of the gloom at the back of the stable.

Sophia jumped. She looked behind her. Steven McCoy was standing at the other end. She couldn't see his face because he was in shadow, but she knew he was staring at her. How long had he been there, she wondered? How long had he been watching her? Spying on her.

"Hello," she said back, keeping her voice as neutral as possible. She was still in her socks. She hadn't put her running shoes back on yet.

He walked toward her, emerging into the soft diffused light that leaked through the stable's weather-stressed wooden walls. He was wearing a T-shirt, jeans, and work boots, not cowboy boots. His clothes were stained with grease, dirt, and sweat. He had taken his hat off, and his wet hair was plastered to his head. It was the sexiest look on a man she had ever seen in her life.

"How was your ride?" he asked. His voice was low and easy. There was no menace to it. He stood near her, a disarming smile on his face. Nothing about the way he presented himself was frightening, yet she felt her nerve endings coming on fire.

"Good." Her lips were dry. She licked them. "It was good."

"My grandmother says you're a good rider." He smiled

again, a king of the world smile. "She says you're a natural."

"I'm all right," she demurred. "I've got a lot to learn."

"You're learning from the master. Can you call a woman a master?" he teased her.

"I guess." Her heart rate was starting to go down. He was just a man. Just a beautiful man. He wasn't going to do anything to her, not with Juanita nearby.

He looked down at her feet. "You shouldn't walk around in your socks in here," he advised her. "There's loose nails lying around, from horseshoes and stuff."

"I was about to put my shoes on." She pointed to her New Balance running shoes that were next to the boots.

He looked at her some more, but didn't say anything. Disconcerted, she sat back down and pulled the running shoes on and laced them up. She stood up again.

"I'm going inside," she told him. "Juanita's making lunch for us." She hesitated for a moment. "Are you going to join us?"

He shook his head. "I'm not supposed to be around you. I could get into trouble if they found out I was in here with you, alone."

"They?"

"The detectives who check up on me. I have to report in every day. Sometimes they come out here unannounced, to see if I'm doing what I tell them I'm doing."

"What do you tell them you're doing?" she asked him.

"Keeping my nose clean."

She smiled at him. "It's dirty now. You must have wiped it with your greasy hand." She picked up a towel she had used to dry herself off with after her ride. "I'll get it for you."

Brazenly, she reached up and wiped the grease off his face. They were close to each other now, inches apart. He gently took her wrist in his hand, as one would hold a captured wild bird.

His mouth was hot on hers. He hadn't shaved—she could feel the rough texture of his beard scraping her cheek. He ground his pelvis against her, between her blue-jeaned legs, and she pushed back equally hard. Their hands were on the backs of each other's heads, pulling them closer, mashing their mouths even more tightly together. His tongue was long and hot, like a snake diving into a hole. She felt like biting it, but she restrained herself.

He broke the kiss. They rocked apart, staring into each other's eyes.

"I can't be here," he said. He was breathing as hard as she was. "It's too close to the house. My grandmother will go ballistic if she finds me in here with you."

She nodded. She didn't want him to go. She wanted to kiss him again, and so much more.

"I'll see you the next time you come out," he said. He smiled. "When no one's around to spy on us."

He looked at her a moment longer, then he turned and walked to the rear of the stable and out the same back door that he'd come in earlier.

She wiped her hand across her mouth. She could feel the stubble burn on her cheek and chin. It would get red later, she'd have to put extra makeup on to cover it.

The next time they were together, she would have sex with him. There was no doubt in her mind. She had been waiting for this for a long time, and now the time had come.

Tina's eyes looked like soup dishes in her face, they were so wide and unblinking. She stared at Jeremy, who was hovering at Sophia's side in the center of a knot of kids. They were outside, near the stage door. The performance was over. It had been excellent; not as fabulous as last night's, but still very good.

"We'll do better tomorrow afternoon," Sophia was saying to the boy who played the Scarecrow. "Tonight was like the lull before the storm."

"I wish I had seen last night's," Jeremy whined. He could sense that Sophia's energy wasn't focused on him.

"Tonight's was just fine," she assured him. She was so in control now. She could do anything she wanted with him. Which, on one level, was a cool feeling, this power over a boy, but on another, a more meaningful one, it felt tacky. She didn't want to have control over Jeremy, especially now. Soon enough, she knew, they were going to have their moment of reckoning. It was going to be an ugly scene.

She had made her decision, earlier in the day. She was going to have to let him know what she knew about him, and more importantly, who her mother was. Maybe she would pretend it had been a coincidence, the two of them getting together, that if he hadn't brought Maria Estrada up, she never would have made the connection. But he wasn't stupid. He would see through that. And he'd be hurt.

He should have gone to the police. This conflict wouldn't exist if he and his roommate had done the right thing. That was her mantra, which her mother had drilled into her. If you do the right thing, you'll never have any regrets.

She caught Tina's eyes on them. "Over there," she mouthed, pointing toward the auditorium.

Jeremy, hearing Sophia greet a friend, looked in Tina's direction. For a moment, Tina froze; then she turned away, but she knew that for a few seconds he had caught a glimpse of her. Oh, God, she prayed, don't let him recognize me.

Something clicked in Jeremy's brain. That girl was vaguely familiar, but he couldn't remember from where. Maybe he'd seen her somewhere else. Or, more likely, she looked like someone else. He turned back to Sophia, dismissing Tina.

Tina, sneaking a glance back at Jeremy, almost collapsed in relief—he hadn't recognized her, or he would be showing some emotion about it. Instead, he was standing there, patiently being Sophia's escort, trying to fit in. So she was safe. She hoped.

What was he doing here, especially with Sophia? That was the burning question.

"Not tonight," Sophia said, in answer to a question from one of the cast members if she was going to go to tonight's party. "I'm beat." She took Jeremy's arm. "I'm going to sit this one out. I'll see you guys tomorrow."

He was driving. Kate had dropped her off, because she knew she would go out with Jeremy afterward, and she didn't want to have to deal with her car. As they were walking across the parking lot, she stopped for a moment and rummaged through her purse.

"I forgot something backstage," she told him. "I'll meet you at the car. I'll just be a second."

"I'm parked over there," he said, pointing. "Do you want me to come with you?"

"You don't have to. Wait for me there. I'll just be a second."

She ran across the parking lot and around the side of the dark building. Tina was waiting, huddling against the wall. Sophia charged up to her. "Are you okay?" she asked in concern. "He didn't recognize you, I'm positive."

Tina was shaking. "What are you doing with him?" she demanded.

"He's my date for tonight."

"Your *date?*" Tina was in shock. "Are you crazy?" She looked like she was about to come completely unglued. "When did you start dating him?"

"The night of the party. After I dropped you off, I went back looking for Rory, the boy I'd been with. He had already left, but Jeremy was still there."

"Jeremy?" Tina asked.

"That's his real name. The boy you were with."

"Jeremy." Tina tried the name out on her tongue. She nodded. "He feels like a Jeremy, more than a Billy. But why . . ."

"Did I hook up with him? To try to find out if he knew anything about Maria Estrada's killing, what do you think?"

Tina collapsed against the wall. "You're going to get me into trouble, Sophia," she moaned. "After you promised you wouldn't. You're not a good friend, Sophia. I trusted you, and you backstabbed me."

"No, no, no," Sophia protested furiously. "I didn't! It's the opposite, don't you get it? If I learned about it from him, you wouldn't have to be involved. That's why I did it, so my mother wouldn't have to out you. I did it to protect you, Tina, I swear it!"

Tina shook her head. "I should never have told you anything," she lamented. "I should have kept my stupid mouth shut."

"No," Sophia said. She put her arm around Tina. She could feel Tina trembling. "You did the right thing. Which is what I'm trying to do." She took a step back, so Tina could have some space. "You can't hide from this, Tina. You can't be here in this country but not be here, do you know what I mean? You can't hide in the shadows for the rest of your life. You won't have a life if you do that."

Tina's head bobbed up and down slowly. "I know that," she said. "But what can I do?" she asked disconsolately. "I have to protect my family."

"Your family won't get hurt. My mom will make sure of that. I promise."

Tina looked at her with wan eyes. "I want to believe you, Sophia. But I can't now. Not when you've already broken a promise to me."

Sophia's heart sank. Tina was the one person in the world she didn't want to hurt, because she was the most vulnerable, and because she had put her trust in Sophia. Who had violated it. She had done it for good cause, because she didn't have a choice; so she had thought. But of course, she did have a choice. She could have stayed out of everything. Her mother and Luke Garrison were the ones who should be doing this, not her. She was just a kid in high school.

But if she hadn't gotten involved, Steven McCoy, an innocent man, might go to jail for the rest of his life for a crime he hadn't committed. Which maybe Jeremy's friend Peter had.

This is why life sucks sometimes, she thought. Because no

matter what decision you make, somebody gets fucked over.

"I'll protect you," she promised Tina. "You won't get hurt. I swear it."

They stared at each other, two new friends, so wanting to trust the other, but not able to now. Sophia started to reach out to Tina, who turned and ran away from her, into the shadows.

They went to the cast party after all. Sophia didn't want to be alone with Jeremy, who had been all over her as soon as they got into his car. She had rebuffed him as nicely as she could, claiming post-play fatigue.

It was after one in the morning by the time he brought her home. They parked on the street in front of her house. A light was on in the kitchen, but the rest of the house was dark.

Jeremy looked at it. "This is where you live?" he asked.

She nodded. "Home sweet home."

"It's nice. I like those old Craftsman cottages."

What a charmer, she thought. He'd say anything to try to please her. She yawned, more noticeably than she needed to.

"It's late," she sighed. "I've had a really long day." She smiled at him. "Thanks for coming. I'm really glad you did."

"Me, too."

The moment was awkward. Sophia gathered herself. "I'd better go in," she said. "I'll call you tomorrow, okay?"

She wouldn't, but he'd call her, leave a message, call again, and again and again and again, like the pathetic loser Jon Favreau played in *Swingers*. She didn't know what was harder, being in love or having somebody be in love with you who you didn't want to be in love with. Love hurts: the song clanged in her head.

"Can I come in?" he asked.

Before she could come up with an excuse—"I don't want to wake my mom up" sounded so sixth grade—he said, "I really need to use the bathroom."

"Okay," she acquiesced. "Just be quiet, okay?"

They entered on tiptoe. Sophia shut the door behind them as

quietly as she could. She led him into the kitchen. "There," she said, pointing to a door off the mudroom that led to the backyard.

Jeremy went into the bathroom, closing the door behind him. Sophia took a carton of orange juice out of the refrigerator and poured herself a glass. As she was about to put it back she caught herself, and poured one for him.

The pipes in the old house groaned as he flushed the toilet. Damn it, she thought, that could wake up the dead. She heard the sink running. Then he came out.

She handed him a glass of juice. "Thanks," he said. He swallowed half of it down in one gulp. He looked around the room. "This is real homey. How long have you lived here?"

"Not too long." She didn't want him to know any of the particulars of her life.

He came close to her. "Where can we go?" he asked.

"Nowhere," she said quietly. "The house is too small. You can hear everything."

"We can be quiet."

He took her in his arms and began to kiss her. Her instinct was to resist, but she managed to hold back on her feelings. A few days ago they had been all over each other. To suddenly become an ice maiden would seem suspicious.

They moved like slow dancers across the room, him pushing her, her giving ground, so that he couldn't get as close as he wanted. As they reached the edge of the wall near the stove he reached up and turned off the light. The room was suddenly dark. Low shafts of moonlight came through the windows over the sink.

"Jeremy . . ." She was trying to keep in control, without making any noise that would wake up her mother.

His hands were on her ass, pulling her to him, the fingers reaching between her legs for the crack of her behind. She squirmed away, pushing up against the cabinet that held the dishes and glasses.

"Jeremy," she whimpered again.

His mouth went to her neck, nibbling the nape below her ear.

She squirmed against him, trying to push him away, but he was bigger and stronger. His free hand snaked under her top, reaching for her breast.

What have I gotten myself into, she thought? This is what happens when you cocktease a boy. He takes you seriously.

A light went on in the front hallway. Padded footsteps made their way toward them. Sophia twisted out of Jeremy's grip. She flicked on the light switch. Her mother, in a robe over her nightgown, was standing in the doorway.

"Oh." Kate put her hand to her mouth.

All three of them froze in place for a moment. Jeremy began backing away, tucking his shirttail into his pants.

"Mom, this is . . ."

"I'm sorry," Kate stammered. "I didn't know you were home. I heard a noise and thought . . ." She smiled apologetically. "Good thing I didn't bring my gun with me," she said, trying to make it sound like a joke.

That would have ripped it, Sophia thought. Poor Jeremy would have gone headfirst out the window.

"Mom, this is Jeremy," she said. "I've told you about him." She was sure her lipstick was smeared all over her face. Her mother was going to get the completely wrong impression about their relationship. "Jeremy, this is my mom, Kate Blanchard."

"Hello, Mrs. Blanchard," Jeremy mumbled. He hoped she wasn't noticing his erection. He dropped his arms in front of his pants to try to hide it.

"I didn't mean to butt in on you like this," Kate said.

Sophia was glad her mother had shown up when she did. She didn't know how far Jeremy would have pushed it.

Jeremy looked from daughter to mother. "Do you really keep a gun in your house?" he asked, his voice almost rising an octave. He was starting to freak from the thought that he could have been mistaken for a burglar. Or worse—that this woman would have caught him forcing himself on her daughter, and applied some immediate frontier justice.

"It's locked up," Kate assured him. "I don't believe in guns lying around the house. People can get accidentally killed that way. Or deliberately."

She glanced at Sophia, who knew they were thinking the same thing: Maria Estrada. She had been killed by a gun that had been negligently lying around.

If Jeremy made the connection, he didn't show it. Now that he wasn't in mortal danger, he was starting to calm down. There was something cool about a woman who keeps a gun in her house, he thought. This woman could take care of herself, that was obvious. And so could her daughter. He had known that about Sophia from the first time they had been together. One of the reasons he was so attracted to her. That, and her pretty face and killer body.

"How many guns do you have?" he asked Kate.

"Just one," she answered matter-of-factly. "It's a Sig Sauer P239, 9 mm. I'm a woman, so my hands aren't that big." She held a hand up to show him. "I want a compact weapon, but one that could stop an elephant." She smiled. "Although I'm opposed to hunting, on principle.

Jeremy was agape. "Are you a cop?" he asked, his eyes darting to Sophia. Jesus, what a monumental blunder this would be, the way he had spilled his guts to her about being with that girl who was murdered. What kind of trouble was he in here?

Kate shook her head. "Not anymore. I'm a private investigator now."

He breathed a sigh of relief. "That must be interesting," he managed to say.

"It can be," Kate answered dryly. She sized up the situation. "Why don't you two go into the living room? I'll make some hot chocolate."

Jeremy looked at Sophia. "I should be going," he stammered. "It's pretty late."

Too late for you now, Sophia thought. I tried to keep you away, but your penis was more powerful than your brain.

"No, stay," she said, grabbing his hand. "You need a hot drink to calm you down, after my mother busted us like that." She turned to Kate. "How would you like it if I walked in on you and some guy?" she asked.

I wouldn't bring him into the house with you here, that's for sure, Kate thought. Her daughter still had a lot to learn, but she was a quick study, that was obvious.

"I wouldn't," she said. "I apologize." She smiled at Jeremy. "I won't mistake you for a burglar again," she told him. "Now that I know you."

How weird is this, Jeremy thought? He hadn't sat up with a girl and her mother since high school. Now here he was with Sophia, who the more he learned about her the more complicated she was turning out to be, and her mother, a pistol-packing detective. His family wasn't into guns—he'd never fired one, or even held one. It would be cool to try it. Maybe Sophia's mother would let him shoot hers.

He and Sophia sat on the couch. Kate sat across from them. One leg was casually crossed over the other. Her nightgown under her robe was resting on her knees. He could see some of her thigh showing underneath. Nice legs, he thought. For an older woman she was pretty sexy.

He could feel Sophia's thigh, grazing his. It felt good. He could feel his hard-on coming back again. He shifted slightly, so that he could cover it with his free leg.

"How's the cocoa?" Kate asked.

"Very good," he answered. He blew on it to cool it off, took another sip.

"Ghirardelli chocolate, from San Francisco," Sophia told him. "You can get it at Trader Joe's."

"It's really good." He took another sip. "Thanks."

Kate got up. "I'll be right back," she told them. "Don't go away."

She left the room. Jeremy put an arm around Sophia's shoulder.

"You're cruising for a bruising, dude," she warned him. "She'll be back in a minute."

"I'm not going any farther than this," he told her. "I've figured that one out."

He sipped more hot chocolate, and leaned over to put his cup down on the coffee table. When he looked back up, Kate was standing in front of him. Her gun was in her hand. It was pointed in his direction, but not directly at him.

He recoiled. "Is that thing *loaded*?" he stammered.

"Yes, but the safety's on, so there's no danger," she said. She looked at Sophia, who was staring at her intently. "I thought you'd like to see it." The barrel drifted toward his face again.

"Uh, sure," he stammered. He looked at the weapon in her hand. It wasn't that big, not like the ones in the movies, the kind Clint Eastwood brandished. *You feeling lucky, punk? Go ahead. Make my day.* One of his favorite expressions. Now that there was an actual gun in his face, he wasn't sure how much he truly liked it.

"Mom, put that thing away," Sophia scolded her. "You're scaring the shit out of Jeremy."

"Sorry," Kate said. She laid the automatic on the table between them. "Want to know a secret?"

"What?" Jeremy asked. He was nervous as hell again.

"It isn't loaded. I took the bullets out before I showed it to you. Because accidents can happen."

If he was going to rise to the bait, this would be the time. But no. Not a twinge, no facial tic. He didn't seem to have a clue.

For Sophia's sake, Kate was glad this boy didn't know the specifics of Maria's murder. But she still had to find out what he did know. She looked at Sophia. "Have you told him anything?" she asked.

Sophia shook her head. "No."

Jeremy looked from one to the other. "What is she talking about?" he asked Sophia.

Sophia girded herself. No more screwing around. "What you

told me about you and your roommate being with Maria Estrada, the day she was killed."

Before Jeremy could begin to absorb that shock, Kate threw in the kicker. "I work with Luke Garrison," she told him. "He's Steven McCoy's lawyer. The man who is on trial for murdering Maria."

Jeremy sat on the edge of the couch, his head between his knees. He had been hyperventilating for several minutes. Kate made him blow into a paper bag to get his breathing under control.

He lifted his head and stared balefully at Sophia. "You are a prime bitch," he spat out at her. He didn't care if her mother was right there, with a gun in front of her—he was going to blast Sophia. "Goddamnit," he self-flagellated, "I should have known better."

Kate regarded him coolly. How many times had she seen this happen? In her experience, betrayal, or the perception of it, was the hardest emotion to deal with.

"I'm sorry, Jeremy," Sophia said. "I didn't have a choice."

"Bullshit," he whined. "You set me up, you scheming little cunt."

"No, I didn't," she fought back. "No one forced you to tell me about your being with Maria. You should have used some self-control, Jeremy, instead of crying on my shoulder," she reproached him.

Kate was glad Jeremy was lashing out, rather than cowering into a ball of unreachable fear. She could deal with this attitude. He might not cooperate, but he would hear what she had to say to him.

"You can continue this argument later," she said, breaking into their catfight. "And you can walk out of here right now, Jeremy," she told him. "But . . ." She raised a hand to stop him before he could get up. "You're going to talk to someone about this. If you walk out of here now, I'll call the police the first thing in the morning, and you'll be talking to them. Which can be extremely unpleasant, believe me. If you've never been the focus of a police grilling, it's no fun. It's a lesson most people don't ever want to learn."

Her threat was a shuck—no way was she going to bring the police in on this. That was the last thing she and Luke wanted. But this boy didn't know that. Visions of jailhouse nightmares were exploding in his mind.

"Or you can talk to me," she told him. "Those are your options. You can talk to me now, or the police tomorrow." She sat back. "Your call, Jeremy. Make it right now."

Eyes downcast, Jeremy told his story in a monosyllabic mumble. When he was finished, he collapsed back against the couch.

"That's it?" Kate probed. "Everything?"

Jeremy nodded. "Yes."

"That's important information. Why didn't you go to the police?"

"Because I was afraid to, what do you think? First of all, I didn't even know about it until I saw her picture on TV," he said defensively. "By that time, they'd arrested this guy who did it."

"Allegedly did it," she corrected him sharply.

"Yeah, whatever," he said grudgingly. "And what were we supposed to tell the police, anyway? That we were with this girl and her friend for a couple of hours and then dropped them off and never saw them again? They would've been all over us. We figured they had the man who killed her, so let sleeping dogs lie. It didn't matter after that."

"It mattered enough that your roommate left town," Sophia sharply threw back at him.

"He didn't leave because of that," Jeremy insisted. "One had nothing to do with the other."

"The police would think differently," Kate told him, keeping the pressure on. "Your actions feel suspicious."

"It was a coincidence," he whined.

"Time will tell about that." She thought about the next step.

It was already after two in the morning. "All right, Jeremy. Here's what we'll do. Monday morning, you're going to meet with me and Luke Garrison, Steven McCoy's lawyer. You're going to tell Luke what you've told me. You're going to tell him everything you know about Maria Estrada," she said pointedly. "Everything," she repeated.

He was shaking again. "Am I going to have to go to the police?"

"That'll be up to Luke. He makes those decisions." She stood up. "I'm sorry I had to put you through the grinder, but it couldn't be helped."

"They got the killer," he cried out. "Why do I have to get dragged into this? This could ruin me."

"Maybe not. Luke Garrison will do his best to help you. But you are going to be involved, there's no getting around that." She thought about what else. "Your roommate. He knew about what happened to her, didn't he?"

His head slumped again. "Yes."

"Before or after he dropped out of school."

"I don't remember," Jeremy answered. "That had nothing to do with her," he said stubbornly.

Kate glanced at Sophia. "The other girl you were with. What's her name?"

He shook his head. "I don't remember. Just some nobody Maria grabbed ahold of, so we'd be a foursome."

She's not a nobody, you asshole, Sophia seethed silently. She's got more integrity than you'll ever have.

"Have you ever seen her again?" Kate asked.

He shook his head. "No."

"Would you recognize her if you did?"

Jeremy thought for a moment. "I don't think so. She was Latino. On the thin side. Pretty enough, but nothing special."

Sophia exhaled. She was relieved, but also, she was angry. How could you be so crass, she thought? She was nothing more to you than someone to get high with and try to fuck? She felt like washing her mouth out from having kissed him earlier.

Jeremy crumpled the paper bag into a ball. "Can I go now?" he asked sullenly. "I've answered all your questions."

"Yes, you can go." Kate scribbled on a piece of scratch paper and handed it to him. "Here's Luke Garrison's address. Be there Monday morning at nine. No excuses. Do you understand me?" she asked him piercingly.

He stared at her. "Yes."

"Make sure you do. If this blows up, you'll be the one picking shrapnel out of his butt, not me."

Jeremy was thoroughly beaten. "I'll be there." He got up and turned to Sophia, as if he was going to say something; then he decided he'd said enough for one night. He went out, closing the door behind him. A moment later, they heard his car start up and drive away.

"You scared his titties off, pulling a gun on him like that," Sophia said.

"I wanted to get his undivided attention."

"You sure did that. I was afraid he was going to crap his pants. Do you think he'll keep his mouth shut? He opened his guts to me, and I was a stranger."

"I think I put the fear of God in him sufficiently." Kate fell back in her chair. "This has been grueling. You must be completely wrung out."

"I'm beat," Sophia admitted.

"That was courageous of you, pulling him into this," Kate praised her. "I don't expect you to do my work for me. I don't even like you to. It's too dangerous for someone your age." She smiled. "But I'm glad you did. You've really helped us, honey."

"Thanks, Mom."

Kate stared at Sophia. "I hate to tell you this, Sophia, but sooner or later, Tina is going to have to tell her story in public."

"I know," Sophia said unhappily. "But what will happen to her? To her family?"

"Luke will work something out," Kate said, making a promise she wasn't sure could be kept. "The District Attorney isn't interested in busting undocumented workers, especially with her family's good credentials."

"I hope so," Sophia said dejectedly. This balancing act she was attempting was excruciating. On one side was Tina, who had become her best friend, and who had really put herself out on a limb. On the other side was Steven, an innocent man who was her future lover. She didn't want either of them to be hurt.

"Let's go to bed," Kate said. She pulled a weary Sophia to her feet. "Tomorrow's a busy day. Your last performance. Juanita's going to bust a gut, she'll be so proud of you."

"I wish Steven could come," Sophia said.

Kate gave her a questioning look. Where did that come from? Sympathy for the underdog, or something more? "They're taping the play, aren't they?" she asked.

"Yes."

"You can give him a tape."

"It won't be the same. But that's a good idea. I'll bring him one the next time I go to the ranch."

29

THE CAST SAVED their best performance for last. Juanita, sitting with Kate, Wanda, and the Garrisons in the center of the fourth row, laughed and squealed and applauded at all the right places.

"Isn't she wonderful!" Juanita trilled loudly at intermission. "She steals the show!"

"I agree heartily," Riva Garrison chimed in. They were all her mothers today.

"Shh," Kate hushed them, looking around nervously to see if any other parents of kids in the show were within earshot. "They're all good," she said.

"Of course they are," Juanita said, lowering her voice. "But there is a quantum gap in quality. I've been attending plays and movies for many years, Kate. Longer than you've been born, by a long shot. This girl has the goods! She should think about majoring in acting in college."

God forbid, Kate thought. Her daughters were going to have professional careers. Wanda, of course, was on her way. She was overwhelmed with her first-year med school classes, but she'd still taken the time to drive down from San Francisco this morning to see her baby sister perform.

"Mrs. McCoy's right, Mom," she whispered, leaning over to Kate. "I never knew Sophia had this talent in her. Did you?"

"No," Kate answered. She was in heaven. "No one did, not even her."

"I'm really happy for her. This is her own thing. It has nothing to do with you or me. It's hers alone."

That's so true, Kate knew. Everyone needed something unique to call their own. She still wasn't sure what hers was, and she didn't know if she'd ever find out. But her daughters had special qualities in spades.

This was as good as being a parent gets, she thought rapturously. The years of not being able to be there for her daughters all the time was washing away on the waves of Sophia's performance. Right now, this moment, was why she was alive.

They went for early dinner to Emilio's, on Cabrillo Boulevard at the beach. Juanita insisted on picking up the tab. "My treat!" she cried out, overriding Kate's and Luke's protestations. "I am going to be able to brag that I was there when Sophia's star was born," she sang out gaily.

"Juanita," Sophia protested. She was blushing, but she was glowing inside. "It was only a high school play."

"I don't care. You have it, my dear. It can be a high school play or a fancy Broadway show, if you have it, you have it. Meryl Streep had to start somewhere, too, didn't she?"

"From your mouth to God's ear," Riva kicked in. She tapped her knife on her wine glass. "A toast." Everyone raised their glasses, except Sophia, who was too embarrassed. "To Sophia Blanchard," Riva pledged. "The first of a long line of wonderful performances."

The entire table seconded her proclamation. Kate looked at her daughters, who were sitting side by side. They were smiling at each other, lost in their own special world.

Jeremy was at Luke's office at a quarter to nine Monday morning. Luke listened attentively as he recited what had happened with him, Peter Baumgartner, Maria Estrada, and the unknown girl who had gone with them up to the Riviera the afternoon of the day when Maria disappeared.

"That's it?" Luke asked, when Jeremy finished.

Jeremy nodded. "Yes."

"You didn't leave anything out."

"No, sir."

"Whose car were you driving that day? Yours or Baumgart-ner's?"

"His," Jeremy replied. "Mine's an old piece of crap. He's got the pussy . . ." He stopped and glanced at Kate, who looked at him without raising an eyebrow. "He has a really nice car."

"What kind, and what color?" Luke asked. This was critical, because the police had an eyewitness who had sworn she'd seen Maria get into a dark SUV with a boy who looked like Steven McCoy. Steven, of course, drove a dark SUV.

"A 328 Beemer convertible. It's silver."

Can't win 'em all, Luke thought philosophically. He looked over at Kate, who gave him a disappointed head-shake.

"After the two girls went their separate ways, what did you and Peter do?" he asked Jeremy.

"Went back to our apartment. We were in the middle of mov-ing in."

"So the two of you were together for the rest of the after-noon."

"Most of it."

Kate almost came out of her chair as Luke said, "*Most* of it? When weren't you?"

"After we got back to the apartment, Peter drove to Robinsons to buy sheets and towels, that kind of stuff. I stayed behind to put up shelves and finish putting away my clothes."

Luke exchanged a fraught glance with Kate. "How long was Peter gone?"

Jeremy shrugged. "Couple of hours. I wasn't paying atten-tion."

"And he definitely went to Robinsons."

"Uh huh."

"You're positive. Couldn't it have been Macy's?"

The distinction was vital. Robinsons was in the La Cumbre

Mall, on upper State Street. Macy's, the other large department store that sold those items, was downtown, in Paseo Nuevo, where they had dropped the girls off, and where Maria had been spotted later on, at the earring store. The two malls were more than five miles from each other.

"How do you know?" Luke pressed. "Because Peter told you Robinsons is where he went?"

Jeremy shook his head. "He showed me the receipts. So I could see how much I owed him for my share."

One step forward, two steps back. First the car, now this. Luke thought for a moment. "Okay," he told Jeremy. "Here's what we're going to do."

Luke escorted Jeremy to the door. "Are you comfortable with the way I proposed handling this?"

"Yes," Jeremy answered gratefully. "I really appreciate this, sir."

"Well, let's hope we don't run into any snags. Any more snags," Luke cautioned him. "You have to do your part, too."

"I know. I will."

"All right, then. We'll be in touch."

Jeremy walked through the reception area and went outside. Luke looked after him, shaking his head. He turned back to Kate. "This muddies the waters, which is good for us," he said, half-thinking out loud. "But let's be realistic, it doesn't change the basic facts on the ground."

"No," she agreed. She gathered up her purse. "What now?"

"We need to get the lowdown on the girl who saw Maria get into an SUV like Steven's. That, the gun, and the gate is their trifecta, so if we can blow a hole in that one, we have more credibility on the other two. If she's a flake or can be discredited, it'll be an uptick for us. Start checking on her. But before you do you need to go to L.A. and interview this Baumgartner kid."

The story they had put together for Jeremy was that he hadn't known about Maria Estrada's disappearance and subsequent murder until recently, when he had seen an article in the *News-Press* about the upcoming trial, which jogged his memory and prompted him to contact Luke, because the article said that Luke Garrison was the accused man's attorney, and he thought that was the proper way to come forward.

"I'm not worried about this moke," Luke said. "He's sufficiently scared that he's under control. You'll have to make a judgment about Baumgartner, after you talk to him."

"What are we going to do about Sophia's friend?" Kate asked. She was concerned for Tina, more for Sophia's sake than Tina's—Sophia was still guilt-tripping herself over betraying a promise. Although she appreciated her daughter's ethics, Kate had a different take on the situation. Illegally or not, Tina was living in this country. If she wanted the benefits of being a citizen, she had to shoulder the responsibilities. Especially in a situation like this one, where a life was literally at stake.

"She's on ice for now," Luke answered. "If I have to use her as a witness at the trial, we'll work it out. Alex Gordon isn't interested in doing the Immigration Service's laundry for them." He stretched, cracking the vertebrae in his lower back. "When can you go to Los Angeles?"

"As soon as it's convenient for Baumgartner to see me. Tomorrow, if I can."

Luke did a drumroll with the tip of his pencil. "Call me after you interview him. Who knows—maybe we'll get lucky."

Kate nodded. "I hope so. We need it."

Friday afternoon was the earliest Kate could schedule an appointment with Peter Baumgartner, who had agreed to meet with her only after she had said the magic words "or you can talk to the Santa Barbara sheriffs." She inched her way along the ridiculously jammed-up southbound I-405 until she made it over the pass, getting off at Sunset Boulevard and heading east, toward the red-brick towers of UCLA. The traffic was still bumper to bumper, but at least it was moving steadily. After a mile she turned onto Stone

Canyon Road and drove into the rarified environs of Bel-Air.

Most of the houses were set well back from the street, so she only caught glimpses as she drove by them, but she knew what they were like. Montecito, in Santa Barbara, was a similar community. The mere rich need not even daydream—to live here you had to have truly serious money, or else had been lucky enough to have bought in decades earlier, before the great southern California housing boom. All the homes were large and beautiful, exquisitely furnished, surrounded by great expanses of perfectly manicured lawns, most with a guest house and swimming pool. There would be a decent smattering of tennis courts, full indoor gyms, and riding rings—whatever could suit the fancy of people with tons of money.

Following the directions Peter Baumgartner had left on her answering service, Kate turned off onto one of the side streets and followed it until she came to the address she'd jotted down. She stopped outside the stone-columned entrance for a moment. The driveway was paved with Italian stone. On either side of it, the manicured lawn was lush in its greenness, as if it had been spray-painted. Low flowering hedges bordered the driveway on either side.

The entrance road was over a hundred yards long. She drove toward a traditional two-story Spanish-style house. As she approached, she saw two Filipino gardeners kneeling on the turf, fixing a sprinkler head. They didn't look up as she passed by.

Off to one side of the main house was a three-car garage. The doors were shut. She parked near the front in a large cul-de-sac area next to two other cars, a black Mercedes CL500 coupe and an electric-blue Aston Martin DB7 GT. One of her wealthy clients in Santa Barbara owned a similar Aston Martin, a rare and exotic machine, particularly in the U.S., where hardly any were imported. *It was more fun to drive than my Ferrari*, he'd remarked casually, which she had no reason to doubt, having never ridden in either car. Something to aspire to. In another lifetime.

She walked up the stone steps to massive double-doors that were inlaid with intricate carvings that looked like hieroglyphics carved on a Mayan stele. She rang the doorbell, shifting in anticipation from one foot to the other. Knowing she was coming to this highfalutin' neighborhood, she had dressed up for the occasion. She was wearing dark lightweight wool slacks, a bone-colored silk blouse, low-heel open-toed suede pumps, and a featherweight Donna Karan sports coat she'd picked up on sale at the Camarillo outlet mall. With the exception of her Jil Sander cocktail dress, this was the fanciest outfit she could throw together. Earlier in the week she'd had her hair cut, and she'd had her nails done, both manicure and pedicure. This was as girly-girl as she got.

The door was opened by a portly middle-aged Chicana wearing a T-shirt, jeans, and beach thongs. She stared quizzically at Kate through thick glasses. "Can I help you?" Her accent was east L.A., not south of the border.

"I'm here to see Peter Baumgartner. I have an appointment."

The woman frowned. "Peter isn't here."

Don't tell me that, she thought in a burst of anger. "He has to be," she said, forcing herself not to lose her temper in front of this woman, who wasn't at fault. "We made this appointment days ago."

The woman's eyes blinked like an owl in daylight. "Wait here a minute, please." She turned and disappeared into the house.

If you stiffed me I'm going to tear your nuts off, you little son of a bitch, Kate seethed. She had never met Peter, and already she was taking a disliking to him. He was obviously a child of privilege. Growing up in this environment, he undoubtedly thought he could break an appointment any time he felt like it, particularly with some woman private eye he had never met and didn't want to.

She heard footsteps approaching. She braced herself for an argument.

The man's Lacoste tennis shirt was damp with sweat. He was wearing a baggy pair of shorts, and Sebago boat shoes without socks.

"Hello," he said. He smiled and extended his hand. "I'm Warren Baumgartner, Peter's father."

"Kate Blanchard." She took a card out of her wallet and handed it to him. He glanced at it and stuck it in a pocket.

"Come in," he said. "Please."

The ceiling in the entranceway was at least twenty feet high. Shaquille O'Neal could have lived here, she thought, as he closed the door behind her.

"You just drove down from Santa Barbara?" he asked.

"Yes."

"That must've been grueling. Friday afternoons . . ." He stuck out his tongue. "Can I get you something to drink?"

"Well . . . okay. Thanks."

"What would you like? I'm going to have a Sierra Nevada. You'll have to excuse my appearance, I just finished taking a tennis lesson," he explained, pulling his damp shirt from his body.

"A Sierra Nevada sounds good," she told him. She didn't normally drink on the job, but one beer wouldn't impair her. Particularly if the subject of her interview wasn't here to be interviewed.

"Consuela," he called out. "Dos Sierras, por favor." He took Kate's elbow. "Follow me."

He led her through the large living room to a small den that overlooked the spacious backyard. In the distance, she could see the tennis court, and a swimming pool. The room they were in was masculine, but comfortably so. The house was decorated in a contemporary southwestern style that matched the architecture. His wife (and her decorator) has a good eye, she thought, as she perused the furnishings. Good, and expensive. Remarkable how well one could live when money didn't matter.

The woman who had opened the front door came into the room with two frosted mugs filled with foam-topped beer on a silver serving tray. He took them off and handed one to Kate.

"Cheers," he toasted.

They sipped the foam from their mugs. "Thanks," Kate said. "I needed that."

He smiled. "Me, too. Please." He indicted two classic Hermann Miller Eames chairs in front of an antique cherry wood desk. "Have a seat."

She sat down, crossing one leg over the other. As she took another sip of beer she checked him out. Late forties to early fifties, she guessed, in good physical shape. Full head of dark, curly hair, starting to gray at the temples. Deep brown eyes, a dazzling white smile. His complexion was wind-beaten, rugged. A handsome man, a man's man. German going back, she guessed, with a name like Baumgartner. Or maybe Russian-Jewish. This was, after all, west Los Angeles.

"Peter didn't call you?" he asked.

"Yes. We exchanged messages. I'm sure this is the right time."

"I meant today. He didn't call and explain he couldn't be here today?"

She shook her head. "No."

"Jesus," he sighed. "I love my son, but sometimes I want to wring his neck. He's in San Diego," he explained. "He's a production assistant on one of our shows that's shooting on location down there. They were supposed to wrap last night and he was driving up this morning, but they went over, so they won't finish shooting until tonight. He'll be back tomorrow morning. I really apologize," he said. "He's very busy, but that's no excuse."

Well, it is, sort of, she thought sourly. Peter Baumgartner had been thoughtless by not calling her, but as least he hadn't deliberately bagged their meeting.

Now what? Go home and come back tomorrow? The idea of fighting Friday afternoon traffic gave her a stomachache, but staying overnight in Los Angeles by herself wasn't an attractive option, either.

"Are you in the movie business?" she asked her host, while

she was deciding which of the lesser evils to choose.

"Television."

The name Warren Baumgartner had been a burr in the back of her brain. Now it clicked. Even a television Neanderthal like her watched E and MTV once in a blue moon. You had to if you were the mother of a teenage daughter, for self-preservation, so you wouldn't be considered a hopeless relic. Along with Dick Wolf, Steven Bochco, Aaron Spelling, and a few others, Warren Baumgartner was one of the most successful producers in dramatic television. She didn't know how many series he had on the air right now, but she guessed there were several.

First Ivan Reitman's line producer, now Warren Baumgartner. Maybe she could get a plug in for Sophia, she thought with a mother's laser-sharp focus. But no, that wouldn't do. She was here on business. Potentially serious business.

"I'm sorry," she apologized. "I should have recognized who you were. Warren Baumgartner. Of course. I've watched your shows for years. They're great." Don't ask me to name any of them, she prayed.

He smiled disarmingly. "That's very nice of you to say. Living in Santa Barbara, you must know people in the business. It's practically Malibu north there now. I'm thinking of getting a place for myself, on Padaro Lane. Something small, for the weekends."

Padaro Lane was Santa Barbara's premier oceanfront community. A small place would go for at least seven or eight million dollars. Or more, the way beach real estate was skyrocketing. This man had thrown that nugget out as casually as if he'd suggested they go to In-N-Out for burgers.

"That would be nice," she said politely. "The beach is great. Isolated." That's what multimillionaires like him wanted more than anything. Privacy.

"Yes, I know. I've stayed with friends." He drained his beer and put the empty mug on a coaster. "Would you mind telling me what this is about?" he asked. "This interview you're going to have with my son."

"I'm sorry, but I can't."

He gave her a perplexed look. "Why not?"

"Because it would be unprofessional."

"Why? Is Peter is some kind of trouble?"

"Not that I know of," she answered carefully. Technically, that was true. For now, Peter Baumgartner was someone who might be helpful to her and Luke. She would reserve judgment about his status until after she had talked to him.

"Does it have to do with a case you're working on for a client?" he asked. "Can you tell me that much?"

"Yes, I can. It does."

"What's the nature of it? Is it a crime?"

"I'm sorry," she answered apologetically. "I would like to tell you more, but that has to be for your son to decide. Please don't jump to any conclusions," she added. "I'm here on a fact-finding mission, nothing more." On his unhappy look, she continued, "I understand your concern as a father, but he's an adult, so this has to be strictly between the two of us, only. If he wants to talk to you about it, that's up to him. But there are legal and ethical procedures I have to adhere to."

"I guess I'll have to wait until tomorrow, then." He sounded put-off and a bit defensive.

"I'm afraid so."

"But he's not in any trouble. Personally," he asked again.

She put her half-finished beer down next to his. "I'm sorry, Mr. Baumgartner. I can't say anything more about it." She picked up her purse. "I'll come back tomorrow morning. When you see your son, tell him I'll be here at ten."

She would fight the traffic and go home, then come back tomorrow. She could take Pacific Coast Highway; it would still be crowded, but at least it would be scenic. She'd wasted half a day on this bullshit. It had happened before, and would again. You have to roll with the punches.

"If that isn't convenient," she added pointedly, "I'd appreciate a call in advance. I don't want to drive down here again for nothing." She stood up. "Thanks for the beer. I can see myself out."

He jumped to his feet. "Please. I apologize for my pushiness. This isn't your fault." He smiled disarmingly. "I'd like to provide accommodations for you for tonight. You don't want to drive back to Santa Barbara and then back down here and back again. My tab, of course."

"Thank you, but that's not necessary."

"It's the least I can do," he said. "Please."

For a moment, she wavered. Then she thought, why the hell not? She didn't relish the extra round trip, and his son had stiffed her. He certainly could afford a hotel room for a night.

"Okay," she told him. "I'll take you up on that offer."

He smiled again. "Good." He glanced at his watch. A Rolex, she noted; what else? "Do you have dinner plans?" he asked, after a check of her left hand to see that she wasn't wearing a wedding ring.

Of course she didn't. Her plan had been to interview Peter Baumgartner, talk to this man and Peter's mother if it could be arranged, and go home.

"No," she answered, "since I wasn't expecting on staying overnight. But I don't want to intrude on yours. I'm sure you and your wife have already made your own." Some party, undoubtedly, with Jack Nicholson and Tom Cruise. Maybe Susan Sarandon and Tim Robbins, if they were in town.

He continued to smile. "Nope, no plans. I thought I'd be having dinner with my son. And I won't be having dinner with my wife. We're divorced."

"I'm sorry," she muttered, pro forma.

He waved off her apology, his smile temporarily fading. "It's ancient history." He brightened again. "I'll call the Hotel Bel-Air, it's practically down the block. They can usually come up with a suite for me, even on short notice."

A suite at the Bel-Air, she thought. What a treat that would be!

"We'll figure it out over dinner," he told her. "Any particular kind of food you prefer?"

Wow, this was fast. "I'm easy."

"California cuisine? Do you like Michael's?"

"I've never been there."

"That's right, you live in Santa Barbara. It's an oldie, but a goodie. One of my favorites. They have a great California wine list."

This had been fast. "I have to call my daughter," she told him. "She's expecting me home tonight."

"How old is she?" he inquired politely.

"Eighteen. She's a senior in high school. She's fine being on her own overnight, but I need to touch base."

"Don't worry, Mom," Sophia told Kate over the phone. "Of course I'll be okay." She listened for a minute. "I don't know. Hang out with friends. Maybe have a dozen kids over here and get stoned and drunk." She scrunched up her face. "I'm kidding, Mom. I don't even have a dozen friends. Tina and a couple of other girls, at the most. Pizza and videos, really wild stuff." She listened again. "I'm riding with Mrs. McCoy in the morning, so I may not be here when you get home. I'll see you tomorrow night, Mom. Have fun."

She hung up. Tina and pizza. What could be more boring? She had a much better way to spend the night. She picked the phone up again and dialed.

"Mrs. McCoy? It's Sophia Blanchard. My mom's out of town tonight, and since you like to ride early in the morning, I thought maybe I could spend the night there, if you have room for me." She listened for a moment. "I can have dinner with you, sure. I'll be there in a couple of hours, is that okay?" A smile spread across her face. "I'll see you. Thanks."

She showered, washed and conditioned her hair, carefully applied her makeup. She brushed her hair until it was gleaming, and took extra care to choose the right clothes. Casual, but a little sexier than usual. She packed an overnight bag with a nightgown, tomorrow's riding clothes, deodorant, toothbrush, and hairbrush.

Standing in front of the full-length mirror in her mother's bedroom, she checked herself out. She looked good, if she did say so herself. Still young, but in all the important ways, a woman. A woman whose time had come to be with a man.

Kate floated through dinner, happy to let Warren orchestrate everything. Talk between them was easy. He told her about the trials and tribulations of his business and about vacations he'd taken—he was an avid sailor, he kept a fifty-nine-foot Hinckley sloop in the British Virgin Islands. She opened up more than she normally did, particularly on a first date (was this a real date, she wondered, or was he making the best of an unfortunate situation), telling him about her work, her past as a police officer with the Oakland PD, about her daughters and their successes. He listened attentively, and seemed to be genuinely interested in what she was telling him. She forgot about how they had gotten together, and relaxed.

The meal was a progression of delightful pleasures, with terrific wines to match. Kate knew her way around a wine list—Cecil, her last serious boyfriend, was a winemaker, so she'd had exposure to good wine—but still, she was knocked out by what they drank: Kistler chardonnay with their first courses, a Harlan Estate cabernet with the entrees, and to cap the evening off, a glass of Graham's Vintage Port with their cappuccinos and dessert. She managed to steal a glimpse of the bill when the check arrived. The wine tab alone was over four hundred dollars.

Warren signed the check without checking the total. "I have a house account," he explained casually.

They rode back to Bel-Air in his Aston Martin. Kate was tipsy. She wasn't drunk by any means, but she wasn't feeling any pain, either. She looked at her watch. It was after eleven. They had been at dinner for over three hours. When midnight comes is

my coach going to turn into a pumpkin? Am I going to wake up
from a beautiful dream?

Be in the moment, she reminded herself. She stretched back
deeper in the seat and watched the night fly by.

Sophia sat across the small dining table from Steven, with Juanita
between them on her left. Now that Steven was a local hero,
Juanita felt comfortable relaxing the rules about having contact
with Sophia; she would be a vigilant chaperone. She was certain
that Kate would feel the same.

She had prepared a simple but delicious meal—buttermilk
fried chicken, mashed potatoes, green beans, homemade biscuits,
and salad. They all drank iced tea. Dessert was apple cobbler
with ice cream.

Steven pushed away from the table. "*No mas.*" He had eaten
twice as much as either of the women. "If I didn't work like a
fieldhand every day, I'd be a blimp," he said, grinning at Sophia.
"As usual, perfect," he complimented his grandmother.

"Thank you, Steven," Juanita answered serenely. As he started to pick up their plates, she said, "You can have tonight off.
Sophia and I will do the dishes."

"Great!" He grinned at Sophia again. "You should come out
here more often. I'm getting washerwoman's hands from all the
dishes I've been washing."

"Very funny," Juanita scolded him. "You can barely keep
your room clean. What are you going to do now?"

"Watch the Lakers, if they're on." He shook his head in disgust. "They're a farce. Golden State beat them like a redheaded
stepchild last night. Golden State, for Christ's sakes! And with
Shaq leading the way, Miami's wiping up the east."

"Do you know what he's talking about?" Juanita asked
Sophia, in the conspiratorial tone women use with each other
when they're talking about men's foibles. "Sports on television!
What a waste, when there are so many great books to read. We've
become a nation of couch potatoes."

"I like basketball," Sophia said, wanting Steven to know that she was on his side, and that she liked what he liked. "But I love to read," she added quickly. "I always have a book in my face." She got up and started clearing the table.

"Don't worry about rinsing, the dishwasher does it for you," Juanita told her. "Do you want to play Scrabble?"

"Sure," Sophia answered diligently. She knew Juanita loved playing Scrabble.

"It's good for your brain," Juanita wise-counseled her. "Like doing crossword puzzles. There's never been a case of Alzheimer's in our family, and it's because everyone read voraciously, and did the *New York Times* crossword puzzle religiously," she proclaimed.

Sophia glanced over at Steven, who was sprawled out on the couch in front of the television set. A game was on, but she couldn't tell what teams were playing. He was shaking his head and grinning.

She and Steven hadn't had a moment alone together. Juanita had dragooned her into the kitchen as soon as she had arrived, so she could teach Sophia her special recipe for fried chicken. Two elements were critical, she explained carefully. The batter had to be light and fluffy, and the oil had to be hot. Sophia had listened diligently, but it was hard, because Steven kept drifting in and out of the house. Back from working out on the ranch for a late-afternoon snack. Out again to help Keith fix the engine on a tractor. Back in again to wash the grease off his hands and arms. Back out in a pair of shorts and Nike running shoes for his daily run through the hills and valleys of the property. Even now, when the fall weather was getting chilly in the evening, he ran without a shirt. Then back in again after the run, all sweaty now, for a shower. His body was lean, rock-hard. He didn't look like he had an ounce of fat on him. A statue, Sophia thought as she ogled him. A masterpiece of flesh-and-blood art.

Steven turned the TV off with the remote. "How did they do?" Sophia asked, looking up from the Scrabble board. This was their second game. Juanita had won the first, but she was going to win this one. They only had a few tiles left, and all the high numbered ones, like Q and Z, that could turn a game around, had been used.

"They sucked, as usual," he answered.

"Did they lose?"

"No, they won, but they still sucked. I can't wait till I get home and can watch the Suns." He stretched and yawned. "I'm going to turn in." He came over and kissed Juanita on the cheek. "Night, Gram."

"Good night, darling," she said, keeping her eyes on the board, still trying to figure a way to eke out a win. Sophia was a good player, better than most. She had a good head on her shoulders, this one.

Steven smiled at Sophia. "See you." He paused. "In the morning."

"See you," she said back to him. "Thanks for letting me use your room."

"No biggie. The horses will whinny me to sleep."

Steven was sleeping in the stable tonight, in a small room in the back that had a bed, which had been used years ago when the ranch had a full-time stable hand. It was rustic, but comfortable. He was sleeping out there, rather than in the house, because Juanita didn't think it was proper for him to spend the night under the same roof as Sophia. It was intuitive on her part: until Steven's trial was over and he had been cleared, he shouldn't be sleeping in the same space with a young girl like Sophia. She worried about any smell of impropriety. If those noisy detectives found out about it, it could mean trouble for Steven. She couldn't put her finger on "why," precisely. But she trusted her intuition. It had served her well for seventy-six years.

Steven went out. Juanita and Sophia sat up a while longer, drinking herb tea and talking about the play. Then they said good night to each other. Sophia changed into her nightgown, used the bathroom, and went into Steven's room. Juanita had put clean sheets on the bed, which smelled of laundry detergent. She lay on the bed on top of the covers, waiting.

"There wasn't a suite available. I hope this is all right."

They were in her room at the Hotel Bel-Air. It was a large single, with French doors that led to a small outdoor patio. This is the most posh hotel I've ever been in in my life, she thought, and he's apologizing?

"It'll do," she told him. She couldn't keep back her smile. "It's lovely."

"Any toiletries you'll need should be in the bathroom. If not, just call the desk and they'll take care of it. If you need a change of clothes for tomorrow, order from the shop and put it on the room bill."

"Thank you." He was being extremely generous, even though he was probably trying to butter her up because of whatever troubles she might be bearing for his son.

"I'll have you picked up tomorrow morning, a little before ten," he said. He smiled—his teeth were dazzling. "Unless there's a problem, in which case I'll definitely call you."

The evening was over. "Good night, Kate," he said. "Again, I'm sorry about the inconvenience."

"Not me," she replied honestly. "This has been one of the nicest evenings I've spent in God knows how long." A real date with a real man.

"Me, too."

You're laying the charm on too thick, she thought. This man was a Hollywood powerhouse, and he was attractive to boot. He could have any woman he wanted, and probably did. His being free tonight had been an accident. She wasn't going to kid herself about that.

"That's sweet of you to say, but . . ." She let it drift.

"I'm serious," he told her. "I spend all my time with people who do what I do. It's refreshing to be with someone who has a life that's different from mine. Real problems and real people, not made-up ones." He smiled. "I make shows based on people like you. I talk the talk, but you walk the walk. I admire that."

I'll trade you places, she thought. Make me an offer.

She could feel the awkwardness between them. It's always hard to say good night, she thought, especially under circumstances like this.

She took the initiative. "Good night, Warren. Again, thank you for a very special evening."

They looked at each other for a moment. He smiled, and turned to go—then he turned back, and they lunged for each other.

And he's a good kisser, she thought deliriously, as their lips and tongues ate at each other. One of his hands was on the back of her head, cradling her, while the other cupped her ass. She pressed up against him, wanting him to feel her breasts on his chest. Their legs parted so they could push up against each other.

Still locked in their embrace, they stumbled across the room, falling onto the bed. She kicked off her shoes. He kneeled above her, straddling her. He leaned down and unbuttoned her blouse from the bottom, at the same time kissing her stomach, his tongue fishing into the crease of her belly button. Her mind flashed haphazardly on what was going on, like lightning skittering across a dry field. If I had known this was going to happen, she thought, I would have worn sexy underwear.

She arched her back so he could reach behind her and unsnap her bra, which he tossed onto the floor. A hand caressed her nipple. She moaned, a deep animalistic growl. His mouth worked its way down her body to her vagina. She writhed under him as he serviced her, feeling an incredible surge of heat all over her body, splotches of red blooming on her chest and legs.

She came in waves, thrusting herself hard against his mouth. She lay there for a moment to catch her breath. Then she grabbed his erection, pulling her knees up and spreading them to take him. "I'm in the middle of my cycle," she whispered. "You'd better use a condom."

"I don't need one," he whispered back. "I had a vasectomy years ago."

She laid back again and guided him in. They rocked slowly, kissing deeply, her hands roaming his back. His mouth was on her eyes, her neck, her ears, her mouth again. She grabbed his ass and pulled him even tighter, like she wanted to pull him into her, all of him, to live inside her.

The orgasm was even more intense this time, she could feel a river of blood rushing to her head. She was afraid she might faint, she was so dizzy with fucking.

He came in one long thrust, then a bunch of smaller ones. She held onto his ass for dear life, pushing her mouth against his.

They collapsed against each other, breathing hard like marathon runners. His mouth was against her neck. His breath was hot and dry. The quivering slowed, then stopped. They lay motionless, one spent creature.

He propped himself up on an elbow and looked at her, his eyes searching her face. "Are you all right?" he asked her.

Are you insane? "Yes, I'm wonderful." Beyond wonderful.

"I never push this hard the first date. I don't know what came over me." He grinned boyishly. "Besides you, of course."

"Me, neither." Meaning, I'm really not that easy a lay. Would he think she was a tramp in the morning? It was too late to worry about that, and she didn't care anyway.

They stood in the open doorway. "Sleep well," he told her. "I'll see you in the morning." A shadow crossed his face. "I hope things go well with Peter."

"I'm sure they will," she said. What she meant was, she *hoped* they would. She didn't want this to be a one-night stand.

One last, lingering kiss. She watched him go until he was gone around the corner, then she closed the door.

She lay on the bed, idly stroking her body where his hands and mouth had caressed her. That was extraordinary, she thought. It was also the most unprofessional thing she had ever done. She had made love to the father of a man who could be a critical witness for or against her client, who, she had to remind herself yet again, was facing a charge of murder.

It had happened. Fate, something you can't avoid. Or more simply, plain human desire. She hoped when the dust settled this wouldn't blow up in her face.

Sandals in hand, Sophia tiptoed across the floor to Juanita's bedroom. All the lights were out in the house; it was after midnight.

She stood at the door. Under the crack between the door and the floor she could see that the room was dark. It had been over an hour since they had said their good nights. The old lady had to be asleep by now. She put her ear to the door. Nothing.

She went into the kitchen and slipped her shoes on. Being careful not to make any noise, she opened the door, making sure she left the lock off. She waited another moment, to make sure Juanita hadn't heard her. Then she was outside, running to the stable.

Steven was by the stable door, waiting for her. He was wearing Levi's, a T-shirt, and flops. In one hand he held a lit joint; in the other, a can of Coors. She ran up to him.

"I was beginning to worry you weren't coming."

"I wanted to make sure she was asleep." She looked at what he held in his hands. "Should you be doing that?"

"No," he said. "But I'm going batshit here, I've got to do something to relax. I only do it late at night. No one's going to know." His smile was easy and bold. "Unless you bust me."

"I don't care," she said, trying to be casual. This was reckless of him, she thought. What if his grandmother caught him? Or the cops?

"Where do you keep it?" she asked.

"In a safe place. This is a big ranch. Plenty of room to hide almost anything." He held the joint up to her. "Want a hit?"

She hesitated—she was nervous already, she didn't want to fuel her edginess any more than was already happening naturally.

"Come on," he cajoled her, holding out the joint. "It'll loosen you up."

She took it gingerly and sucked in a small amount of smoke. It burned going down her throat. She held her breath for a few seconds, then exhaled with a hack.

"Strong," she wheezed.

"Killer shit," he agreed. "Could paralyze an elephant." He handed her the beer. "This'll help."

She swigged down a mouthful. That was better. "Want some more?" he asked, holding the joint up again.

She shook her head. She was already feeling the effects. "I'm cool."

He took one more hit, then wet his thumb and forefinger and extinguished the joint, putting the roach into the pocket of his jeans. "It's cold out," he said, taking her hand. "Let's go inside."

The little room he was sleeping in was cozy. They sat side by side on the rough blanket on the bed. He reached over and took her hand in his, stroking it gently. His calluses felt like sandpaper on her smooth skin.

She wasn't wearing anything under her nightgown. It slid off over her shoulders. He was out of his T-shirt and jeans. He, too, wasn't wearing anything underneath.

He caressed her body as they kissed. She moved easily to his touch, as if they had been lovers for a long time. "Is this your first time?" he asked her.

She'd thought he might ask that, and she'd debated about lying. She had broken her membrane years ago in gym class, so she could fake it if she wanted to. But she wanted him to know he was the first.

"Yes," she answered.

"I'm honored." He hesitated. "Are you sure you want to do this?"

"Positive."

He picked his jeans up off the floor, reached into a pocket, and pulled out the small package. Deftly, he tore it open and pulled the rubber out. She watched as he unrolled it down the length of his penis.

"You look big," she said. "Are you bigger than average?"

"How would you know?" he teased her. "I thought you were a virgin."

She blushed. "I've seen pictures."

"It's bigger than normal," he confirmed modestly. "It's not that big that it's going to hurt you, if that's what you're worried about."

"I don't care if it does. I'm expecting it to."

She laid down. He hovered above her for a moment. Then he guided himself into her with a long, slow thrust.

It did hurt. She winced. She could feel her muscles tightening, which made it hurt more. Try not to be tense, she told herself. Every woman since Eve has done this.

He was on his elbows, pumping up and down, his eyes open, staring into hers, which stared back. She started to feel better, more relaxed. She put her arms around him and drew him closer to her, feeling his rhythm, starting to move with it. His finger massaged her clitoris. Her body rose up to meet it.

The orgasm was better than when she did it to herself. Stronger, and longer. The muscles of her vagina contracted without any effort from her, it was a force of nature.

He came shortly after she did, a series of strong thrusts. He pushed up on his elbows again and looked at her. "Was it all right?" he asked with concern. "Not too painful?"

"It was fine." She smiled. "Better than fine. Better than I thought it would be."

It had been good, very good. Some of her friends, describing their first times, had said they'd felt unfulfilled, as if there should have been something more. The earth moving, or some other cliché. The earth hadn't moved for her, but she hadn't expected it to. This had been as good as she'd thought it would be. And the next time would be better.

THE DRIVER WAS waiting in the lobby. He was a young man, dressed in a freshly pressed oxford button-down shirt and khakis. "Mrs. Blanchard?" he asked politely.

"It's Ms.," Kate said between clenched teeth.

Her exasperated correction sailed right by him. "I'm Nate," he identified himself cheerfully. "Mr. Baumgartner sent me to bring you to the house. You're all checked out. Do you have any bags?"

"Just this." She handed him a small overnight carry-bag. Earlier that morning she had bought a T-shirt and a pair of knee-length shorts from the hotel shop (she had hand-washed her undergarments in the sink after Warren left), along with this small duffel to stash her dirty clothes. When she tried to pay for the items, the clerk had informed her that all of her expenses had already been covered. Given that carte blanche, she'd been tempted to buy a swimsuit so she could take a dip in the pool, but the least expensive one was over a hundred dollars, and even on a millionaire's money that was too rich for her blood for one half-hour swim.

Her only regret was that there hadn't been someone to share it all with. It would have been blissful to wake up next to Warren Baumgartner, but that was too much to ask for. Maybe, if his son Peter turned out to be clean, they would see each other again. If not, it had been a great one-night stand.

Before she'd left her room to go to the lobby she had phoned Angela Baumgartner to confirm the appointment they had made before she came down. The reception she got from Peter's mother was chilly—Angela had forgotten about the meeting. This would mess up her timetable. Couldn't they do it another time?

What was with this family and their laissez-faire attitude about appointments, Kate had thought with a flash of anger. It was her status, that was obvious. This woman didn't think of her as an equal, not close.

She had almost rudely rebuffed the woman. She wasn't going to make another trip down here to accommodate someone who wasn't thoughtful enough to remember their meeting, particularly since her reason for wanting to cancel was so trivial. After venting for a moment, Angela had agreed to meet her at the Starbucks on San Vicente Boulevard, in Brentwood.

Nate the chauffeur pulled in front of the house. As Kate got out of the car, she spotted a silver BMW convertible parked in the driveway. She was conflicted that Peter was here. She had been half-hoping he wouldn't be, so she could have more time with Warren.

The housekeeper was more cordial when she opened the front door this time. "Mr. Baumgartner is waiting for you on the back patio. Please follow me."

Although she was happy about the prospect of seeing Warren again, she would have to be firm with him about his not being present when she interviewed Peter. Afterwards, they could talk. She knew Warren would have questions for her, but she needed to deal with Peter first.

She followed the housekeeper to the rear of the house, where a covered patio overlooked a large expanse of manicured lawn, beyond which there was a black-bottom lap pool and a large stone-and-tile barbeque area. On the other side of the pool there was a pool house in the same architectural style as the main residence. She knew that the pool house would be fancier than her home. This morning, that didn't bother her.

"Would you like something to eat?" the housekeeper offered as she opened the French doors that led outside. "Coffee or juice?"

"No, thanks," Kate declined. "I had breakfast at the hotel." Room service: Orange juice, yogurt with fruit, English muffin, coffee. Twenty-four dollars. She had signed for it, and had left a generous tip.

To her surprise, it wasn't Warren waiting for her—it was Peter. He was turned three-quarters away from her, looking out over the yard. He was barefoot, wearing shorts and T-shirt. He had a mug of coffee in his hand.

Kate stopped in her tracks. From this angle, Peter Baumgartner could pass for Steven McCoy. Unlike his father, who was dark, almost swarthy, Peter was fair. His hair color was similar to Steven's, as was the length. They were the same approximate height and weight. They shared the same lanky, athletic build.

Peter heard her approaching and turned to meet her. As soon as she looked at him full in the face she could see the lack of similarities. Peter's face was fuller than Steven's, and his features were different—the color of his eyes, the shape of his nose, his jaw. Put the two of them side by side, and no one would mistake one for the other. But from a distance, or from behind, they were a decent match.

"I'm sorry I didn't call yesterday," he said sheepishly. "I was up to my ass in alligators, and I spaced."

"That's all right. I've forgotten appointments, too," she told him graciously. *You don't know how all right it was that you weren't here yesterday. I should be thanking you.*

"My dad said you wanted to meet with me alone," he told her. He pointed in the direction of the pool house. "He's over there, in his office. When you want to talk to him, I'll call him."

She wondered if Warren was spying on them. She would, if it was her daughter who was being questioned by a private investigator. She pointed to a glass table on the patio. "Is this a convenient place?"

He shrugged. "I guess."

They sat across from each other. She sized him up. "You know why I'm here," she said. "You talked to Jeremy, didn't you?"

He nodded.

"Did he tell you what he told the lawyer?"

Peter was obviously uncomfortable. "That we were with that girl who was murdered."

"Maria Estrada. You knew her name, didn't you?"

He squirmed in his chair. "She told me, but I'd forgotten."

"Because you'd given her a phony name, so you assumed she would use one, too?"

He stared at her in surprise. "How did you know that?" He caught himself. "Who says I used a phony name? Was it Jeremy?"

The question hadn't been put to Jeremy. The thought had occurred to Kate later, when she remembered Sophia had mentioned that Tina had told her the boys had used fake names.

"So you did," she confronted him.

Peter hung his head. "Yeah."

"Why?"

He almost laughed in her face. "You think I want some little high school bitch to know my real name? If she had a brain, she'd figure out who my father is. She could have screwed me over good."

"Except she was killed, so she missed out on that chance," Kate replied acidly. She didn't like this boy. That could complicate any relationship that might develop between her and his father, but that couldn't be helped. The job came first.

"I didn't mean it like that," he said defensively. "I mean, any girl."

"I know what you mean." She sat back. "Tell me what happened with you and Maria."

With a few inconsequential differences, Peter's account was the same as Jeremy's. The boys had talked this through, Kate thought as she listened, there was no question about that. She had to remind herself that didn't mean either one of them was lying.

"Did you drink with her?" she asked.

He nodded.

"What?"

"Beer." He hesitated. "And tequila."

"Even though you knew she was underage."

"Yes."

"Did you do any drugs?"

He nodded again. He looked miserable.

"Which ones? Marijuana?"

"Yes."

"Any other drugs?"

He shook his head. "I had a tab of Ecstasy on me, but we didn't do it."

"She didn't want to?"

"We didn't get around to it."

"But she would have? Did you ask her?"

"She was up for anything, basically."

"So you had sex with her."

Peter almost fell out of his chair. "No!" he protested. "Who told you that? Did Jeremy tell you that?"

"Did you or didn't you?" Kate leaned toward him. "Listen to me carefully, Peter. The worst thing you can do is lie. About anything. You're in too much trouble now. And don't forget, Maria wasn't the only girl who was with you boys."

He collapsed like a straw house in a stiff breeze. "That other girl. You talked to her?"

Kate shook her head. "No."

Not a lie. She hadn't talked with Tina about this—yet. But she would. And although it would be frightening for Tina, she would tell the truth. Her reason for not coming clean wasn't the same as this boy's, and Jeremy's. No matter what turned up, she would never be linked to Maria's murder. At this point, who knew about these two, especially Peter?

"Do you remember the other girl?" she asked. "Her name, what she looked like?"

"Not really," he answered. "Your basic Chicano girl. She was there for the ride, so Jeremy wouldn't be a fifth wheel."

What a sad put-down, Kate thought. As Jeremy's had been. Tina the cipher. The fill-in, the kid you picked because the teams had to be equal in size. There was nothing wrong with Tina. She was a presentable, attractive girl. Her problem was that she had no pizzazz, for fear of standing out and calling attention to herself.

Her heart went out to Tina. Not only because no one should go unnoticed, but until recently, her own daughter had been in the same boat.

"Let's get back to what I asked you about. You did or didn't have sex with Maria Estrada."

"I didn't," he answered emphatically.

"Including oral sex, or a hand job."

His eyes popped. "Jesus, lady."

"Come on, Peter," she told him firmly. "Don't go all shy on me. Did she blow you or jerk you off?"

His face clouded. "No. She didn't do anything."

"She wouldn't put out?" Kate pressed him. "That must have ticked you off."

He glared at her. "She couldn't. The other girl freaked out before me and Maria could get it on. She made us take her back to town."

Jeremy had left that detail out. Or maybe he hadn't known. The two couples had been physically separated.

This next part was delicate. "So when you got back to town, why didn't you and Maria take off again, if she was so hot to trot?"

"She didn't want to anymore. The moment had passed." Peter scowled. "Dumb bitch."

His answer both puzzled and offended her. "Why was Maria a dumb bitch? Because she didn't want to go on with you?"

Peter shook his head. "I'm talking about the other one, the timid little mouse. She screwed everything up." For the first time since they began talking he looked her straight in the eyes. "You know what's really fucked about this? If me and Maria had hung together that afternoon, she wouldn't have gone off with whoever killed her. She might still be alive."

Kate and Peter walked across the wide expanse of the backyard to his father's home office. Warren listened intently as Peter told him what had happened between him and the girl who was later found murdered out in the Santa Ynez Valley. The more Peter got into his story the deeper Warren slumped in his chair, his head dropping to his chest.

When Peter was finished, he looked up. "Jesus, Peter," he lamented. "Why the hell didn't you tell me about this?"

Peter looked like he was about to cry. "I was afraid to, Dad."

"Is that why you dropped out of school so abruptly?"

"No!" Peter protested heatedly. "It had nothing to do with that. I swear it!"

Warren was pallid. "What do we do now?" he asked Kate.

"I think you should talk to your lawyer," she suggested.

"We will." He hesitated before asking the next question. "Is Peter under suspicion?"

"I'm not with the police, so that's not up to me to decide," she answered. "If Peter's story holds up, I would say probably not. Legally, he wasn't bound to come forward, although withholding information is never good. It can make someone look like they have something to hide. Again, your lawyer can advise you about that."

She shouldn't have made love to Warren. She shouldn't have gone to dinner with him, or let him pay for her hotel. She had let her emotions supersede her professional ethics. You were stupid, she chastised herself harshly.

Well, she had done it. In the long run, she hoped it wouldn't matter. But she had compromised herself, nonetheless.

She got up. "Thanks for your time. Both of you." She reached into her bag and took out her digital camera. "Do you mind if I take a couple of pictures, for our files?" she asked Peter.

He looked at his father, who nodded grudgingly. "Okay," Warren agreed.

She took a couple of head shots, and one from each side. "One more, from behind," she requested. "Might as well get all the angles."

Peter turned his back to her. She took the picture, and put the camera back into the bag.

"I'm done now."

"I'll see you out," Warren said. "Don't move," he ordered Peter sternly.

Warren escorted her outside. "I'm sorry about this," she told him. She hoped he believed her.

"It's not your fault. Although I do think you weren't entirely straight me with yesterday." He shook his head. "Stupid bastard."

"He was scared." She felt she had to defend Peter, now that she had burned him.

"I'm talking about me, not him. Do you know the line from *Othello*, before he kills himself? *I loved not wisely, but too well.* That's me. I've been overly indulgent toward Peter, especially since I left his mother. I've never made him stand behind his actions, I've always let him off the hook. Like his dropping out of school this quarter. I knew the reasons he gave me were bullshit, but I didn't press him on them. Now he's in real trouble."

She couldn't help herself—she took his hand. He grasped hers firmly. "You can't beat yourself up over being too lenient toward your child, Warren. I do the same with mine. It's better than the opposite."

Because we want them to love us, she thought despairingly. And are so afraid they won't.

"Thank you," he said gratefully. "I needed that."

She opened her car door. "Please keep me abreast of what's going on," he pleaded with her. "I'm scared for Peter."

"Of course I will," she promised him. "And Warren—I didn't deceive you. Not intentionally."

He stared at her. Then he looked toward the house. No one was in sight. He pulled her to him and kissed her on the mouth.

"I hope I see you again," he told her, when they broke. "I hope we'll be able to. Honestly, without any bullshit."

"I do, too," she answered. "I really hope we can."

Angela Baumgartner was already at Starbucks, sitting at an outdoor table. Her tanned legs were crossed, and an expensive-looking sandal dangled off an impatiently wiggling foot. She was easily recognizable to Kate; she looked like her son—the same fair coloring, the same facial features. A tall, athletic-looking woman, she appeared to be in her late forties. To Kate's unsophisticated eye it looked like she'd had some facial work done. If not plastic surgery, at least Botox. She was drinking a cappuccino from a takeout cup. She didn't stand when Kate introduced herself.

"I didn't order you anything, because I didn't know if you'd be on time," she told Kate rudely.

Kate sat down at the wrought-iron table. Five seconds and the woman had already laid down her marker. "I've had my morning fix," she replied easily. Sticks and stones, lady, she thought with delicious upsmanship. I just fucked Warren Baumgartner, and you didn't.

Angela sipped some foam off the top of her cup. "How's my son? Is he in trouble again?"

No beating around the bush with this woman. "Why? Has he been?"

Angela shrugged theatrically. "Not recently, to my knowledge. But since he doesn't live with me and we hardly spend any time together, I don't know what's going on with him. He dropped out of school, so I assumed he was up to no good of some kind."

"He didn't tell you why?"

"No. He doesn't confide in me. He saves that for his father."

Not a lot of love between mother and son, at least from her end. It had to do with the divorce and Warren having custody of Peter, Kate was sure of that. She knew how hurtful it was for a parent to be rejected by a child. Particularly a mother, who had suffered the pain of bringing him into the world.

"So you don't see him that much?" she asked.

The woman shook her head. "We have dinner together once a month. I always have to be the one to call and ask. Beg, practically. Occasionally he'll drop by if he needs money. His father gives him a healthy allowance, but Peter doesn't know from budgeting. He sees something he wants he goes out and gets it, whether he can afford it or not."

Like the high school girl he saw and wanted to have sex with.

"Actually, I'm being a bit dramatic," Angela confessed. "Our relationship has thawed somewhat in the past year. Peter finally realized I wasn't the monster Warren has made me out to be. Our divorce was brutal," she confided, grimacing. "I had to fight tooth and nail for every dime. And Warren still got primary custody of our only child. I finally got tired of fighting his lawyers," she lamented resentfully.

"So he's always lived with his father."

"We shared him for a while, but Peter understandably wanted to be in one place, not shunting back and forth. And once he turned eighteen, he could choose where he wanted to be. He chose Warren. I was left with whatever bones they were willing to throw me."

She has reason to be bitter, Kate thought. Someone always has to lose. "But you're seeing him more now?" she asked.

"Bit by bit," Angela answered. "I did visit him in Santa Barbara a couple of times last spring. It was easier for us to be with each other up there, away from the shadow of his father. Another reason I was sorry he dropped out." She sipped some coffee. "Anyway, that's our personal business, and none of yours. So tell me—why are we here, Ms. Blanchard? Something to do with Peter, obviously."

"I'm investigating a murder that happened in Santa Barbara County earlier this year. The beginning of September."

Angela's eyes widened. "A murder? Are you with the police? I thought you told me you were a private investigator."

"I am. I'm working for the lawyer who's defending the man who has been accused of the murder."

Angela looked at her with suspicion. "Is Peter involved in this? Is that the reason you're here?"

Kate chose her words carefully. "To my knowledge, he isn't involved." Yet, she added silently.

"Then what?"

"We thought he might have seen or known something about the victim that could help our defense."

She wasn't going to tell Angela about Peter's involvement with Maria Estrada. If he wanted to, that would be his choice. She was sure Angela would be on his case about it.

"And did he?"

"It doesn't appear that he was."

"So he's in the clear?" Angela persisted.

The concern was real. You can't fake that, Kate knew. Estranged from her son or not, Angela still had strong maternal feelings for him. It made her, if not likable, at least an object for sympathy.

"I think so," Kate answered. She pushed back from the table. This unfortunate woman didn't know enough about her son's life to be of any help. "I'm sorry to have inconvenienced you. Thanks for your time."

"That's all right," Angela told her, relieved. "You put a scare into me for a moment. I'm parked down the street. I'll walk with you."

The two of them strolled down San Vicente Boulevard toward the ocean. Young families were pushing children in strollers, couples were having a late breakfast or shopping, still others perambulated aimlessly, enjoying the day. All of them were white—not a black or Latino face could be seen. Kate had worked on cases that had sent her to Los Angeles, and she had been surprised at the rigidity and durability of its racial separations.

Angela remote-keyed the doors to a freshly washed Lincoln Navigator that was parked on the street. "I'm sorry for being a bitch earlier," she apologized. "I'm always on the defensive when it comes to Peter."

"Don't worry. I understand." Kate glanced at Angela's truck. "Nice car. Is it new?"

"I got it a year ago. I have a small landscaping business, so I'm always hauling big plants and bags of fertilizer. I wanted something that could take a lot of cargo, but that was still smart-looking." Angela laughed. "It's important to impress the valet parking attendants."

An unexpected sense of humor. She really isn't so bad, Kate thought. "I envy you about the landscaping," she told Angela. "I love to garden, but I have a tiny yard." And no free time.

"It's amazing what you can do in a small space," Angela replied airily. "The next time I come up to Santa Barbara—assuming Peter starts back again next quarter—I'll come by and show you what you could do."

"Well . . . thank you," Kate answered, surprised at the woman's sudden congeniality. She's like me, she realized with a pang. A middle-aged woman who's alone. Money can't buy everything, she thought. Immediately followed by "what will her attitude be if she finds out I'm fucking her former husband?" Probably not sweet.

That was for the future, if there was one, an always unpredictable state of affairs.

Angela checked the time. "I have to run. It was nice meeting you, Kate. I hope the next time we can start out on a better footing."

"Me, too," Kate told her. "Oh, I forgot. One more thing."

Angela turned to her. "Yes?"

"When you were in Santa Barbara, did you ever go to a ranch

in the Santa Ynez Valley called Rancho San Gennaro?"

Angela thought for a moment. "Yes, I did. Why?"

"Just covering all the bases," Kate said, improvised off the top of her head. "A friend of mine owns it."

"Mrs. McCoy?"

"Yes." Her heart was suddenly palpitating like a humming-bird's. "Do you know her? I think she may have dropped your name in conversation."

Angela shook her head. "I only met her once."

"When was that?"

"Last spring. It was a charity benefit, sponsored by the university," Angela explained. "For native plant preservation, one of my pet causes. Mrs. McCoy was a charming hostess."

"Yes, she's great," Kate agreed. "So you drove up there?"

"Yes."

"Did you take Peter with you?" Kate asked, trying not to sound frantic.

"As a matter of fact, I did. He wanted to go about as much as he wanted a root canal, but I insisted. I was only in Santa Barbara overnight, and I wanted to spend as much time with him as I could. Fortunately, once he got there, he liked it. There were other students with their parents, and the old house and grounds are beautiful. That's where the event was held, at Mrs. McCoy's old family estate," she explained. "It's only used for functions such as that one now. I'm sure you know it, if you and Mrs. McCoy are friends."

"I know it well," Kate replied. As if off the top of her head: "When you went there, did you drive by a gate at the entrance to the property?"

Angela thought for a moment. "I don't recall a gate. Is there one?"

"Yes," Kate answered. "They usually keep it locked."

"It wasn't locked when I was there," Angela said with certainty. "They must have opened it so the guests could drive in."

She frowned in thought. "To tell you the truth, I didn't even notice there was one. Why do you ask?"

"Just curious." Kate extended her hand. "Very nice meeting you."

Angela smiled. "Me, too. I'm sorry I couldn't help you out," she said, almost apologetically.

"Don't worry about it," Kate told her. "And you never know," she added cheerfully. "Every bit helps."

Peter Baumgartner's face stared into the camera lens. A mouse click, and there was his left profile. Then his right profile joined it. Finally, the back of his head. The images formed a picket line.

Kate had loaded the pictures from her camera into Luke's PowerBook. They sat side by side at his desk, looking at them intently.

"Damn strong likeness," Luke commented as he stared at the pictures. "If you put the shot of the back of Peter's head next to one of Steven's it would be hard to tell the difference, if you didn't know which was which."

"No shit, Sherlock!" Kate couldn't sit still, she was so antsy with excitement. "When I first saw him from the back, it felt like a ghost coming to life. And then, when I found out from the mother that Peter had been at the ranch, I almost wet myself."

Luke laughed, but his eyes remained riveted to the screen. "Great work, kiddo."

"Thanks." Kate's mind was in overdrive. "Are you going to confront Alex Gordon with this? It puts everything in a whole new light—doesn't it?"

"Yes and no," Luke said cautiously. "Peter Baumgartner's being with Maria Estrada the day she was killed doesn't establish a nexus that he had anything to do with it. We know the girl was loose. Who knows who else she was with that day?"

He turned away from the images on the screen. "I don't buy Alex dismissing from this," he said, thinking out loud, "and short of that, I don't know what practical good it does us to give this to him now." He leaned back, thinking out his options. "I could whistle Dixie in three-quarters time and Alex wouldn't walk from this case on this evidence, he's too invested in it. And it isn't bulletproof, at least not yet."

He straightened up. "First things first. I need to talk to our client."

Steven and Luke sat at Juanita's kitchen table. Juanita had gone to the stable to give them privacy, although Luke knew that as soon as he left she would be all over Steven, wanting the lowdown. There was nothing he could do about that. He would impress on Steven the importance of keeping this confidential, but he didn't know if Steven could keep any secrets from his grandmother.

"Kate Blanchard, my detective, has come up with some new information," he told Steven. "Stuff the police don't know about."

"What kind of information?" Steven asked eagerly. He leaned forward with expectation.

Luke played it cagey. "Some potential witnesses who *might*—let me emphasis *might*—know about other people who were with Maria that day. That could have a bearing on our defense."

"You mean whoever really killed her?" Steven asked eagerly. "Damn! Finally."

"We can't make that direct a connection, not so far," Luke cautioned him, "so don't get your hopes up that high. But it will help us."

Steven beamed. "Great! What do we do about it?"

"That's the million-dollar question," Luke told him. "The D.A. isn't going to dismiss the case against you based on this material. He's in too deep with what he has, and it doesn't absolve you, although it raises substantial doubts." He hesitated. "The question is, do we tell him anything about it, or wait and use it at the trial."

Steven frowned. "You're the lawyer. You tell me."

Luke smiled. "I don't want to show our hole cards until we have to. But I needed to run this by you. At the end of the day, it's your decision."

Steven nodded thoughtfully. "Thank you, but these are your choices to make. I'll go with whatever decision you think is right."

PART IV

31

MARCH ARRIVED, BRINGING monsoon-force rain. It came late—January and February are the normal wet months for Santa Barbara, but they had been dry, so this later-than-usual precipitation was a source for joy and relief: the drought was finally over. But in the areas where the fire had wasted everything in its path, the runoff created massive mud slides that swept down the hillsides, carrying tons of raw dirt into the swollen rivers and onto home sites and roads, creating an equally vicious disaster. Highway 154, the main artery from Santa Barbara into the Santa Ynez Valley, was shut down for over two weeks. Crews from Caltrans, the state highway agency, labored to clear the mud, rocks, and other detritus that buried the narrow two-lane highway for almost ten miles.

The State of California v. *Steven McCoy*, scheduled to begin in the middle of the month, had to be postponed. Steven, Juanita, and the others on the ranch, as well as dozens of families in neighboring areas, were shut off from any access, in or out.

Finally, the highway was opened. Juanita and Steven were able to navigate over the pass into the city. They, along with Steven's parents, would stay at a hotel in town for the duration of the trial.

Luke had alerted the court that Steven would be staying in town, rather than at the ranch. Permission had been granted as long as Steven stayed in the direct custody and control of his grandmother, as his bail stipulation required.

Judge Martindale's courtroom was the largest Superior Court chamber in the courthouse. It was high-ceilinged, over twenty feet tall. Large south-facing windows, now streaked from the rain, took up almost an entire wall, from the low wainscoting to the pressed-tin ceiling. The other three walls were faded adobe in color, bordered by dark wood trim. All the seating fixtures were the same rich, dark wood—judge's bench, witness stand and chair, jury box, prosecution and defendant's table and chairs. Behind the railing that separated the participants from the spectators there were eight rows of benches made of the same wood as in the rest of the room, divided down the middle by a wide aisle. The benches were deep and comfortable, like those in an old-fashioned train station. Spectators had been known to fall asleep during boring parts of trials. As long as they didn't snore, the bailiffs left them alone.

Jury selection had taken three days. There were seven women and five men, two-thirds of whom were middle-aged or older. Eight were white, four were Latino. There were no blacks or Asians—they were such a small segment of the county population that neither ethnic group rarely served.

Alex Gordon stood tall at the podium. He was wearing a dark-blue Hugo Boss suit, a crisp white shirt with French cuffs, a silk tie in a subtle pattern. His hair was freshly cut, and he'd had a manicure.

Behind him, seated at the prosecution table, one crossed leg nervously jiggling up and down, Elise Hobson was wound up tight. Elise always had a queasy stomach at the beginning of a new trial, like an athlete waiting for the starting gun to fire. She snuck a few glances across the aisle to Luke, who was leaning back in his chair, a picture of easy composure. When he felt her energy directed toward him and turned to look at her she twisted away abruptly, not wanting him to see her staring. This was going to be a war. Luke was the enemy. She didn't want him to see or feel any sign of weakness, of uncertainty.

Not that there were any. She felt good about this case. Better than good—terrific. She and Alex had prosecuted dozens of high-level cases, and had won over ninety-five percent of them. They had this one nailed, she was confident of that. This victory would be especially savory, because Luke Garrison was the opposing lawyer. His shadow still hung heavy over her, and on Alex, too. Kicking his ass would go a long way toward casting it off.

Alex began his opening statement to the jury.

"I want to thank you in advance for your time, your energy, your devotion to the belief in one of the most basic rights a citizen has in this country—the right to an open trial by his or her peers. When all the facts and arguments in this trial are over, you are going to deliberate the guilt or innocence of the defendant in this case, Steven McCoy."

He turned and looked at Steven, who returned his gaze without expression. Luke, sitting at Steven's right, kept his eyes on Alex as well. No casting glimpses at the jury box, no looking away. You are not arrogant, but neither are you afraid. You are innocent. You can stare anyone in the face without cringing.

Alex turned away, his attention on the members of the jury again. "And when all the facts and arguments in this case are over, your decision about Steven McCoy's guilt or innocence is going to be an easy one. You are going to find him guilty of murder, in the first degree. You are going to do so not because of any emotional sway I or my colleague, Ms. Hobson, can have over you—we can't. Nor will you be persuaded of any possible innocence on his part due to the oratorical skills of his lawyer, Mr. Garrison. You may be entertained by Mr. Garrison, who has a great courtroom presence. He has been known to charm birds out of trees. You will find him witty, original, and seductive. But he will not be able to convince you that his client, Mr. McCoy, is innocent of the murder of Maria Estrada, for a good and compelling reason—he can't. The overwhelming evidence in this case will override any courtroom magic Mr. Garrison can call up. You will evaluate this evidence, and you will conclude, as the police who painstakingly investigated this case have, and I and my colleagues have, that only one person could have murdered Maria Estrada—Steven McCoy."

He stopped for a moment to look back at Steven, so that the people sitting in the jury box would look at him, also. Then he turned to them again.

"Here is what we are going to prove. That hardly anyone except Steven McCoy even knew about the remote area on the McCoy ranch where Maria Estrada's murdered body was found. We will prove that no one except Steven McCoy had access to that remote area during the time that Maria Estrada disappeared and was killed. That is vitally important, ladies and gentlemen, it is critical. Please understand how critical that is. I mean that literally—no one else could have physically gotten to that area, and we'll prove that to you, with the aid of convincing, credible witnesses. We will also put eyewitnesses before you who will testify to the whereabouts of Maria Estrada on the day she disappeared and was killed, all of whom will link the defendant to her.

"And finally . . ." He paused for a moment, to give the coup de grace its proper weight. "We will present irrefutable evidence, backed up by unimpeachable experts, that the bullet that killed Maria Estrada came from a gun that had Steven McCoy's fingerprints on it." Another pause. "As well as the victim's."

Alex stepped back for a moment. He glanced over at Elise, who gave him a supportive smile.

"Maria's killer's fingerprints are on the murder weapon. That's absolutely unassailable. Now I know that his lawyer will come up with a cockamamie story about how they innocently got there, and aren't connected to Maria Estrada's murder. And I know, when you hear this fable, that you will be astounded that it's the best Mr. Garrison and his client could come up with. And I'll let you judge whether it's an insult to your intelligence."

He leaned forward on the podium, resting on his forearms, as if he was your next-door neighbor leaning on the fence that divides his property from yours, so the two of you can have a friendly Saturday morning chat about the prospects of this year's UCSB basketball team.

"I know Luke Garrison well," Alex continued. "He used to

be my boss. I learned my craft from him, and let me tell you, he was one terrific teacher. He's about as good a lawyer as you can find. If a member of my family or one of my friends got into trouble and needed a great defense lawyer, Luke would be the first one I'd call. But folks . . . no one bats a thousand. Not Barry Bonds, and not Luke Garrison. Even the greatest hitter will sometimes strike out. And that's what my esteemed adversary is going to do here, with that desperate flimflam he's going to try to fake you out with. Because that's all he has—smoke and mirrors. He won't have a real defense for Steven McCoy, because there isn't one."

Alex took a quick sip of water, then pushed forward. "Maria Estrada is dead. She was buried six months ago, the pitiable remains of what was left of her. Nothing that anyone can do will bring her back to life. Her family will grieve for her forever, and there is nothing we can do to ease their pain."

He stopped and looked off past the prosecution table to the spectators who were sitting in the rows on his side of the aisle. Maria's entire family had come for this. They sat mutely, watching and listening, their faces contorted with grief and anger. Mrs. Estrada was sobbing quietly into a handkerchief. Women on either side of her were trying to comfort her, although they, too, had tears in their eyes. Hector Torres, sitting apart from them, was a smoldering force. All his attention was on Steven McCoy's back.

Alex stared at them for a long moment. Then he turned to the jury again. "We must do what the law requires us, *mandates us*, to do. We must convict Maria's murderer and put him in prison for the rest of his life, so that he can't kill again. So that the body of another Maria Estrada will not be found rotting under a merciless sun. So that justice, at last, will be served."

"Good morning," Luke began. He looked at each juror individually for a second, smiling at each one. A friendly smile, meant to put them at ease.

"I liked the way the District Attorney talked to you at the

beginning of his opening," Luke told them. "Reminding you that one of the bedrock tenets in this great and free country of ours is the right to an impartial and fair trial. It's what he said afterwards that made me sit up straighter in my chair. That after you give Steven McCoy his fair and impartial trial you're going to summarily convict him. And that his evidence is foolproof, while anything I say or show you is—how did he put it?—some kind of flimflam. A carny trick. Sleight of hand. Sizzle, but no steak."

He looked over at the prosecution table. Alex turned away reflexively. Elise stared at him fiercely, her eyes locked onto him. He smiled at her. Her face turned dark, an instinctive scowl.

Luke brought his attention back to the jury. "I'm not going to get into specifics with you now," he told them "and I'm not going to make you any promises. I know that Steven McCoy is innocent, and I'm confident that when the steak stops sizzling and the smoke clears, you'll agree with me. Because contrary to what Mr. Gordon told you, his case isn't as strong as he'd like you to believe it is. As you will see, it's all circumstantial. And we will rebut every single piece of evidence the prosecution will throw at you. And we will also show you, with real witnesses and real evidence, that any number of men, known and unknown, could be Maria's real killer."

He left the podium and walked to the jury-box railing. Gripping it lightly with both hands, he looked up and down the double row. "I ask one thing of you," he told the jurors. "Keep an open mind. Examine the evidence carefully, and objectively. And when you have, ladies and gentlemen, I am confident that you will do the right thing. You will find Steven McCoy innocent of the crime for which he's been charged."

An aerial view of the section of the ranch, encompassing the old house and the location where the body had been found, was projected onto a large overhead screen, positioned so that everyone in the courtroom could see it. It covered an area about half a mile square. The house was in the bottom quadrant of the slide. Near the top was the culvert where Keith Morton had stumbled upon Maria's remains.

Keith was on the stand. He was wearing city clothes, but he still looked like a cowboy. Even in the middle of winter, his face was the color of burnt amber. He flexed his large hands as he looked back and forth from the image on the screen to Alex Gordon.

Alex walked Keith through the process of how he had found the body. Keith described his revulsion and horror at what he had seen. He then told of how he had called the police, and waited until they arrived, to show them what he had found. As he was telling this to the jury, other slides were projected onto the screen, closer versions of the initial overlay—the house, and in particular, the area where the body was discovered.

Alex brandished a handful of eight-by-ten photographs. "People's exhibits seven through eighteen. Pictures of what we are seeing up on the screen, with some others showing closer detail," he explained. "Taken by a sheriff's detective at the time the body was seen by the sheriffs who arrived on the scene."

Luke, rising briefly, stipulated that the pictures were acceptable. Alex handed them to the members of the jury, who passed them around to each other. A few turned away in disgust.

Another series of slides came up: the living room of the old house, a full shot made with a wide-angle lens. With Alex's prompting, Keith identified what they were looking at. Next came a picture of the gun case. Then a tighter one, showing where the murder weapon had been found. Then a photo of the revolver itself.

"Detective Perdue pointed that weapon out to you, is that correct?" Alex asked.

"Yes."

"And you knew right away there was something wrong with what you were looking at?"

"Yes, I did."

"Why was that?"

"The pistol was in the wrong place. Someone had moved it. If you knew where the different guns were supposed to be, it was easy to spot."

Alex walked over to the evidence table. He picked up the Colt revolver, which had been tagged. "Is this the gun he showed you?" He handed it to Keith, who turned it over in his hands.

"Yes, it is," Keith answered.

Alex took the gun from Keith and walked it over to Luke, who glanced at it, but didn't touch it.

"No objections," he said mildly.

"People's exhibit J," Alex announced. He walked over to the jury box, held the revolver up so they could all get a good look at it, then placed it back on the evidence table.

He returned to the podium. "Approximately how often do you check the placement of the pistols and rifles in those cases?" he asked. "They are locked, aren't they?"

"Yes, sir. They're locked up. It depends," he said, responding to the first part of Alex's question. "Whenever I'm in the old house, I check to make sure everything's where it's supposed to be. Especially the weapons. About once a month or so."

"So we can say with a strong degree of certainty that the murder weapon had been out of its proper place in the gun cabinet for a month or less."

Luke got to his feet. "Your honor. We can cut through this. We will produce a witness who will testify under oath that she took the gun out earlier on the day that my client arrived at her ranch, which is the same day the victim was last seen."

He wanted to take the jurors' attention off the gun. Guns are powerful tools, not only physically, but symbolically. The more you brandish a gun in peoples' faces, especially one that is connected to a murder, the larger it looms in their consciousness.

Martindale looked at Alex, who nodded reluctantly. "Fine," he said. He turned to the court aide who was running the slide projector. "Next set of slides, please."

The slides that now came up showed the entrance to the

property, from both outside, taken from the road, and inside, shot back toward the road. In both pictures, the gate was closed.

Alex walked over and stood at the side of the screen. Using a pointer, he touched both pictures, first outside the gate, and then inside. Remaining at the screen, he asked Keith, "Is this the entrance to the section of the property where the body, and later the gun, was found?"

Keith nodded. "Yes, it is."

"Is this the only road that leads in and out of that section?"

Another nod. "Yes."

"So this is the only way to drive to that old house."

"Yes."

Alex nodded, as if Keith's reply resolved a particularly important question. "Next slide, please," he requested.

A slide of the gate, taken from outside the property, came up on the screen. "Is this gate normally kept closed and locked?" Alex asked.

"Yes."

"So when the gate is closed, you can't get in."

"Not with a vehicle," Keith answered. "You could get around it on foot, but you couldn't drive in."

"Is the purpose to keep out intruders? Do you have No Trespassing signs posted on the gate?"

"We sure do. And that is the reason, to keep people out."

"Does it work? Does the locked gate keep unwelcome people out? Poachers, hunters, birdwatchers, whoever?"

"Very well," Keith answered. "It's solid. You'd have to be driving a tank to bust through."

"Next slide, please."

A tighter shot came up, featuring the combination lock. Alex touched the lock with his pointer. "Do you know how many people have the combination to this lock?"

"Just me and Mrs. McCoy," Keith answered. "And my wife. Mrs. McCoy would know if anyone else does. You have to ask her."

"But to your knowledge, only you and your wife, who are long-time employees of Rancho San Gennaro, and Mrs. McCoy, the owner, know the combination to that lock."

"To my knowledge, yes. But like I said, you need to check with Mrs. McCoy." He looked out into the audience, past the defense table, to where Juanita was sitting with Steven's parents. "I don't want to say anything I don't know about for sure," he added defensively, feeling her disapprobation. "I work for her. She's the boss."

The screen went blank. The courtroom lights came back up. "Thank you, Mr. Morton," Alex said. As he returned to the prosecution table he looked at Luke and said, "Your witness."

Luke stood up. He glanced down at his notepad, then strolled to the podium. "Good morning, Mr. Morton," he said pleasantly.

Keith greeted him cordially.

Luke turned to the aide who was manning the slide machine. "Would you put up that overview again?" he requested. "The one that shows the house and the ravine where the body was found."

The courtroom lights dimmed as the slide came up again. Luke stared at it for a moment. He crossed the room to the screen and picked up the pointer. "From here to here," he said, touching first the house, then the ravine, "how far would you say it is?"

"About a quarter mile," Keith answered. "Maybe a bit longer."

"Fairly flat, the layout between the two?"

"Pretty flat," Keith agreed. "Slight upgrade."

"Walking it, how long would it take? In dry weather."

"Five or six minutes."

"What if you were carrying something heavy?" Like a body, which he left unspoken.

The jury reacted to that. They sat up straighter, leaning forward.

"Another couple of minutes, I suppose," Keith answered.

"Double? Ten minutes? If it was someone like you, in good condition."

Keith nodded. "I'd think so. Ten, twelve minutes, tops."

Luke turned to the projectionist. "Could you put up the slide of the location where the body was found?" he asked. "One that doesn't have any people in it."

The first slide came off the screen, the requested one came on. Luke turned to the bailiff deputy sheriff. "Would you get me the evidence picture that corresponds to this slide, please?"

The deputy, a solidly built woman whose hair was pulled back in a tight French braid, crossed to the evidence table. She sifted through the photographs until she came up with the right one. Crossing the room, she handed it to Luke, who thanked her. He looked at the picture, at the screen, at the image in his hand again.

"This location where you found the body. It's out in the open, isn't it?"

"Pretty much. It was under some heavy brush."

"But it wasn't buried, was it? It was more like it was just put there. In a hurry."

"Objection!" Alex called out, rising from his seat. "Calls for conjecture."

"Sustained," the judge agreed.

Luke crossed the room to the jury box. He handed the picture to juror number one, who looked at it closely for a moment, then passed it on. While the jurors were examining the photo, one after another, he returned to the podium. "Except that the remains were in a patch of brush, they were visible. Is that right?" he asked. "It didn't look like there was any attempt to bury them, or to hide them, did it?"

"No," Keith answered. "It didn't appear that there was."

Luke looked at the jury, then back to Keith. "Thank you. No further questions."

Marlon Perdue, the forensic detective from the coroner's office, sat comfortably on the stand. This was nothing new to him—he had testified in dozens of trials, including several murder trials.

After establishing Perdue's bona fides, Alex walked him

through the sequence of events from the precise time he arrived at the ranch, supervised the transfer of the remains to the autopsy room at Cottage Hospital, and learned that the victim had been shot. Several slides and photographs clarified his testimony. Then Alex took him back to the day when he returned to the ranch to continue his investigation, noticed that the Colt revolver was out of place in the gun case, discovered that the case was unlocked, discussed with Keith Morton the suspicious nature of that, and took the gun into evidence and delivered it to the testing lab in Goleta. It was a straightforward presentation, unemotional, clinical. A professional doing his job.

When Alex was finished, Luke walked to the podium. "Good morning, Detective Perdue," he greeted Marlon cordially.

"Good morning, counselor," Perdue replied.

"We've known each other for some time, haven't we?"

Perdue nodded and smiled. "Going on two decades."

"You were one of my favorite detectives," Luke told Perdue. "A straight shooter and a total pro. I told you that on more than one occasion, didn't I?" It was a statement, not a question.

"You did," Perdue confirmed. "And I appreciated it."

Alex rose from his chair. "With all due respect to the mutual admiration society these men have for each other, where is this going?" he asked. "What does it have to do with this trial?"

Judge Martindale peered down from the bench to Luke, as if to ask, "What does it?"

"It doesn't," Luke said affably. "I just want everyone to know that I think Detective Perdue is first-rate, and that I have never, or almost never, questioned his veracity."

At the prosecution table, Alex and Elise exchanged a glance. Where is this going, they wondered. Alex thought about getting up again to move this along, but decided to wait it out and see what developed.

Luke turned to the court aide who was manning the slide projector. "Would you put up the slides that show where the remains were discovered," he asked.

The lights dimmed slightly as the slides were projected onto the screen. Luke looked at them for a moment, then turned back to Perdue.

"How many situations such as this one have you been involved in, detective?" he asked. "Finding the remains of a body that turned out to have been deliberately killed, rather than having died by accident."

Perdue thought for a moment. "About a dozen, I'd guess."

"So you're an expert on the subject, as the District Attorney earlier proclaimed."

"I think I know what I'm doing, after all these years," Perdue responded modestly.

Luke turned to the screen. "Take a look at these pictures for a moment, will you? The remains are clearly visible, aren't they."

"Yes, they are."

"There wasn't much attempt to conceal them, was there? The body was just dumped there."

Alex half-rose in his chair, as if to object that this was speculation, but thought better of it—Perdue was his witness. He didn't want to disparage his own witness's credibility. It could undercut the credibility of his other expert witnesses. He eased back into his chair.

"I'd say that's right," Perdue answered. "Whoever tossed it there didn't try to cover it up."

"Somebody carried the body out there from somewhere else, tossed it into the bushes, and took off. Would that be how you'd imagine it happened?"

"Yes."

"When you arrived on the scene . . ." Luke paused. "Let me take a step back. Were you the first officer on the scene?"

Perdue shook his head. "No. Some sheriffs from the local office got there before I did."

"Had they secured the crime scene?"

Perdue frowned. "More or less."

"More or less?" Luke pounced. "What does that mean?"

Before Perdue could answer, he continued, "Was it secured as tightly as you would have liked? As you would have done, if you'd gotten there first?"

Perdue shook his head. "No."

"There had been a fair amount of milling around, wasn't there."

"Yes."

"So you weren't able to check the area for distinctive foot-prints, were you? Because too many people had already tramped around on the ground."

Unhappily, Perdue answered, "That's correct."

"So you were never able to match up any footprints to any of Steven McCoy's shoes. Or anyone else's."

"No," Perdue acknowledged. "We didn't get any."

"Did you get any footprints that led from the house to where the remains were discovered?"

Again, a shake of the head. "No."

"That would have been helpful, wouldn't it?" Luke asked. "If you had found footprints leading from the house to the ravine? If they had matched up with the defendant's that would have been a solid piece of evidence, correct?"

"It would have been, yes," Perdue answered.

"Or conversely, if a different set had been found, it would have been pretty good evidence that someone else carried that body out there."

"That would have been a possibility," Perdue conceded.

Luke leaned back from the podium. "No further questions. At this time."

He walked back to the defense table. As he passed Alex and Elise, he noticed, to his enjoyment, that they were slumped down in their chairs.

"I want to caution you in advance," Alex Gordon warned the jurors. "The pictures I'm about to show you are graphic and hor-rific. I doubt that any of you have ever seen anything this disgusting, but unfortunately you're going to have to now."

Judge Martindale intervened. "I want to throw in my warning, too," he said, looking first at the people sitting in the jury box, then out to the spectators, particularly the members of Maria's family and her supporters. "If you can't handle this, leave now. I won't tolerate any outbursts in this courtroom."

The room went dark as a series of images of Maria Estrada came up, taken first where she was found, out on the ranch, and then at the autopsy room at the hospital. She looked more like a collection of protoplasmic slime that had been thrown into a bag than a human being. Her arms and legs were like cooked strands of spaghetti. You could barely tell there was a face.

There was a moment of hushed silence, a collective gathering of breath: then a wail erupted from the section behind the prosecution table. Maria's mother was shrieking, her body rocking back and forth.

She's never seen these, Luke thought in anger. Alex hadn't shown them to her. He had sacrificed any shred of decency toward this grieving mother to make sure he'd get maximum outrage now.

You want to win this too badly, he thought. There are lines you don't cross. You just crossed one.

He felt Steven slumping next to him. He put a hand on his shoulder. "Hang in," he whispered. "This is as bad as it's going to get."

Throughout the courtroom there was muted sobbing and murmuring, but the only loud noise came from Maria's mother. Judge Martindale tolerated her outburst for a few seconds, then he brought down his gavel.

"I can understand how terrible this must be for you, Mrs. Estrada," he said, addressing her. "But you have to control yourself, or I'm going to be forced to remove you from my courtroom."

The distraught woman either didn't hear him, or was incapable of stopping. Her sobbing became louder, more pitiable. As if to further punctuate the darkness and despair of the moment, a rolling clap of thunder boomed into the room.

Martindale rapped for order. "I'm sorry, but I'm going to have you taken out, Mrs. Estrada," he told her. He signaled to a couple of courtroom deputies who were standing against the wall.

Luke stood up. "Your honor," he called out over the commotion.

Martindale looked at him. "What is it?"

Luke glanced at the prosecution table. Oh, how you're loving this, he thought. "We don't object to this show of emotion," he told the judge. "Any mother would react the same way. If I may suggest a five- or ten-minute recess, so she can regain some composure, I think we could move on. It's her daughter. More than anyone, she deserves to be here."

The mood was muted. The slides were no longer projected onto the screen. Mrs. Estrada was still crying, but quietly, into a handkerchief. Her friends and family hovered around her, forming a protective cocoon.

Alex walked Dr. Atchison through the autopsy process. The condition of the body, how he had quickly found the bullet, the events that transpired after that. When he was finished his questioning he walked back to his seat without looking at Luke.

Luke, sitting at the defense table, leafed through some notes. A feeling of antsiness pervaded the chamber as he paged through them, his face down. "Are you going to cross-examine this witness?" the judge finally asked him.

Luke looked up. "Of course I am, your honor." He found what he was looking for. He approached the podium, carrying a few pages in his hand. "When you examined the victim, did you check to see if she had ingested any drugs prior to her death?" he asked.

"Yes, I did," Atchison answered.

"What did you find?"

"There were traces of Tetrahydrocannabinol in her system."

"Which is commonly known as THC, the active ingredient in marijuana, is that correct?"

"That's right."

"So shortly before she died, Maria Estrada smoked marijuana."

"That would be my conclusion, that's correct," Atchison answered.

"What about semen?" Luke continued. "Did you find any samples of semen in the body?"

Alex stood up quickly. "Objection, your honor," he said forcefully. "The victim's sexual conduct isn't relevant. We are not alleging rape, or any other sexual activity in conjunction with the charges."

Martindale gave Luke a "show-me" look.

"Her sexual conduct is important, for two reasons, your honor," Luke argued. "First, it shows a pattern of promiscuity. An eighteen-year-old girl who had semen DNA in her remains, particularly if there were multiple samples, could be characterized as someone who had easy dalliances with men, any one of whom could be as strong a candidate for having killed her as my client. And second, if none of those samples matched up with his, that would exonerate him as having had sex, and would cast aspersions on whether he was ever with her at all."

Martindale looked at Alex, then back at Luke again. "I assumed this might come in, so I've already thought about it," he said. He looked at the jury. "I'm going to overrule the prosecution's objection and allow this line of questioning."

Alex shook his head angrily. "Exception," he barked.

"Noted," Martindale answered calmly. "You may proceed," he told Luke.

"Thank you." Luke turned to Atchison again. "Did you find semen samples in the victim?" he asked again.

"Yes," Atchison answered.

"How may different strands of DNA did you find, doctor? In

other words, how many different men did Maria Estrada have sexual intercourse with shortly before she was killed."

Atchison glanced at his notes. "I found three distinct samples."

"So she had sex with at least three men shortly before she died," Luke pressed.

"Yes. There could have been more," Atchison amplified. "If she had sexual partners who used a condom, their DNA would not be present."

Luke stepped back for a moment. "You seem to be saying she didn't practice safe sex, is that right?" he asked. "Having sex with multiple partners and not using protection isn't very smart, is it?"

Alex jumped up again. "Objection!" he called out. "Calls for speculation."

"Sustained," Martindale ruled. "Strike the question. Do you want to rephrase?" he asked Luke.

Luke shook his head. "No, that's all right." The jury had heard it—that was all he cared about. "Getting back to the DNA," he said to Atchison. "Where you able to match the DNA you recovered from Maria Estrada to anyone?"

"No," Atchison answered. "We weren't."

"Did you take a DNA sample from Steven McCoy?"

Atchison nodded. "We did that immediately after his arrest."

Luke gathered his notes. "Did his DNA match up with the samples you got from the victim?" he asked.

"No," the doctor answered conclusively. "There was no match."

The other technicians made their brief appearances: the expert who took and matched Steven's fingerprints to the murder weapon, and Dana Wiseman, the bullet expert. They gave their findings crisply, concisely, professionally. Luke's cross-examinations of them were perfunctory—you can't argue hard facts, so you don't. Get the witnesses off the stage as fast as you can. At a quarter to five in the afternoon, Judge Martindale brought the trial to a close for the day.

Overnight, the rain had stopped. The sky was still low and leaden, but for the moment, the city was dry.

The redheaded salesgirl who had sold Maria the earrings fidgeted as she sat on the witness stand. She was overdressed and had too much makeup on; she looked like a runner-up from a television reality show. She described the events as she had told them to Detective Rebeck. She knew Maria Estrada by sight—Maria was a frequent shopper, and sometime shoplifter, from their store. They kept a sharp eye on Maria whenever she came in.

When Alex was finished, Luke got up and took the podium. "How're you doing, Ione?" he asked. Her name was Ione Skye Purcell. Her parents had been Donovan fans, Luke assumed. A piece of particularly obscure trivia from the rock 'n' roll memory shelf of his brain.

"Okay," the girl answered.

"I only have a few questions," he told the girl, giving her a friendly smile to put her at ease. "I know how you can get nervous sitting up there, especially if you never have before."

"No kidding," the girl answered with a shy smile of her own, as if to say, *at least somebody knows what this feels like.*

"When Detective Rebeck first interviewed you, did she ask you if you could identify the man who was with Maria?" he asked her.

"Yes," she recalled.

"And did you tell her you couldn't?"

The girl nodded affirmatively. "Uh huh."

"Why couldn't you?"

"Because I wasn't paying as much attention to him as I was to her."

"Because of her history of theft in the store."

"You got it," the girl answered sprightly.

"Before or after Steven McCoy was arrested, did anyone in law enforcement show you a picture of him and ask if you could identify him as the man who had been in the store with the man they'd arrested."

"Yes, after," the girl said. "The lady cop came in with a picture and asked me if it was the man who was with Maria."

"What did you tell her?"

"That I didn't know. It kind of looked like him, but I wasn't going to swear to it."

"And you still wouldn't?"

She shook her head. "I couldn't."

"Did the police ever ask you to come down to the jail and look at a lineup of possible suspects?"

"No. I was never asked to do anything like that."

"So to this day, you couldn't swear that Steven McCoy was the man who bought Maria Estrada the earrings."

She stared at Steven. He gave her a blank stare. "No," she said steadfastly. She looked at the prosecution table for an instant, then turned back to Luke. "No matter how hard they wanted me to."

Ione the shopgirl had at least tried to come in with what she thought was the proper attire for a murder trial. Katrina, the girl who had seen Maria get into the SUV with a man who resembled Steven McCoy, didn't care about protocol. In the fall, when she had met with Rebeck and Watson, she'd been a typical Jennifer Aniston wannabe. Now she was in full Goth attire and makeup. Black-on-black clothes, featuring lace-up-to-the-knees boots. Black lipstick, black mascara, black and red eye shadow, black eyeliner. Each ear had at least half a dozen piercings, along with her nose (and God knows where else, Kate thought, looking at the girl from her seat behind the defense table). With the darkness around her eyes and mouth, contrasted with the white heat she'd applied to the rest of her face, and her punk-spiked hair, she looked like a raccoon on a drug cocktail. She was, however, alert and coherent in her remembrance of what she had seen, as Elise questioned her about it.

When Elise sat down, Luke took over. He had a sheaf of eight-by-ten glossies in his hand, which he gave to the bailiff to be marked for exhibit. He handed a set to the judge, and put another down on the defense table.

Alex and Elise looked at them for a moment. "What are these?" Alex asked, looking at Judge Martindale, who was leafing through his own set. The judge gave Luke a questioning look.

"They're for the purpose of trying to make an identification," Luke said, somewhat cryptically.

Both Martindale and Alex could see where this was going. "In my chambers," Martindale said, standing up. "Ten-minute recess."

"What the fuck is this?" Alex exploded.

"Exhibits," Luke answered calmly, leaning against the side of the judge's desk. He suppressed the urge to smile.

"Lame look-alikes of your client? Except there aren't any front shots, only sides and backs," he complained. Elise, standing so close to him they were touching at the shoulders, had a scowl plastered on her face. "What kind of game are you running with this, Luke?" Alex asked aggressively. "What is this, judge?" he fumed.

Judge Martindale was the senior judge of the Santa Barbara Superior Court. He had been on the bench for over twenty years. He had known Luke when Luke had the job Alex occupied now, so he was inclined to give Luke more rope than he gave most other lawyers, since Luke usually delivered. Still, he expected a sound answer.

"Some of the most important pieces of this case hinge on identification, your honor," Luke responded. "This is going to be the second witness who will testify that she saw Maria Estrada with a man who looked like Steven McCoy. I don't know how credible this girl is. So I want to test it."

"What do you mean, how credible?" Elise asked. She looked at Alex—what was this all about?

"Listen and learn," Luke threw back at them. "Give me a little space, judge," he implored. "If my line isn't working, you can cut me off, no arguments."

Martindale thought it over for a moment. He looked at the pictures again. "I'm going to let you introduce this," he told Luke, to Alex and Elise's disgust. "But I'd better see a clear path, or I will stop it in its tracks."

"Katrina, how are you?" Luke asked the witness from the podium.

"Okay," she answered. "How about you?"

There were a few titters from the gallery. Luke smiled. "Doing good," he told her. "Thanks for asking." He squared the photographs on the stand. "Do you go to the high school?" he asked. "Santa Barbara High?"

"Uh huh," she confirmed. A feral tongue darted out to lick the dark lips. Luke caught a glimpse of a tongue stud.

"Senior?" he asked. "Close to graduating?"

"Glory be, yes!" she sang out.

"Going to college in the fall?"

She nodded. "Design school, in L.A. I'm into fashion."

"So I see," Luke answered dryly. He looked at a typed page of notes. "You've been at the high school for four years, since ninth grade?"

"Uh huh."

"So you were a classmate of Maria Estrada's for the whole time she was there."

The girl's face darkened. "Yeah, I was, from way back. Before high school. Junior high, too."

Luke glanced at his notes again. "Were you friends?"

She snorted. "Hardly."

"Why was that? Because she was Latina, and you aren't?"

Katrina shook her head heatedly. "No way! I got plenty of friends who're Mexican. I ain't prejudiced, like some of the dorks from Montecito who don't know any Mexicans at all, except for their maids and gardeners. That's bogus, judging people by where they come from, or what they look like," she said righteously.

"Commendable of you," Luke congratulated her. "So what was it about Maria you didn't like?"

The girl fidgeted in the chair. "Lots of stuff."

"Would poaching other girl's boyfriends be one of them?"

She drew back, scrunching down in the chair. "What do you mean?"

He looked at his notes, not that he needed them. "Did you date a boy named Eli Herrera last year? Go steady with him for three or four months?"

Alex Gordon got up. "Your honor, what's the point of this?" He looked at Elise, who was as baffled as he was.

"You'll see in a minute," Luke answered quickly, not waiting for the judge to answer. "Did you?" he pressed Katrina.

"Yeah," she admitted. "So what?"

"He dumped you for Maria Estrada, didn't he?"

She shot daggers at him with her dark-ringed eyes. "We were breaking up anyway."

"Didn't you tell your friends that you were going to get her?"

She was clearly uncomfortable now. "Maybe I did. People say shit like that all the time. It don't mean nothing."

Martindale's gavel came down. "There will be no profanity in this courtroom," he admonished Katrina. "Do you understand?" he asked harshly.

She nodded meekly. "Yes, sir. I'm sorry."

Luke pressed on. "After Maria's death became known, didn't you say to a friend . . ." he looked at Martindale. "Excuse me, your honor. I know you don't like profanity in your courtroom, but I have to get this quote exact."

"Go ahead," Martindale allowed him.

"Didn't you say, 'The cunt deserved it'?"

Katrina was slumping lower and lower in her chair. "I didn't really mean it. I didn't want her to get killed," she whimpered.

Luke paused. "I'm sure you didn't. It was an expression. Because your feelings had been hurt."

She grasped the straw. "Yes."

"But until then, you were angry at her. You wanted to get back at her. You wanted her to look like she was . . . how shall I put it? Loose. A whore, I believe you said about her."

"She was one!" the girl answered darkly.

"If people found out she had just picked up some guy at random and gone off with him, that would make what you said true, wouldn't it?"

She didn't answer.

Alex got up again. "This is pointless," he protested. "I move this entire testimony be stricken, and the jury instructed to ignore it." He turned to Luke. "Give it up. This isn't a fishing expedition."

"I'm getting to my point," Luke insisted. He looked earnestly at Martindale.

"Make it now, or move on," Martindale admonished him.

"That's exactly what I'm going to do, your honor." Luke picked up the photographs and walked them over to Katrina. A court aide carried a cork-backed easel to the witness area and set it up in front of Katrina, while also making it easily visible to the jurors.

"You're sure it was Maria Estrada you saw that day at the mall," he began.

"Absolutely," Katrina responded firmly.

"You were watching her closely, weren't you. To see what she was up to."

"You bet I was."

"So you would have had a good look at the man she was with, since you were tracking her. You stalked her all the way from the mall out to Chapala Street, didn't you?"

Katrina was clearly discomfited by Luke's use of the term *stalked*, because that was precisely what she'd been doing, and now he had publicly busted her.

"Yes," she answered resentfully.

"You watched her walk up the street with this man, until they got to a car, is that right?"

"Yes."

"Until they got in the car—together—and drove away."

"Yes! Okay?" she blurted out. "I spied on them the whole time!"

Luke turned away from her for a moment and thumbtacked the pictures onto the easel. They were pictures of young men, taken from behind. All had longish dark-blond hair. Luke pushed the easel closer to Katrina.

"Take a look at these," he instructed her. "Look at them carefully."

She leaned forward, looking at the pictures. Above her, Judge Martindale looked down on them as well. Luke positioned himself next to the easel.

"Can you pick out which of these men was the one with Maria that day?" he asked.

"Objection!" Alex called out. "Your honor, this is a fishing . . ."

Martindale cut him off. "Overruled," he said curtly. He peered down at Katrina from above. "Answer the question, if you can," he directed her.

She squinted hard at the photographs. "I think . . . maybe . . ." She slumped back. "I can't tell. It's the back of their heads."

"Because you never saw the man's face, did you?" Luke pushed her. "This angle, from the back, is all you saw, isn't that true?"

"Yes, it's true," she answered in a soft, barely audible voice.

"You followed Maria Estrada clear across the mall, out of the mall, and watched her go down the street and get into a car, but you never saw the man's face?" he asked, clearly not believing her. "How is that possible?"

"It just is," she answered stubbornly. "He never turned around."

"But she did? Enough, certainly, that you could see her, and know for sure that it was her you were watching? For sure?" he repeated.

"Yes, for sure," she answered doggedly. "I wasn't paying him any attention," she said in a rising tone. "I didn't care about him. I wanted to see what that bitch was up to, screw whoever guy she was with!"

SLAM! The explosion of Martindale's gavel was like a rifle shot. "Do not use words like that in this courtroom," he warned her again. "It isn't acceptable. Do you understand."

"Yes, I understand. Jesus," she muttered under her breath.

"How far did you follow them, once you spotted Maria?" he asked.

Sullenly: "I don't know."

"From near Elaine's, the earring store?"

"Near there, yeah."

"Through the mall, out the mall to the street, and then to the car they got into."

"That's what I said, isn't it?" she answered.

"How far was that?" he asked.

She shook her head. "How should I know? Who cares?"

"I do," he answered. "Because it's a pretty good distance. I went down there the other day and paced it off myself." He turned to Judge Martindale. "From outside Elaine's to the entrance to Chapala Street is over a hundred yards. A darn long distance to be following someone and never once see his face." He turned back to Katrina. "You saw Maria with a man, who you can't identify, except for the color of his hair and his general height, because . . ." he dropped his voice dramatically. ". . . *He never once looked around*. But you followed them all the way through the mall, out to the street, and watched them get into his car, which you described in some detail. The only thing you didn't get was the license number and the make of the car. But you knew the color, and the style." He stopped for brief moment. "That's what you're telling this court? Under oath? You've sworn that is the truth?"

"It is!" she insisted.

Luke turned away from her to face the jury. "You saw Maria

Estrada, who you had a real problem with." His eyes were on the
jurors, and theirs were on him. "You followed her all the way
through the mall to the street, where she got into a car with a
man. You watched them drive off. You were able to see what kind
of car it was. *But you couldn't begin to describe the man, except
that he had blond hair*," he ranted. "A detail, I'll bet, people had
been talking about at school, since Steven McCoy, who has blond
hair, had already been arrested."

"No!" she cried out. "That's not true."

"It wouldn't have been hard to find out what kind of car he
was driving, either," Luke pressed. "So it would have been easy
for you, long after the body was discovered and a man was arrested, to tailor your story to fit some angry agenda of yours,
wouldn't it! You even told your friends, after she was killed that
she deserved it, didn't you? You wanted to get back at Maria in
the worst way. But since she had been killed you couldn't get it
directly, you could only get it by smearing her memory." He
turned to face her. "Which is what you did, isn't it, Katrina?"

The girl's face was beet-red under her white Goth makeup.
She flew out of the witness chair. "I hated her, okay! She was a
first-class bitch! And if she hadn't wanted to fuck every guy she
could get her hands on, she might be alive today! But that doesn't
mean I didn't see her, didn't see the guy she was with, and didn't
see the car they got into. Because I did! And whatever feelings I
had toward her can't change that!"

32

STEVEN AND JUANITA had been living on room service, which was getting old. They needed a break, so tonight Juanita was hosting a dinner at an Italian restaurant a few blocks from their hotel. The restaurant's owner set them up in a private room, so they wouldn't be disturbed. Besides the McCoys, Kate, Luke, Riva, and Sophia had been invited. A small payback, Juanita announced, for the great work Luke and Kate had been doing for Steven.

"Don't get ahead of yourself," Luke cautioned her as he dug into his risotto. "It's still a steep hill to climb."

"I think you're doing very well," she disagreed. "You made mincemeat out of that last witness."

Luke smiled. "Thanks to Kate's great assistant," he said, beaming at Sophia, who was sitting between her mother and Steven.

Sophia looked up, and blushed.

"No one's going to believe that girl now," Juanita said. "Which is an important part of their case, isn't it?"

"Yes," Luke agreed. "But she may not have been totally discredited. Even people with agendas aren't necessarily liars."

He didn't want her testimony to be completely discredited. He was sowing the seeds of doubt. Later, when he brought his own witnesses forward, he wanted her description of the vehicle Maria had gotten into to have validity. But for now he wanted to rock Alex and Elise back on their heels, as often as he could. He looked at Sophia, across the table.

"Good work," he praised her again. "I'm glad you're on our side, Sophia."

Again, she smiled, ducking her head and leaning toward Steven, who seemed to be more comfortable and less anxious than he had been at any time during the trial so far. He leaned closer to Sophia and whispered something in her ear. She smiled, and laughed softly.

Sophia had had a wonderful winter. From feeling like an outcast at the start of the school year she had become, after her triumph in the play, almost too popular. She had more friends than she had time to be with, and she had also done well academically; so well that she had summoned the guts to apply for early admission to Stanford. She had debated the pros and cons of trying to get in there, because she hadn't wanted to be seen as Wanda's little sister—a tough act to follow—but the two of them had talked it over during several intense phone conversations, and Wanda's advice had overcome whatever qualms Sophia had: it was a big school, Wanda was gone, and they were interested in different disciplines. Wanda had gone heavy on the sciences, and Sophia was going to be a liberal arts student, with a major in drama. She would chart her own course.

In October, Sophia had sent in her application, and the week before Christmas, the thick FedEx envelope arrived—she'd been accepted. She and Kate had celebrated deep into the night. She was also, by now, an accomplished rider. She went up to the ranch almost every weekend to ride with Juanita, and to help with her winter garden and other ranch chores.

None of that could compare, though, to her relationship with Steven. The two had been white-hot since their first sexual encounter. They were careful not to give Juanita any reason to be suspicious; it was always done away from any prying eyes. Steven used a rubber conscientiously, even though Sophia had volunteered to go on the pill so they could have bareback sex. But he didn't want her to—why mess with your system if you don't have to, he reasoned. He was a pre-med student, he knew about health.

She didn't know if she was in love with him, but she thought she might be. Once this trial was over and he was free, they would see what would happen. For now she was going with the flow, and loving every minute of it.

She squeezed his hand under the table. He squeezed hers back. If only they knew, she thought deliciously. Her mother would have a heart attack.

Riva leaned over to Luke. "She's balling him," she whispered into his ear.

He looked up, startled. "What?"

"Or he's balling her. Or they're both doing each other. However you want to say it," she told him.

Luke looked across the table at Sophia and Steven, who seemed to be engaged in their food. "How do you know that?" he whispered back in alarm. If that was true, and Kate knew about it, the shit would fly.

And even if she didn't, he was distressed over the possibility. Steven was on trial for murder. No good could come of a relationship between him and a girl who was the same age as the girl he was accused of murdering. That she was the daughter of his coworker, and one of his best friends, could only compound the misery.

"Do you really think so?" he whispered.

"I *know* so," she said, keeping her voice down. "A woman's radar for stuff like that is infallible, if you're looking for it."

"Jesus H. Christ," he muttered, looking at Steven and Sophia again. "Do you think Kate knows?"

Riva shook her head. "She doesn't want to know. If she has any suspicions, she's buried them."

His eyes swept the table, coming to rest on Juanita, who was talking to her son. "What about Juanita?" he asked. "Does she? Could she?"

"I've been wondering about that," Riva said. "I'd bet they're taking great pains to conceal anything from her. She's a very moral woman. She wouldn't countenance it, even if Steven wasn't on trial. I'm sure she feels protective toward Sophia, almost as if Sophia was her own granddaughter."

Luke took a sip of wine to steady himself. He looked across the table at Steven and Sophia again. There was a glow between them. Now that Riva had alerted him to it, it was impossible to miss.

"Are you going to say anything to Kate?" he asked Riva.

Her eyebrows shot up. "Are you crazy? That's the last thing I'd do. The best that could happen, aside from Sophia not getting pregnant, God forbid, would be for Kate to not know anything, at least until this trial is over, and Steven is free."

"If he's free," he had to caution her.

Riva was a lawyer's wife. She knew it was never over until it was over, no matter how sweet it smelled. "Yes. Until it's over." She squeezed Luke's hand under the table. "Don't you think you're doing well? Looking at it objectively?"

"I do," he allowed himself to say. "But who knows what a jury will do?" He pushed his plate away—his appetite was gone. "Do you think I should say something to Juanita? Make sure she keeps them separated?"

She shook her head. "It's too late. Horse is out of the barn." She glanced at Steven. "You might want to have a come-to-Jesus meeting with your client. Not about him bonking Sophia, specifically, but about keeping his nose extra clean in general, especially now that you're in trial. All the great groundwork you've laid could blow up in your face if this came out."

She didn't have to tell him why. If a rumor ever got started that Steven McCoy was such a reckless womanizer that he would initiate an affair with a girl in high school, the daughter of his lawyer's private investigator, in the middle of his trial, the adverse publicity could be crushing.

"It's weird," he mused. "It's like he has a bipolar personality. He's done some wonderful things, like risking his life to save that couple during the fire, but then he turns around and does something totally irresponsible, like having an affair with the woman he rescued while her husband was recuperating in the hospital. He has this mind-set of privilege and entitlement that makes him look arrogant and thoughtless. If he cops an attitude on the stand when Alex is cross-examining him, he could blow it." He swigged another mouthful of wine. "I'm going to talk to him about Sophia. And about pretending to look humble, even if he doesn't feel it."

Cindy Rebeck sat down in the witness chair. Despite the forecast for more rain she was wearing a short skirt over sheer black tights, and as she crossed one long leg over the other, the skirt rode halfway up her thigh. She demurely tugged it down, folded her hands in her lap, and gave Elise Hobson, who was standing at the podium, her undivided attention.

Elise walked Rebeck through the process that led to Steven's arrest, beginning with hers and Watson's first visit to the ranch, the day after the body was found. She read excerpts from the interviews the deputies had with Steven and Tyler, when the boys came back to Santa Barbara. Rebeck was precise and assured in her answers to all the questions. She should have been—Alex, Elise, and several other assistant D.A.'s had been coaching her for days.

"When did you and Detective Watson first think that either of these men might be suspects, rather than material witnesses?" Elise asked. They were in the second hour of Rebeck's testimony by now.

"When we learned about the gun that was found in the house," Rebeck answered smoothly.

As she reached for a drink of water, her eyes left Elise's face and drifted over to Steven, who was staring at her. She wet her lips and looked away. "Until then, there was no reason to," she told Elise.

"So until the murder weapon was found, and the defendant's fingerprints showed up on it, you had no cause for suspicion. Is that correct?"

Rebeck shifted in her chair and crossed one leg over the other again. "There came a time when we had some doubts about what they were telling us, but they were less of a suspicious nature than a curious one. That's more a cop's intuition thing than anything. You're always assuming that nothing is exactly as it seems, not even one and one equals two. Finding out they hadn't spent all their time together presented a set of circumstances that we had to nail down, but not because we had any suspicions about them. It was thorough police work, that's all. Any officer in our position would have done it exactly the same way."

"So to repeat, suspicion didn't fall on Steven McCoy until the murder weapon was found at the ranch, tested, and his finger-prints turned up on it."

"That's correct."

This back-and-forth was one of the most important parts of Elise's interrogation of her witness. She and Alex were sure Luke would try to claim that the boys' Miranda rights had been vio-lated, and she wanted to head that option off at the pass. Even though the Supreme Court had been giving the police more lati-tude in questioning suspects before they were Mirandized, it was still a touchy issue, particularly in a case like this, where the defendant wasn't some scumbag gangbanger off the street, but the scion of a wealthy and important family. The deputies had played by the rules. The jury needed to be made clear about that.

The rest of the interrogation went as Alex and Elise had planned it—the confirming of the fingerprints, and the other damning pieces of evidence that led to Steven's arrest. The most damaging items, aside from the fingerprints on the murder weapon, were Tyler's initial statement that the gate leading to the property had been locked, his obvious, reluctant acquiescence to Steven's insistence that it wasn't, and the information that had come in later from Katrina, who had seen Maria and somebody who looked like Steven McCoy get into a dark SUV that matched Steven's.

It was past noon by the time Elise was finished with Rebeck. Cross-examination would begin after lunch. Rebeck climbed down from the stand and walked out the side door. Before she left, she couldn't help but throw a parting look back at Steven. He was still staring at her.

Luke ushered Steven into a small conference room off the courtroom that was reserved for defendants and their lawyers. They sat across from each other at a square metal table that had been rescued from the pits of the basement.

"She's full of shit," Steven complained. "They were trying to pin this on me from the minute I stepped foot in the station. Did you see the way she was showing off her body? She was like that when she interviewed me. I was wondering if she was going to put the make on me. Which wouldn't have been that hard to take, she's a fox. But cops aren't supposed to act like that, are they?"

"No, they're not." Was there anything to this, for real? Rebeck had shown a lot of skin, but that was her style. Luke knew more than one man who had tumbled into bed with her. She got A's across the board. That didn't make her any less of a detective, though. She got high marks in that department, too.

"Did anything physical actually occur between you and her, when the two of you were alone?" he asked.

"She touched me a couple of times. A very friendly kind of touch."

Why hadn't this come up before? Was this a product of Steven's imagination, or was there some truth to it?

"What kind of touching?" he asked. "Where?"

"Her fingertips on the back of my hand. To make me feel at ease, so she claimed. I've been around enough women to know when they're coming on to me. She was," he said emphatically.

"But nothing happened? No sexual contact of any kind? Nothing more than a few friendly touches, to put you at ease?"

"Nothing sexual, that's right," Steven said. "But I'd bet you if I hadn't been arrested she would have been happy to meet me for a drink later on." He leaned back in his rickety metal chair, which threatened to come out from under him.

"Well, she didn't, so it doesn't matter. But that's what I want to talk to you about."

"Me and the lady cop?" Steven asked. "There's nothing more to tell."

"You and women in general. You have to stay away from them. Completely away," he said with emphasis.

Steven's face screwed up. "Like my grandmother? My mother? How could I avoid them? I don't want to, anyway. My grandmother's been a rock for me. I'd be up shit's creek without her. I'm not going to stay away from her. Or my mom, either. Why should I?"

"I'm not referring to them. I'm talking about other women."

"Like who?" Steven asked. He looked past Luke to the door that led to the outside.

"Sophia Blanchard, for openers. I don't want you near her. Which you were yesterday, at dinner."

He had hit a nerve—he could see it in Steven's face. Riva had been right. Her intuition was unfailing.

"We happened to wind up sitting next to each other," Steven protested feebly. "What's the harm?"

"It looks bad, that's the harm," Luke scolded him. "You're on trial for murdering a girl her age, in case you've forgotten. And it could be a technical violation of your parole."

"I didn't murder anybody," Steven shot back.

Luke fought the temptation to slap Steven across his face. "I said *on trial*. Which is exactly the truth. So don't get wise with me, it doesn't play. And it looks bad, you and her together. Let's not give the police or the press any more fodder for their cannons."

Steven shook his head as if to imply that Luke was a hopeless relic. "Fine. But you'd better lay down the law to her, too. Tell her to stay away from me." He smiled thinly. "If she can."

Luke's hand slammed down on the table. The impact reverberated in the small room. "Listen to me, Steven, and listen damn well," he said with heat. "I'm not here to facilitate you, or be your friend, or your stooge, either. I'm here for one reason—to get you acquitted."

"I'm the one who was arrested," Steven snapped back with equal force. "I'm the one who's had a year of his life stolen. I'm the one whose reputation will be doubted forever, even after I win. So don't come on salty to me. If seeing Sophia is going to hurt my chances of getting off, then I won't see her. It's only a few more weeks, I can handle that."

"See that you do." Luke looked at his watch. "Go have some lunch. I need to prepare for my cross of your imagined conquest. Just remember what I told you. You don't want me talking to your grandmother about this."

Steven nodded—that would rip it, and they both knew it. "Don't worry. I won't go near Sophia."

By the time the afternoon session got underway it had started raining again. Outside, seen through the high south-facing windows, the sky was dark. Pellets of rain slammed against the glass. Luke stood at the podium in front of Cindy Rebeck, who was back on the witness stand.

"Good afternoon, detective," he greeted her.

"Good afternoon," she replied. She stared at him calmly, almost aloofly.

Luke looked at the material in front of him. Besides his own notes, he had the transcripts of the interviews that Steven and Tyler had given the deputies when they had returned to Santa Barbara for questioning.

Months ago, when he had started preparing for this trial, Luke had considered asking the court to exclude everything the boys had told the police from the record, and that it not be allowed in at the trial, because their Miranda rights may have been violated. But after he debated with himself about whether or not to take that route, which under most circumstances would have been standard procedure in a situation such as this one, he decided not to. Ultimately, Steven hadn't been arrested because he gave the cops any damaging information. That had only hastened the process. He was on trial because his fingerprints were on the murder weapon, and he had the means and the opportunity to kill Maria. So it would be better, he had concluded, to keep this stuff in the record, and try to turn it against the prosecution.

"When Steven McCoy and Tyler Woodruff came to Santa Barbara last September to discuss this case with you, they did so voluntarily, isn't that right?" he led off.

She nodded curtly. "That's correct."

"They were not suspects, either of them. They came to Santa Barbara from their home in Tucson, Arizona, to help your department try to solve an important case that hadn't produced any acceptable leads. Which was putting a lot of pressure on the department."

"Yes," she agreed. "That was why we brought them out. To help us, if they could. Not because of any pressure." She turned to the jury box. "We don't allow outside pressure to affect our work."

"That's commendable," Luke deadpanned. "You and your partner, Detective Louis Watson, interviewed them, is that right?"

"Yes," she answered comfortably. "We were the lead detectives assigned to the case."

"Together?"

"Yes." She paused. "Initially."

"Initially," Luke repeated. "We'll get back to that in a moment. Where did you interview them, Detective Rebeck?"

"In our conference room, in the detectives' area. We normally interview people in there, particularly when there is more than one person. It's the roomiest space."

"And because you can videotape them, is that right? That room is set up for taping, video and audio."

She looked at him evenly. "Yes."

"When you started questioning them . . ." He paused. "Before you started interrogating them . . ."

"We were questioning them, not interrogating them," she corrected him.

"Questioning, okay," he replied. "Before you started, did you tell them you were taping them?"

Rebeck shook her head. "No."

"Why not?" he asked. "Why would you tape someone and not let them know they were being taped?" He glanced over at the jury. A few of them were writing in their notepads.

"It's standard procedure," she answered. "There's nothing illegal about it," she added, turning to the jury as she spoke. "We do it with everyone. It's for their protection as well as ours," she added. "Sheriff Griffin runs a transparent department. We don't want anything to be secret. We think that's the right way to do it," she said with a tight, self-satisfied smile. "Nothing hidden."

"But why didn't you tell them? What harm would it have done?"

She shook her head. "It's just how we do it. As I said, it's completely legal. The courts have ruled that way, many times."

"I know, thank you," he told her. "But isn't that normally when you are dealing with suspects? These men were there voluntarily." He paused. "Unless you thought they might be suspects." He leaned forward, toward her. "Did you?"

"We did not," she answered strongly. "They weren't suspects then."

Luke leafed through the papers in front of him. "When did you first think Steven McCoy might be a suspect?"

She shifted in her chair, recrossing her legs. They are damn nice, Luke observed. He wondered if the judge was sneaking a look from up high. Hard not to. "It was a gradual development," she said. "Until, or if, we got more substantial evidence, we weren't going to consider Steven McCoy or Tyler Woodruff as suspects."

"Considering, or thinking?" he pressed. "I'm asking about what you were *thinking*, detective. You've been in the department for several years. You were assigned this important and sensitive case because of your skill and know-how. You've developed a strong sense of intuitive feel, haven't you? From my experience, most good cops do. So let me ask you again—did you have any intuitive feelings that Steven McCoy might be a suspect, before you formally charged him?"

"No," she answered firmly.

"You didn't look at him when he first walked through the door to your office and think, 'He looks like the description we got from the girl at the jewelry store'? That didn't set off any internal alarms? Since you knew he had been at the location where the deceased's body was found?"

Again, she decisively answered, "No. I did not think that. No alarms, not even false ones," she added.

"Neither you nor Detective Watson said anything about that."

"I've already answered that question. The answer is no."

Luke stood at the podium for a moment, staring at her. She rearranged herself in the chair.

"If that's your answer, then fine," Luke told her, in a tone that clearly implied that he didn't believe her. He picked up another sheet of paper. "Did Steven McCoy tell you that he knew the combination on the lock for the gate that guarded the entrance to the McCoy ranch?"

"Yes, he did."

"He volunteered that information. You didn't have to pull it out of him."

"He told us without prompting, that's correct."

"Did that upset you and Detective Watson? That he knew the combination to the lock, and you didn't know that he knew it?"

She flinched, just for a second. Luke didn't think any of the jurors had noticed it, but he had. He looked back at the prosecution table. Alex and Elise had seen it, too.

"We were surprised, yes," Rebeck admitted.

"And when you found that out, he still wasn't a suspect?"

"No," she said reluctantly.

"What does it take to arouse your suspicion, Detective Rebeck?" Luke asked sarcastically. "A smoking gun and a body on the floor?"

"Objection!" This time it was Alex who jumped up. "This is completely out of line!"

"Sustained," Martindale agreed. He leaned over the top of his perch. "Don't force me to cite you, Mr. Garrison. You know better than that."

"Sorry, your honor," Luke apologized. "It just slipped out."

"No more slips," Martindale admonished him. "Strike that comment," he instructed the court reporter. Turning to the jury, he told them, "Forget you heard that. It won't be part of the record."

Luke looked behind the defense table, where Kate was sitting, in the first row behind Steven. She was grinning. He gave her a quick smile back. Then he turned to Rebeck again.

"At a particular point during this interview, you and Detective Watson decided to question Mr. McCoy and Mr. Woodruff separately, is that correct?"

She nodded. "Yes."

"When?"

"When . . ." She seemed to be temporarily flummoxed. "When it seemed appropriate."

"And I am asking when that was," he repeated. "*Why* it was, to be more precise. Why did you and Detective Watson decide to question my client and Mr. Woodruff separately, instead of together, as you had been doing. Since they weren't suspects, but rather volunteer witnesses. They still weren't suspects, right? You still didn't have any feelings in that direction?"

Rebeck shifted in her chair. "No," she answered stubbornly. "We still didn't think of them as suspects."

"So you felt there was no need to advise them of their Miranda rights," Luke went on. "Because they weren't suspects. There was no doubt about that."

She stared at him. "That is correct," she answered stiffly.

Luke turned to Martindale, on the bench. "I want to read something out loud. It's part of the prosecution's exhibit, but I want the jury to hear it."

He put on his reading glasses and picked up a transcript of the interview Watson and Rebeck had conducted with Steven and Tyler. "At this point in the questioning, the detectives have shown Mr. McCoy and Mr. Woodruff a picture of the deceased," he told the jurors. "Detective Watson asks, and I'm quoting here, from their transcript, 'So now you're at Paseo Nuevo. Did you see her? Any chance at all?' Mr. Woodruff answers first. His direct quote is, 'I didn't see this girl. I'm sorry, but I don't recognize her, at all.' Then Watson asks Mr. McCoy the same thing. 'What about you?' And Mr. McCoy answers, 'No. I never saw her.'"

Luke looked up. Brandishing the pages, he said, "On the record, both of these men have told the detectives that they hadn't seen Maria Estrada. Ever. So Watson changes direction in his questioning, because he isn't getting anywhere. He asks, and again, this is a direct quote, 'So how long were you there . . .' —meaning the Paseo Nuevo Mall—'What did you do, where did you go after that?' And Woodruff replies, 'Which one of us?' Watson then asks, 'What do you mean?' And Woodruff replies, 'We split up.'"

Luke took his glasses off and looked at Rebeck. "Now Detective Rebeck," he said. "Is this not the precise moment when you and Detective Watson decided to question the two men separately? To split them up, so they wouldn't be in contact with each other?"

She pursed her lips. "Yes," she said tightly. "It was."

"Which meant, of course, that one or the other was now under suspicion. Correct?"

Rebeck looked at the prosecution table. Then she turned back to Luke again. "No," she answered. "They were not suspects at that time."

Luke regarded her with incredulity. "How is that possible? That still didn't ring any bells?"

"No, it didn't," she said doggedly. "They were not suspects at that time."

"Then why did you separate them?"

Rebeck's top leg began to jiggle involuntarily. "To speed up the process." Her voice sounded strangled.

Luke's look to her could have shattered glass. "Do you expect anyone in this courtroom to believe that?"

"Objection!" Alex and Elise both jumped up. "That is prejudicial and inflammatory, your honor," Elise cried out.

"*I'm* inflammatory?" Luke fired back. "This witness is testifying under oath that she disregarded; strike that—that she and her partner deliberately violated one of the most fundamental rules of law, your honor. They had to have had suspicions by that time, but they didn't offer Mr. McCoy or Mr. Woodruff their right to counsel." Before Martindale could rule on the prosecution's objection, he fired his next question at Rebeck. "Why didn't you Mirandize them?"

"Your honor!" Alex yelled. "Are we going to . . ."

Martindale put up a restraining hand. "One thing at a time. Answer the last question first, Detective Rebeck. Why didn't you and Detective Watson apply Miranda at this point?"

"Because we didn't consider that they were suspects yet," she answered doggedly. She slumped in her chair. Her legs splayed out in front of her. She tugged at her skirt.

She should have admitted they fucked up and taken her lumps, Luke thought. Now she's in a snare of her own making. "I'm sorry, detective," he told her, "but you can't have it both ways. Either they were suspects, or they weren't. If they weren't, why did you separate them? And if they were, why didn't you Mirandize them? It can't be both. It has to be one or the other."

She stared at him sullenly. "They were not yet suspects," she repeated. "And we felt it would be better to interview them separately. We made that decision. We make decisions like that every day. Don't read more into it than is there."

"I'm reading into it what you're telling us," Luke retaliated. "Your words, not mine. Let's move on," he said crisply. "We're not going to get any further with this." He put his notes aside and walked toward her, stopping a few feet from the witness stand.

"You interrogated Steven McCoy privately, is that correct?"

"Yes, that is correct," she replied. "I interviewed McCoy, Detective Watson interviewed Woodruff."

"How long was your interview with Steven McCoy?"

"About twenty minutes. Half an hour at the most."

"You were alone with him? It was just the two of you?"

"Yes."

"Did you tape that part of the interview?"

She shook her head. "No, I didn't."

"Why not?" Luke asked. "You just testified that you tape everything."

She squiggled around in her seat some more. "That room wasn't equipped for taping."

"Was the door open? Was anyone observing you?"

She shook her head slowly. "No."

"To both questions," he said, making sure to pin her down.

"Yes. The answer is no to both questions. The door was shut, so no one could have seen us."

"So anything could have gone on in there."

"What do you mean by that?" she asked sharply.

"I don't know," he parried. "What should I mean?"

"You seem to be implying something," she spat out at him.

Luke felt like giving her a hug. That was a big mistake, lady. You just opened up a nasty can of worms. He looked back into the room. Alex was massaging his temples. Elise was staring fiercely at Rebeck, her eyes two black accusers.

"I'm not *implying* anything," Luke said. "Let me put the question to you directly. Did anything go on between you and Steven McCoy, while you were alone in the room with him?"

Rebeck flushed red. "That's preposterous!"

"You didn't answer the question," Luke came back calmly. "Was there any physical contact between you and the defendant?"

"No," she answered tightly. "There was not."

"Nothing?" he pressed. "Not a touch, an accidental bump, a handshake? There was zero contact between the two of you?"

He was close enough to her to see that she was shaking. So Steven hadn't been lying about that after all. Something had happened between them. Maybe they had done nothing more than exchange implied signals. But there had been something.

All twelve members of the jury were looking intently at Detective Cindy Rebeck. She sat up in the witness chair, and faced Luke directly.

"I touched him," she admitted.

A low murmur went through the courtroom. From the corner of his eye Luke could see Steven. He was locked into Rebeck.

"Where?" Luke asked her. "How?"

"On the arm and shoulder. I may have brushed his neck accidentally with my fingers. I was trying to put him at ease," she said quietly. The fight was out of her now. "He was becoming agitated, and uncommunicative. I was trying to calm him down."

"By stroking his neck? I'm sure he reacted to that, but I don't believe it would have calmed him down. More the reverse, I'd think."

Someone in the large room tittered. Rebeck sat up straight. "My intention was to calm him down. Nothing more."

Elise tried to apply damage control on redirect. "When did you read the defendant his Miranda rights?" she asked Rebeck.

"As soon as I finished interviewing him."

"That was before a gun had been found at the murder site that had his fingerprints on it?"

"Yes. I didn't know anything about the gun at that time."

You're lying, Luke thought darkly. You damn well knew about the gun by then. He made a note to check the logs for the exact time Steven's interrogation had ended, as well as when

Perdue had found the weapon and taken it to the lab for testing.

"Why did you read the defendant his Miranda rights, and not Tyler Woodruff?" Elise asked. She knew Luke would hammer Watson with that, and she wanted to beat him to the punch.

"Woodruff had an alibi for what he had done that day, and where he had been," Rebeck explained. "McCoy didn't."

"You did everything by the book, didn't you?" Elise asked.

"Objection." Luke didn't bother getting up. "Leading the witness."

"I'll rephrase, your honor," Elise said, before Martindale could sustain Luke's motion. "Did you follow proper and established police procedures in your handling of Steven McCoy, in regards to informing him of his Miranda rights on a timely basis?"

"Absolutely," Rebeck answered resolutely. "To the letter."

Watson followed Rebeck. He didn't have anything new to add, although he did admit that Tyler's knee-jerk reaction to whether the gate had been open or locked when the boys left the ranch to go to town had rung a bell in the back of his mind; but he had ignored it, because McCoy had insisted the gate had been open, and Woodruff had agreed. It was only later, when the gun and the other hard evidence came in, that he thought Woodruff's initial reaction had validity.

Luke didn't spend much time on cross. Watson didn't have anything to add that he hadn't already gotten from Rebeck, and he wanted the jury to keep his interrogation of Rebeck as fresh in their memories as possible.

The rain let up overnight, but by morning it was coming down in sheets again. The courtroom smelled of wet clothes. Umbrellas were stacked outside in the hallway like sentries.

Tyler was sworn in and took the stand. As he sat down he gave Steven a hangdog look, as if to say "I didn't want to be here. They made me."

The two friends hadn't seen each other since Steven's arrest. During the fall they had spoken on the phone and had exchanged e-mails, but after the first of the year there had been no communication: once Tyler reluctantly agreed to testify as a prosecution witness, the two weren't allowed to have any contact.

Alex Gordon strode forward to the podium. Tyler was the prosecution's key witness. He was the only person who could physically place Steven at the ranch (except for the brief interlude with Juanita, which had taken place hours before Maria Estrada was last seen), the only one who had gone from the ranch to Santa Barbara and back with Steven, and had been with Steven after they returned. He had driven in and out of the security gate with Steven, and had been inside the house when Steven supposedly handled the revolver that turned out to be the murder weapon.

Alex squared his notes. "Thank you for coming out here from Tucson and testifying in this matter," he began, as if Tyler was here of his own free will.

Tyler nodded and muttered, "You're welcome."

Alex's questioning was brisk. "When you arrived at the ranch, the security gate was closed and locked, is that correct?" he asked Tyler.

"Yes. It was locked," Tyler answered.

"And how did you get it open?"

"Steven opened it."

"With a key, or was there a combination lock?" Alex asked.

"A combination."

"Which Steven knew? He knew the combination to the lock?"

Tyler nodded. "Yes."

"Did he tell you how he had got the combination?"

"He said he remembered from the last time he had been there, over the Christmas holidays."

"He unlocked the gate and you drove in. Is that correct?"

"Yes."

"Did you close the gate behind you and lock it back up?"

"No. We left it open."

"So between eleven o'clock in the morning and noon on the day in question, the security gate was unlocked and open. A vehicle could drive in and out."

Tyler nodded, and answered, "Yes."

"What did you do after you entered the property?" Alex continued. He pointed to a map of the ranch that was mounted on an easel between the witness stand and the jury box. "Did you drive along this road?" He picked up his baton and ran it along the access road. "To here? This house?" He touched the picture of the old house with the pointer.

"Yes."

"And when you got there, did you see anyone?"

"Steven's grandmother was there."

"At the old ranch house? Inside the old ranch house?"

"Yes. She was inside. She came out when she heard us drive up."

"Was she expecting you?"

"No. She was surprised."

"Steven McCoy hadn't called ahead to let her know you were coming?"

Another "No."

"Did she express surprise that you had been able to get through the security gate?"

As he waited for the answer, Alex looked over at the jury box. The jurors were paying close attention.

"At first," Tyler answered. "She was worried that it had been left open. Steven had to tell her how he knew about the combination. Then she was okay."

Alex shuffled through his notes for a moment. "About how much time did you spend on the property that morning?"

"Hardly any," Tyler told him. "Ten or twenty minutes."

"Did you go inside the house?"

"No, we didn't."

"What did you do?"

"Steven and Mrs. McCoy talked. He told her we were going into Santa Barbara, and that we wanted to come back at night and stay there, at the old house. He had good memories of it."

"All right. You and Steven McCoy were there for a few minutes, then you drove into Santa Barbara."

"Yes."

"You left the property the same way you came in? Through the security gate?"

Tyler nodded. "I think it's the only way in and out."

"Did Mrs. McCoy say anything to you about the gate?"

"She asked us to close and lock it behind us. She didn't like people having access to her property."

"Okay," Alex said. He'd come back to the gate later, so it would have the maximum impact on the jury. "What happened when you got to Santa Barbara?"

Tyler explained that they had gone to Super Rica for lunch, then drove to the mall. They had wandered around for a short time, and he then bumped into Serena Hopkins, an old girlfriend of his, who was starting her last year at UCSB.

"You and this girl took off together?"

Tyler nodded. "Yes."

"Leaving Steven McCoy by himself?"

Another "Yes."

"What time was that, do you recall?"

"About two."

Alex made a show of writing that down. "Two o'clock in the afternoon, you and Steven McCoy separated." He looked up. "When did you and Steven hook up again?"

Tyler glanced toward the defense table. Steven was staring at him. Tyler looked away, to Alex Gordon in front of him.

"Eight o'clock," he answered.

"Eight in the evening."

"Yes."

"So for about six hours you didn't see each other, at all. Did you talk on your cell phones?"

Tyler shook his head. "No."

Alex glanced at his notes again. "Did you try, at any time, to reach Steven McCoy on his cell phone?"

"Yes."

"When was that?"

"About seven-fifteen."

"Seven-fifteen in the evening. Why did you try to call him then?"

Tyler shifted in the chair. "He was late. I was beginning to wonder where he was."

"He was late," Alex repeated. "Does that mean that you and he had set a time earlier for when the two of you would get back together?"

"Yes," Tyler answered.

"What time was that?"

"Seven."

Alex paused for a moment. Then he asked, "What were you thinking when he didn't show up?"

Tyler squirmed in his chair. "First I thought I'd gotten confused about where we had agreed to meet up. But I was pretty sure I remembered, because it was where we had separated. Then I thought he must have met someone and gone off, and lost track of the time."

"Was part of the reason you were worried was because he had the car? You had taken this road trip in his car, right?"

"Yes."

"A dark-blue Nissan Pathfinder SUV, is that correct? Steven McCoy's car was a Nissan Pathfinder?"

"Yes."

"Okay." Alex shuffled the papers on the stand. "When McCoy showed up at eight o'clock, what was his excuse for being late?"

Tyler shifted around again. "He said he had gone to a movie and had lost track of the time."

"A movie." Alex thought about that for a moment. "Did he tell you about anything else he had done that day? Anywhere he had been, anyone he had seen?"

"He told me he went to the beach and had a beer after that."

"In the six hours that you and he were apart he went to the beach, had a beer, and went to a movie. That's all he said he did?"

"Yes. That's what he said," Tyler told him.

"Okay. So now you're back together. What did you do then?"

"We got dinner. Brophy's, down at the beach."

"And then?"

"We drove back to the ranch."

"You drove back to the ranch," Alex repeated. "When you got there, was the gate open, or locked?"

Luke leaned forward. This was going to be some of the most important, and potentially, the most damaging testimony in the trial. Steven, sitting next to him, was particularly alert: he, too, knew the importance of what was about to come.

Luke took a quick look behind him. Kate, sitting in the first row behind the barrier, was visibly tense. Seated behind her, Steven's parents and Juanita were watching attentively. Steven's parents looked worried, but they had looked worried from day one, even when Luke was scoring points for Steven.

Juanita was the only spectator who didn't seem to be upset or concerned. She was intent on the process, but her face was tranquil. This woman has incredible inner serenity, Luke thought in admiration. She could weather anything. He turned his attention back to the front of the room, to hear Tyler's answer.

There was no doubt in Tyler's voice. "It was open."

"Opened. Not locked."

"Yes."

"Were you surprised?"

Tyler hesitated.

"Because you had remembered that you locked it behind you

when you drove into town, isn't that right?" Alex continued, before Tyler could answer. "That Mrs. McCoy had reminded Steven—warned him, really—to make sure and lock the gate?"

"I remembered that she had reminded us to lock it," Tyler answered.

"So when you returned, and saw that the security gate was unlocked, you were surprised," Alex stated yet again.

Tyler looked away from him for a moment, toward the defense side of the courtroom. Then he turned back to Alex. "No."

For a second, Tyler's answer didn't register with Alex; then it did, and Alex looked like he had just taken an unexpected step off a cliff. He turned around to Elise, who was feverishly digging through a thick stack of notes in front of her.

Alex leaned forward on the podium. "How could you not have been surprised?" he asked Tyler harshly. "You had locked the gate behind you when you left, and ten hours later, when you returned, it was open." *What was this fucking kid doing?* "What did you think, that someone else had opened it?"

"No, I didn't think that," Tyler said. "I remembered that we had left it open."

Alex swayed on his feet. "That's not what you told the police." He was livid. "That's not what you told me. Several times, may I remind you."

Tyler ducked his head.

Elise came forward from the prosecution table with a sheaf of notes in her hand. She gave them to Alex, pointing to various places on the pages. Alex looked at them, then turned to Tyler again.

"I'm going to read some of your own recorded testimony to you, Mr. Woodruff." His tone was aggressive now. He looked up at Judge Martindale, who was peering down at them with more intensity than he had shown at any time during the trial. "Everything I'm going to read is an exact quote, from tapes and transcripts. Steven McCoy: 'Then we drove into Santa Barbara.'"

He looked up at Martindale again. "He's referring to them leaving the property for the first time. Page sixteen in people's exhibit five, your honor."

He waited until Martindale nodded that he'd found the quote, then continued. "Detective Watson: 'And you locked the gate behind you when you left.' Answer from Tyler Woodruff: 'Yes.' Do you recall answering the question that way, Mr. Woodruff?"

Again, Tyler shifted uncomfortably in the witness chair. "Yes, but . . ."

Alex put a hand up to stop him. "You don't need to qualify it. Your answer was 'yes.' It's here in the record. Now later, you were being questioned alone, by Detective Watson. Watson asked you, referring to arriving back at the ranch that night, 'When you got there, the security gate at the entrance to the property was unlocked. You're positive about that?' And you answered, 'yes.' He then asked, 'And you were surprised, because you thought it had been locked. That was what you remembered.' And you answered, 'At first, I did.' And then you said that only after Steven McCoy insisted that he hadn't locked it that you decided it had been left unlocked. That's what you told Detective Watson, isn't it?" He brandished the pages in Tyler's face. "Do you want to look at it? Refresh your memory?"

Tyler shook his head. "I don't have to look at it. I remember."

"It's as I've recounted it?"

"Yes. It's what I said."

Alex looked at the transcript again. "Then Detective Watson went on to ask, 'But your initial reaction was that he had locked it when you left earlier.' And your answer . . ." He tapped the page, and held it up in front of the jurors. "Your answer was, 'Yes.'"

He put the page down. "Since then, I and other members of my staff have interviewed you, haven't we? And you have been consistent that to the best of your recollection the gate had been locked, and the only reason you changed your mind was because Steven McCoy pushed you to change your mind." He gave Tyler a ferocious stare. "Isn't that true, Mr. Woodruff."

Tyler nodded nervously. "It's what I told you, that's right." He looked off again, toward Steven. "But it wasn't what happened."

"What wasn't what happened?" Alex asked menacingly. He looked like he was going to strangle his own witness.

"The gate," Tyler answered. "I was confused about it."

"Confused?" Alex practically shouted at him. "What were you confused about?"

"About the sequence of the gate being locked and unlocked," Tyler said defensively. "What happened was, when the detectives were questioning us, I was thinking about the gate, and how it was when we got there, which was locked, and I got that confused with later on, when we left."

"You were confused," Alex said icily.

"At the sequence."

Alex left the podium and strode toward Tyler, until he was standing practically nose to nose in front of him. "Three separate times you told the detectives the gate had been locked. Not once, not twice, but three times. How could you have been confused every one of those times?" he demanded.

"It was a hostile environment in there," Tyler erupted. "Steven and I came to help them out, and as soon as we walked into the station they treated us like we'd done something wrong. Like we had something to do with that girl being killed, just because we were where the body was found. Those detectives weren't friendly with us, they were pushing us, hard. I started to get nervous, so I said something off the top of my head that wasn't true." He sat up straight in the chair and looked behind him, at Judge Martindale. "I've been going over and over this in my head. And I finally remembered what the truth was." He turned back to Alex, who was holding onto the sides of the podium, looking like he'd been poleaxed. "The gate was open when we left, and it was open when we returned."

Alex pulled himself together and finished his interrogation. He badgered Tyler into admitting that they had smoked marijuana when they got back to the house. Then he brought up the murder weapon, and Steven's account of how his fingerprints had gotten on it. On this point, Tyler was more helpful; or at least, less destructive. It had been dark inside the house when they returned. He hadn't seen a gun, so he could not have seen Steven pick it up and put it in the gun case. They had slept outside, and hadn't noticed anyone coming or going that night or the following morning.

Luke practically floated to the podium. "I only have a few questions for this witness," he told Judge Martindale. Turning to Tyler, he asked, "You spent the night sleeping outside the old ranch house?"

Tyler nodded. "Yes."

"No more than a quarter mile from where the murdered girl was later found," Luke reminded the courtroom. "Did Steven exhibit any anxiety that night while you were camped out? Any nervousness?" The implication being that a man who killed someone and dumped her body practically right next to them would not be calm and placid.

"No," Tyler answered. "He was easy and relaxed. His usual self."

Luke nodded. "Going back earlier. When you returned to the ranch that night, was the security gate locked, or open?"

"It was open."

"There's no doubt in your mind."

"No," Tyler answered firmly. "None at all. It was open."

"No further questions."

Luke turned and walked back to the defense table. For the first time since the trial had begun, Steven was smiling. Before he sat down, he looked past Steven to the family. The parents seemed less anxious than they normally were, but they were still tense. Juanita, sitting next to her son, was beaming.

Kate was both ecstatic and bewildered. "Where the hell did that come from?"

"Who knows?" Luke replied. He had been as surprised as anyone. "Maybe it's like Tyler said it was. He felt he was under pressure and told them what he thought they wanted to hear. Or he made an honest mistake and figured it out." He twirled his pencil between his fingers. "I could give a shit less," he said happily. "It was a *coup* of humongous proportions, that's what matters."

They were in his office. Court was adjourned for the day. Steven had gone off with his grandmother and his parents to have dinner. It wouldn't be a celebratory meal—it was too early for that—but the food would taste damn good, of that Luke was sure.

Kate flopped down on his couch. She shook her head as if she was suffering from tinnitus. "But look," she said. "Months later, I went out to see Tyler in Tucson. When I was interviewing all those people."

"Right." He waited. "So?"

"He wasn't in a hostile environment with me—we're on Steven's side. I asked him, again. Was the gate open, or locked. And he couldn't swear it was open, which he wanted to do, believe me! He wanted to protect Steven, but his conscience wouldn't let him. He told me that his best recollection was that it was locked." She stared at Luke. "Why would he say that then, and change his mind now, at the eleventh hour and fifty-ninth minute?" She shook her head again. "It doesn't feel right to me, Luke."

He knew she was right. Now that the euphoria had blown off, he could see there was something wrong about this. He hadn't been there when Kate talked to Tyler, so he had to go by what she told him, but that was golden, as far as he was concerned.

"What do you want me to do about it?" he asked her. "Do you think he lied?"

"To help Steven?" she conjectured. "Could be. They are best of friends. And he wasn't certain, either way." She hesitated. "But my clear memory was that he was leaning toward locked, and let Steven convince him it was open."

Luke tossed the pencil onto his desk. "If it turns out there's a problem, it'll be Alex's, not ours. He was their witness, thank God."

"The witness from Hell," Kate said.

Luke smiled. "Or from Heaven, depending on where you're sitting."

33

OVER THE WEEKEND the rains moved on, and the skies cleared. Monday sailed in crisp and clear.

Luke got to the courthouse an hour early. The courtroom, located on the second floor, was empty. He sat at the defense table, waiting to begin presenting his case. He loved being here. This was his church, his shrine. Except for being with his family, he was more at home here, more centered, more invigorated, than anywhere else on earth.

On Friday, the day after Tyler threw his Molotov cocktail into the proceedings, Alex had brought in more forensic experts to try to counter the damage Tyler had done to their case. They had hit hard on Steven McCoy's fingerprints being on the murder weapon. And on that note the prosecution had rested, pending rebuttal.

Now it was his turn. He was primed, ready to go. A few early arrivals straggled into the room. He got up and walked into the hallway. When Steven arrived they would go off together by themselves. Luke would deliver a pep talk, and instruct Steven on his courtroom demeanor. Then they would enter the arena together.

Kate Blanchard came up the wide tile stairway and walked toward him. Sophia was with her. She looked like a woman today, not a girl. The change comes fast, Luke thought. Sophia was ahead of schedule—it usually didn't kick in until college, when the parental ties were cut. But he knew the history of the Blanchard women. Sophia had been self-reliant for long time.

Kate was proud of her daughter, it radiated from her whenever the two were together. And she was scared shitless of her daughter's sudden maturity; that, too, was obvious. In a few months Sophia would be off to college, and Kate would be on her own again. He wondered if she'd be lonely. Some of the time, probably; everyone in her situation was. She was so independent, that was the problem. She had never learned you can be independent and still be in a deep and loving relationship. Some people could never build that bridge. He hoped, as a friend, that she wasn't one of them.

"It's a beautiful morning," Kate sang out. "Ready to take names and kick ass?"

"Gonna try." He smiled at Sophia. "How come you're here?" he asked pleasantly.

"We're off school for three days of teachers' conferences, so I decided to come and watch," she answered. "Is that all right?"

"It's fine. I'm sure Steven will be happy to see you. The more supporters in his corner, the stronger he'll feel."

Sophia colored. "He won't even notice me."

Like hell he won't, Luke thought. He could practically smell the pheromones coming off her. How could Kate not know?

Or maybe she does, was his next thought. Either way, it was none of his business, other than how it affected the trial. Once it was over (assuming they won), the two of them could do whatever they wanted. He would be finished with Steven, and Sophia would be Kate's problem.

The elevator doors opened at the other end of the corridor. Juanita, looking jaunty, came out first, followed by Steven's parents, and then the star attraction himself. He had gotten his hair cut over the weekend and was wearing a conservative suit, shirt, and tie that Riva had picked out for him at the Men's Wearhouse in the mall. They walked down the long hallway toward Luke and the Blanchard women.

Luke nudged Kate. "You and Sophia go inside and grab good seats. I need a few minutes alone with Steven."

She nodded. "Come on," she said to Sophia.

Sophia was looking off, toward Steven. He had been talking to his grandmother, their heads huddled together. When he looked up and saw her, he stopped. Juanita looked off, also. She gave them all a big smile. Then she turned and said something to her grandson, who nodded distractedly.

"Go inside," Luke urged Kate.

Kate nodded. "Follow me," she told her daughter, who was rooted to the floor. Kate took her by the arm and gently but forcefully led her away.

Luke approached the McCoys. "Go get your seats," he told Steven's parents. "Steven and I need some private time."

Juanita leaned up and kissed Steven on the cheek. "Good luck," she said cheerfully. She was on the defense witness list, so she couldn't be in court during this part of the trial until after she testified. "I'll see you over lunch." She turned and walked away. Steven's mother and father pushed in through the heavy door.

"What's Sophia doing here?" Steven asked Luke, once they were alone.

"She's off school, so she came to see the trial. Is that a problem?"

"I thought you didn't want me seeing her. Us seeing each other."

"You know what I meant. This is different. It's public."

Steven cocked an eyebrow. "I hope she behaves herself."

Luke gave him a dark look. "She's not the one who's on trial for her life. It's you I'm worried about."

"I'll take care of me," Steven assured Luke. "I promised you I'd stay away from her until this was over." He gave Luke a flat stare. "I keep my promises."

Luke stood at the podium. He gave Tina a reassuring smile. "Please state your name, for the record."

"Tina Ayala."

"How old are you, Tina?"

"Eighteen," she answered quietly.

Judge Martindale leaned over. "You'll have to speak up, so the court reporter and the jurors can hear you clearly."

She nodded and cleared her throat. "Eighteen," she said, raising her voice a notch.

Tina's citizenship status had been rendered a nonissue. When Luke had turned over his witness list he'd told Alex and Elise that one of his potentials was undocumented. If that was going to be a problem, they should let him know now and he'd drop her, even at the risk of weakening his case—he didn't want to put her at jeopardy. Alex, to his credit, had given his word that the matter wouldn't come up as long as she wasn't on the Justice Department's watch list, and as long as she was truthful. Luke assured him she was clean, had no gang ties, no vendettas to settle.

Even with this reassurance, convincing Tina to come forward publicly had been a hard sell. Luke explained to her and her parents that she could be subpoenaed as a hostile witness and compelled to testify, but that would make things worse for them. He would have to tell the judge why she was a hostile witness, and then the INS might find out. If she came forward voluntarily, she would be protected.

They had no choice, and besides, her father wanted her to testify. It was what a real American would do.

Still, she was painfully nervous. She had never been in a courtroom, much less testified in a trial. All her fears of the police roiled in her mind.

Calmly, Luke led her through the sequence of her time together with Maria Estrada: how Maria had met two college boys over lunch, had asked Tina to be the fourth, so they'd be matched up, boy-girl, how Maria had snuck off so she wouldn't be seen with the boys, who were unknown to her friends.

"We drove up to Franceschi Park, on the Riviera," Tina recalled. "I was paired off with one of the boys. Maria went ahead of us with the other one."

Luke crossed the front of the room to the evidence table,

picked up two eight-by-ten photographs, and brought them over to Tina.

"Defense exhibits eleven and twelve," he stated.

Judge Martindale nodded and looked through his evidence book. Alex and Elise, at their table, did the same.

Luke handed the pictures to Tina. "Do you recognize either of these men?" he asked.

She looked at them. "Yes."

"Are these the two boys you were with?"

Another "Yes."

"You have no doubts about that."

"No," she said without hesitation. "It's them."

Luke stepped back. "I want you to look over at the defense table," he told Tina. Turning to Steven, he called, "Would you please rise, Mr. McCoy?"

Steven got up, buttoning the middle button of his new suit coat. He looked toward Tina. Luke paused momentarily, so the room could feel the weight of witness and defendant looking at each other. Then he asked Tina, "Is the defendant in this case either of the two men who were with you and Maria Estrada that day?"

She shook her head. "No."

"Are you positive?"

"Yes," she answered firmly. "He wasn't with us."

"Until this morning, had you ever seen this man before?"

"I saw his picture in the paper," Tina said.

"Have you ever seen him in person?"

"No," she told him. "I haven't."

"Thank you." Luke looked at Steven. "You may be seated, Mr. McCoy."

Steven sat down. Luke handed the photographs up to Martindale. "The names of these two men are Jeremy Musgrove and Peter Baumgartner, as noted on the record. They're on our witness list."

He had given his witness list to the prosecution a month ago, the latest he could turn it in. He assumed Alex's office had done background checks, but he didn't think they had known of the specific connection between the boys and Maria Estrada. Although Peter and Angela Baumgartner would have to be subpoenaed as hostile witnesses, Jeremy was testifying voluntarily, and Luke had had numerous sessions with him. Jeremy hadn't been formally approached by anyone from the prosecution side, so Luke hoped that was the case with Peter and Angela as well.

He turned back to Tina. "At any time when you were with Maria Estrada, did she indicate that she was willing to engage in sexual activity with either of the men who drove with you to Franceschi Park?"

Alex jumped up. "Objection, your honor. Calls for speculation."

"Sustained," Martindale agreed. "Rephrase your question, counselor."

Luke looked at the jurors, then back at Tina again. "Did you *hear* her say that she was willing to have sex with both or either of these men you identified in the photos, and if she did, what was it she said, as best as you can recall."

Tina flushed red. "She said . . ." She stopped.

"Finish your answer," Martindale instructed her. "Use the exact words that were said, no matter how graphic. We understand they won't be your words, that you're repeating what you heard."

She swallowed and licked her lips, which were bone-dry. In a small voice, she quoted, "'If the shit is as good as you say it is, I'll give you the best blow job you've ever had.'" Her face turned a darker shade of red. She ducked her head.

"By shit, did she mean marijuana?"

"Yes," Tina peeped.

"She said this to the boy she was with? The one who called himself Tom?"

Tina nodded. She kept her head down. Judge Martindale leaned toward her. "You'll have to speak your answer," he told her sympathetically. "I know it's difficult, but you have to say these things, for the record."

Tina, looking miserable, nodded. "Yes," she answered. "That boy."

"Was there anything else?"

Another tortured nod. "Later, when we got up there, they were going to have sex. She told him to put on a rubber, so she wouldn't have a baby."

"That was her reason?" Luke asked. "So she wouldn't have a baby?"

"Yes. She said she'd already had to get rid of one, she didn't want to have to do that again. That they had to use protection, because it was the wrong time of the month for her to have unprotected sex."

A low buzz hummed in the courtroom. Luke let it build for a moment before he continued. "Then what happened?"

"He had left them in his car, so he went to get one. That's when I decided I had to get out of there."

"Because you were too embarrassed?"

"Yes, and because I couldn't do that with the one I was with."

"The other man whose picture I showed you."

"Yes." She looked up at the judge. "I didn't want to do anything, your honor. Not just the sex part, but the drugs, too. I don't do those things."

"That's good to hear," Martindale told her. "Keep going," he instructed Luke as he stared at Tina.

"Then what happened?" Luke asked.

"They drove us back into town."

"They drove you straight back into town? No stops along the way?"

"No," she answered. "Straight back."

"What was Maria's mood? How did she take having her sexual encounter stopped because of you?"

Again, Alex was on his feet. "This is speculative. The witness isn't a mind reader, your honor."

"Hold on," Luke said sharply. "This witness was right there. That's a question she can answer."

"Agreed," Martindale ruled. "Please answer the question," he directed Tina.

Tina was rigid in the witness chair. "She was angry. She cursed me out. Told me I wouldn't have a friend in school. She called me a bitch," she said with surprising strength and candor.

Luke suppressed a smile. Good for you, he thought. He'd been worried that Tina might fall apart and blow it, but she was coming through like a champ.

"When you got back to town, where did they drop you off?"

"Across the street from Paseo Nuevo, on De La Guerra Plaza."

"What did you do?"

"I got out of the car and walked away. I wanted to get away from them as fast as I could."

"Which direction? Toward the mall, or away from it?"

"Away. Toward Milpas Street."

"Was Maria still with them when you left?"

"For a minute. She and the boy called Tom talked for a short time."

"Did they exchange anything? Cell numbers, anything like that?"

"I don't know."

"But they could have. You just didn't see it."

"Objection!" Alex bellowed.

This time, Martindale sustained him. Luke didn't rephrase his question. Instead, he asked, "Did Maria leave in the same direction you did?"

Tina shook her head. "No. She went the other way."

"Into the mall?"

"Yes."

"You saw her go into the Paseo Nuevo mall. You're sure of that."

She nodded emphatically. "I saw her cross State Street and go in."

Alex stood at the podium, staring at Tina. She averted his look, her eyes on her shoes. After letting her hang uncomfortably for a moment, Alex leaned forward. "What time did the four of you return to the mall?" he asked her.

"About one o'clock," she answered. "Or maybe one-thirty. I didn't have a watch."

"No later?"

"No."

"So by one-thirty in the afternoon, you and Maria Estrada and these two men parted company. You went one way, Maria went the other. Did the men follow her?"

"I don't know," Tina answered.

"You saw Maria walk into the mall."

"Yes."

"At any time when you saw her, did either or both of these men follow her?"

"No," Tina answered. "Not when I saw her."

"That's all, your honor," Alex said curtly. He walked back to the prosecution table.

Judge Martindale smiled at Tina. "You're excused. Thank you for coming forward."

Tina got up and left the courtroom without looking at anyone. Luke heaved a sigh of relief when the door closed behind her. His fingers had been crossed against Alex thinking of the golden question: "Did you ever see either of those men again?" She would have had to answer "Yes, she had seen Billy (Jeremy) later in the year," and that would have opened a Pandora's box that could have derailed the body of his defense. Thank God Alex had been too angry and off-balance to think outside the box.

He looked across the aisle to Elise, who was frowning. No doubt wondering why her boss had let this shaky witness off so

easily. She knew Alex was shaken by Tyler's destructive about-
face, but they had a long way to go. She'd have to give him a
bracing during the next break. She glanced over at Luke, who
was flipping through some notes. Now there was a boss you
could depend on, she thought, almost wistfully. The fastest
lawyer on his feet that she had ever known. He would have figured out a way to break Tyler down and gotten him to recant, or
at least would have made him look foolish and duplicitous.

Steven tapped Luke on the forearm. "Good job," he whispered. "Where did you find her? She was dynamite."

"Basic detective work," Luke answered obliquely. He wasn't
going to inform Steven that Sophia Blanchard had been the cata-
lyst of his defense, that without her connection to Tina, and from
Tina to Jeremy Musgrove and Peter Baumgartner, the odds of
them winning would have been much slimmer.

To some degree, Maria Estrada was still on trial—witness
Katrina's condemnatory outburst—but the trial wasn't going to
be as balls-out ugly as he'd been afraid it might be, back when
they first started. When he had shaved this morning he hadn't had
to flinch from the face that looked back at him in the mirror.

After the lunch break, Juanita was sworn in. She acknowledged
Martindale warmly, and he broke protocol to extend his personal welcome in return. She sat up in the witness stand like an alert
bird on a wire, her hands folded neatly in her lap.

"Good afternoon, Mrs. McCoy," Luke greeted her.

"Good afternoon," she greeted him back.

"I want to go back to last September 14," he began. "Do you
remember the events of that day?"

"Clearly."

"Would you describe your morning? From the time you
arrived at the old house on your property."

Juanita sat up even straighter. "I went there around eleven
o'clock. I rode my horse. It's a pleasant ride, and the easiest way
to get there from my own residence. My dog accompanied me.

On the way, I stopped to pick some wild sage."

She adjusted her position. "I had gone there to catalog some old photo albums that had gotten disorganized over the years. We have pictures that were taken on the ranch that date back to the Civil War. I had been putting off getting them in order. I had resolved to start on that job the night before, and once I get an idea in my head I have to take care of it. As you get older, you become more fastidious. At least I have," she said with a self-deprecating smile.

"Go on," he prompted her.

"I don't recall how long I'd been working," she continued. "Not very long. Then I heard a vehicle approaching on the road, so I stopped what I was doing."

"Were you expecting someone?" Luke asked.

She shook her head. "No."

"What did you do then?" he asked. "What was your reaction?"

"I was concerned." She glanced up at Martindale for a moment, as if doing so would confirm what she was saying.

"Why was that?" Luke asked.

"No one should have been there. Our private road that leads to that section of property from the county road has a security gate at the road head. We keep it locked, to keep intruders out. Over the years we've had hunters trespassing on the property; others, too. We don't want anyone coming onto our private property who doesn't belong," she said, almost defiantly. "Who hasn't been invited."

"This locked gate. Who knows how to open it?"

"Normally, only me, my foreman, and his wife."

Luke nodded. "Why didn't you think it was one of them?"

"Because I know the sound of their vehicles," she said with surety. "And it wasn't one of theirs."

"Okay," Luke said. "Then what did you do?"

"Like I said, I was worried. Either the gate had been left open by accident, which almost never happens, or someone had broken in. Whichever it was, I didn't feel right about it. I assumed it had to be an intruder." She paused for a moment. "It's isolated out there. I was by myself. I'm very capable of taking care of myself, but I am seventy-six years old. At my age, you worry about some weirdo coming around your property and doing something bad."

She continued. "I opened one of the gun cases in the living room, and took out a pistol, an old revolver." She looked toward the jurors. "We have an extensive gun collection, going back over a century," she told them. "It's mostly for show, although some of the pieces, the rifles and shotguns, are fired occasionally." She came back on point. "I wasn't going to actually use the pistol, of course. I didn't think it was loaded, to tell you the truth. Most of the weapons aren't. But when you live on a ranch all your life you learn early that a gun is a handy and necessary tool." She grinned. "Like Al Capone said, much can be accomplished with a smile, but more can be accomplished with a smile and a gun."

Some nervous laughter broke out. Martindale gaveled for silence.

"And of course, I know about guns," Juanita went on. "I've been shooting since I was a girl. In fact, I had killed a feral boar earlier that very morning," she said proudly. "He was tearing my garden up something fierce, and I wasn't going to tolerate that."

Luke smiled. What a character, he thought. He looked at the jurors. They were eating out of her hand. "What happened then?" he prompted her.

"A car drove up."

"Did you recognize it?"

"No, I didn't."

"So what did you do?"

"I watched from inside the house to see who it was. I must confess, I was a tad scared."

"And who was it?"

"My grandson. Steven McCoy." She pointed to the defense table and smiled broadly. "Him. And his friend, Tyler Woodruff."

Steven smiled back at her.

"Aha," Luke exclaimed, watching this touching display of familial love. "So then what did you do?"

"I threw the gun down and ran outside."

"You just tossed it aside."

"I put it down," she corrected him primly. "I didn't actually throw it."

This was going well. He waited a few seconds for the good feeling to sink in, then began again. "Were you expecting him?"

She shook her head. "Not at all. I was totally surprised. And delighted. He's a wonderful young man." She grinned, almost shyly. "Don't tell my other grandchildren, but he's my favorite," she confided.

Now she was starting to lay it on too thick. Better rein her in. "Did you ask him how he had gotten in through a locked gate? I assume it was locked, and not left open accidentally."

She nodded in agreement. "Yes, I asked him. He told me his father had given him the combination when they had been out the previous Christmas holiday, and he'd remembered it."

"You were satisfied with that explanation?"

"Of course," she answered staunchly. "He's family."

One issue down. "What happened then?"

"We talked for a few minutes. They told me what they'd been doing that summer. They were going to spend the day and evening in Santa Barbara, and return later that night. They wanted to spend the night camping outside the old house, for nostalgic reasons, which was fine with me. We made plans to have breakfast together the following morning."

"Then they left? Before you did?"

"Yes. I stayed there and worked on my photography project."

"Before they left, did you remind Steven to lock the security gate behind him?" Luke asked.

He glimpsed toward the jury. They were listening carefully.

"Yes."

"And he told you he would?"

A nod. "Yes, he did."

Luke paused again for a second. "Now when you left there and returned to your own house at another section of your property, did you leave by that road? The one that has the security gate?"

"No," she answered. "I went back the way I came."

"So you never saw if Steven had locked the gate, or not."

"No, I didn't."

So far so great. "You were in the old ranch house by yourself for a spell before you went home." It was a statement, not a question. He wanted that detail to be firmly lodged in the jury's collective mind.

"Yes. I was by myself."

"Did you remember to put the revolver back in the gun case? The one you took out when you thought Steven might be an intruder?"

"No. I forgot to," she told him.

"Did you also forget to lock the gun case back up?"

"Yes," she answered again. "I completely forgot about all that."

"So you never put the gun back, and you never relocked the case."

"No, I didn't," she confirmed. Her voice started quivering. "It was a terrible mistake. That poor girl might be alive today if I hadn't forgotten."

"It's not your fault," he assured her. "Nobody thinks that." Another look at the jury. They were totally sympathetic to this poor old woman. Just the way he wanted it.

"The house itself," he said. "Do you keep it locked up?"

"Of course we do. We have many valuable collections in it. Not just the guns," she said, with another look at the jurors, then up to Martindale. "Art. Books. Furniture. It's irreplaceable, much of it. Not only our family's history, but that of the county, and the state. It goes back almost two hundred and fifty years," she added proudly.

"I've been there. It's a beautiful and unique place," Luke

agreed. "So when you left later that day, you locked the house up behind you, I assume."

She shook her head. "No, I didn't."

He feigned surprise. "You didn't? Why not?"

"Because Steven was coming back that night. I wanted him to be able to go inside, if he wanted to."

"You weren't worried about it being left open, with all that valuable stuff inside?"

She stared at him as if he were the slowest kid in the class. "Of course not."

"Why?"

"Because I had reminded Steven to lock the gate behind him when he left," she explained patiently. "Nobody would be able to get in, because they wouldn't have access to the property."

"Of course," he agreed. He shuffled through some notes to let that permeate. Then he asked her, "When did you next go there?"

"The morning after. To make Steven and Tyler breakfast, as we had planned."

"And then?"

"We talked for a little while. They didn't have much time, they had to get on the road. They were driving straight through to Tucson, to register for their fall classes at the university."

"You returned to your house then."

"Yes."

"You locked the old house up."

"Most definitely I did."

Luke waited a moment before introducing his next topic. "At any time when he was there, did Steven tell you he had forgotten to lock the security gate behind him when he went to Santa Barbara earlier?"

A strong head-shake. "He certainly did not," she said reproachfully.

"He was afraid you'd be mad?"

"He *knew* I'd be mad."

Luke chuckled. He looked over at Steven, who was hanging

his head with just the right amount of sheepishness. "I want to get back to the historic nature of that house for a moment," he told her. "Do you always keep it closed to the public?"

"No," she answered.

"When do you open it? How often?"

"A few times a year. I'm on several boards—art, music, non-profits, the university. We also have some open houses for our valley neighbors, other ranchers. The county rodeo association."

"How many people attend these events?"

"It varies," she replied. "Sometimes a dozen or less, sometimes as many as a hundred or more."

"So every year, a couple or three hundred outsiders come onto your property. Do those numbers sound right?"

"About right," she agreed.

"Do you know all these people?"

"No, I don't. In many cases, I hardly know any of them."

"There have been hundreds of people you don't know and have never met, except for on whatever particular occasion they're there for?"

"Yes. I know the organizers, of course. And we have someone in the house during those times, to keep an eye on things."

"When you host these events, Mrs. McCoy, do you leave the security gate open and unlocked?" he asked.

"Yes, we do," she answered, "because it's the only way in. We used to post one of our ranch people there to open it as guests arrived, but that was too cumbersome. So now we leave it open."

"For the duration of the event only?" he led her.

She nodded forcefully. "Absolutely. As soon as they're out . . ." She clapped her hands together in a dismissive motion, ". . . it's locked back up."

"Any other occasions when the gate would be opened?" Luke asked.

"During spring roundup, friends come to the ranch to help out. It's a valley thing, neighbors helping neighbors." She smiled.

"And it's fun. You get to be a cowboy for a day. We leave the gate open then, for convenience."

"How many people participate in that?" Luke asked.

"It depends on how large a herd we have in any particular year," she told him. "But dozens. We often have more help than we need. Afterwards, I cook for them, a big barbeque. It's one of my favorite events of the year," she said, looking over at the jurors and smiling.

"Of those neighbors," Luke continued, "how many are men?"

"Most of them," she replied. "More women now than in the old days, but it's still a man's thing. Although that's changing, like everything in society."

Luke gathered up his notes. He was almost finished; only a couple more questions. "What was your reaction when you were told a body had been found on your property?" he asked.

Juanita shuddered. "I was horrified."

"How did you think it had gotten there?"

She shook her head. "I had no idea."

"Weren't you surprised, since you keep the ranch locked up and off-limits from intruders?"

"Yes," she agreed. "I was very surprised."

Elise handled Juanita's cross-examination. There wasn't much she could do to poke holes in it. Juanita hadn't said anything that could be turned around against the defense. More importantly, a blind man could see that the old lady had won the jury over about thirty seconds after she sat down in the witness chair. Anybody dumb enough to screw around with a seventy-six-year-old grandmotherly icon should never have been admitted to the bar. Elise wasn't nearly that stupid.

At a quarter to five in the afternoon, court was adjourned for the day.

It was well past midnight, but Kate couldn't sleep. Worrying about the trial wasn't keeping her awake; it was Sophia. It had finally hit her this morning, when she saw how Sophia reacted when Steven McCoy came into the courthouse. Her baby was hung up on him, badly. She might as well have stamped the news on her forehead, it was so obvious. She had fallen right down into the well; Kate had realized that as soon as she'd seen that look on her face.

No wonder Sophia was spending all her free time at the ranch. Horseback riding couldn't be that compelling. She was sleeping with Steven. She had to be, you can't hold back hormones that are raging that fiercely.

By now, having discovered Peter Baumgartner, she was convinced that Steven hadn't killed Maria Estrada, so the issue wasn't that Sophia was involved with a murderer. Steven was the grandson of one of the finest people she had ever known, which had to rub off, even if his parents were cut from lesser cloth: genes often skipped a generation. He was bright, with a good future; he was going to be a doctor, like Wanda. And in many ways, he was a good person. Look how he had gone out and rescued that couple during the fire. He could have been caught in a backdraft and killed. They had been lucky, but it was Steven's grit that had gotten them through. A heroic act, and selfless. There were many checkmarks on the positive side of Steven McCoy's ledger.

The problem was, some of those strong qualities were the very things a mother feared for her daughter. Steven was a man, and Sophia, despite her maturity, was still a girl. She hadn't even graduated from high school. And regardless of how much Steven liked her, whatever was happening between them couldn't last. In a couple of weeks the trial would be over, and he'd be going back to Arizona, to the real life he'd had to suspend for over half a year.

She knew that Sophia had to be on edge about her affair, but she also had to be happy, out of her mind with rapture. She remembered the feeling from when she was that age. It was like no emotion could ever be that powerful again. And maybe it never was. A woman never forgot her first love, even if it turned out to be less than the real thing—how many of those were there?

Well, there was nothing she could do about it. It was time for this to happen. She hoped that when Sophia crashed, she wouldn't break. What she did know was that she'd be there to pick up the pieces. But maybe that wouldn't happen. Sophia was strong. She had to be; it had been forced on her.

Sophia would be all right. She was the one who was going to suffer. September, when Sophia would leave home for college, was coming in the blink of an eye. She would be alone again. She had forgotten, over these months, what it was like to be alone. Before, it had been bearable, often comfortable. It wouldn't be like that this time.

She thought, again, as she halfheartedly fingered herself, about Warren Baumgartner. They had talked on the phone a couple of times, but she hadn't seen him. Ethically she couldn't, until the trial was over. But that wasn't the real reason. They were on opposite sides of what could turn out to be a wall too high to climb. She wondered if he would show up in the courtroom, now that his son was going to be a principal in the case. She wanted him to, and at the same time, she didn't. She didn't want to be distracted, and his presence would do that. But she wanted to see him, anyway.

If he showed up, she'd deal with it. Right now, all her energy was centered on her daughter.

34

JEREMY MUSGROVE, STIFF as a marionette, was sworn in and took his seat in the witness chair. He blinked nervously as he looked up at Luke. The courtroom was humid from the recent rains. He could feel sweat starting to form in his armpits.

As Luke greeted Jeremy, the rear door to the courtroom opened and a man quietly slipped in. Kate, sitting in her customary seat in the first row behind the defendant's table, glanced behind her. Warren Baumgartner, at the back of the room, saw her staring at him, and stared back without expression.

She closed her eyes, then opened them. He was still there. She started to smile—partly in greeting, partly in recognition, partly in welcome, and most urgently, partly with desire—but her mind overrode her emotions, and her lips didn't turn up, for which she was very glad. She had to bury her feelings toward him. To open herself to emotion, even a crack, could be awful, both personally and professionally.

If Warren picked up on the distress his showing up caused her, he didn't show any sign of it. He turned away, scanned the room for a moment, then took a seat in the last row.

Luke was oblivious to the emotional psychodrama that was playing behind his back. He greeted Jeremy, and after a mumbled "hello" in return, asked his first question: "Where and when did you first meet Maria Estrada?"

"Last September 14, at Chico's Restaurant in Santa Barbara," Jeremy answered. His voice was flat and low.

Luke led Jeremy through the series of events that had

occurred after the boys met Maria, up until the time when they brought her and Tina Ayala back to town. His account corresponded closely with Tina's, the only difference being the spin he put on the interaction between the two of them. His version was that they hadn't done anything because *he* didn't want to, not because she stopped him. He hadn't been the least bit interested in her, he claimed; he went along to help his friend Peter out. Salve for his ego.

"Okay," Luke said. "You got back to town around when?"

"Around one-thirty," Jeremy answered.

"What did the girls do then?" Luke probed.

"The one I was with headed back toward where we met her," Jeremy said. "Maria went to the mall."

"Before Maria went into Paseo Nuevo, did she and Peter spend any time together that you weren't part of?"

Jeremy nodded. "They talked off to the side, away from me."

"For about how long?"

Jeremy shrugged. "A minute? Not long."

"Did they exchange any information? Phone numbers?"

"I couldn't tell," Jeremy answered.

Luke stared at his notes for a moment. "After the girls left, what did you and Peter do?"

"We drove back to our apartment."

"In Peter's car. His BMW convertible."

Jeremy nodded. "Right."

"Then what? After you got back?"

"We started setting things up. We'd just moved in, so stuff was all over the place."

"And that's what you did for the rest of the day, you and Peter? Worked on your apartment?"

The tip of Jeremy's tongue played with his upper front teeth. "That's what *I* did."

"What you did?" Luke repeated. "What did Peter do?"

"He went out to buy stuff we needed."

For a moment, there was a sense of suspension in the courtroom. Luke filled the void. "Peter went *out*?" he repeated. "To get things for your apartment? What did he get?"

Jeremy twisted uncomfortably in the hard chair. "Sheets, towels, dishrags. We had plates and utensils from his mother, but we needed garbage bags, dishwash detergent. A spaghetti pot."

"Small household items," Luke certified. "How long was Peter gone on these errands?" he asked.

"A couple of hours."

"A *couple*?" Luke said doubtfully. "Could it have been three? Four?"

Jeremy face's contorted as he recalled. "I don't know if it was that long."

"A few hours, does that sound right?"

"That's about right," Jeremy confirmed.

Luke stopped for a moment to steal a look toward the jury box. This startling disclosure had captured their attention, as he had hoped it would. He turned to Jeremy again. "Besides these basic household things, did Peter buy anything else for your apartment?"

Jeremy waited a moment before answering. "Yes."

"And what was that?"

Jeremy paused again. "A kitchen table," he told Luke. "One of those square butcher-block jobs."

Luke's face showed confusion. He was sure everyone else in the courtroom was manifesting the same expression, especially Alex and Elise. "A kitchen table?" he repeated back.

Jeremy nodded. "From the Pottery Barn. It's next to Robinsons, at La Cumbre Plaza. They were having a sale, so Peter bought it," he explained. "And a couple of chairs that went with it. We already had our beds, a couch, TV. That was the last thing we needed."

"So besides the small items you've told us about, Peter also bought a table and chairs," Luke catalogued. "When did the Pottery Barn deliver it?"

"Nobody delivered it," Jeremy answered. "Peter brought it

back with him that afternoon, with the rest of the stuff."

Luke left the podium and walked a few steps closer to Jeremy. "Peter came back to your apartment with the pots and pans and sheets and the other stuff he had bought. *And* the table and chairs?"

Jeremy was getting more and more nervous. He could feel his underarm sweat dripping down his sides. "Yes."

Luke nodded slowly, as if something wasn't computing, and he was trying to figure out what it was. He glanced at his notes again. "How did Peter get a table and chairs into a BMW convertible?" he asked Jeremy.

Jeremy's throat was dry from anxiety. "He didn't take the Beemer."

Luke took another step forward. "He didn't drive his BMW? Then what car did he take?"

"His mom's Lincoln Navigator."

Luke took a short pause to let that depth-charge sink in. Then he asked: "His mother's Lincoln Navigator? That's an SUV, right? Pretty big, isn't it?"

Jeremy nodded. "Yeah, it's almost as big as a Suburban. His mom lent it to him for a couple of days, so we could haul our big stuff up from L.A.," he explained. "Beds and dressers, those things."

Luke scanned the room. He had everyone's undivided attention now. Judge Martindale was leaning over his perch at an angle so severe it looked like he might topple off. Alex and Elise, too, were literally on the edges of their chairs.

"So that afternoon," Luke went on, "*after* you and Peter came back to your apartment, *after* you dropped Maria Estrada and the other girl at Paseo Nuevo, Peter went out again in a Lincoln Navigator SUV, rather than his BMW convertible? Is that right?"

"Yes," Jeremy answered.

"Alone?"

Again, "Yes."

At the prosecution table, Alex and Elise looked like they had been nuked. Alex's face was purple in rage. He leaned over and said something in Elise's ear. She shook her head. Then he turned to Watson and Rebeck, sitting in the row behind them. They were frozen in stunned disbelief.

Luke returned to the podium. "So for a few hours that afternoon, after you and Peter and those two girls parted company outside the Paseo Nuevo mall, your roommate Peter Baumgartner was driving around Santa Barbara in a Lincoln Navigator Sports Utility Vehicle. By himself."

"Yes," Jeremy answered. "That's correct." He backtracked. "I don't know if he was alone," he clarified. "I know that I wasn't with him."

Luke left the podium and walked over to the defense table. He took some eight-by-ten photographs out of a manila envelope. Looking at them, he smiled.

Months earlier, when Jeremy had dropped this bomb in their laps, Kate hightailed it back to Los Angeles and shot a roll of film of Angela Baumgartner's Navigator. Now Luke held a stack of them in his hand. He handed a photo to Judge Martindale, dropped a second on the prosecution table, and crossed to the jury box, where he passed several of the pictures out to the jurors. Then he walked to the stand and held one up to Jeremy.

"Is this the vehicle Peter Baumgartner was driving that afternoon?" he asked his witness.

Jeremy looked at the photo. "Yes, it is."

Luke leaned forward on the railing. "Tell me, Jeremy. What color is this Lincoln Navigator SUV that Peter was driving that afternoon?"

Jeremy didn't have to look at the picture again to know the answer. "Charcoal gray," he stated in a clear, emphatic voice. "Dark gray. Almost black."

Court was adjourned for the day. Luke and Kate had gone back to his office. Luke was nursing a Laphroaig over ice. Kate sipped a half-glass of sauvignon blanc.

"I wonder how Alex's mood is right about now," she mused gleefully.

"The same as Elise's and all the rest of theirs," he answered with equal relish. "Terrible. It's a bitch when you're blindsided. I know, I've been there. Nice to be on the other side for a change," he gloated.

Alex hadn't done a stellar job on Jeremy's cross-examination. Off-balance, and lacking any damaging factual information, he had tried to bully Jeremy into making a mistake. Jeremy had held firm—Luke had thoroughly prepped him for rough tactics. By the time Jeremy was excused you could almost see a black cloud forming over the prosecution's side of the courtroom.

"Alex took too much for granted," Kate said. "Once he had his bird in hand, he didn't keep on digging. You wouldn't have stopped there," she told Luke.

"Thanks for the support," Luke said appreciatively, "but I would have prosecuted this case in a heartbeat, just as it was." He sipped some whiskey. "We caught a one-in-a-million break with Tina connecting Sophia up with Jeremy. Without that, and Tyler's turning around out of the blue, we'd be the ones with acid in our stomachs." He stirred his drink with a finger. "We've been luckier than anyone deserves."

"Steven McCoy," Kate corrected him. "He's the lucky one."

Angela Baumgartner, reluctantly testifying under subpoena, stated that she had lent her Lincoln Navigator to her son Peter at the beginning of the fall term. She also grudgingly admitted that she and Peter had visited Rancho San Gennaro six months before Maria Estrada's body was found there.

Warren Baumgartner didn't show up for his ex-wife's testimony. Kate had been on the lookout, hanging back in the corridor outside the courtroom until the last possible moment. Either he didn't want to be in the same space with Angela, a reasonable assumption, or he didn't want to be in the courtroom at all, given the thunderstorm that had started to gather over his son. Or, Kate dolefully thought, he doesn't want to be near me. He had to be harboring resentment toward her for bringing Peter into this mess.

Her professional job had trumped the personal one. Not for the first time or surely the last, but it still wasn't a happy thought. That it had been inevitable didn't mean she had to like it. Of course, if she hadn't been working the case they never would have met at all, and she wouldn't have had that glorious night.

When she was being honest with herself, something she was loath to do, because she hated introspection, she knew that nothing could happen between her and Warren. He was a multimillionaire who lived a glamorous life. His hangout buddies were George Clooney and Larry David. She was a working woman who struggled to make her mortgage payments. After the giddiness wore off, what would they talk about?

There was a man out there for her; there had to be. But his name wasn't Warren Baumgartner.

Steven McCoy, finally given the chance to speak in his own defense, was an assured and credible witness. Under Luke's gentle questioning, he calmly recited his version of what happened that afternoon, and as calmly rebutted Alex's attempts, during a long and grueling cross-examination, to rattle him.

Alex valiantly tried to stem the tide in his closing summation. But he could tell from the reception he was getting that his efforts were like trying to put out a fire with a water pistol.

Luke didn't have to break any new ground when it was his turn to address the jury. He reminded them of Steven's heroics during last fall's conflagration, and made the compelling argument that if Steven was guilty, that would have been the perfect time to flee—he could have been in Timbuktu by the time his disappearance was discovered. He had stayed right where he was supposed to be, because he wanted his innocence to be validated.

Elise, all electric nerve endings, delivered the rebuttal summation for the prosecution. You could almost see the energy radiating out from her as she paced back and forth in front of the jury box.

"In all my years of prosecuting murder cases," she said, her heels tap-dancing a fast rhythm to the staccato tempo of her speech, "I've never been involved in one that had so much evidence against the accused. Forget all the mumbo jumbo, the last-minute suspects from out of left field. Here's all you need to remember: Steven McCoy knew where this isolated location was. He could get into it, *whether or not the gate was locked*. And most importantly: his fingerprints are on the murder weapon. That alone convicts him!"

She ran a hand through her hair. "Here's just one glaring example of how shallow the defense's case is: their invention of how Steven McCoy returned the murder weapon to the gun cabinet. The defendant's own grandmother waxed eloquent about how ranch people are almost pathological about gun safety. She's right, they are. So how in the world can we believe that Steven McCoy, after supposedly finding the murder weapon in a dark house, went right to the gun cabinet and opened the door? He would have known that door was locked." She shook her head disdainfully. "Only if he had picked that weapon up *with premeditation*, killed Maria, and then taken the time to see if the cabinet was unlocked—in the daytime, when there was enough available light for him to be able to see—would he have been able to put the gun away."

She came to an abrupt, almost screeching stop. Her look to the jurors was one of primal ferocity, as if she was daring each one of them to challenge her point of view. She pointed dramatically across the room at Steven, her blood-red inch-long fingernail an accusing beacon.

"This man killed Maria Estrada," she spat out. "He flung her body away in the hot, merciless sun for the coyotes and vultures to pick clean. He has never shown one iota of remorse toward his victim. Even if he hadn't done it, wouldn't you think he would have taken a moment when he was on the stand to offer his condolences? Wouldn't anyone with a heart and a soul do that? A tiny token of sympathy to a grieving mother?"

Elsie shook her head in sad remorse. "Nope. Wouldn't do it. Because that would be a sign of weakness. A sign of guilt. An admission that he did it. That he killed her. And left her poor broken body out in the sun to be savaged by wild animals."

As he watched Elsie, Luke didn't know whether he wanted to laugh, cry, or applaud. Not since Johnnie Cochran had immortally declared, "If the glove don't fit, you must acquit," had he seen such over-the-top histrionics.

She had it going, he had to give her credit. But she didn't have momentum on her side. From long experience, Luke could tell that the jurors were enjoying her performance, but weren't buying the supporting evidence. He hoped.

Elise wrapped it up. "Steven McCoy was there. The gun was in his hand. The body was dumped on his grandmother's property. Ladies and gentlemen, if this isn't conclusive enough evidence that Steven McCoy killed Maria Estrada, then no one is ever going to be convicted of murder in Santa Barbara County."

She cocked her wrists and pointed her fingers at the jurors, like she was pointing two loaded guns at them. "Access, knowledge, fingerprints on the murder weapon, and no alibi." She paused. "Those are the facts. That's what's logical. All the rest is baloney."

Finally, she mustered a smile. It was a tight, uneasy gesture, more a grimace than an invitation. "All we're asking you to do is use the common sense you were born with. This is not brain surgery. We can all figure this one out. And when we do, we'll come to the same conclusion: Steven McCoy killed Maria Estrada, and must be found guilty of her murder."

The case went to the jury at 5:15 on Thursday. By one the next afternoon, they had reached their verdict.

Judge Martindale entered the courtroom. Everyone else was already in place. Although the rainstorms had passed there was a feeling of clamminess in the air, a heaviness that was as much spiritual as it was physical.

"Has the jury reached a verdict?" Martindale asked.

The foreperson, a middle-aged white woman who looked like a cook in a school cafeteria, stood up. "We have, your honor," she said in a firm, almost Biblical voice.

She handed the verdict slip to the clerk, who brought it to Martindale. He unfolded it and read it. Showing no emotion, he looked up, glancing first at Alex and Elise, then at Luke and Steven. "The defendant will rise," he proclaimed.

Luke and Steven stood up. Luke put a supportive hand on Steven's shoulder.

Time was at a standstill. Kate almost felt surprised when she glanced at the clock on the wall behind Martindale's head and saw the second hand moving. She looked down the row to Juanita, who was sitting in the aisle seat, closest to the wall. The old woman was a picture of serenity, almost beatitude, Kate thought in admiration.

Martindale cleared his throat. "What is your verdict?" he asked.

The foreperson's words came out plain. "We find the defendant not guilty."

For a second nothing happened, as if they were all frozen in aspic. Then everyone converged on them—his parents, his grandmother, Tyler, Kate. "You did it, bro!" Tyler screamed. "You freaking pulled it off!"

Steven hugged Luke in a fierce embrace. Luke hugged him back. "Thank you, man," Steven choked out in a voice laden with emotion and relief.

Martindale brought his gavel. "Order!" he called out. "Hold their celebration," he admonished Luke.

Luke pried the family off Steven. "Cool it," he warned them. They could celebrate later. He wanted Steven out of here as quickly as possible, without incident.

As if waking from a nightmare, Alex and Elise began stuffing eight months of now-useless work into their briefcases. Behind them, Watson, Rebeck, and the rest of the sheriffs' detectives and staff that had been involved in the case milled about aimlessly, shaking their heads in angry denial. Further back, Maria's family and friends were huddled together, as if at a funeral.

"The defendant is free to go," Martindale pronounced. "You can go on with your life, son," he told Steven with a personal grace note. He thumped his gavel again. "Court is adjourned."

The news crews were stacked up three-deep outside the courthouse. Luke and Kate shepherded the McCoys and Tyler out the door. The mob was immediately upon them, scrambling for position.

"I'll stay with Steven and give the vultures a statement," Luke told Kate. "You get the family out of here."

He guided Steven to the center of the throng. "Stand behind me, and keep your mouth shut," he instructed Steven. He walked to the bank of microphones. "My client is not going to make a statement, so I will make a short one for him. This has been an exhausting ordeal for everyone. Mr. McCoy and his family are happy and relieved that it's over, and they can move on with their lives. They extend their condolences to the Estrada family, and pray that the real killer will someday be brought to justice."

As reporters began yelling out questions, he put up his hands to quiet them down. "We're not going to make any more statements, and we're not going to answer any questions," he told them firmly. "Mr. McCoy is a private citizen who wants to return to his private life. Now please show some decency and let us through."

He signaled to a pair of off-duty CHP officers he'd hired as security. The bodyguards flanked them, forming a human shield. They pushed their way through the knot of reporters to a Hummer with dark-tinted windows that was waiting for them at the corner. Juanita, Tyler, and Steven's parents were already inside. The security men hustled Steven into the backseat and jumped in after him. The car pulled away into the street. A policeman held up traffic so they could make their escape down Anapamu Street.

Kate joined Luke as he walked back to the press conference. He led her to the edge of the media convergence, where the foreperson and two other jurors were being escorted out of the courthouse. They stood at the back of the crowd as the jurors were led to the beehive of pressed bodies.

The foreperson leaned in to the microphones. "When the trial started, we thought the prosecution had a strong case," she said, her voice echoing from the amplification. "But they didn't present it as well as we thought they could have. They didn't manage their witnesses well," she elaborated. "You should know exactly what your witnesses are going to say. When they change their minds on the stand, it weakens your case. The defense did a better job presenting their side."

Another juror stepped up next to her. "Once we started hearing all these different stories, everything became too murky. It was like Rashomon. We decided that the prosecutors didn't prove their case beyond a reasonable doubt, which is what the judge told us they had to do."

God bless you, Luke thanked them silently. You did the job right.

"Did you consider that Peter Baumgartner could be the real killer?" a reporter called out.

"Not that it was him specifically," the foreperson explained carefully, "but that there could be plausible alternatives." She looked at the other two, who nodded in agreement. "If Baumgartner *hadn't* existed, there's a chance our verdict wouldn't have been the same," she declared.

Luke had heard enough. "I'm out of here," he told Kate. "I'm going for a run. I need to clean this out of my system. We'll check in later."

He walked away. Kate took out her cell phone to call Sophia.

"Kate."

She jumped. Warren Baumgartner was standing a few feet

behind her. "You startled me," she said, as she turned to him. "I didn't know you were here. Were you inside?"

"In the back on the other side, where you couldn't see me." He smiled thinly. "Congratulations. Your lawyer did a great job."

Kate smiled back. "That's what he does."

"A lot of people are going to say he got a guilty man off."

Her smile froze. She felt acid beginning to drip into her stomach. "Steven isn't guilty." She paused. "Do you think he is?"

"It wasn't up to me. Fortunately, for your side."

That ripped it. It had been a great one-night stand. She'd remember it, and move on.

Warren sighed heavily. "I like you, Kate. Who you are, what you believe in, even if it's misguided."

"I was doing my job. And I didn't deceive you. Not deliberately."

He kept looking at her. "I'm going back to L.A.," he said. "Let's see how we feel when this dies down, if it does."

A faint hope was better than none. Although she wasn't sure if that was what she wanted. "Are you worried about Peter?" she asked, knowing the answer, but unable to hold her tongue.

Warren looked like he'd been gut-punched. "Of course I am. But do I think he killed that girl? Absolutely not. He would have come up with a better story if he had." He looked away. "He has problems. I've spoiled him, way too much. But he could never kill anyone, not like that. It isn't in him."

Then why did he drop out of school so suddenly, Kate thought. Why hadn't he said anything for months? How can you explain away all the incredible coincidences?

She didn't need to go there now. "I don't think he did, either," she told Warren, trying to sound convincing. She didn't know whether or not he believed her, but there was no point in ripping the scab off. "For what it's worth, I doubt that Alex Gordon will come after him. He blew his wad on Steven McCoy. He can't come back and argue to another jury that he was convinced Steven was the killer, but now he's sure it's someone else. His credibility's shot on this case. Maybe his whole career."

"I hope you're right," Warren said. He stuck out his hand. "Good luck, Kate. Maybe somewhere down the line."

He leaned over and kissed her on the cheek. She almost twisted so that their mouths touched, but she restrained herself. He stared at her again for a moment, then walked away. Kate watched him leave. Then she took her cell phone out of her purse, and called Sophia.

35

ALL AROUND THE exterior of the old ranch house, luminaries had been lit, bathing the grounds in a soft, shimmering glow. Inside, dozens of candles burnished the main rooms with muted, diffused light. It was as if the ghosts from centuries past had come to life to join with the living in celebration of the family's ongoing history and recent good fortune.

Juanita had spent the day preparing the festive dinner. Sophia had been her energetic helper. Early in the morning she had assembled all the lights, inside and out, then had joined Juanita in the kitchen. Over the past few months, with Juanita's help and encouragement, she had been learning how to cook a real meal from scratch. Although the complexity of preparing tonight's banquet without the modern benefits of electricity or gas was intimidating to her, what she lacked in experience she made up for with enthusiasm.

The day before, Juanita had thawed out a loin of wild boar that had been stored in the large freezer back at her house. It was a portion of the feral pig she had killed the previous September, the day the tragedy had unfolded. The meat had marinated overnight in her secret concoction. Her mother had passed the recipe on to her, and someday she would pass it on to Sophia, who she was more and more beginning to think of as her logical heir. Now it was slow-braising in a reduction of onions, mushrooms, leeks, tomatoes, and herbs from her garden.

The two women, one old, wise, and patient, the other young and eager to learn, had labored side by side from midmorning to early evening. Accompanying the pork roast would be a salad of greens from Juanita's garden, broccoli-and-cheddar soufflé, beets and green beans she had put up over the winter, potatoes au gratin (Steven's favorite), and to cap off the meal, a homemade chocolate cake (his other favorite). Everything would be cooked on the old wood-burning stove.

"Back in the old days it would take two cooks a couple of days to make a meal like this," Juanita informed Sophia, as she stirred the cake mixture. She sipped from a glass of sherry. "But we can do it in one day. Because we are strong women," she sang out merrily. "And have modern appliances, like freezers," she added pragmatically.

"And because we're tough women," Sophia said in giddy refrain. "Bold women. Take-no-prisoners, ass-kicking women." She giggled as she drank her Coke straight from the can. "I shouldn't say stuff like that around you," she apologized.

"You can say anything you want," Juanita told her indulgently. "I'm not preserved under glass. Not yet."

"Not ever!" Sophia looked about the kitchen, at all the food in various stages of preparation, everything arranged in orderly precision. She hugged Juanita. "I've learned so much from you."

Juanita blinked her eyes, so the tears wouldn't show. "And I from you." She took another sip of sherry to settle her emotions. "We need to get a move-on," she said briskly. "We have a ton of work ahead of us."

The guests arrived as the sun was going down. They mingled outside in the dappled light, drinking a local sauvignon blanc and munching on raw vegetables and dip.

In a few days, Steven would finally be going home to Arizona. This was his last chance to say goodbye to those who had been his life during his ordeal, particularly Luke, Kate, and Sophia. And to thank them, for hanging in, and believing in him.

Before Steven's parents and Tyler headed back to Tucson they had celebrated in a restaurant in Los Olivos, one of the small towns near the ranch. The meal had been a subdued affair, but toward the end it became contentious. Even though their son had been acquitted, it was as if a fog of stigma hovered over Steven's parents, that the very act of being charged, regardless of the outcome, was a black mark on all of them.

Steven had picked up on their disapprobation and they had fought, first quietly, then openly. It was inevitable—he was a different man now. There was almost nothing left of his carefree boyishness, his openness. His ordeal had hardened him in some indefinable but conscious way. He still enjoyed life—it tasted better now, he felt and appreciated things more clearly, every day was a new possibility—but there was a guardedness about him that hung on him like an invisible mourner's shroud.

He had been happy when he and Juanita saw his parents off the next day. Juanita had tried to cheer him up.

"They'll come around," she promised him. "It takes time."

"I don't care anymore, Grandma," he'd told her. "I'm moving on. I've got your support. That's enough for me."

She hadn't pressed the issue, because she knew he was right.

Tyler had gone back a day later. The two friends had partied hard before he left, hitting half the bars on lower State Street. Steven felt a strong debt of gratitude toward Tyler. He had been there for Steven, putting his ass on the line, fighting off the D.A.'s attempts to break him. He had spent the entire school year without his best friend, the year they were going to sow their last wild oats. Still, this ordeal had bonded them in a way they hadn't expected or desired, but would glue them together for life.

Juanita, who was in the kitchen putting the final touches on her masterpiece, came outside. Her face was flushed from standing over the hot stove.

"Come in, please," she invited everyone. "It's time to eat."

The old oak-plank table was almost bent over with the weight of all the food, dishes, glasses, serving plates, and candelabra. Shadows from the candles danced on the dark walls. They had eaten and drunk to excess, which was just enough.

As Sophia cut slices of the chocolate cake and passed the plates around, Juanita stood and raised her glass of pinot noir. Juanita had been drinking more than usual—she normally didn't have more than a sherry and an occasional glass of wine with dinner—and the alcohol had loosened her inhibitions, so she could open her heart without embarrassment.

"When the prodigal son returned to his family, his father killed a fatted calf to celebrate his homecoming. Here, tonight, it was a mean old pig, shot dead by yours truly, but the sentiment's the same."

As everyone laughed, she continued, "Now that Steven has been delivered from the hell of these past eight months, we celebrate his reentry into what we all know will be a productive and fruitful life."

The guests raised their glasses in toast. "To Steven," someone spoke out.

"To Steven," came the full-throated refrain.

Steven grinned and raised his glass in thanks. He had been imbibing all afternoon. He stood up unsteadily, holding on to the edge of the table for support.

"Back at ya," he said thickly. "Especially you, Grandma. Couldn't have done it without you." He looked across the table to Luke. "And to my ass-kickin' lawyer." He shifted his gaze over to Sophia, who was sitting alongside her mother. "And a special thanks to you, Sophia. For being there for Grandma. And for me, too."

Sophia turned crimson. "Thank you," she said in a quiet voice.

"And to all of you," Steven said, saving Sophia from further embarrassment. "From the bottom of my heart, I thank you all." He sat down heavily, forking a chunk of cake into his mouth.

Kate looked across the table. Riva was watching her and Sophia with a knowing smile on her face. She raised an eyebrow, as if to say, "Haven't you figured it out yet?"

Kate swiveled to see her daughter, who was busy with her

dessert, her head low to her plate. I can't hide from this anymore, she realized. She had been in denial for too long. Steven was a vibrant young man. Sophia was a desirable young woman. The electricity between them was obvious.

She could do worse, Kate thought philosophically. Steven came from good stock. And he was leaving the day after tomorrow. Sophia would go on with her life, and Steven would fade in her memory. First crushes never lasted.

There was a low murmur of easy chatter as everyone had their dessert and coffee. Kate looked up as she heard Juanita telling her seatmate that Tyler was going to veterinary school in the fall.

"He was accepted at Davis, which is one of the top schools in the country," Juanita was saying. "It's a lucky thing I'm friendly with some of the regents, they pushed his application right to the top." She smiled knowingly. "When he's finished, we'll set him up in practice right here in the valley. Lord knows we need good vets out here. He's going to specialize in livestock," she added, "so he can help Steven run the ranch, after I'm gone."

"You're going into ranching now?" Luke asked Steven. He hadn't heard that one before. "I thought you were still headed for medical school."

"He's going to do both," Juanita interjected. "He'll be a doctor, and also a rancher. My husband double-dipped. It's not hard. You hire good help and let them do the heavy lifting." She smiled at Steven. "And you know I'm ornery enough to stay alive to see it all happen." She squeezed his elbow affectionately.

"That's great, Grandma," he said with a mouthful of cake. "Hang in there." He swallowed and smiled. "Tyler and me. We're a great team, aren't we? Like brothers. He saved my life, the way he stuck it to that D.A. Served them right for the way they screwed us."

Luke and Kate exchanged looks of concern. This was not a topic for public discussion.

"Steven, let's table it," Luke said easily. He didn't want to draw more attention to this.

"Whatever you say." He grinned lopsidedly. "Tyler and animals. Who'd a thunk it?" He patted Juanita on the arm. "Give her credit. It was her idea. "Hey," he said brightly, "she's paying for it. Tyler's getting a free grad school education. No way he was going to turn that down." He gave Juanita a sloppy kiss on the cheek. "You're the best, Grandma."

Juanita sipped her coffee. "I'm glad I can help Tyler," she said. "He surely deserves it."

Steven raised his glass again. "To Tyler, and me, and my grandmother. Living happily ever after. Or at least for a damn long time."

Kate had driven up with the Garrisons. They stood outside, by their car. The other guests had left; they were the last to go.

Sophia came out to say good night. She was spending the night with Juanita. There was a ton of cleaning up to do here, and tomorrow morning they were going riding.

"Did you have fun?" she asked.

"Yes," Riva answered, "it was lovely. You're going to be a great hostess someday if you keep hanging around with Juanita."

Sophia smiled. "She's a great role model. Almost as good as you, Mommy," she said, giving Kate a tired hug.

"Where's Steven?" Kate asked, trying to sound nonchalant.

"Inside, helping out." She laughed. "He's not very much help. He had too much fun tonight. Making up for lost time."

"You're not going to keep up with him, I hope," Kate fretted.

Sophia rolled her eyes dramatically. "Knowing Steven, he'll fall asleep before his head hits his bed. Or maybe he'll stay here. He likes it here, out under the stars."

That would be fine with me, Kate thought. If it were up to her, he would sleep it off until Sophia came home tomorrow. Although she knew that was wishful thinking. They were going to have a last night together. It was out of her hands, and her daughter was a good kid. She trusted Sophia.

"So Steven's going to be a rancher," Luke mused. "That's a surprise to me. He never said anything about that."

Sophia made a face. "Don't believe everything you hear. He wants to be a big-city boy. No horseshit on his loafers. He's gone loony, isolated out here." Instinctively, she looked over her shoulder. "Don't tell Juanita I said that. Steven's like a god to her. She's got all her hopes piled up on him. And it isn't like he's shining her on," she said defensively. "He knows she has these fantasies, so he tells her what she wants to hear. He figures he'll deal with the reality of it later. Or he'll keep playing out the string until her memory's gone, or she dies."

She looked back at the house again. "I need to get back inside and help Juanita. See you tomorrow." She gave Kate a kiss, waved goodbye to Riva and Luke, and went back inside.

The three stragglers stood together for a moment, breathing in the fragrant night air. Riva broke the silence.

"Juanita bought Tyler off."

Kate stared at her. "That's a heavy accusation, Riva."

"We don't know anything," Luke said heatedly. He didn't need to hear this shit tonight, especially from his wife. "Juanita is a generous woman, and she's rich. She can easily afford it. They probably have an arrangement that he'll pay her back after he's established."

"She'll be a hundred when he's in a position to do that," Riva told him. "But maybe I'm too cynical. And you know what? Her helping Tyler doesn't mean he lied. Maybe it was . . ."

"Insurance?"

"If you want to call it that. Gratitude." She nuzzled her husband's neck. "You won, Luke, fairly and legitimately. You kicked their sorry asses from here to Bakersfield. You would have worked around it regardless of what Tyler had said," she assured him.

"Riva's right," Kate chimed in. "You outplayed them, Luke. And whatever strings Juanita pulled, if she did, Steven's innocent. Nothing else counts."

Juanita was exhausted. She had been on a forced high from the months of waiting, the trial, the verdict, and now the entertaining to celebrate the end of it all, and she was ready to collapse, at least until tomorrow morning.

Sophia sat alongside her on her high wooden bed as the old woman, wearing a flannel nightgown that had been through so many washings it was almost transparent, brushed out her hair.

"We're getting an early start," Juanita reminded her. "So don't stay up late." She cocked an ear as if listening for something. "Did you hear a noise?" she asked. "I wonder if Steven's all right."

When they had returned, Steven had given his grandmother a sloppy kiss and staggered across the yard to his room in the back of the stable. He insisted he wasn't drunk, but he wanted to lie down.

"No, I don't hear anything," Sophia answered. "He's probably conked out. Boy doesn't know the meaning of the word moderation."

"Unfortunately, that's true," Juanita concurred. He had been indulging himself too much recently for her satisfaction, but she knew by now he didn't take criticism well, so she'd left it alone. "He needs to be careful. It's dangerous to be drunk and go wandering around out here." She laughed. "But Steven can take care of himself. We know that, don't we?"

"Yes," Sophia agreed. "He can definitely take care of himself."

She knew that Steven wasn't sleeping. He was awake, waiting for her. She would go to him after she was satisfied that Juanita was asleep. Although she was pretty sure that by now Juanita had figured it out about her and Steven. That Juanita hadn't said anything about it, hadn't tried to be all grandmotherly and protect her, was another reason she loved Juanita. She was living proof that you could be old and still be cool.

Juanita ran the brush through her hair. "Fetch me that box, please." She pointed to a large, square, black onyx jewelry box on the top shelf of the old triangular bookcase in the far corner of the room.

Sophia got up from the high bed and walked over to the bookcase. She reached up and took hold of the box. It wasn't as heavy as she had expected. She brought it over, set it down on the bed next to Juanita, and climbed up on the bed again.

Juanita picked the box up and placed it in her lap. She opened the top. "Take a look."

Sophia edged closer, so she could see inside. The box was two-tiered. The top section was hinged, so both levels were easily accessible. In the bottom level there were bracelets, mostly silver with turquoise inlays. The top level contained several sets of earrings: diamond, pearl, ruby, sapphire. Two sets were deep turquoise, in silver settings.

Juanita delicately took out one of the turquoise sets. She held them in the palm of her hand. "Beautiful, aren't they?"

"Very," Sophia said. They looked like turquoise stars in Juanita's feathery hand.

"I got them in Santa Fe, over fifty years ago. My husband and I were out there on a visit. Have you ever been there?"

Sophia shook her head. "No."

"It's beautiful. If I didn't live here, that's somewhere I'd enjoy spending time." Juanita twisted her hand so the earrings caught the light. "We should go there, after you graduate. I love to travel, but I don't have a companion to do it with anymore. You can be my companion," she decided. "Would you like that?'

Sophia was taken aback. "Yes. Thank you," Sophia told her.

"Good. I'll start looking into it."

She picked the earrings up between her thumbs and forefingers and held them against Sophia's earlobes. "Excellent," she enthused. "See for yourself."

Sophia got off the bed and went to the mirror of Juanita's dresser. She held the jewels up to her ears.

"Put them on."

Sophia took out her studs and replaced them with Juanita's heirlooms. She stared at herself in the mirror.

"Let me see."

Sophia walked over to Juanita and stood in front of her. Juanita was beaming. "Perfect. They fit your face much better than mine." She took both of Sophia's hands in hers. "Wear them in good health."

Sophia's jaw dropped. "I can't take these."

"Why not?"

"Because . . ." She was overwhelmed. "They must cost a fortune."

"So what?" Juanita said. "They didn't, actually, but what does that matter? They should be worn, not hidden away in an old lady's keepsake box." She squeezed Sophia's hands. "I'll be very hurt if you don't take these."

Sophia was shaking. "I . . ."

"You must."

Sophia touched the earrings. They felt like fairy wings on her ears. "I'll take perfect care of them," she promised. She leaned over and kissed Juanita on the forehead. "I can't believe how good you are to me."

Juanita began brushing her hair again, long, forceful strokes. "You bring me joy every moment I'm with you, Sophia." She brushed more vigorously. "You've been a great comfort and support to me." The brush dropped into her lap. "As I hope I will always be for you."

Sophia quietly closed the door behind her and ran on tiptoes to the stable. It was a clear, starry night and the moon was only a day past full, so there was ample light to see by.

Steven sat on the edge of his bed. A lantern cast his long shadow against the far wall. He was sucking on a sweaty bottle of Corona. A baggie of marijuana and his pipe were on the edge of the blanket. His shirt and shoes were off, and his jeans rode low on his hips. Damn, he's beautiful, she thought yet again.

He looked up with a lazy smile as she came to the doorway. "What took you so long?"

"I had to make sure she was asleep." She breathed in the

sticky air. It was warm and sweet, the smell of smoked weed. At his feet she spied a couple of empty beer bottles. "Don't you think you ought to slow down?" she cautioned him. "You've been hammering it pretty good tonight."

"More like you need to catch up." His words were slightly slurred. He pulled a cold bottle from his Igloo and held it out to her. "Here."

She shook her head. "I don't want to drink. I want to be clear."

He shrugged. "Suit yourself." He patted the bedcover. "C'mere."

She remained in the doorway. They hadn't had any time alone since the trial ended. Partly because of their schedules, but more because Steven was withdrawing. It was a natural reaction, she understood that; but it still hurt. Although he had used her, she had used him as well, so that wasn't what upset her. The difference was emotional. On a pretty deep level she was committed to Steven, but she had come to understand he had never been committed to her; not honestly.

Despite that, he still enflamed her. She had been aching for this. She wanted their final times together to be romantic. This wasn't romantic.

"Put the marijuana and beer away, and I will."

He brought the bottle to his lips and drank the rest of it in long gulps, his Adam's apple bobbing up and down. He tossed the empty across the room.

"Okay. It's gone."

"The marijuana, too."

"What a party pooper!" He stuffed the baggie under the mattress. "Happy now?"

"Yes." She made him wait a moment longer; then she walked across the small room and sat down next to him, kicking off her sandals.

He put his arm around her and drew her close. "I've missed you," he sweet-talked her clumsily. "All these people wanting a piece of me. My parents, my grandmother, my lawyer, your mother. Why can't they all leave me alone?"

Jesus, she thought—you won. Give it up. "Those are the people who stood behind you," she reminded him, feeling put off by his lack of graciousness. "Your grandmother's been a saint through all this. Where would you have been without her?"

"You're right," he gave in. "It's just . . . arrghh . . . that stupid girl! Why did she have to be such a cunt?"

She stared at him. "What's that supposed to mean?"

"You weren't in the courtroom to hear all the garbage they said about her," he told her, his voice rising in anger. "She lets some bozo she's never met pick her up in the morning, an hour later she's hot to trot to fuck him, but it got fucked up so she picks up some other guy and goes off to fuck him. Or maybe it was the first guy, who knows. If she hadn't been a little whore, none of this would have happened." He spat onto the floor. "She'd still be alive if she wasn't such a slut."

Sophia felt a chill, hearing Maria described that way. She knew of Maria's reputation, but it still hurt to hear such harsh, unfeeling words. She had said those exact words herself, and now she was ashamed that she had.

"You shouldn't talk about her like that," she admonished him. "She's dead. Think of her poor family and what they've gone through."

He slumped back against the rough plank wall. "You're right, it's petty of me. But I lost eight months out of my life that I'll never get back. And there's always going to be a cloud over my head."

Sophia leaned back so she was resting against him. She could feel the heat coming off his body. "Maybe they'll find the real killer someday. Maybe it's that other boy."

Steven shook his head as if trying to shake away the memories of the last eight months. "They never will. It's always going to be a mystery." He turned to her. "We don't have much time left. Let's not talk about it anymore, okay?"

She was happy to let the ugliness go. They stretched out on the thin bed. He was naked under his jeans, which slid off his narrow hips onto the floor. He lifted her dress up over her head and tossed it on top of his pants. Reaching behind her, he unsnapped her bra. It joined her dress and his jeans.

They rolled around on the bed. He kissed her swollen nipples. As his hand slid under the band of her panties, she began stroking his erection. "I have to tell you something," she whispered into his ear.

"What?" The hand snaked lower, caressing the moist curliness of the top of her pubic hair.

She should have told him earlier, but she had been afraid he would withdraw, not want to be with her. "I'm having my period."

He stopped moving. She felt him tense up.

"It's almost done." There was no one around, but she was whispering. "I'll be finished by tomorrow. We can have regular sex tomorrow night."

He pulled away. She raised up on her elbow. "Come on, Steven. I can't help it." She put her hand on his chest and pushed him back. "Let me do you."

She put both hands on his shoulders and pushed him down onto his back. Leaning over him, her swaying breasts grazing his chest, she held her hair back with one hand, braced herself with the other, and took his cock in her mouth.

She started sucking him, her head bobbing up and down on his shaft. He pushed up into her mouth, his penis ramming against the back of her throat. She gagged and pulled away.

"I'm sorry," she apologized. "I couldn't help it." She took a deep breath and started to go down on him again.

He pushed her away and sat up. "Roll over onto your hands and knees," he ordered her.

Sophia shook her head. "I don't want you in me, Steven," she protested. "Not while I'm on my period."

It was as if he hadn't heard her; or more truthfully, that whatever she said and wanted didn't matter. He grabbed her and spun her around so that she was on her hands and knees, facing away from him.

"Steven," she cried softly, "I don't want to."

He jerked her panties down past her knees. "I'm not going to fuck you in the pussy, Sophia," he breathed into her ear. His breath felt like fire on her skin. He grabbed her hips and started to push into her anus.

"No, please," she whimpered.

"Don't fight it," he told her. "You're going to like this, I promise."

He pushed her down, onto her stomach. She tried to punch at him, but he was on top of her, straddling her. She managed to turn her head and bite his hand.

He yanked it away. "You bit me!" He stared at his hand. "It's bleeding!" He grabbed her by the neck and shoved her down. "Stop fighting me," he roughly told her again. His breath was scorching her face. It smelled like gasoline, he had so much alcohol in him. He pulled her up, so that she was in the doggie position. "This how all you high school girls like it, isn't it," he said, his voice low and thick.

She felt herself becoming hysterical. "I don't want to do this," she wailed. "Don't do this, please. Please, Steven, don't!" she screamed.

Before she could cry out again, he forced himself into her. His thrust was hard and fast, no gentleness, no easing his way in—the opposite of how they normally made love. Incredibly, in some deep recess of her mind she was excusing him: it was the drinking and the dope that was making him act this way. This wasn't the Steven she knew. But the pain, not just the physical pain, but the humiliation and helplessness to stop him because he was stronger obliterated all that, and also the flash that went through her mind again, about what he had said—that high school girls liked it up the ass.

She screamed and tried to kick him off as he pushed her down again, one hand on the back of her head, smashing her face into the blanket. She started bucking, and he grabbed her by the shoulders to control her. As his hand came away from her head, she screamed again.

The explosion sounded like thunder clapping between her ears. Steven's body slammed against hers, his face smashing into the back of her head. His teeth cracked against her skull as if he was trying to bite through to her brain.

There was blood. She knew her anus was bleeding from his harsh penetration, but this was different blood, she could feel it on her back, it was spreading down her lower back, down her ass and legs, and then he wasn't moving, and she could hear a heavy rattle coming from somewhere deep inside of him.

He was like a set of weights on top of her. Unmoving, heavy, inanimate. Summoning all the strength she had left, she rolled over, forcing him off her. He fell in a heap on the floor.

The bullet had entered his body below his left shoulder blade. The blood was oozing out, not pumping fast, but already he was covered in it.

"Steven!" she screamed. She looked around wildly. "Steven!" she screamed again.

She heard someone running. Hurriedly, she put her panties back on, and reached for her bra. Her panties began staining with her blood, but she had nothing to staunch it.

She looked up as the footsteps approached. Juanita, her long hair streaming down her back, ran into the room. She stared in horror at Sophia, cowering on the narrow bed. Then her eyes went to Steven, naked and bloody on the floor.

"Somebody shot him," Sophia ghost-whispered. She was shaking uncontrollably.

Juanita looked at her grandson. Her face was bloodless. She knelt down and put her fingers on Steven's throat. She hovered there for a moment, as if in prayer.

"Put your clothes back on, Sophia," she told the hysterical girl.

While Sophia fumbled into her clothes, Juanita laid a blanket over Steven. Then she took Sophia's shaking hand and brought her back to the house. They went into the bathroom. Juanita drew Sophia a hot bath.

"Wash yourself up thoroughly," she ordered Sophia. "You aren't bleeding too badly."

She eased Sophia into the steaming water. While Sophia collapsed in the tub, Juanita went into her kitchen, picked up the telephone, and dialed 911.

"This is Mrs. McCoy, out at Rancho San Gennaro," she told the dispatcher in a voice that was eerily disembodied. "An intruder has murdered my grandson."

REBECK AND WATSON blew in as if propelled by a hurricane. Sophia was out of the bath, smothered in an old robe of Juanita's. She was huddled into herself in a chair. Her face was blank, as if she was in a catatonic state.

Rebeck crouched down next to her. She could see the girl was an emotional mess, but she had no time for civility. "Did you see anything?" she asked urgently. Every minute was critical.

Sophia shook her head.

"She didn't see anything," Juanita interjected. She hovered over Sophia. "Can't you see she's in shock? I don't want you asking her any questions," she told them with a fierce protectiveness. "I'll answer whatever questions I can."

She led Sophia into her bedroom. "Stay here and don't say anything. I've called your mother. She'll be here shortly."

"But shouldn't I . . . ?"

"Hush," Juanita whispered. She put a finger to Sophia's lips. "This has been a terrible time of suffering," she said gravely. "Don't you think we've all suffered enough?"

Sophia stared at her, dumbstruck.

"Steven's gone now," Juanita said in a quiet, authoritative voice. "He can't defend himself. Just as that poor girl couldn't defend herself." She stared into Sophia's eyes as if looking into her soul. "It's time to let them go. We need to let them take their secrets to the grave."

She leaned in closer. "You saw nothing," she repeated intensely. "I'm doing this to protect you, Sophia. Do you understand that?"

Sophia nodded. "I didn't see anything," she repeated by rote.

Juanita shut the bedroom door behind her and went back into her living room. She sat down on her couch.

"I was about to go to sleep," she told the detectives. "I was exhausted. We all were. We'd had a party this evening to celebrate the verdict, and to bid farewell to Steven, who was going home to Arizona tomorrow." She stopped for a moment. "It was his last night here," she said in a choked voice.

Gathering herself, she continued. "Steven said good night to us and went to his room in the back of the stable. Sophia wanted to take a bath, and I got ready for bed. Just as I was about to get under the covers, I heard some voices outside."

"What kind of voices?" Watson asked. "How many were there?"

"It sounded like there were two," Juanita answered slowly. "I'm not positive. You'll have to excuse me. I'm not completely straight in my head right now." Although her eyes were dry, she dabbed at them with a handkerchief.

"Did you recognize them?" Watson pressed. "Both, or either?"

"One of them sounded like Steven's."

Watson huddled down right next to her. "What did he say?"

She shivered. "I heard a voice cry out, 'No! Don't!' Like that."

"And what did the other person say?" Watson continued. Both he and Rebeck were scribbling notes as fast as they could.

Juanita closed her eyes in thought. "I didn't hear it clearly. It might have been, 'It's your turn,' or 'It's your time.'"

The detectives exchanged loaded glances. "Then what happened?" Watson asked.

"I heard a gunshot." She started to say more, then stopped.

"Go on," Rebeck prompted.

"I ran to the front door and threw it open. I was afraid to run out, because I didn't know who was out there." She paused for a moment. "Then I thought I saw someone running away."

"Did you see who it was?" Rebeck asked feverishly.

Juanita shook her head. "It was too dark, and the figure was too far away." The handkerchief twisted in Juanita's hands. "I ran to the stable . . ." She hesitated for a second, then went on. "I could see right away that Steven was dead." She rubbed her dry eyes. "All that grief he went through. That we all went through." She buried her head in her hands. "For nothing."

Kate, frantic with worry, pulled up in front of Juanita's house in a cloud of dust. Half a dozen police cars were parked there, along with the coroner's van. She ran inside, pushing past the clustered detectives.

Juanita was in the living room, waiting for her. "She's in my bedroom. It's been a terrible ordeal, but she's all right. She's sleeping now."

Kate sagged. "My God. What about you? Is Steven . . . ?" Her face registered shock and horror.

Juanita nodded somberly. "Someone killed him."

Kate gathered Juanita in her arms. "Oh, Juanita," she lamented. "I'm so sorry."

The tears finally came. "He almost made it," Juanita said, in a voice as soft as a cloud. "He was so close to getting on with his life and putting this ugliness behind him." She bowed her head as if in prayer. "It's all such a tragedy," she whispered. "Such a needless, wasteful tragedy."

Three weeks after Steven was buried in a quiet ceremony at the family's ancestral graveyard, Rancho San Gennaro had its annual spring roundup. Cowboys from all over the valley came to help out. After a long and exhausting day, two hundred and thirty-seven calves were branded and inoculated. The males were castrated, and twenty prize heifers were culled out to be used as future breeding cows.

In the evening, Juanita threw a barbeque to feed all her helpers. Sophia was right in the mix. During the day she helped move the six-month-old calves from the holding pasture to the pens, and then worked alongside Juanita and a dozen other women to prepare the meal. When it was all over and everyone had departed, she and her surrogate grandmother collapsed in fatigue and satisfaction in a job well done. Sitting outside Juanita's house, they toasted each other with apple cider.

"You are now an official cowboy of the female gender," Juanita anointed her. "How does it feel?"

"Really good," Sophia answered. "It really felt right to be here."

"The first of many, I hope," Juanita told her. "That would make me very happy."

"That's what I want, too."

Sophia had survived the physical part of being raped better than she and Juanita had feared. The morning after, Juanita had taken her to a private gynecologist. The doctor, a family friend and confidant, had cleaned her up and took cultures and blood samples to make sure she hadn't contracted any disease. A few days later, the lab report came back—a clean bill of health. Although the penetration had been painful, and was still uncomfortable, she knew it would pass.

The emotional and psychological scars would last longer. She couldn't bury her rage at Steven for having violated her, but he was dead now, so there wasn't a living presence she could vent against. And she knew that Juanita was suffering terrible pain for her part in what had happened, a pain she would always carry with her. So the two of them were bonded that way, too. She didn't tell anyone, not even her mother, about Steven's deathbed confession, and she still wasn't completely willing to believe that it had been a true confession. Maria's being anally raped was common knowledge, so he might have been referring to the circumstance, not that he was the direct cause of it. But that was trying to give the benefit of the doubt to a man she had fallen in love with, her first love. In her heart, she was sure she knew the truth.

Kate and Luke had lunch on the patio of a new restaurant near the Art Museum. It was a glorious spring day. As usual, Luke's caseload was larger than he wanted it to be, and as usual, he had a hard time turning down clients.

"How's school going?" he asked Kate.

"Good," she answered. She picked at her Cobb salad. "I've got a torts class and an environmental law seminar. I'm thinking of making that my specialty. You can do good without having to deal with killings and maimings and mourners. It seems more civilized than rubbing elbows with drug dealers and homicidal maniacs." She broke off a chunk of focaccia and dipped it in olive oil. "I'm getting weary of blood."

"I hear you," he answered. "The trouble is, it gets in your own blood. And sometimes you actually make an honest-to-God life-and-death difference."

"Like with Steven McCoy," Kate said ironically.

"Yes," he answered heavily. "Like Steven."

Steven's murder had been stunning. Everyone who had been involved in the case felt betrayed. Why go to all that trouble, all that time, all that anxiety, as well as money, to see it end like that? It was the ugliest example of vigilantism Luke had known, let alone been involved in. Even Alex Gordon, who had been convinced of Steven's guilt, was enraged at the usurpation of the process.

There were no suspects in Steven's shooting. Hector Torres, the obvious candidate, had a firm alibi. The police found no footprints, no tire tracks. The bullet that killed Steven came from a 30-30 rifle, one of the most common in circulation.

Rebeck and Watson weren't getting anywhere. They had interviewed Sophia, but she stonewalled them. She insisted she had seen and heard nothing. It was as if the shooter was a ghost, or as Rebeck ghoulishly characterized it, an avenging phantom, a dark angel who for once had been on the right side.

Kate had tried to question Sophia, but she had to go gingerly. Her daughter hadn't been as traumatized by the experience as she had feared she could be, but it was clearly an open wound on her psyche. After Sophia had rebuffed her a few times, Kate left the subject alone. If she ever wanted to talk to her about anything, she'd be there.

It would be hot later today, but now, just after sunrise, the temperature was mild and inviting. Sophia had spent the night at the ranch, so she and Juanita could get an early start. It would be their last ride of the summer. Tomorrow, Sophia and Kate were driving up to Palo Alto for the start of Sophia's freshman year. Wanda, who was already deep into her second year of medical school, would come down from San Francisco to join them. Sophia was excited, nervous, apprehensive, jittery, eager—all the emotions Kate remembered Wanda had felt when she had started college.

Sophia had invited Juanita to join them on the drive up, but Juanita had graciously declined. This should be a special occasion for the three Blanchard women to savor among themselves, she explained. She would come up in a couple of months, for Homecoming. They would spend the weekend together, when Juanita could also get reacquainted with whichever remaining classmates she had who were still alive and kicking. She didn't expect there would be very many.

On the night of Sophia's high school graduation, when the three of them and Wanda had gone out to dinner, Juanita had pulled Kate aside. She was going to pay for Sophia's college education, and she didn't want any argument about it from Kate. She knew that Sophia had a generous financial aid package, so it wasn't like she would have to pay full freight, but she insisted that she make up the difference.

Kate had been stunned by Juanita's offer, and had tried to dissuade her, but Juanita was adamant. Sophia was like a granddaughter to her now. They all knew that. She could easily afford it, and Kate couldn't. She not only wanted to do this, she *needed* to, she implored Kate.

It was a relief not to have to worry about the money, and Kate knew how important this was to Juanita. Sophia had replaced Steven in the old woman's heart; they were as close as blood kin, except literally. As close as Sophia is to me, Kate thought with some ambiguity. But that was her own jealousy, her possessiveness—Juanita and Sophia truly loved each other. The building of their relationship had been a long and arduous journey, yet it was just beginning.

As the sun was breaking over the low mountains to the southeast, they mounted up and rode out into the open range. The winter rains had brought an end to the drought, and there was an abundance of water in the springs. They followed a wide trail that passed by a grassy pasture. The cows, heavy in their pregnancies, grazed and drank and shooed flies away with their tails. In the next few months they would begin calving, and by Thanksgiving there would be the beginning of the new herd. Sophia would come down on the weekends when the cows started dropping their calves. Ranching was in her blood now, and she wanted to take part in all of the operations.

A month earlier, Juanita had revised her will. She was leaving Rancho San Gennaro to Sophia Blanchard, to be held in trust with her mother, Kate Blanchard. She did attach a condition: it was to be Sophia's as long as she was alive and actively worked it, once she had graduated from college and pursued whatever occupation she chose. If Sophia decided ranch life was not for her, it would revert to Juanita's heirs. Juanita was certain the ranch would remain in Sophia's hands for a long, long time.

High above, a red-tailed hawk floated in the thermals. Sophia reached into her saddlebag and took out a digital camera, her graduation present from Luke and Riva. She sighted the bird and took a picture. Riding alongside Juanita, she showed her the image.

"That's a keeper," Juanita told her approvingly.

Sophia pointed the camera at Juanita. They looked at the picture on the screen. "This one's a keeper, too," Sophia said with a smile.

The trail rose at a gentle slope, leading them toward a grove of pines, eucalyptus, and live oak. They could feel the sun warming their backs. The hawk drifted away with the wind.

Thanks to Markus Wilhelm, Gail Hochman, Carole Baron, and Kathy Kiernan for their encouragement and support. I also wish to thank Michael Galvin, Joyce Dudley, Terrence Lammers, Dr. Robert Anthony of the Santa Barbara County Sheriff-Coroner's Office, Lt. Chris Pappas of the Santa Barbara County Sheriff's Department, and Rick Dodge of Dodge City Gun Shop, for their help.